GRACE

J. S. McInroy

Published by : Slate Run Publishing, LLC.
www.slaterunpub.com

Cover Design : Dayna Winter

ISBN:0692555996 (paperback version)
ISBN-13: 978-0692555996 (paperback version)

DEDICATION:

John Flynn, after my father, the most important man in my life.

ACKNOWLEDGEMENTS:

Those who have had the good Grace to let me be myself while I complicated their lives.

AMBITION:

Move to San Diego and swim into the sunset.

GRACE

The road ends at the undifferentiatable onset of Erie and horizon. The Hellcat mutters away. Father turns to Son. Son to Father.

"I still don't understand why we had to pass him by. He was obviously alone. Obviously distressed. Am I not the Savior? Or is it just a convenient name for those — such as I — who cannot understand?"

"Don't play dumb with me, kid. Save that for your sister. You know how it goes. And you understand why. It — everything — has already happened. We try moving every stray we see from one flightpath to another and we fu… screw everything up. You're getting a chance again. But now take to heart the Calvinist concept of preterism. Not all are "elect," but that in no way means those same are not chosen. Just passed by."

"And so…are they not not chosen?"

Save it, Jay! Each and everyone's arrow has been loosed. Sometimes gravity is the sole determinant."

"But…."

"No buts. Let's fire this beast up and head on back to Jersey. Your sister's about to get into the middle of something I want you to watch. You're going to see our hiker again. Name's Arthur. Watch for him."

The charger snorts its readiness and the dad and kid hole about in a perfect 180 headed at two-hundred plus away from the great blue waters. Ancient voices stir in Canadian woods. Sapphic sisters welcome a prospect into their company. Pamela Bruno laughs as her father participates in her conception. A White Heron is intercepted by an errant arrow above the great lake. Pale feathers drift behind its fall from grace.

"Dark Star" eases the Son's mind toward clarity.

The worm turns and inserts its male end into its female mouth.

All is.

Dance of Despair
Ruth
2013

She, only Scarecrow Anna, goes on and on as to how her music teacher touched her breast when she was seven, the teacher a "Lesbos" as the dweeb would always put it. Always — three times a week, Monday, Wednesday, Friday, 11:00 AM, St. John's Episcopal. The stupid little twit has no breasts of any noticeable substance, even now at twenty-something. What did the butch feel anyway? A boy chest on a scrawny little chick, probably hoping for some smidgen of drama in her already impoverished life? So what if she turned to weed at twelve and Hydro, Lortab and any other painkillers she could find by the time she turned eighteen? *Suck it up, you anorexic cow. Lose some more weight, get a life. Every week or so you add another substance to your list; today it's Percodan rather than the Percocet of last week. What do you do anyway, search out new doctors, pharmacies, dealers? Or do you simply imagine new evils to spice up your presentation? You're pathetic.*

"Might I interrupt here?" I intrude, causing consternation to flash just a moment across the too timid Anna's face and a momentary slump of disapproval to betray the bland features of Paloma, the not so dove-like social worker in charge of, *No.... Not in charge of, rather, moderator of,* the group of, this day, thirteen women in her substance-abuse session. Tuesdays she moderates Domestic Violence, and freaking Anna is in that too. Is there no escape? Not really, at least not unless one takes steps, firm, determined steps. Such I just have done, striding right into the numbing drone of Scarecrow's litany of imagined pains and analgesic solutions.

We are all women. Sometimes, I wish there were some men; men seem stronger, their drugs more lethal, their experiences more private even while most public. Once upon that long-ago time back in college — Williams, if you must know — a professor of something or other, no doubt Psych, stressed the point that sometimes pop-psychology is not all wrong, that John Gray had a point. Men do retreat when hurt, go into a cave alone while, on the other hand, women seek to share, to vent, to find comfort and strength in the communal experience even of grief and such horrors as abuse and humiliation. I have always thought that a weakness, preferring the male approach to my own gender-induced urge to cry rather than to rage, to find comfort for my own pain in the agony of others. But, here I am. Sharing again.

"I too have suffered abuse," I shout in my most masculine tones. I've told the story before, and it is no casual brush with something that might have been. It occurred. Over and over again for years...three to the best of my recollection... until my mother caught us. They are familiar with the details: my screams...of hunger, orgiastic wails most primitive, both of us certain she was not at home. But home she was, her own screams drowning mine into silence.

"Unlike you, Dotty, and you, Carla, I was responsible for my parents' divorce. And unlike the lot of you, my transgressions are most real. I seduced him. Not the other way around."

Admittedly, in the strictest legal sense of the term, it was rape; I was just fourteen, but the poor man never had a chance. I was every bit as much the woman then as I am now, and I was desperate for love, and love does express itself through sex, and I knew what I needed. Reveled in what I got.

As I relate it, when she discovered us, I was a senior in high school. They sent me off to live with my aunt, and my mother has not spoken so much as a word to me since. Others saw to my education, provided more than adequate funds, undoubtedly in concert with my father, for my upkeep, including the best of clothes....

I could take these Troglodytes for a stroll down a memory lane depraved enough to darken their dreams forever....

"Thank you, Lottie," Paloma interrupts, "but, as we have agreed, the time has passed for the past. Remember Linda's motto, 'There is no past; there is no future; there's only here; there's only now....'"

Just like all the rest of them, Paloma is really just too, too simple. Did she think I wouldn't look into that? "A facile and misleading, misquoted line from a song," I reply, not without a certain smugness, adding a lyric of my own, complete with snarky comment, "She might just as well have stolen, 'sha-la-la-la-la-la, live for today.'" I'm all dark and serious now, "I thought this was supposed to be a more therapeutic approach, perhaps touching upon the reasons for our addictions rather than this 'one day at a time bullshit.' I've been to NA, you know. And quit."

Let them deal with that for a while. "So, if you will, on this today, this here, this only now, I think I need to say something. Your troubles, no doubt are real, your pain excruciating.... But they're not mine. To be truthful, I could care less about" (turning to each in turn) "your imagined addictions, your kleptomania, your incipient lesbianism" (two of them here), "your depression" (three), "your old man's need to put on your clothes" (*probably too big for him unless he's a gorilla too*), "and your manic depression" (four and out).

11

"I'm here for me, Paloma... we all are... for therapy, something that may not cure me or even heal a few of my wounds, but which may make my life a bit more bearable, keep me a little bit straight, maybe even lead to the possibility of an uninterrupted night's sleep... just six blessed hours."

The freaks all sigh. God, I hate sympathy or empathy or whatever their pseudo-authenticity might be termed, and I am goaded into escalating into one of my patented outbursts, once naturally springing from my pain and despair, but now calculated, designed to shock. Something they never fail to do even with an audience such as these slugs who have been subjected to my theatrics more than once. By this time, a man probably would have told me to zip it. These drama queens just settle back to listen, to identify, to store up in their pouchy little cheeks for later vicarious experience (As part of their own imagined catalog of degradations?), and above all to reinforce that unique sense of superiority shared by born-agains, recovering addicts, and high-tech geeks.

"I seduced my father, you know. Not my step-dad or any of those half measures. My real, my biological progenitor. I fucked...."

"That will be quite enough," the pigeon pussyfooter coos. "Please, Lottie, for your own sake, don't go there. Might we not better move past the angry words, words I fear are chosen not only for their shock-value, but as a disguise as well? If you push us away, you must understand, we (the winged rat here pauses dramatically, casting her walleyed gaze about the circle, never truly addressing me sitting directly in front of her, so comfortable is she lurking at the periphery of things) shall be unable in any way to assist you, to help you grow."

"Fuck, you," a man would say and walk out. "Whatever," I choke, my anger and resentment, their caustic acid suppressed before it can bubble its sulfuric menace up through the gathering reflux of my soul. "My," the septic stench of the words fuming into my sinuses, causing my always too-dry eyes to water, "apologies. I suppose I might just chill a bit."

Much to their great relief, one would imagine, I arise rather clumsily from the stupid folding chair, nearly stumble over my flip-flop feet, and stalk out of group, emphatically snapping the door behind me. Once in the hall, walled away from their simpering, their emotionally bloated anorexia, I let it all go. Maybe my nose drips just a bit before I can reach the tissue, a brown napkin from Starbucks, wadded in the tight pocket of my shorts; perhaps my eyes leak just a drop or two; I can't truly say, and don't really care. I do care though, really do hope, that my words, echoing in that church basement hallway, break through the barriers now between me and the group, that the whole murder of Scarecrows, Pigeons, *et al*, not only hear, but take them to heart, add them to

12

their own impotent lists of goals and action plans, "Fuck, you," I holler, just getting warmed up, "And may you all fuck your daddies. Wherever they may be. Even in their graves."

APPARITION? VISITATION? ANNUNCIATION? Do the Anglicans worship the Virgin? Anyway, there she stands. One of God's more beautiful creatures. Around her radiates light — from a window behind and above her to be sure. The effect is undoubtedly auric, a golden aura, so much more than a halo.

"Shh," the angel murmurs.

I do. I have no other choice.

"Forgive me for prying," the presence whispers, "but I can't help but feel that you are troubled."

Life! Sometimes the living just isn't worth the effort. By choice I stand alone, trembling with anger one minute, accosted by a divine being the next. Then thrown right back into the plague-pit of mundanity. As always, my impulse is to act, to speak harsh words, to pull away from such encounters. The vision extends a delicate brown arm, ringed at its tiny wrist by three silver bangles, and lays a small, expressive hand upon my bare shoulder. I give her my most acerbic look. Directly into fathomless black eyes. I am lost. The silver hoops in her ears, flickering above her bare shoulders, play a sparkling song in concert with the words those eyes need not utter. This angel, under other circumstances, could be myself.

Without prelude, with no thought whatsoever, I blurt, as if in some Episcopal confessional, High-Church all the way, "I seduced my father." As taught by the nuns of my own denomination, I begin to rattle off the rest. "He was drunk. As he often was, and I.... I loved him so. I didn't really mean it, you know. I just helped him into his bed. Mom, always the princess, had her own bed...her own room. Anyway, he was so sweet, and the alcohol of his breath enticed me. It still has that effect. At times at least. I was in my summer jammies...just a T-shirt really, and when I crawled in beside him, felt his hard body, so strong and yet so helpless against me, all I did was snuggle up to him as we both slept.

"The next morning, the early, early morning, I awoke to his return from the bathroom. I could hear the toilet running. He had on a pair of boxer shorts, and, well... his penis, hard and no doubt dream-inspired, took on a supernatural aspect. It was the treasure I had always sought, the salvation from all my childhood disappointments, from my childhood itself. No girl — I was quite adult developmentally, physically, I mean — could fail to achieve my objective.

"Afterward, we both cried, vowed to keep our secret, and the very next week, my own, as well as his, inhibitions anesthetized by just the proper amount of alcohol, we set sail once again upon the dark sea of incest...."

"Shh," the apparition cautions. "A church is no place for such talk. Now, shut your whore's mouth. If your life's so fucking bad, why don't you kill yourself? Why didn't you once it all fell apart?

Eventually, the therapy session over, the imbeciles stumble upon me, back against the wall, needle remarkable thighs revealed by my skimpy attire, my fists buried in my dirty hair. The pigeon is called. By the scarecrow no less. And despite my protests, I soon find myself once again in SPARC despite being straight for at least two months. Well... except for Memorial Day. Really, Dad was a veteran. What was I supposed to do? I lay all that night with him. My beloved. Got quite a chill too. Maybe the next day too, you know. Not since then. I swear.

EVERYTHING IN LIFE is so damned clichéd. The imbeciles at St. John's have no corner on that one. Really! I may be the clichéd addict and alcoholic, but, to twist their inane phraseology just the tiniest bit, I walk the walk, but refuse to talk the talk. The first cliché about this place is its address, Mercycare lane. Or maybe it's the name itself, SPARC: St. Peters Alcohol Recovery Center. I wish to God I hadn't, but one of the very few pieces of useful information I have gleaned from my journey through the life I have fallen into is that there is a "process" of recovery, but no actual moment when the addict or alcoholic dare claim to actually have recovered. No day shall come when a beer or two will be possible, a hit from a communal joint, a pleasant respite, if only for an evening, morning or afternoon, from the incessant pain of simply being whoever one is. Even hoping for such is a first step down the road to relapse. Just who the hell do these sanctimonious hypocrites think they're fooling anyway? Any addict can see through them. Only an idiot believes anything they have to say, let alone "turns it over" as they always require. I'd rather be an HIV positive crack whore than one of them. If I make it, it'll be on my own. As more than one somebody has said, I don't need nobody, and the old dude, Catfish John I think, loves to sing to himself while we're, you know...together, "I ain't askin' nobody for nothin'." How he goes on and on. He has money though...and a great sense of humor.

Anyway, SPARC can be good for a little R & R. All I need do is bullshit my way through group, pretend to believe. I even pray along at the end of meetings. Damn, I might even let myself cry toward the end of my stay. Once again, I shall excel. *Summa cum laude* for sure.

Today they're bussing several of us down to the hospital for, at least in my case, routine physicals, Pap smears, blood work, etc. etc. This could not have come at a better moment. I was really getting sick of group, individual therapy, more group and then one of the idiotic Life Skills things. Where do they get these ideas from anyway? When I was in Four Winds they let me skip most of the crap. Not at St. Pete's. Today, however.... Freedom!

I expect the doctor to inquire about my tracks, but she says nothing. I expect only a brief uncomfortable moment with speculum and intrusive hand. What I do not expect is her nervous laugh, trembling lip, and downcast eyes. "I need to call Dr. Parker," she mumbles. "Don't worry. I won't be gone long."

She's not; she returns in less time than it takes to open a bottle of Percocet, trailed almost immediately by a little Asian chewing upon whatever grains she has chosen for lunch. "This is Dr. Kim," announces the first one, who it turns out is just a Nurse Practitioner. She should be able to clear this up."

"Clear what up?" I choke from the table. "Isn't this just...."

"Shh," the little yellow thing breathes. "It's probably nothing."

WELL, IT WASN'T nothing. They didn't even need the Pap smear, but they ran all the tests anyway, and here I am newly settled in my new room, awaiting treatment decisions for the cancer which has been eating at me for, I guess, quite some time: Stage four Cervical. Spread all to hell and gone. At last I've found it, the one sure escape if not recovery from addiction. Death.

It must be a busy time of year for medical services; I'm not even on an oncology ward; instead I'm sharing some kind of general medical room with an old lady lying comatose in the bed next to mine. There won't even be someone to talk to as I lie dying. I comfort myself with the thoughts that her condition saves me from having to deal with an inquisitive old crone full of stories about grandchildren, brimming over with questions, and no doubt expressing the usual platitudes such as perpetually overflow from the likes of her. Mary Elizabeth Bruno is her name. Please, Mary Elizabeth, do not wake up. At least not until I'm out of here.

Ratso! I'm not here two hours and the old fool stirs; then she calls out to God, and then to someone named Pam. No one answers and in almost no time she quiets and returns to sleep. I follow suit. Come morning I awaken. So has Mary Bruno. In the light of the new day, for the first time I see more than her night shrouded form. She sits upright. Her posture, the expression on her surprisingly young and beautiful face radiate something akin to the aura around my visitation in the hallway of St. John's. Is she too a figment of my imagination, a semi-spiritual being sent to torment me with another bogus sort of inspiration which makes absolutely no sense, especially now that my future has become so compressed?

I have heard the staff talking; Mary Elizabeth is somewhere around seventy years old, but looks not a day over forty...well, maybe forty five. Anyway, she sure looks better than I feel at the moment. She is a controversial figure they whisper. A lesbian, who, with her embarrassingly semi-celebrity of a "spouse," once hijacked the Cathedral and the Bishop himself. Bare as the day she was born, her mate, one Pamela Bruno, proclaimed to the multitude that she was truly the daughter of God, and continued on to declare the two them, she and Mary Elizabeth, to be if not lawfully at least spiritually wed until death might them part. Some of the nurses think this is pretty cool...even awesome, while others would mutter execrations such as "abomination," were their vocabularies sufficient to the task. She has suffered a fall. Not from grace. Just down her cellar stairs and has four broken ribs as well as numerous bruises and lacerations. Perhaps even a concussion.

This is not her first time in St. Peter's. The whispers grow so loud as to echo up and down the merciless halls and intrude into my forgotten section of our hopeless room. The old lady has in the past few years been brutally raped, suffered injuries even more grievous than those which have prompted her current visit to Wellness Central. And the senile old fool just keeps on smiling.

Forgive me, but so have I been raped. More than once. And the last thing I felt at those times was the obvious joy so angelic in her countenance. Pain begets little else than more pain. The end of pain is nothing but a temporary numbness, and then comes more god damned pain. The rape has no end.

INTO MY TEMPESTUOUS little interlude croaks the crackly voice so many old women develop, maybe from smoking. This is not quite the same. This voice has a depth not at all old womanish It originates in some far-off place where the truth dwells and beings are lighter than the air we breathe. "You are not alone," she says.

Oh, man, what're they giving me? I'm hearing things. Cancer might not be half bad if this is how you live with it. I haven't been so stoned since Daddy's birthday. Or was that Memorial Day? Who in all this sunshine can really care?

Maybe no one else. But I really do...despite wishing that I did not. I'm an addict not a fool. I'm getting nothing even resembling a mood altering or perception enhancing drug, no pain killers, not even a minor dose of Ambien. I am an addict and as such will be left to suffer through this alone and unaided. So much for the rewards of sobriety. I haven't leapt into the abyss, rather have I been tossed over the precipice edge, and, as I tumble through the dark, no inkling of my proximity to life's harsh bottom other than the awareness that it accelerates toward me with each passing second per second, there is no prayer can save me, no hand to catch, no arms to cradle me. Not at all lost, neither will I be found.

Something gets me high, and I am not afraid.

THEY MUST BE slipping me something. Last night I slept at least ten solid hours, maybe awakened from time to time by the night nurse. I don't remember. Tonight, from out the emptiness only drugs can impart to sleep I am nuzzled into a fuzzy awakening. Someone is beside me, her face like an October moon full to mine. "She's awake," Luna whispers behind her into the dark side.

I would prefer to feign unconsciousness, but that would not be the right thing. Instead, "Who are you?" I exhale into the luminous countenance.

Shattering into golden splinters, her luminescence scatters wild photons through the shadows of my room. They reassemble, eidetic tracings into fading images, little cat trails through which shimmer the fading notes of a bright voice. "Pam! You will want to see me again."

I return to sleep.

I surmise that I caused some consternation among the staff. To all observers, I slept the rest of the night, and for the next few days, despite repeated attempts to awaken me, remained disconnected. I had, according to their cant, slipped into a near vegetative state. Nothing they did had any effect. Lacking apparent cause for my condition, all they could do was shove an NG tube up my nose and down my throat so that they might provide me nourishment. What idiots these bio-technicians be. I was totally aware of their misinistrations; I simply preferred to be elsewhere, safe and comfortable in a place they could never know.

For her own time, not that of the attending idiots nor for that matter of my own, Pamela Bruno, Mary Elizabeth's spouse and my bright new angel, wrapped me in her mystery and told me of the ways I might find salvation. Not the salvation of the soul. Not at all. One of the many precious bits of knowledge remaining me after I return to my hospital room and the befuddled faces of my long ignored if not forgotten mother and sister is the certainty that my soul needs no salvation. My body does. I am cancer struck and addiction plagued, but my soul and the souls even of the dunces surrounding me need no saving. It — they — are immortal, free, and of great amusement, often despair, and sometimes joy to God, but never damned, despised, and cast into any lake of any kind let alone hellfire. Even the dunces'. Damn, the blessed Pamela held nothing from me, "There is fire...and ice," she revealed. "For sure, some are lost, but eventually all will be found. There is life. That is your eternal reward. It is yours to do with as you will. My place, and I might add, that of Jesus, Prince Siddhartha, and a whole bunch of others...? The best I can say is that God sends us to find you. To change some of you. So, even if you may run, you can't hide.... Grateful Dead. I love that song." A little depressing though, don't you think?

"I leave you, Ruthie, with that song as your key. Don't overthink things; study the lyrics and they will lead you away from the trite simplicity of the song's message. So, when you've had enough of running and there's seems no place to offer you refuge, use it to find me inside yourself. I am there, now and forever. Whenever you need me, whenever your cravings, the depravity in which you immerse yourself or simply the banality of this existence drives you to despair, all you need do is chant it, along with the band or not, all you need do is sing in your own voice to your own rhythms, 'I can run, but I can't hide,' something of a paraphrase to be sure. But there you are. Do as I say, and I will become known to you."

At least those are the words I choose to have heard the girl speak. Actually, I think she communicated through those splatters of light rather than words, but my mind requires words, even when alone with only my second self as companion. I've come to know that words are really limiting... but then language is all we have.... Isn't it?

I lie, facing up into the splotched with something or other hospital ceiling, the gibbous face and form of Mom peering foul perfume into my awakening. I can feel her breath all warm and thick as bloody stool. She shrieks, "She's awake." I am discovered.

The time for fabrications, at least important ones, has obviously drummed its final beat. I guess I shall no longer lie, at least to myself. My story about my Daddy and Mother catching the two of us makes for great recovery sharing.

They all believe it. Dunces, the lot. True, my father is dead, but none of the other things I have built up into my own tragic saga bear any resemblance to the actual events of my life as I sometimes misremember them. Let me begin with Daddy. We'll eventually get around to Mom and Felicia the pumpkin, but later as befits truly minor yet unforgettable characters.

When I was a senior in high school my numbskull mother, ever retarded, came to the realization that I was — to employ her platitude — troubled. The school psychologist finally, after one of my better episodes, convinced her I needed treatment. So off I went for a week to Four Winds Rehabilitation Hospital in Saratoga where they assessed my circumstances and diagnosed me as suffering from bi-polar disease possibly related to chemical dependency. So much wisdom gleaned in just a week. After my discharge I began to see Dr. Altman who most memorably prided herself on her kinship to the director Robert Altman, an entity whom, of course, she had never met. Her office, however, did boast an autographed photo of the great man, boasting the sentiments, "To a great cousin and valuable fan." It was signed, "Bob." All so terribly intimate, so pretentious, so inexplicably sad. But even now I feel just a dim catch of empathy. We all need somebody. We really do.

I needed my Daddy. Every little girl does, but he left us when I was three. All I remember of him, I think, is made up, the result of my imagination, leavened perhaps by family stories. The Marines took him from me. By his own choosing, I suppose, but not before Mother drove him away. They never divorced; she simply made his life miserable. How do I know this, you may ask. If you knew the bitch — yes that's the nicest descriptive adjective available...at least to me — you would entertain no doubts. All her stories, even the ones not pointedly critical? Filled with venom.

An Annapolis graduate from a wealthy family, Dad met my mother at a Christmas party in 1975. He was First Lieutenant Francis X Kelleher of the low-key but influential Import/Export Kellehers. Just like the Kennedys, Mother would sneer, they achieved prominence by disreputable means. She needed always to imply if not directly assert the superior lineage of her family of retailers, Coopers Shoes, for Christ's sake. As for me, I'm proud to be descended from bootleggers and possibly importers of substances even dearer to my heart. Mother would always allude to yet never elaborate upon Dad's family's connection with certain elements of the American irregular financing of indigenous tribespeople in you know where.... Or Iran Contra for that matter. How possibly does owning a couple of shoe stores stack up against that? From what I have gathered, Dad's company helped bail them out during the Carter recession, maybe even secured a controlling interest.... Whatever! All my problems, according to my mother, are traceable to genetic predispositions inherited from — you guessed it — Dad.

Anyway, all of it matters not a whit to me. In 1983 Daddy went off to Lebanon, and left me behind. With my mother, and my stupid little sister.

Here I lie, no Daddy, but one mother and one sister too many. It's bad enough to be on one's deathbed, but then comes the intolerable. I can talk with this stupid thing down my throat and all, but they don't know that, and I brilliantly feign extreme discomfort if not outright pain even uttering the simplest of phrases, and soon, it is all them. Nevertheless, I still have to listen, and eventually regret my dumb show. How good it would feel to just yell or even softly say, "Shut the hell up. Please...please...please. No more!" How they do natter on. Platitude after platitude. Ignorant of the inescapable logic of following the axiom that if silence is golden then, of necessity, talk is dross. They slop words all around me, and I am bound to listen, captive of my own deception, my egregious mortality, too far removed from blessed death.

In the middle of some Pumpkin twaddle a striking shaft of music inserts itself, fine and precise, a scalpel wielded by an artist of sonic surgery. The melody is unfamiliar, the instrumentation decidedly oldies rock and roll, but the words.... When the words come, I fall through the brittle ice of my circumstances into a place I have been before although not awake, and I sense rather than see her. Pam. Part of me still clings to the crackling surface of the hospital reality; I see my mother's blank face as she nods agreement with something Flea says, and Felicia, as bulbous as always, lights with that inner light which glimmers so sickly through her gaping pores. She has said something sensitive no doubt. They both love to gush. Soon (soon I am proven right) they will blubber false tears and hug and seek to comfort me. Imagine yourself embraced by a Polish tuber and an American squash of huge proportions, and you might just be able to imagine the revulsion promised here. So many things really are worse than....

The Pam in my mind shushes me. Actually shuts me up, and disappears. I climb up out of my shallow pond, shuddering in the gelid warmth the two creatures squish about me. The music continues; annoyance sours Mother's sweet compassion. Then it absolutely curdles. At first unrecognizable even to me — remember she is my dream girl, not someone I have ever seen with my actual eyes — a vision of ultimate slutishness approaches preceded by a most pleasing essence of herbal delight. She wears a white beater and no bra. The rest of her is barely covered by a miniscule green skirt — dark like a forest glade I remember from some movie about Nazis and Greek mythological figures — and she wears no shoes. Mother's protest is drowned in the amplitude of the girl's little white phone.

"We can run, but we can't hide," she mouths along with the Dead, as right between the Pumpkin and the squash she inserts herself into my waking reality. "Mary just insisted that I come over," she beams, and turning to the befuddled duo, continues to Mother, "Are you by some improbable chance Isadora Kelleher, Ellie Cooper's daughter?"

Mother has always loved using the word "floored" for the general condition commonly referred to as "taken aback." I have always hated such idiosyncrasies of common speech, but this time Mother's word happens to be appropriate. If not for the Pumpkin's big, round shoulder, she is sure to have fallen, or at least sunk decorously (for her anyway) to the.... You guessed it.

"Yes...yes...yes, I am," she stutters into the tissue she has produced from thin air and pressed to her lips. "But...but how...who?"

"Not me. It's my old lady over there," the blessed intruder laughs. "She thinks she knows you."

I can't see her face, but upon turning to my roommate's side of the room where Mary Elizabeth sits dwarfed by her chair, Mother's entire bodily attitude bespeaks confusion. "I...I, yes, I think I know her.... And... and.... Yes... I am Dora Kelleher. Could she... I mean...is she Mary Elizabeth Foster by any chance?"

By this time Mother is turned completely around and back to me; I detect not just confusion but actual panic in her face. The tissue conceals nothing, and her dissembling eyes are blank with truth. Why is she so (here comes another of her words) discombobulated by this old woman? Half turning back, she gives Mary a trembling little fingertip wave as her tissue drifts to the floor.

"Don't be troubled," Pam murmurs, "Mary harbors no ill-will at all. All she asks is that you stop over and say 'hello,' so that she can...." Pam breaks off here. In confusion?

Discombobulated or not, Mother has always been able to summon another of her favorite states "high dudgeon," and this she accomplishes most admirably now. "Why? So she can accuse me? Of what? I ask. I spoke my mind; that is all. We all were, and I still am, Catholic, Women of Mary, for Pete's sake. She defiled the temple, the name of Jesus Himself when she married you, as if such were possible in the eyes of the Lord. Then...then, she, both of you, continued to receive. It was my duty to do as I did, and Father Murray agreed."

"We just went over to RPI," Pamela smiles. "You achieved nothing. Anyway, that's not the point. If I had any choice in the matter, I would never forgive you, but, unlike you and my Mary, I have no choice. I must forgive, and, admirably, I guess, Mary Elizabeth chooses to. Times have seriously changed since that whole thing. I guess the question now is can you make your peace with an old lady? Who, I might among other things add, has been raped and has forgiven the pig who did it to her," at which Pam gently swivels Mom toward the smiling little Mary Elizabeth, compelling her gaze upon that beatific countenance (forgive me the grandiloquence, but all this talk has me thinking in Catholic patterns.), and prods her toward the other side of the room.

Not Mother. Not my mother! Not Felicia's either I would bet. Stumbling upon her little buds of heels, she accelerates almost to a run and, upon reaching Mary Elizabeth, falls to her knees and kisses the other's hands, shakes with sobs, and even utters one long wail, like the death song of a coyote or some such animal.

Not my mother!

Felicia takes a hesitant step toward the tableaux; Pam glides inside the circle of my bed, swishing the privacy curtain about us with what seems a nod rather than a handling. I say seems a nod, but perhaps not even that. Over at SPARC I have taken up the distraction of TV. One of my current favorites is a story line following some teenage witches. They can do things. So can Pam. I swear, the curtain, without even so much as a glance from her, recognizes its mission and upon its own volition carries it out. I have no time for speculation, however, because that totally bold little thing has whisked down my sheets and gathered my gown up about my throat. Her hands begin to explore my thighs. I've been molested before. I'm used to it. I hate it. Almost always I submit.

This time, Mother, Felicia, the abused Mary, and a hospital full of saviors just beyond the flimsy draperies of our privacy, are the cause of my making no exception. On my death bed I open myself to the depredations of another's will, this time her instead of his sickness. Let there be no mistake; this is a rape. Of sorts. I never say no, but does that really matter when no questions are asked, no opportunities for demurral afforded.

In my experience there is always an initial spasm of fear. Some might say rush, but my word is well chosen. I freeze solid at the event's horizon, abandon all hope, am drained of any will and am drawn into darkness. At its inception, this present is not unique, but quickly manifests substantial digression from the expected. Her hands, her light fingers move about my most intimate places as might soft shadows of some holy music. I am alive and warm as never before, except perhaps in Mother's womb. Her fundus, yes, even Mother's, must have been an Edenic place. After all I dwelt there until she tired of my parasitical presence and expelled me into a world I never in a million years would have chosen had I the authority to make such decisions.

Pam's hand grows still. "Not so, Ruth," she exclaims without, I swear, verbalization. "You did choose exactly the life you have been given." The hand resumes its tracings upon my warming flesh. That this being is, to say the least, exceptional, is undeniable, but in no way does she, again in my less than humble opinion, have any clue whatsoever as to any choices I have or have not made while alive let alone in some never ever land of fantastic pre-natal existence. Anyway, just what in hell am I doing lying in a Catholic Hospital surrounded by a hundred or so prying eyes, including my mother's, allowing some flagrant lesbian to do me in my sick-bed? I'll just screech. Really loud and the whole thing will be over. Actually, I'll warn her first. That might possibly save us all embarrassment.

"Open your eyes first," her Marijuana voice breathes into my ears. "Believe me," you won't be so anxious to call in the Swiss Guard once you see."

No surprise. I submit, and do her bidding.

They're gone. "They" being the multiple track marks on my thighs and arms (I hadn't even felt her touch on my arms). At last count, I had twenty two red and/or black buds up and down the insides of my thighs just above the knee and countless others running up and down my arms, some faded, some quite fresh. They are gone.

"So are the ones on your neck," the amazing thing laughs. "You're clean as a baby's backside. For now," The smile disappears, a blackness assuming its place. "Mary believes in you. She remembers you from happier times. She sent me over. I know you now too, and I'm not so sure. There are things in you that don't go away all that easily. I'd suggest an exorcist, but getting rid of your Demons might also be the end of you as well. I'd do anything for Mary though, especially now when I can't do anything at all except such little shit as this. Know what I mean?"

Never.... I have never, never, never, despite all my submission, my own depravity.... Never have I and never shall I consider my situation (I'm dying for good Christ's sake) or myself as just a little shit or for that matter a little anything at all, especially shit. Yes, I have a fine command of the language, but my circumstances have taught me a great deal, and I fucking explode into the language so especially favored by all those scumbag mothers who have taken me to all those places I regret having visited — all except Catfish that is. He has the language too: high and low. He favors "jizbag" over "scumbag" for instance, but these are minor semantic differences; we both mean the same thing, and we both can picture the used Trojan slick and wrinkled from use, its bulbous end cradling like so much pneumococcal sputum the pathetic dribblings of someone else's wasted love. "Fuck you, jizbag," rolls up my throat like the first dawn of childhood's joy, and I begin an oedipal follow up with reference to her firstborn son and her own bloody ass, but her laughter slaps my words back down my throat.

"You might be worth it after all," she manages between what seem like mini-seizures, and placing a magic hand upon my bunched shoulder, purrs in a most flirtatious manner, "I think you might take some getting used to, but it could be worth it."

I have nothing to say. Words stop up in my esophagus; I feel as if they may simply burst past my larynx, spewing bloody bits of vocal apparatus along with them as they force their way into being. She touches my throat, and it is all the chicken soup of all the Jewish mothers, one of whom most definitely, although she once attempted to deny it, was my own mother's grandmother, her Bobeshi according to Aunt Julia (who now spells her name with a Y). Once again I submit, giving way to some need within myself to be at someone else's (usually his but this time her) mercy, which almost always ends up unhappily. This time perhaps.... I let myself go, and (surprise surprise) the little whore climbs right up into bed with me, lays herself down beside me, takes my face in her no longer magical, not merciful at all, just urgent hands, draws me to her, and riding my just recently healed thigh kisses me deeply, and, unhindered by the medical apparatus, laps way down my throat into that place where bitter words are no doubt lurking. Then just as quickly, and truly surprisingly, she is catlike barefoot once again on the floor, her smile an Alice vision of something occult, promising, possibly evil, but more likely good unto mystical.

"See ya," she gloats over her bony shoulder as once again without motion she whisks the curtains back open. About two gliding steps away she turns. I'll be back tonight. Try to go to sleep early....Oh, yeah. Don't get your hopes up. I can do many things, difficult as well as easy, like sweeping away those tracks, but the real thing this time, at least for now, is denied me. Believe me, I just tried it. He won't let me at the cancer. There's more going on with you, I guess anyway, than I suspected. I wonder if Mary knew. I'll have to ask the old witch. Sometimes she won't tell me everything. Me? I'm a motherhumping open book."

What kind of witch is this Pam herself? Mary be damned. My eyes follow her across the room, and, as she goes, my vision expands. Against the near wall, the one with the windows, slumps the Pumpkin melting into a heating unit, and I see clearly over the receding Hecate's shoulder my mother's face appear, pale and faded as a February moon.

MOTHER RETURNS ALL wooly from her *tete a tete* with her old frenemy. I swear to myself, unbelievable as it is, that she has not only been crying, but smiling through her tears. Ignoring the Pumpkin, she manages to shed all the scales and Armadillo armor of so many bygone years, perhaps including even the three-quarters of that year I spent unfolding inside her, and implores (I choose the word advisedly) my forgiveness, cries out from behind her veil of tears for a new beginning, a mother and child reunion between two strangers who have not as yet achieved any sort of unity to be renewed. I must not laugh, and in fact, except for just a second's prompting from somewhere dark in my soul, I do not feel remotely like doing so. I tolerate her kiss upon the cheek, the improbably tender caress of her hand something akin to that of a blind woman searching for just the right touch necessary to convey a reality to her brain that her eyes for so long have failed to deliver. "Forgive me," she sobs again, and I am what you might call totally freaked.

The last time I wanted her love I think I might have been all of twelve or thirteen, and then, I am totally aware, my need was the sentimentality of a young girl victim of way too many raging hormones. I have gotten on just fine without her, have even imagined her as dead. Now, I had best play along. Whatever is to come for me will probably be long drawn out, unpleasant, and expensive; that is unless I should most foolishly choose to assert my individuality, embrace my essential independence, and submit to the low-rent, sub-par options of Medicaid. Oh, Mom, your little girl certainly is able to find it deep down in her heart of hearts to forgive you. So without choking or even a minor convulsive swallow, I croak past my tubes, "I love you," and open my arms to her who has so abused me that at one time I might rather have hugged a Komodo Dragon, and almost sincerely I utter a silent thank you to Pam and Mary. In their minor way they have brought me some minimal form of salvation.

MOTHER, AT LEAST her money, as well as her contacts among, by her own reckoning, some very elite people, before the afternoon is out, has effected the services of a Dr. Bhatti, or some outlandish name such as that, who, according to the little nurse assigned me this day, is not just the foremost oncologist in the Capitol District, but possibly, as she put it, "the whole country. Who knows? Maybe the whole world?" Such a simpering little twit, full of her own low-level jabber which she has seen fit to foist upon me, impossibly assuming I might really care who is who or what might be what in a community that, even just a few moments with Mother's I-phone has revealed, is astoundingly ineffective when confronted with circumstances such as mine.

Nevertheless, the way those same few moments with Mother's precious voodoo device have led me to a truth far beyond the mundanities of patient care, medical diagnosis, and best-case scenarios is curious indeed. That brief excursion into interconnectivity has allowed a most profound understanding to settle into a small corner of my consciousness. All the nattering of RN's and the pronouncements of MD's, even those reputed to be the least ineffective members of their profession, are of little or no consequence. *Que sera, sera!* Life goes on. Until it doesn't. I really do not love having to say it, but Mother's change of heart beats them all. Her most maternal concern for my well-being constitutes something of a miracle in itself. Her penitence, her tears of remorse, the newly kindled warmth behind her thin smile, may not have healed my body, but immediately they have soothed my soul and over time may heal my aching and once empty heart.

Well... that last bit is a bit extreme, but then must I not be forgiven as one *in extremis?*

Bullshit. Mother cannot help it. She, even in her weaker moments, is always faithful to her one true self. She is, after all, and always shall be, a bitch. That I am able even to think such pap (a real smear here) speaks ill of me. She came to me out of guilt. Whatever. She did her bounden duty. It is the rare mother who finds it possible to turn from the fruit of her womb in that little drupe's moment of most dire need, and mine is no different. Cut me up at St. Peters or at Memorial Sloan-Kettering; it's all the same to me. Shove your poison seeds as far up my blind vagina as you may wish; broad-band or shaped beam me; poison me with chemicals designed to keep me alive in misery for perhaps an extra year or so. I am no-one's fool. The mind behind the treatment, the site of its administration are of no significance. In truth they will have pierced more than my hands and feet; they no doubt will also have numbered all my bones. However.... Mother is the one most able to ease the horror of my last pathetic days. In my extremity I find her invaluable. Thank you, Ladies.

AS PROMISED, PAM returns that evening. Just not for me. It's not because she's so deeply engaged with Mary either. No sound other than the gurgle of something being drunk stands out from the background white of the room. Fuck her, then.

As soon as that thought works its way toward vocalization but before I utter even a preliminary sound, a shadow appears; it approaches the still form of Pam. Taking her by the shoulders, the insubstance jerks her most solid form to its feet. The rapist?

I reach for the call button.

What unfolds is not rape. Rather it is a long and mutual exchange of kisses and random yet hardly purposeless pawings. No wonder Pam always wears a skirt. In no time I find her seated, back toward him, for such I perceive the phantom's gender to be, upon his lap, and a dance of extreme sensuality featuring the quietest of rustles, the softest of moans commences. It is only when she is firmly seated and has begun some sort of thrust which appears isolated within her pelvis that the witch looks over. My eyes already seeing more than the gloom should reveal are blinded by their glare. I laugh. Of all the insane infidelities in the entire world, this, as Mother might say, takes the cake. I understand. Mary lies passive, awake and fully aware of her mate's indiscretion. She feels no resentment. My eyes seeing yet still blind, I am allowed to perceive the hot coals of her awareness casting violet shafts of their own blind comprehension up into the spotted ceiling. Pam will never, indeed can never, be faithful. Nonetheless, she is a most wondrous creation, and this night, as she submits her own will, her desires, her love to another inevitable expression of the too universal for exclusivity nature of her spouse, Mary Elizabeth's dark fire kindles in me a form of hope, and God forgive me, perhaps the incipience of not only forgiveness but also of love for my most unworthy Mother.

They come to my bedside, the shadow and his mate. He is real. His name is Lenard. "I can't stay," Pam whispers. "This boy and I'r just getting started. I'll leave you with this. You can see the power of my intercession written as the clear flesh of your arms and legs, and I know you comprehend the message of Mary's eyes. Sleep well tonight. You will know all you need know when you awake." At that she turns, lifts her skirt to flash me a most pale and magical moon, and skitters on bare feet out the door always just beyond the reach of her lover's questing hand.

ALMOST ALWAYS I am competent enough to be aware of the difference between reality and unreality, to be more precise, the distinctions existing between the world of my dreams and that of my waking self. For some time, I have been aware that they overlap in multitudinous manners, and said awareness has been sufficient to dispel any confusion unconventional habits and active imagination may have ushered my way. Until last night that is. I now am constrained to make choices, life or death decisions, but have naught but shadow upon which to base them. If I am being given no drugs, the presence of which in my system might explain my confusion, of what verifiable substance have been these most recent visitations of the little ho who might be Jesus? Or at least his sister? Or some thing of some superordinary nature? Religiously have I eschewed feeble-minded, week-willed explanations for indecision. My will is paralyzed. I do not know. Am unable to understand. Am I awake or dreaming? Alive, dying or already dead? Am I the object of a divine visitation? Is Pam holy or demonic? Succubus or angel? I do not know. Am unable to decide. Is all darkness? Or is it light?

I have always scorned the vacillations so common to the elite and hyper-educated which serve no function but to debilitate. Someone, Mark Twain I would guess or maybe Bukowski, I don't much care, wrote that a problem in this world is that the intelligent are full of doubt while the idiots are full of confidence. I find this observation tragically accurate. The world is led by the likes of Mother and Felicia while the rest of us wonder what we might do, filled with "further considerations" and "the need for more exhaustive research." I would despair but cannot decide even to do that.

Not all investigation, however, is futile dithering. Since my years at Williams, one of my favorite resources—when I am straight—has been a marvelous ethereal entity entitled *The Skeptic's Dictionary*. Earlier in the day I employed Mother's iPhone to access scientific information concerning my situation, but I must confess I also looked into some, as they are so blandly termed, *Alternative and Complementary* therapies, and just for a moment, perhaps even somewhat longer, I allowed myself to be seduced by the possibility of non-invasive, non-toxic, non-radiological treatment for my cancer. Then, as if of its own will, the skeptic appeared, and from page one, entitled **The Touch That Doesn't HEAL:** *From Abracadabra to Zombies*, emerged the truth, page after page of idiocy debunked. Perhaps someday I shall thank some doctor, possibly even God, I cannot say, but for now I thank the Prime Skeptic Robert Todd Carroll whose unique contribution to a sanity more multitudinous than mine alone is truly invaluable.

Specifically, I had visited a website entitled *Independent Cancer Research Foundation* headed by one R. Webster Kehr who among many other publications presents a near miraculous yet ultimately mundane approach in *The Overnight Cure For Cancer.* Were I to subscribe to his approach, there would be no need for surgery, radiation, or Chemo. In a natural way in this natural world I would be healed. The appeal was irresistible; as have Paloma's little cote, I too was led to coo my acceptance of a power both greater and more mysterious than I had imagined might exist in the material world. Why not? If nature, either our own or that catchall entity out there all around us, causes such as cancer, then doesn't it stand to reason that nature also holds the cure? If only we accept. If only we turn our lives over to this higher power, this savior, God, as we might understand her, shall not all good things, including health, flow? Aye! There's the rub: the more I read on the site, the more questions and doubts niggled at my mind.

To date, Paloma's way has been absolutely no help to me at all. As for Kehr? Who might he be anyway? I found quite quickly that Mr. Kehr is no doctor, not even a veterinarian. He has two degrees from Brigham Young, one in Math and one in Accounting. Hell, even Paloma is as qualified as this ex-Marine, former Mormon Missionary to treat my problem. So, not quite by magic or coincidence, but rather by the return of my questioning nature, I turned to Mr. Carroll and was quickly disabused of the notion that somewhere, anywhere, out there lay recovery from my most dread disease. My only faint hope seems to lie with the scalpel, linear accelerator, and IV drip. God help me, I don't want that. Quite possibly, I might have slid into accepting demonstratively false hope as preferable to established yet hopeless procedures....

Fortunately, I fell asleep.

THE WOMAN FROM the church hallway, she who might have been one of my possible selves awaits me. She is so real. Too real. I am not sleeping. I cannot be. Never in dreams have I experienced another's odors, not the occult personal musk nor the public essences of various *parfumeries*, neither have I so memorably felt such soul-deep warmth as wrapped itself about my so very corpus that decidedly non-malignant night. She does not speak; she need not.

I will not survive this cancer. I will not outlive my mother, the Pumpkin, not Paloma or the Scarecrow. I may not even have as much as a year.

"Where in all bloody hell is Pam?" I think I scream this out into the empty hospital darkness not just into the abyss becoming of myself. The beautiful me smiles. She casts her eyes down and beckons me to follow. I have read Lewis Carroll, have innocently believed in the possibly of passing through a magic mirror. A fifth floor pane of window glass? Really? Nonetheless, here we are, above it all. Or at least some of it. Off to the east lights rise higher than we. The moon pales far above us all. We move beyond, above and below but no longer around. It is desert. There is light but no sun to be seen; the sky is blinding; the sand below as well. We glide softly to a raised shelf of rock. I know I have visited this place before. As confirmation, upon a pock-marked oval stone lies the pink with yellow flowers flip-flop I have been unable to find for months. And spent needles, stacked, a dozen or more, clean picked bones once a part of life, one time filled with joyous fluid motion. I have huddled upon this promontory before. I have faded into here from many dreams. This, however, is no dream. Ruth, the lovely one, kneels before me. "Here you truly are Lottie," she asserts. Tears glisten at the corners of her eyes for a mere second before the sere atmosphere sucks them into the thirsting void.

"May I tell you a story," she asks, "one you already know? Will you hear it out despite its familiar and simplistic nature?"

Freedom of choice is a complex phenomenon. I am in this place against my will. I am doomed to an early death, and this being, myself or whoever, asks my permission to relate some trite little parable or other that I probably have no desire to hear, and also requests that I freely relinquish my freedom to opt out once the ridiculous thing is begun. As I've said, I am far too compliant, too submissive. "Lay it on," I breathe into the glittering air

"The tale is of a recalcitrant sheep and her shepherd as it works itself out in a land such as this."

Whatever.

Dance of Destruction
Arthur
2012

"I first dropped acid in October of 1970, just twenty-three years old, but well past the prime age for such things. I had first heard of Lysergic Acid Diethylamide several years earlier, subsequent to my discovery of Ken Kesey's *One Flew over the Cuckoo's Nest*. Kesey was a genius of substance far more than literary, if you know what I mean. The man was more than the appellation human suggests. In my particular circumstance, one might assert that he came to live in my soul. I admire a precious few, if any, of my fellow — for such they claim to be — human beings. Mr. Kesey is the grand exception. I thirsted for the Kool Aid and hungered for the sacrament of liberation he most assuredly promised to be. I was not disappointed. My subsequent disaffection with such pedestrian pursuits as enlightenment and transformation through the cyclopean lens of LSD implies no diminution of the stature of the author. He was a pioneer. The fact that continents exist beyond the one he opened to those of us bold enough to venture where very few other than he had gone before, does not diminish his achievement. "LSD opened my eyes to the miracle of that which we name reality. Kesey knew there was more, that to see beyond the horizon one has to fly.

He never discovered the way. I burn to do so.

"Now many such as my parents claim that Jesus, or his spirit or Paraclete or some esoteric being of similarly unlikely otherworldly nature, dwells within them and offers up unto them Eternity…Infinity, if you prefer. That their Bible is the roadmap to Heaven and unity with the divine. Do such, however, truly follow their master's voice? Would they willingly drag their own death up a hill beyond their climbing? I absolutely would not. I could go on the rest of my existence without any sort of God, but especially one such as theirs. Indeed, my parents, each alone and both together could serve as authenticating evidence for Thoreau's observation that 'Any fool can make a rule, and any fool will mind it.' I'm no Bible scholar, but what I've learned about Jesus is that all he basically suggested was that we love God and each other. Admittedly I have fallen short in both cases. However, I must inquire: Is it possible to fall short of a goal one has never set for oneself? From my perspective, Jesus is no more than an interesting character in a tedious if tragic story. I do like the way Scorsese did him. I'd probably be like that too. However, as did my parents, and as do all their remaining foldfellows, such believers blindly, they would say faithfully, follow the earthborn rules of that outworn creed called Christianity in hopes of some eternal reward so depressingly like the drudgery they already experience that the only reason to eschew suicide is the fact that death only gets you there sooner than is absolutely necessary. Should I truly give a tinker's farthing?

Anyway, back to basics. It took me some time, consideration and reconsideration, before I dropped my first tab. By the time I finished my third reading of *Cuckoo* and channeled Kesey I had already tried pot and as an initial compromise increased my usage, adding more exotic and potent manifestations of the weed as well as pure, or so I believed, THC. Into this I blended alcohol along with a positive fondness for any form of Amphetamine — mostly diet pills. I actually became proud of the fact that, in my own mind, I was developing into quite the speed freak.

"I had a decent job as a reading specialist in a local school system, but that soon ran afoul of my increasingly obvious countercultural leanings. Ours was a small school in a small town, New Lebanon, NY, and I could perceive hostility coming from all sides, students, parents, administration, and other faculty. Consequently, in June of 1970, I dropped out. I had tuned in to the Beatles, the Stones, Simon and Garfunkel, but that summer, adrift upon the streets of nearby Albany, I came to know more of the 60's spirit than ever before. I was able to insinuate myself into a Grateful Dead concert, and experienced the Jefferson Airplane at SUNY Albany in a small room, maybe two-hundred people. I was really drunk and stoned with some hot shit meth I had just zoomed right up into my brain of brains. Gracie sang and pinned me right up against the wall, a helpless motherfucker caught in some kind of pull greater than all the moon shadows of all the tides of all this life. Or something akin to that. They say I ran up on stage, that Jorma laughed and offered me a tambourine. I guess I may have staggered around up there a while before my friends came and retrieved me. So it went. I think I almost remember.

"Anyway, due to the devolution of my communication skills, perhaps it is not so obvious as once it was, but I am very well educated. My Bachelor's is from Cornell, Master's in English from SUNY Albany, and an ABD in communications from RPI. These experiences and near accomplishments encouraged in me a nascent supercilious attitude only worthy of someone who had earned a PhD and then gone beyond. However, having always found it difficult to think less of myself for any reason whatsoever, I choose to view deciding not to finish my PhD as the result of having achieved an awareness of a higher order than academia can engender or a degree certify. I simply had moved beyond such vanities.

"Thank you Kesey, Gracie, Jerry, *et al* for the truth you helped me find. No lie such as that broadcast about by academic credentials could deceive me any longer. By October I had already dropped out of RPI and had dropped into my authentic self. October 12, a great day for explorers all, I dropped my first acid. From that moment the real I began to live. You may call me Randle McMurphy. No, I am not some fictionalized version of a fictionalized character. I am McMurphy subsequent to the lobotomy; I am the Randle of my mind, alone and separate from any mundane concept such as awareness, and I am more alive than before you pressed that pillow to my face and stopped up the hallucinogenic imaginings we all, but no longer I, recognize as reality. I am more alive than ever you thought of being, than ever you could comprehend—unless that is, you are like me.

"How likely is that?

"I walk among you. Here I sit in your pathetic group, fourteen zombies and one truly dead who nonetheless strolls upon your tedious pathways. So, why not settle back and listen to my story. No ear buds, no phones, no i-Pads allowed. It is my turn, and I will speak from beyond my grave.

"I possess many talents, not all of them socially acceptable, not all of them of any value or interest to me. One of them is a charismatic personality. If I wish, and rarely do I so, I am able to charm almost anyone, male, female…bi. No matter the form in which you imagine yourself, I most likely can glamour you. The other is a sporadic interest in technical theatre. I am an accomplished stage carpenter, lighting designer, electrician, and sound tech. I have worked for several major artists on tour, including *America, The Association,* and *Jim Croce.* I still travel the more mundane highway south and west to New Orleans for *Jazz Fest* every spring. I've been around, and still am whenever I want to be. I once held a spot on Jim Morrison and stumbled part of the way to where I am accompanied by his song *Break on Through….* Because of the Doors as much as anyone else I broke into the place where I am now and I ain't never coming back.

"Enough of playtime! Let my story be told."

"Again?" rings multithroated about the room, resounding ever louder as it bounces back and forth into a cacophony of discontent.

"Now people," Paloma soothes. Allow Arthur his say.

"Randal," I assert. "You will call me by my true name. I am Randal."

"Of course you are," the sparrow squeaks. "I apologize. Go on…if you would."

Of course I will, and I do. "If who I have become has a defining moment, and it absolutely does not, it is that night of the TV."

"Of course..." once again echoes.

"Please, group," the dove coos.

Fuck them all, I think. For all their impatience maybe I should give them the full story not merely the prologue I tend to share.

I cannot. I never shall.

"We were at a friend's apartment. Mitch was his name. He too worked in theatre, and he wrote plays as well. The occasion was the after party after the after party after the party after the premier of his one-act *Just a Sad Song* at the Cohoes Music Hall, a professional production with lighting by Yours Truly. A grand success it was, running for two weeks more without either of us in attendance. Possibly a very good thing, you might intuit, given the state of our consciousnesses. That night at Mitch's I entered the reality of the space between and within myself. Hadron be damned. I am WIMP. I am Dark Matter. I am not space nor am I time. You cannot find me, for I may not exist. I am, however, Randal McMurphy, and for a nonexistent instant I partied well.

"In some slow molasses of time and the nonvacant void, four or five of us dwelt in a perceived world of immense possibility. True, it may have been engendered by an overabundance of alcohol and drugs, especially Orange Sunshine and some four-way blotter of more minor credentials, but truth be told, the truth was revealed at least for those circumstances, as differently imagined as they may have been, and the never ending dance of destruction began.

"A favorite musician of mine, with whom I never worked, styled a Bob Dylan song in a most unforgettable fashion; no, it was not superior to Dylan's, an artist with whom I might have worked, just different, and in its own way was able to lay the fat old cliché out upon the Higgs field of all my particulate matter and make it assume reality within the unreality and hypothetical probability all caught up in the slumping amber of possibility. 'Death is not the end,' the Master wrote and his interpreter sang in just one of the different linguistic forms the English language, especially when coupled with music, may assume. A tired old cliché. Who has not heard of the laws of conservation of matter and energy? Who does not understand that Quantum and particle physics render the concept of 'end' as absurd? If there is no end, then Death, while possibly extant in more than one guise in a multitude of imagined universes, offers no possibility of termination in any of them.

"Your blank faces amuse me; the ricocheting squabble of your empty-headed objections causes me pleasure. You must know that were I to leap from my chair, or remain seated for that matter, pull a pistol, nine millimeter would be my choice today, I could not put an end to even one of your miserable little lives. Yes, you'd die, you'd all die, but nothing would end. Even were I to turn....

"Ok, Paloma. I hear you. Sorry folks. I just let myself carry myself away from myself at times.... You all know that.... You're fuckin' used....

"Again, sorry! I'll continue from the still place from which I so magically just now fell away.

"Teddy, you're always quoting Jesus. I know you know at least in some way that I must be telling the truth. No doubt both Dylan and Cave believe in some sort of savior. Of Heaven? And Hell? I hope the fuck not.... Again...sorry.

"My wish here is to transition into that party, the dance of destruction. Perhaps a more accurate term would be dance of superpositional states, but a simple form of expression for the very complex nature of such concepts serves best when one addresses such as you. Thus I use destruction. I hope as well to reveal the eternal and ubiquitous nature, as real as real can ever be, and so achingly simple, of Death. You see me before you. I am Randal Patrick McMurphy. I am dead.

"Snicker your doubts and misunderstandings, you fools. You know not me, you blocks, you stones, you worse than senseless.... No, Paloma, I will not cease nor will I desist. Were I a common man, I wouldst assay to cobble you, but I am no commoner, nor Marullus either. I cannot drive you vulgar from your path, and neither am I Caesar. I lie eyeless, breathless upon a bed of stone within a stone garden from which I observe you blind about your business, within which I am not allowed to linger, from which I cannot escape. The Bard had it right, as far as it goes. He just never went far enough. If death truly is not the end, and I avow that it is not, then Marullus, Flavius, Brutus, Antony, even Caesar himself fit the metaphor. Were they all not equally blind, dense, and pathetically human?"

WHERE DO YOU imagine we must be off to, Dovey? Are we all not involunteers here? All save you, of course. Where might you be in such a hurry to fly away to?

Your apartment? If I must know, your cat?

Really sweet one? How long can a dove cohabitate with a feline. Unless.... Declawed, fanged and balled....

Really, now that was uncalled for.

FOR THE PAST nano-minute, if there exists such category of nothingness, I have been communicating intensely with Paloma, my little dove. She is gone now as must necessarily be the case, and I am left with my own leavings greasing my bull-goose-bumped upper lower extremities as well as slicking down the wild nest of my pubic hair. She is achingly magnificent, and her parting words unspoken, I read them in her tragic eyes. Yes, you filthy slut I know. That's what they all say. Pull your wings tight about you; go home and bleed your asshole drippings into your birdbath commode, and when you are able, when you can take it again, you may return, and I will rip your delicate being into cosmic shrieks and feather stripping howls of that draught of joy and agony which only I am capable of brewing in the female soul.

"It's all right," I say. "You most assuredly are welcome."

No doubt I should arise and shower or at least clean myself up a bit, but there is something profoundly erotic in wallowing about in coital expenditures even if they are the result of solitary associations. Besides, I have to get to a meeting, the one just down the hall. But first, a meeting before the meeting as they like to call it. Just the three of us, Me, Myself, and I. Sometimes there are others. Paloma has been here, for instance, dressed as she was that afternoon when for her our session was to be followed up by another of some professional significance. She hoped, she revealed with a smile wide enough to slip a cow's tongue through, it would lead to a full-time position on the faculty at Albany Medical College. For my own reasons I hoped she wouldn't get it. She still doesn't know, she claims, but I think I do. She'll soon be long gone. That's why the venture into buggery this afternoon. Fuck her in the ass and she'll always remember me.

I think.

I am; I am three actually. At least this day, but then I am also one as am Myself and Me. We're so similar in fact that none of us is able to delineate, at least logically and coherently, any difference at all. The three of us together? We fucking know.

Yes, our language has somewhat coarsened, perhaps, most probably due to the descent into common carnality the Dove occasioned, and afterward also. Our physical pail has slopped over, and, hogs that we are, we have wallowed in the swill. Pleasurable as such may be, I can't go down there smelling of sex and her various essences. There is time. A shower will be a delight after a particularly sweaty and fetid coupling such as was ours. A stall, unlike a common sty, is also a fine solitary place for intrapersonal communication. As we wash away the detritus of every day, our understanding is elutriated as well.

Perhaps this day will offer a clearer vision a new perception of exactly who it is we are.

I am not Randal, we know that, but neither are we Arthur, king, real or fictional.

Just who we are though....

Ah, god, the water is hot. My back, my scalp burn alive through whatever haze has enveloped them. My thighs, my feet, even my grumpy old ass. God is pleasure.

The aftermath. I sit toward the back on a classically scarred up VA folding chair. There is no Dove this evening. This is straight recovery crap. AA this time. I attend them all. But I do not belong. *Je refuse!* Just like all AA meetings, this one technically is open to all who qualify as alcoholics and even to those simply wishing to vacation in a foreign, even occult, land, but actually, only those of us, both residents and day-care, who are clients of the VA ever find their way into these rooms. Just as well. We're a completely insane lot with memories, practices, sins and compulsions the citizens of this fair land are best spared any knowledge of. For instance, at least two-thirds of us at this meeting have, not always in the heat of battle, killed a fellow human being, and more than one or two of us have done worse than those poor Gyrenes videotaped pissing on the corpses of those whom they have freshly wasted. Ever heard the threat, "I'll cut off your head and shit down your neck"? I've seen it done. *Hoo Rah!* as they say in the lesser branch of the Navy. Hoo far reeking rah!

How is it that I have achieved so many academic degrees you may ask, given this latest information concerning my apparent resident status at a Veterans Administration Hospital, and a combat-informed military record? I must admit that the preceding is both a relevant and misguided question. Here I sit, smiling outward as well as inward while maintaining the non-communicative posture I have adopted over the course of my three-week's enforced attendance at this meeting of the no-minds. Perhaps my reticence is due to my smug superiority—notice I say "superiority" not sense of same. Perhaps, but then how would one account for my volubility in Paloma's more therapeutic sessions? I can only say that they know me here in a particularly limiting sense of that term. They have all my records. Even from high school. I am a historical character, compulsively recorded in an official SRB. I do have a college degree. Two actually. The first, pre-Vietnam, a BA in History, no graduate work, not even an almost-Master's, let alone an ABD. I did work at the school. That is until I danced up the front walk one seven AM or so and with great efficiency dispatched the double-glass from three of the main office windows, following that up by urinating all over the imbecile's desk...or...now that I think of it, into the bottom drawer of his precious filing cabinet. Whatever, it was a far, far better course of action than was the one I had originally plotted the evening and pre-dawn before. I had been listening to Pink Floyd — more about them later — Ummagumma. How that disk doth draw me directly into the heart of the sun of my own divine inspiration....

If I don't stop, I'll laugh out loud. As the minivan's stickers proclaim, *Life is good.*

Sid, we all call him Vicious, long and not so lean with a gravid cirrhotic abdomen and true Asian coloration incongruous in one named Wingate, expounds upon his virtuous refusal during his own imagined mini My Lai. I had a Zippo; everybody did. Sid kept his in his pocket. His guilt trip, by which he means the long and winding course of the last forty years or so, his self-defined cowardly decision not to report his fellow Marines, is, by his own eye-witness account, not just the primary, but the sole reason for his, again by his own estimation, over-indulgence in alcohol, first Schaeffer and then Genesee Beer. Poor Bloke, as British Bob has quipped, is killing himself with a low-end manifestation of the High Life. I refuse to scoff at Sid with the unrestrained contempt his pathetic tale warrants, however. Surely there is no soul upon this overpopulated planet more prone than am I to extravagant visions of himself, excited imaginings of fact and fiction, actuality and imagination, real and oh so possible as to loom more likely probable.

So.... Back to the reality of a folding chair and a dreadful cup of cooling coffee.

I am beginning the third week of my projected stay, a short timer at last. The circumstances of my commitment, for that is its exact nature — in the 1950's sense of the term — are irrelevant to the nature of my presently perceived circumstances. I have always been odd, at least from the moment of my imagining myself as separate from the fog surrounding the three-year-old being staring into the slack features of the creature he somehow identified as Mother while she slept. Dark and pocked, that face, matted upon black hair wrought in twisted patterns upon a yellow pillow, for the first time seemed *Other*, and from its sudden individuality I drew my own. From that day forward I have known myself, grown myself, and remembered the self I have chosen from day to present day. I have ever known our reality as conceptually similar to that of the ancient holy trinity of those or that being both one and many, both present and eternal, all-encompassing in its irrationality yet, surprisingly, in a limited sense, impossibly possible. Simply, I too am three, as I have already revealed, but am more than three as well. I am alone. Individual, yet never only one. Donne wrote that "No man is an island," and the Airplane answered, "He's a peninsula." I love the poem despite the fact that Donne had no real inspiration or insight, and even the snarky response of the drummer is an empty jest. If Spencer Dryden was really Charlie Chaplin's nephew, the joke becomes even more worthy of silent mimicry. Should one really wish to X out the letters, n,u,l,a, in order to be confronted with this child's view of his nature, of the nature of us all? I love you Spence, but I search for more awareness than that. Might I not just as well be affirming that no man is a fruitcake; he's a currant, thereby eliminating the need for eliminating an entire irrelevant letter. What if one were to X away the C and the r in the Great Pretender's common appellation, then rearrange the remaining letters? So too might the whole of humanity and his/her/our (?) multitudinous worlds be reduced to puns of little consequence other than to amuse the stoned awareness of someone even more removed from sophistication than am I (all three of us).

So far I have smiled through half a meeting. Is there any future here? Of course not. Just as does the past, so too does the future, so does the present as well offer only convenient phraseology for the desperate fumblings of the mundane consciousness, itself possibly more than possibly yet probably quite improbably either eternal or infinite or possibly impossibly simultaneously both.

I truly could have been that other man that I know I am not. I much admire the ABD, and I know I could have done exactly that which my imaginative construct has done so effortlessly. After *Nam* (I despise this particular appellation, but even here it holds a certain *cachet*), I got my MA, assumed a role in the semi-professional workforce, and embarked upon a distinguished career as a counter-cultural misfit. I do mean misfit. I fit nowhere, neither a hippy nor a hawk, neither square nor TTI (totally tuned in). I did, however, manage to completely drop out. Even Robert Hunter recognized the allure of *Home*, but even the Dead could not lead me there. I have no home, neither external nor internal, and my only guide has ever been myself, at least one of me. So here I am, the actual me, entering the last week of my VA stay, and I am quiet. I must set out upon the dark road of my destiny again, either that or into the uncertain and weightless present of one who has fallen over the edge and for whom there can be no solace, no sense of anything other than being. Whatever that is.

Some cowboy clown or other begins its drone. He is someone who flits in and out of Paloma's sessions as well as the droning hive of AA, someone who may have achieved an even higher degree of PTSD than that incorporated into the persona most would assume to be myself. We have never so much as exchanged "Keep on coming backs." While of no relevance to me and my own concerns, he has impressed several of the Troglodytes here (and I include staff, professional and support, within this group) with his imagined insights. They refer to him and his halting phrasings with a piety worthy of a Pentecostal preacher of the tent show variety. His name is Lenny or something like that, and I think his surname might be Cohan or (more likely) Cohen.... No matter, he seems to have over the course of time spewed forth enough doggerel to fill a ten-cut C&W CD. One in particular occurs to me at this moment: *But you see, I was a soldier....* Interesting if not fascinating is it not how we (all humans, that is) remember so well so many songs and pathetic rhymes that we despise with every wave of our rational brains. Damn those Amygdalae anyway. I refuse to be slave to my biology. Yet, again come those possibly stress-intensified words, *You see, I was a soldier!*

THE LITHIUM IS working. They give me meds every day, and the fools (or possibly they're too busy) trust me to take them. Over the past three weeks I have amassed an impressive stock for resale, but as of yesterday I have begun using them for personal advantage. Sometime within the next several days some functionary will check my levels, and my discharge might possibly depend upon their being high enough to attest to my compliance with medication protocols. As ever there must be, however, problems attend. The less than worthless Med. immediately tickles a trembling into my hands, and a need to stretch the tendons in my neck. Sadly, I am a walking casebook for Lithium sides. I am thirsty all the time and would urinate myself dry by noon if it were not for an appalling intake of anything resembling salt. Given the opportunity, like some old dog, I would most probably chew incessantly upon a piece of rawhide. And coffee! I love a good, hot mug of strong coffee; I might find it easier to give up both alcohol and drugs than go forever without, not just caffeine, but whatever else it is that sets coffee so far above even a most potent, faux Black Beauty. Problematically, the brew reduces Lithium levels, and even here in AA, I must abstain. Soon, thank all the higher powers, the situation will be reversed. I require Lithium for no purpose other than to limit the duration of this latest incarceration; I do not need meetings, nor do I require therapy. I do need....

"No thank you, Phil." I do not wish to share.

I assiduously try to maintain the language of my thoughts as well as that of their external manifestations at a certain level, but, inwardly at least, I sometimes allow it all to slump into a deep pile of excremental verbiage. *There, that makes it better, offers a blessing of sorts upon that which is to come. Fuck you*, I howl inwardly, but, (could it be the lithium?) outwardly I remain unmoved, ostensibly the compliant alcoholic, as I add, "I think I need to listen. Today." B*ig emphasis upon this word, today, they love it here.* On and on they drone, all of them once soldiers except, of course, those who call themselves sailors, and Marines, and just what do you call someone who once was Air Force? We all — pardon the effluvia — once were in that same boat or whatever you desire to christen your particular mode of once-upon-a- time military transport. We all were motherfucking soldiers, even that Dyke Lois over by the window with her GI Jane hair. No, she would never fuck Daddy, but I would wager, *as* Daddy she would most lustily have her vacuous way with Mommy. What think you of that Siggy? Elektra all the way? She simply fails to qualify as Oedipus. Would not the response be most enlightening if sadly manipulated Orestes were asked if killing Mommy might not be the equivalent of doing her most sinfully? As Clytemnestra bares her breast, imploring his mercy, does not his peninsula grow long? And hard?

I AM ON the street. Alone and free, four dollars and sixty-two cents in my pocket and hope in my heart. As I amble hardly without aim in the direction of Holland Av. I anticipate the fateful turn toward New Scotland and the already open sports bar. Recovery Room I do believe it is called. Corporate types are really so profoundly clever are they not? Whoever would have thought, just around the corner from the VA and directly opposed to Albany Medical Center, to have called their bar the Recovery Room, a name oh so pregnant with possible interpretations. It is to there I must repair if I am to recover from the dreary weeks in the psych ward, the endless sessions and meetings. But what to do? I am effectively broke. There is no possibility of running a tab at a yuppie place such as the Room.

To a more than minimal degree, I do possess within my repertoire, a charismatic persona which finds its optimal expression in such straited circumstances. As Mr. Vicious is often (too often) wont to say, I could charm the tits off a witch or the balls off a horny bull. Coarse, indeed, but also perceptive. No doubt, I shall soon be delivered into more comfortable circumstances.

Ah, Mr. Burns how aft do this rodent's best schemed lays go agley. I am free, my eyes stung by the cruel April breeze for but a moment, when from the nearby walkway which leads to even deeper donjons of recovery, issues forth a voice, part Johnny Cash and part British Bob. If such be possible! "Where to, my friend?" the unseen visitor into my land of sad hopes and forlorn dreams intrudes an unexpected question. That is no one's business but my own, but, given the nature of this sidewalk interrogation, perhaps Cowboy Bob is simply another I. Such manifestations of myself are not infrequent, and my best choice when confronted by such in potentially public circumstances has always been to ignore them or, should one such grow insistent, answer privately within the shared expanses of my own consciousness. I choose to ignore the Oxford twang and diligently assess my possibilities as with equal determination I pursue my course along the avenue.

"You, Artie!" the voice calls in its annoying hybrid tone. "Over here. I need a word with you."

My mother called me Artie. My sisters. My brother. Nobody else. They would never dare. Only during those brief times when one or multiples of them emerge from wherever they are hidden does that name ever find resonance in the chambers of my awareness. This most assuredly is some form of an other. Damn all those meetings I have attended and all the dregs of human procreativity who have in some insidious form or other attached themselves to me as a result of my misadventures. No doubt it is one of such who hails me now. As I expected, a thing of vaguely recognizable countenance appears. He manifests as a grey and wrinkling scarecrow — for he is exceedingly thin with overly broad, impossibly square shoulders. Of course, he is the poetry dude from group. Hell and all sorts of damnation.

"Mr. Woolf.... Arthur," the man from Oz commences in a most formal English tone, poor Johnny dead within him as he most inescapably is within our currently shared plane of reality. "Please, might you perhaps grant me a moment of your time? I shan't detain you for any great extent of same...."

He mocks me. This is no saccharine Bobby. This motherfucker's mocking me. Nevertheless, at this moment of anger, of testosterone rising, I must admit to a certain appreciation for his artistry. He could be, might be.... Me. He has followed me from the hospital. Whatthefuckever, he's gonna wish to Christ he'd stayed where he belongs. I have been looking his way over my right shoulder, but now I turn full front with just the hint of an angle, left foot forward, weight slightly to the rear, ready for either....

"Hold on, partner," the Mooky cautions, Johnny Cash once again alive and well within his now subdued tonality. "I'm a friend."

Yet on guard, the unrefined heart of the darkness who I am present in my expression, I counter, "Yeah? So you say. There's nobody calls me Artie no more. Nobody."

"Not your brother?"

"My fuckin' brother's dead. I come away from the places I been and live. Billy's dead. I fuckin' survived Holloway back in '65. That poor bastard bought it in Saigon, *Tan Son Nhut* in 66 for God's sake. About a year after Holloway. Not even real combat. Mortar round took him out while he slept. He was a good one, but 'was' is the word. You ain't him. You are askin' to join him though. Right fuckin' quick."

Again with the Johnny Cash or maybe it's some even more cowboy accent, "Whoa," he cautions, "I've seen you around, and once I was sure it was you, I thought I'd have a word. I knew Billy, you know...or parbly you don't. Anyhow, I thought maybe I could help an old brother's brother out. Know what I'm sayin'?"

Billy always attracted the freaks, and this guy obviously is no exception. Probably extremely annoying, perhaps, especially at times like this, unfortunately importunate, but dimwits of like nature have been one of the multitudinous banes of my existence for most if not all of my adult life. Even Billy could be more than a trifle trying at times. All his buddy here wants, no doubt, is some comfortable reminiscence of the type deemed by some therapists, the whorish dove among them, to be therapeutic. Perhaps the stickman has money....

"Perhaps," I suggest, "you would care to accompany me to the Recovery Room for a morning's ablution?"

"Perhaps," the supercilious bastard counters, "you might be suggesting a libation."

In fact libation is the term I intended, but upon occasion, especially when I have recently descended into that unrefined and impervious to such processes core of myself, my higher facilities require a period of recovery from the shock of recognition that the very beast which they have been charged with suppressing has so easily burst its chains, and a time as well to suppress the nagging doubt that they are sufficient to the task, for they know full well that their prisoner is they themselves. Not one of me will ever admit to some semi-literate fool that I am either confused or wrong. "I meant," I sneer, "precisely to use ablution, meaning, my new found acquaintance, to wash away the dreary antiseptic film of the medical establishment there to our rear, and to ablute from our individual and collective consciousnesses the comical proscriptions of all the talk and all the therapies of those who profess to know and understand others who themselves are of a nature not recognized in their textbooks nor understood by their orgulous intellects."

That last got him. I love the word "orgulous." Nobody knows what it means, so I use it at will whenever I mean proud as to be taken in its pejorative sense. I am back. "Totally, totally!" as some TV clown used to say on some program one of me actually has deigned to watch upon the television machine.

This orgulous clown, inartistic as only the unconsciously ridiculous can be, transforming three syllables into four and mispronouncing the perfectly simple second syllable as if it were two, adding an "ig" as in "pig," nonetheless stumbles upon the correct denotation of the word. "Origulous, he muses; parbly means proud or somethin' like that?"

Ending as he does with the lifted tone of a possibly insincere question, the fool knows full well that I am required to answer. For just a moment I wonder, does this blatantly uneducated member of the eternally recovering underclass somehow actually know the word? No. His pronunciation has trumpeted that fact to all within earshot. Has he somehow, miraculously for one of his ilk, intuited the meaning from context? Possible, I must assume. Or could he possibly be, unthinkable as such might be, merely toying with my sense of my own superiority, valid as that perception certainly is? Impossible. In a way the once real Johnny Cash was a real cowboy. No real intellect to be sure, but a man of talent, artistry, and supreme dignity. I would wager that Mooky here is no better than an alcoholic rodeo clown, one stumble-step ahead of the bull's horns, whose sad business is to distract destiny for a moment's time away from the fallen riders whose hope is to pick themselves up from the dirt and limp off to give their insane craft another try on some impossibly brighter day.

I'm about to go somewhere I haven't been for a while. No doubt the lithium has spared me such visits. Here I go. Back to Mitch's apartment in Cohoes...the drugs, the booze. The night of the TV. The night of that which might have been....

"Listen, pardner," Mook intrudes. "We, neither one of us needs a drink. How about just a door further down?"

Of course, they're all so wearyingly predictable. Nothing better than a cup of coffee. In their universe that may be so. But not in mine. At least not this day. I say "No."

"Sorry then to have detained you," he chirps not really British Bob or Johnny Cash.

I know the accent. "Are you Canadian?" I ask. "Quebec maybe?"

"Nope," he responds with a wide smile. "Not since I 'as a kid. Oklahoma most a my life. Goodwell. The real thing. Born up north. S'possible a man can't git rid of the things he's born with no matter how he tries."

I find it serendipitous that in this latest round of my continuing saga with the VA two of the three or so people (Paloma for certain. Never shall I forget the silk of her skin, the soft fragrance from between her newly parted thighs.) I might remember for more than a day or two are this clown and British Bob, neither born in the United States, both, apparently in Mook's case, actually in Bob's, US military combat veterans.

More in jest than from actual curiosity I ask, "Are you legal?"

"After my first tour," his flat reply.

We round the corner onto New Scotland; how we got here I cannot say. Oblivious to its seduction, we pass the Recovery Room, soon finding ourselves pouring creamer and scads of sugar into Grande dark roasts. I am not this easily led. I can only attribute my docility to the lithium. Back in a little hallway leading to the restrooms stands a table, half in the dark, half-light. Mooky imperiously, yes imperiously as were he a dowager empress, coincidentally providing substance for my term orgulous, gestures its way.

I hate myself. Sometimes I find myself a fool. I have been seduced in a most unromantic fashion by this chameleon. I wonder.... Is it possible he is even more I than I am myself? Whatever that means. I have been asking such stupefying questions in sessions and meetings for so long that now in my lonely times I have begun to ask them of myself. As if there could be an answer. Just what more might this clown, this cowboy, this fellow sufferer from whatever combat-related illnesses the VA has assigned us, prove to possibly, actually and not-so-actually be? Such flashes through my mind as we arrange our cups, as he sighs, again somewhat in the nature of that old bag over in England, and looks directly into what might have been my unguarded eyes had I not long ago learned the technique of shutting down their naturally too indiscriminant standards for admission through their gateway into my consciousness. This morning in the strangely filtered sunlight of a Starbucks, curtained against the dawn and its aftermath, they hang mirrors beneath my brow, speak nothing, offer no hint of that which peers through them.

"Yer pretty guarded, ain't cha?" Johnny asks in his most Mooky voice, deceiving me not a whit. "What ya hidin' in there anyhow?"

I gaze directly into his glittering — I imagine snakelike — blue eyes, move not a muscle, facial or otherwise. Silence prevails for some time. I will not speak first.

He does. "Perhaps," he begins, "I should introduce myself."

I move not. Inert is a very powerful word in its negation. A powerful state as well. I might just go there. Let them haul me back to the hospital. Catatonic — reminds me of Premature Burial, of Poe, of all the dark possibilities of the human condition. Yes I might just find that amusing.

"My name," he drones "is Lenard Cohan. Like the *Yankee Doodle Dandy* Irishman, not the *Hallelujah* Canadian.... *a* instead of *e*. I seen you the room an' thought I'd take the opportunity to see how you was doin'. Me and your brother Billy was kind a close, know what I mean? Brothers is more like it. He thought you was pretty special, you know. Talked quite a bit about you. Proud a what you done."

Despite the turmoil in my mind, I maintain silence, immobility. My eyes stare unblinking, unmoving forward directly into, through and past his own. Soon I shall have no need of focusing upon my own emergent catatonia. He will be present as I bring upon myself not only catalepsy but perhaps the first self-induced and temporary onset of *Fibrodysplasia Ossificans Progressiva*. I have no need (read necessity born of circumstances) to physically contract these or any other manifestations of so-called altered states from any tangental source. I am an altered state, and I contain the infinite possibility of all other such modes of existence. My muscles need not become calcified through the medium of some disease or other sort of external stimulus. They already contain that reality within themselves. As do I (we). My (our) parts are both part of all that exists, and the totality of that existence as well. I am become stone.

"You need not respond," Mooky Len announces calmly and directly into my statue eyes. Obviously, despite their petrine nature, they see his lips move, and my equally stone-deaf ears hear, as does my ossified mind comprehend. I shall not move, but I shall be required to listen. No doubt I could shut my perceptions down so as to spare myself the tedium of attendance upon his upcoming inanities, but I have never totally mastered my curiosity. I, for my own sake, need to hear, but I need not respond.

"I know you better than you might guess," he announces, "and so, I think, maybe I oughta tell you a bit about myself before we get down to business. And let me tell ya, we got some serious business to do."

It all comes in something of a jumble, but my stone-cold concentration makes perfect sense and impeccable logic of it. Ourselves are most amazed.

"My name's Lenard Cohan, Irish, an' originally illegal alien. My parents snuck us over from Canada, settled down in the panhandle where, it was a college town, they found like-minded others not too far off from themselves. They was Communists, or maybe they eventually evolved into Anarchists. Don't know. Don't really care. I grew up. Come north. Thought I might give engineering a try, RPI. Only got's far as Hudson Valley Community College the first time at it. Enlisted. Two tours. The second time I'as a sniper. Hear you took a shot at that one too...." He pauses, chuckles, invites response.

I do not demur.

"Anyways, like I told ya, I'as at Tan Son Nhut with yer brother. Me an' him done some crazy things fer a time there. Until.... You know!"

I am unable to refrain from wondering how this clod possibly could have considered himself RPI material. I hope that amazement has not begun to manifest itself via some inadvertent tic or even a lavafication of my eyes. I suppose even a stone must maintain some degree of vigilance in order to remain true to that which it essentially is.

"Maybe some time we'll talk about the sniper part of war, but of more importance right now is my experience that night at the airbase. Now, shut up fer just a minute" (he is so impossibly foolish), he drawls, "an' let me tell ya. I know you've discovered somethin' 'bout who 'zackly you are, and I think I know what that's about. Even if I'm wrong, appears to me yer gonna set here an' listen, and (again) even if I'm wrong, I'll still be kinda right. I ain't here cause a myself. Somebody ast me to talk ta ya. Seems yer 'bout ta find you a new focus in life.... Whether you want to or not.

"Anyway, that'll come later. Fer now listen. Back there in '66, April 13 to be precise, I found out something about myself that might be similar to something I've kind of picked up about you around the circuit. I know you've been outside of yourself, and have met yourself out there where normal people do not go. I wonder if you know how that happened."

I know alright, but I shall never give this transforming into something neither British nor red-neck cowboy the satisfaction of my perceptible interest.

He gazes calmly into my blankness and continues. "It was the middle of the night. I was asleep. Soundly. The last time such has been my good fortune, unaided that is. When the RPG's hit, not really close at first, I kind of sat stunned, confused, but then I heard small-arms fire, and I knew some real bad shit was comin' down. You know. You gotta grab yer weapon. An' ya gotta git out into it. Rat in a hole ain't no way to go.

"So up and out I run. The night was all flashes and flares. Kinda beautiful, and by the sound a things I knew where to go. I was barefoot, but that made no difference. My feet got cut all to hell, but I never felt it. Things got louder and started to smell. I knew what came next. There was a shed in front of me reflecting some kind of pale light. Like maybe it was the moon or something, and I knew I was going there, and I knew what lay around its backside. How I knew I couldn't say, but there I was. I slowed down both inside n out. All by itself my finger selected auto. How, I don't to this day know. I can shoot Sharpshooter in my sleep and Expert while stoned. Auto's fer clerks and messenger boys, but there I went, kind of gliding, not running, not creeping, no caution, no fear, fully automatic at the ready.

"By the time I come 'round the building, I was three steps ahead of myself. Charlie, all six a him, had stopped to regroup an' find some other game. Two dead Airmen lay off to one side. Naked as when they was born. Had their weapons. Just didn't really know how ta use 'em. Probly mechanics or somethin'. Anyways, by the time I come round the corner, I already knew what to do. Somewheres outsida it all I kind a floated, already at the end of the thing just getting started. Curious. Even then I musta wondered, but nothing interfered with the inevitability of this time seeming already to have passed. That which had to happen worked its destined way as I understood that it must. I gotta say, I had no idea what the end result might be. I experienced death that night, at that time, and in that place. It has remained with me forever. I smiled as I felt the rounds tear my chest apart, splash my blood across the moonshine walls of the unreal shed....

"I got them all. I stood laughing beside myself for a moment until a couple of guys come running up shouting shit like they'd been watching a football game or something. We left the dead guys lay. They say I got four more that night. I only know, and I can feel it even now. Not remember it. Feel it... the sense of being connected to something so profound as to maybe be God

"Or at least Qi in its universal sense.

"I was connected.... You know?"

"That I do."

"Caught ya," the clown beams.

Dance of Oblivion
Lyndi and Edward
1994

Edward woke up this morning wondering if Lyndi would mind. Last night she had been in such a terrible mood that when, as usual, he rolled half his weight atop her, his yearning knee pressed urgently into her warm nexus, she had cursed him, softly as was her wont when seriously angry, and dug her enameled nails into the soft flesh of his left shoulder as she thrust him from her, abruptly and with undue force. "Give it a rest," her parting words as she turned away, bundling the summer weight comforter about her pale shoulders, thereby depriving him of its embrace as well.

Ignoring his wounds, realizing that he had been only half-hard anyway, Edward offered an olive branch. "What's wrong, honey?" he whined in his most concerned voice. "Is there anything I can do?" That should have gotten to her, at least have elicited a smiling response somewhat of the nature of an apology or the tender promise of a new day.

Instead, she mumbled into her bunched up comfort pillow, the one she would hold between her legs for most of the night, "I'm tired," effectively terminating all options for discussion and compromise.

Edward had not been all that ready for the arms of Morpheus. He had followed Lyndi into their room, undressed, accoutered himself in just PJ bottoms, man-satin soft, deepest maroon, all the better to contrast to his pearl tone skin, his hairless chest, built and rebuilt to perfection three days a week without fail at Planet Fitness. His Bi's and Tri's as well — perfect, taut skin over smooth muscle, the essential masculinity of which more often than not set his Lyndi's heart racing and her other organs... well set them at the ready, prepared for his "go." Not this evening.

At a loss for any significant response to her mood and feeling something of a child, he had resorted to the TV and his ear-buds. She never even offered her usual half-hearted objection to the "annoying light" or any acknowledgment of his orphan state. Instead she breathed herself softly and regularly off to sleep.

Morning was already well on its sunny way to more than a new dawn, "beginning," if you will when he awoke. Before he was even half aware of what he was doing, he found himself between her fragrant, unfolding legs, his need at her gates, her adit performing its accustomed AM function for him who would mine deeper within.

OFTEN LYNDI IMAGINED herself an organic board covered with the most luscious of offerings: ropes of grapes, green, pink, red, and dark, cherry, plum, black as the soul of god's most delicious sinner. And oranges, California sunshine, Florida Tropicana delights, and the holy red blood of the Sanguinello.... Winter fruit as well, not her favorite, but at times most satisfying, hard pears and the crisp mush of out of season apples. Yes, Lyndi was an overabundant offering of sweet and colorful delight. But her shoulders had begun to ache, and her hips felt displaced.... Of course, she was belly-up with her arms twisted back to form two pillars of four, the other two, her legs cramped back uncomfortably and widened to immodest extreme. Her back as well...it was arched; she ached all over.

She was no table. Tables have no feelings; tables cannot observe themselves as from outside themselves...from above. They don't have to pee. Their bowels do not ever feel the pressure.... For the love of all that's holy, tables have no minds, no bladders, hips, knees, backs, elbows, shoulders or bowels threatening to gather themselves for disgusting explosive emissions.... Just what in the merry hell? What gnome or other unsightly, unseen creature is doing this? She feels it, knows its nature. Dopey, Grumpy or Horsesassey is shoving a banana...a freaking plantain, rough skin and all right up there into another place which tables never ever possess....

Didn't the idiot get the message last night? Men! Especially Eddie. He knew she loathed morning sex. He smells; she smells. This morning? Last night was in some ways forgivable. Her appointment was scheduled for this afternoon, and.... She could have been a bit more generous last night. For maybe half a second she had entertained the notion. After all, last night was last night, the day before, not the day of. Even so, the risk was too great. In no way could she go to her appointment smelling of sex, oozing its last leavings out upon the speculum, Anna's blessedly gloved hand....

With that thought, Lyndi flung her black eyes open, filling them, she hoped, with reproach rather than sleepy bemusement. It did feel kind of nice. But she couldn't...just could not. "No!" she shouted loud enough to wake the neighbors had there been any within half a mile of their place. "Stop it. You know I can't...."

His grin filled her vision, the barely discernible cleft of his chin, taupe colored, and vulnerable nestled within the dark AM shading of his oh so sensuous jaw. His soft breath teased her sensitive eyes; his fingers, so gentle when he wanted them to be, traced her left nipple as sensuously as ever could have the silk of her new four hundred plus *Agent Provocateur* silk pyjama top which somehow had disappeared from her person. She was naked. Totally, her legs already clasped about his hips precisely in that sweet boyish spot where his slim, athletic waist offered the perfect little groove for their purchase. That was the spot where she was able to hold him to her, to squeeze him and clasp him tight up against her while she did the work, if that is what you should call it. No gross in and out, no sound but her own, no being used, no using. Just man and woman together. Ed and Lyndi.

Oh, she could scream. And scream she did. Let him come all deep, dark, and intimate within her. Then she exploded with the last, the greatest, the absolutely most profound orgasm she would ever have. But then.... She did not, needed not, know that.

DAMN! I HATE it when she does that. It's like whackin' off the third or fourth time in the same day. No exciting action, no real pleasure. The shit just sort of dribbles out, and you're tired.

A SMILE ON her face, Lyndi canceled her Gyno appointment. She could reschedule at a later date. Some other time. Lyndi smiled through the rest of her sunny day.

Edward motored off in his new, 1994 Volvo to his State Street office.

Tara and Smitty
1992

Tara could have been their daughter had that time, August of '94, been this time. For Tara, as Lyndi eventually also would understand deeper within herself than ever had Edward or anyone else, both times had become all time.... Or something akin to that in some otherwise completely unrelated way. As with all passed-on-through or simply dead children, Tara, somewhere else far removed and yet ever so close to the reality shared by Lyndi and Edward, would haunt her traumatically adoptive parents. Her birth into their lives as profoundly painful as was the birth of Christ himself upon the garbage hill, both for him and for the father who had sent him to that place. Mary...Lyndi? Do they not yet weep?

Not Edward. A devoted agnostic in matters relevant to the Old Testament, he, nevertheless, was a born again believer in the daydreams of such prophetic songsters as Pete Seeger, and as relevant to the Tara situation, The Byrds' adaption of Ecclesiastes. Never one to overthink things, he may have asked himself once or twice if everything truly has its season, especially weeping and laughing. More susceptible to the lures of commonly professed morality, Lyndi embraced her internal *Mater Dolorosa* and mourned her own sacrificial offspring far beyond her husband's tolerance. Who dare claim that only a boy might become Jesus? Who might dare affirm that all innocent lambs, male or female, are either truly innocent or, for that matter, really sacrifices? Do not we all just run out of this one particular sort of temporality we so blindly name time and claim for our own? Hoping for and aspiring toward eternity while living for each day as if it held the key to happiness, do we not go about the business of our lives blind to all except that which we choose to see? Listen to this. Could Lyndi possibly be Arty's sister? Pam's?

No way.

TARA WAS BORN to an unmarried pair of transient souls taking some little comfort where they could, expecting nothing more profound than just a momentary release from the chains of themselves, wholly unprepared for even the most basic necessities of parenthood. Nine months, three days and some hours after the fatal coupling, December 13, 1973, little Tara was delivered headfirst into a toilet in the yellow and brown *Chicks* of Mahar's South Troy tavern. Ella was totally fucked up on rock and JD, so wasted that she had somehow missed the whole procedure, and, had she not been trailing blood and a dangling umbilical cord, might have succeeded in sitting, not the least bit uncomfortably, at Billy's well-worn bar long enough for her daughter to drown. *Oh, dear God, if only....* She'd of gotten off. Maybe probation, rehab.... She'd a gotten off. Damn her carelessness.

Little Tara — her mother, a petite five-foot-three, one-hundred-and-one-pound humanoid, drug-addicted, alcoholic, eighteen-tooth manifestation of dysfunctionality to such an extreme as to be uncommon even in their devolving neighborhood, known as the Burg — somehow managed to remain drug, alcohol, and sex free until sometime around her eighth on ninth birthday. Holy miracle of all holy miracles, she never, ever, or at least not more than once or twice, injected heroin. Never pregnant, God, after all does at times show a modicum of mercy, Tara, despite extended tours of unprotected sex, also remained forever HIV negative. Again...thank God for his mysterious grace. Crack...? Now, we all know: Crack Rules.

There was more to Tara than this, and one day in her seventeenth summer she heard the call of something just over her left shoulder. Or was it in the back of her head? It consisted of words; that was for certain. And music...she thought...but nothing she had ever heard before. Anyway, the words were from a most unmusical book, one she had been forced to read, one which had stretched her comprehension into places where only incomprehension dwelt. Thanks, Smitty. Now she was hearing things.

Smitty, Agnes Smith, a former nun, had experienced her own epiphany one rainy day as, obscured by the gloom and the dripping, drooping foliage of the plum tree beside which she had parked, one of a beautiful set of lovely early spring bloomers planted in their own little island smack dab in the middle of the St. Augustine parking lot, she had observed Father Lawrence and the Sacristan, a lovely young man of fifteen years or so, bid each the other farewell in a most unspeakably erotic fashion.

Her faith must not have been of any great substance. For thereupon she resigned.... Not really. It took her about a year of inquiry and meditation, but that evening, set in a nearly Edenic environment, Sister Agnes' faith began its sure and certain erosion into the secular humanism it was destined to become. Truly, as her sister Dolores had quipped in her most sacrilegious, wantonly sarcastic fashion, "It seems the snake in the garden was hidden in Father Larry's pants."

Incipient Secular Humanist or not, Smitty could not help but cringe, inadvertently whisper an ejaculation, and experience just a miniscule sense of the wrongness of it all. In such fashion did her epiphany achieve its fullness. The simple truth of all life, human or not, secular, divine, or anything else it might just happen to be: It is all warped and twisted, and she...we...are powerless to do one darn thing about it. We must simply be. Dare we also hope? As for those of us, such as Smitty, who know things the rest of us do not? Is not their knowledge torment? Our ignorance?

You know.

Following her separation from the Benedictines, Ms. Smith, not as yet Smitty, no longer Sister began to flower anew, to shed the blessedly sacrificial nature of her previous existence and to resurrect herself as one of whom Zarathustra just might have spoken, had that particular holy man actually possessed the profound insights so satirically imputed to him by the foremost Prussian comedian of the nineteenth-century whose "God is dead" would ring forever strong in the cavern of Smitty's subconscious, until, that is, she had no subconscious any longer. In many pedagogical fashions and along many avenues of the mind Ms. Smith created from the devastation of her once pious soul the New Woman most women or men can never hope to become. Smitty metamorphosed into *überlerher,* and forever altered Tara. Maybe some others as well.

The field of their jousting, for such best describes their early interactions, was School11, perhaps best recognized as The Former School 11. No longer an integral part of the Enlarged City School District of Troy, NY, neither was it situated in the Burg nor was it part of that system. Former School 11, known within each city district, as LA, the Losers Academy, was specifically attuned to the needs of classically "troubled" students and dropouts. Tara was no dropout, but, boy, was she ever classically troubled.

Überlerher and Subterranean, as Smitty came to call Tara, not because she had confused the child with terra and was thus prompted to nickname this classic underachieving student as somehow sunk beneath the earth into some Kerouackian subcultural intellectual anti-intellectual pit of teenage drug-addled rebellion, but rather because one of the meanings of Tara is star, and she, whom the überteacher came to think of as her little star, had been born into this world under the influence of the darkest star of all the black holes out there in the firmament, so empty, so desperate for something with which to fulfill themselves that they vacuum up all the garbage along with the rare bits of anything worthwhile until soon all they have to offer as well as aspire to is the void which they themselves have created. The Tara of mythology was the site of the Stone of Destiny. For Smitty's dear, little one, that destiny, all destiny it just might be, was much the same as her own view of life itself. Somewhere she had read of Sylvia Plath that she saw the "human experience as horrid and ungovernable" and all relationships as "puppet like and meaningless." These words precisely expressed the teacher's recent awareness, the true fate of us all, to be mired within the trivial, the pathetic, and the doomed fulfillment of our own experiences, to fall victim to the emergence of our depraved human nature. Tara, her dearest one, stood as the physical manifestation of that dreary nature. She had sat there, such a dirty little Sylvia, her knees etched with sand, her grim white blouse stained with gruesome blots under each freckled arm. She wore a dirndl, its bodice tight beneath her breasts, their already defeated youth merely a sad memory as they drooped beneath the confining elastic. The blouse, deeply cloven, revealed drops of moisture scattering tiny trails and tails in the dust enshrouding her entire person. The skirt, extravagantly flowered in huge orange blooms resembling poorly mutated poppies of some gigantic species defacing the deep blue of the fabric upon which they squatted, could only be termed understated when opposed to the riot of lemon, valentine's pink, lurid red, and bilious green of her plastic fantastic flip-flops. In Smitty's own words, "She was a sight," a discombobulation of the senses, such that, upon first glance the überlerher felt her resistance sucked up in some great maw of possibly obscene, decidedly lethal übergravity. Left only with a most unprofessional, unsisterlike surrender to the same impulse which had overcome Father Lawrence, Smitty fell in love with one of God's dirtiest little girls.

Lyndi and Edward
1994

Friday evening. An entire week lay before them, and contrary to their usual habit, it was not at all mapped out in elaborate detail. Saturday, Edward would work half the day while she treated herself to a mani-pedi followed by a session with her new Elizabeth George, *Playing for the Ashes*. Sunday, not too late she hoped, they would depart Sonny and Cher's, the Mangold's, anniversary party in Saugerties, cruise back to Poestenkill at a moderate speed, and then Veg for an entire seven days. They might trek up to Maine. They might not.

The firm had forced poor Eddie to adopt a fragmented vacation plan. The two weeks in June, an ocean voyage from Vancouver up to Alaska and back, had been magical. This week promised to be a pleasant breather from all responsibility, an opportunity to recharge batteries and possibly open some unexpected doors into experiences one could never plan for.

As capstone, the week after Labor Day, they would be off for ten days in Argentina, Edward's ancestral home. He had never been to his parents' homeland, and it was too bad there was no time for a stopover in Buenos Aires. That would have to await another time. They only had a few days, four of them to be consumed by travelling and recovering as well as by the idiotic trivialities of accommodating oneself to the importunities placed upon a person by any foreign place, ancestral or not. They would be skiing on Mt. Castor in Tierra del Fuego, would visit the southernmost city in all the world, Ushuaia, and perhaps even sample some very ethnic cuisine. Edward had told her stories of the stories told by his father about the less than civilized tastes of the Patagonians, and he most devoutly hoped to experience the roasting and partaking of the flesh of a whole goat, *chivito*, as well as sampling authentic *chimichurri*. Lyndi was not so sure of that one, but she loved to ski and positively adored travelling to out of the way places no one of her friends had the faintest hope of ever visiting. It was all so mysterious. Exciting. Words always failed her. It would be, it would really be.... Something!

Of course the future beckons. Is that not all it is capable of doing? Anyway, while all futures are not yet, and some more than others may beckon with the oh so nice aura that word exhales about all it encompasses, most do not. In fact, were the future to be explored to its absurd universal conclusion....

Lyndi needed none of that. Why, oh why, into the middle of her pleasant rainy-day reverie did such thoughts never fail to intrude? This night was certain to be amazing, first cocktails at the Gideon, then the Philadelphia Orchestra, seventh row center, and then... The night would still be young. Lyndi could not help but smile remembering two summers ago. Along with Edward's friend Alan, decidedly gay and unabashedly flamboyant, they had stayed at the Gideon, had dined in the most extravagant of Saratoga restaurants, other than the Gideon of course, the legendary Siro's, had lost and won big at the track, had attended a concert or had it been two?

That amazing night.... Can booze and prolonged proximity not only loosen the moral strictures of the most contentedly married but also convert the decidedly one-way temporarily to the other? Undoubtedly that entire evening Lyndi had wavered, and, she was certain, Alan had been most accommodating. They might so easily have tripped blithely across some line or other had not the very spirits which prompted them to the edge in the first place have shown some mercy as well. Lyndi could not remember. Alan would never tell.

Sometimes the smell of horses became, just exactly as one might expect, the smell of horses, their sweat, their uncontrollable, odiferous, yet in some way almost cute, droppings. What must...? Oh, my God, imagine. How must Saratoga and all the cities have smelled in those depressingly primitive good old days everyone finds so romantic? A horrid word plopped itself into her consciousness. *Horseshitty*. God forgive her. So gross yet so undeniably true. The horseshitty of Saratoga... of New York. Even the parfumerie of all the world's parfumeries, the horseshitty of Paris.

Edward, ever the trusting innocent, had met a man who knew a man who knew a trainer at the harness track, and had been let in on the big secret. House of Hanover or Silly Sulkyvan or some other equine of equally asinine name was a sure thing in the eighth race. He or it, a gelding she thought it might have been, was going off at least twenty to one, whatever that actually meant. "What is OTB for?" she had asked her husband in the face of his insistence that they just must go, but he had kept on insisting until he drove her right into the arms of a headache.

OPENING A BOTTLE of cheap Rosé almost immediately upon Edward's departure, Lyndi took the first step down the long-time untrodden path of solitary entertainment. Fate, however, would not leave her to herself for long. Always in her life outside factors had intruded, and that evening was to be no exception to her less than golden rule. She would soak, abandoned and luxurious in the deep, long tub. Her wine would glow warm as a candle flame within her. Soft music, borne by gentle vapors would cleanse her heart...her soul. She might sleep, rocked and buoyant in the still waters, and, when her bath was finished? Well, she simply could not say. Perhaps she might sleep on into early morning, dream the dreams of her childhood, once again sit in her swing, the scent of lilacs quiet in the air, the sun golden halos about the enchanted yard. Or better, she would arise with the last wisps of steam, reborn into the tiger lily, the huntress of the night. Perhaps....

Other factors, however, always exist. As was the case that night, one other factor perched in an extravagant nest several furlongs along the tree-lined way into town, that being Chance in the guise of a certain blonde and blue jawed married man by the name of Howard, his actual name it turned out, whose wife came upon him and Alan in fragranté.... Yes she knew the proper word, but that evening had been so overwhelmingly fragrant: The ubiquitous pines lining the roadway, marching everywhere in single files across the landscape, and inside, the thirty six roses, Cara Mia, Floribunda, and the truly lavender Blue Curiosa, a most elegant and emblematic gift from Edward, set about the room in silver carafes, and then, about an hour after the rose-penitent had left for his appointment with Certitude, in slipped Alan, mixing a decidedly masculine essence to her own Bulgari Rose, so hastily purchased at the hotel's gift shop, her own travel selections, chosen for outdoor exposures and horse tinctured atmospheres, wholly inadequate to her more civilized set of anticipated female indulgences.

Alan, black of mood, red of eye, yet smelling most appealingly of juniper and liquorice. Poor man. What can a woman possibly find more attractive than wooing, charming, cajoling, comforting, and eventually bringing a sad little smile to the face of a magnificently structured, silken-skinned, gay man, so handsome that she is unable to help but wonder...? Enough, she was not going there. Poor Alan needed her help, not her vanity, not an emergence of that lower nature which in these situations inevitably rears its ugly head. Usually in men, but were they not about to enter a new century, the twenty-first, most possibly the century of the woman? Whatever. She'd be old and as good as gone before that ever happened. For now she would play the part, assume the role of dutiful and supportive friend: the woman, ever the giver, ever in support, and her pleasure would be the reemergence of the sun, the smile on her Alan's face.

One of the ever-loving God's gifts both to women and gay men, Lyndi firmly believed, was their ability to find in laughter a cure for most of life's emotional ills. Such was especially true of her best friend and soul mate Cherish

Mangold. Cherish no longer taught at Bell Top, and their communication had become one of ever more infrequent phone calls. Cherish's husband, unbeknown to all but a select few, sadly not including Lyndi and Edward, had been writing short stories and novels for years. Suddenly, success was his. He had a best-seller. It was to be made into a movie, and, no longer needing Cher's once cherished employment in the East Greenbush School System, the two of them had departed for environs more suited to his new station, Saugerties, close enough to Woodstock to share in its aura as well as to provide Sonny, Endwell, as he now insisted upon in public, with valuable contacts and possible social situations most advantageous to the advancement of his marketing as well as his artistic aspirations.

For Cher? Her friend had long dabbled in acrylics, both formless and repetitive. Since Endwell's rise to moderate celebrity, however, she had achieved a measure of recognition herself, having been on at least two occasions mentioned in *The New York Times* as "An experimental artist worthy of attention." She, according to the paper, had managed to integrate diverse genres such as natural sound, digital recording, photography, even architecture into a cohesive and affective artistic vision "revolutionary in nature." Lyndi, who still appreciated Andrew Wyeth, had not seen or perhaps "experienced" this new material and knew better than to ask for explanation when speaking with her friend on the telephone. She had, after all, read *The Painted Word*, and, despite being no great fan of satire, had, as a result, developed a certain caution concerning questions relating to the "meaning" of an artist's work. She once had fallen in behind a pickup truck, emblazoned across the rear window with the slogan "HARLEY DAVIDSON, IF YOU HAVE TO ASK YOU WOULDN'T UNDERSTAND. Is that not ever the way with those who are unable to explain something, be it a machine or a work of art? If you are unable to explain whatever it is you do or create, charge those who might ask you to do so with invincible ignorance, and leave them ashamed rather than informed.

Tears slid down her kitchen window, eaves dripped like woodpeckers in chorus upon her deck, and Lyndi reached out in memory to Alan's sad, rejected face. Upon his knees, as he almost shyly had told her, upon a most extravagantly expensive rug, Nain Persian he would bet, at least $10,000.00, the most delicious Howard so randy upon him as if they were two vernal goats in rut, Alan had begun to feel for at least the hundredth time the stirrings of true love within his never too calloused heart. At exactly the same nanosecond as he crossed over into epiphany, as all the feelings from his loins, the man-musk of their coupling weaving its dusk about them both, wrapping them up in the aura of the powerful *Yang* opposites so simply yet so inadequately expressed by the term paradox, just at that god damned, cock sucking… *Forgive me Lyn.* Just at the magic moment, in banged the bovine little thing. Howard's wife Julia. Herself, it turned out, a himself in drag. Had not Alan been quite so large and intimidating, even while in fragranté, violence might have ensued. Instead the pathetic little girlie-man shrieked, demanded, and then pouted as Alan righted himself and, the truth be told, fled the scene.

He was Lyndi's to do with as she would, but first, might he have a drink of something? Anything strong. Gin would, of course, be best.

Tara and Smitty
1992

"You look just like Sylvia Plath," Smitty had blurted before she could catch herself. Immediately, confusion began its reign within her. "What I mean is," she continued, careful not to stutter, praying not to flush, "I have a picture…. Do you know who Sylvia Plath is…was?"

Of course she didn't. The two of them stood, alone in a classroom about to fill with the leavings of all the county's failed systems, this child just one more of the multitude. *The great unwashed*, Smitty could not refrain from thinking, and neither could she censure the smile breaking upon her face nor stifle the most disrespectful chuckle gurgling down deep in her throat. Who might take her to task for this? Most assuredly the little girl before her had visited neither shower nor tub for quite some time.

No teacher and most certainly no nun, even one considered "former," should play favorites, adopt a human child as one would a stray kitten, but so did the teacher assay.

SUCH COULD NEVER be. Tara was well beyond the point of becoming some dried-up old woman's lap dog, not even for the promise of the elusive GED. Tara needed no diploma, no certificate of completion, no New York State documentation of any kind. Neither did she need any friends, especially not some teacher, at least forty years old, and probably a lesbian. This first day in former school 11 she would make her last. The stupid old thing was acting like she was a schoolgirl herself. And her hands. Really. Tara did not need to be steered to a front desk. On her own, she would find the spot where she belonged. At the back. Hopefully some cute guys sitting there, and maybe even some cool ones. Instead, the pathetic pig literally pushed her down into a rickety front seat, smiled a gap-tooth smile, and clumped back to her own teacher place at the front of the room. Probably hoped to get a good look up her skirt. Worse than a man, some of these bitches.

"The rest of the class will be here soon," the idiot cawed in her old witch voice, "and I asked that you come in early so that there might be some time during which we could get to know each other, feel each other out, if you know what I mean.

There it was. Not even subtle.

"What I mean is you probably would like to know just what is expected from you and what is expected from me in this class."

With that, her rainbow hung glasses bouncing all over her udders, the lesbo produced from some beige bag of some negligible origin a sheaf of papers, four to be exact, detailing course content which included "Language Arts: Reading, Language Arts: Writing, Science, Social Studies," and "Mathematics," as well as a detailed summary of each subject including the amount of class time as well as study time devoted to each. In addition the old hag handed her a separate sheet detailing attendance and "deportment" requirements. Shit, this looked harder than regular school ever was. Tara wasn't waiting for the end of the day. She was outta there at lunch.

It was all too freakin' much. The teacher stood over her, peering nowhere except into her eyes. "I knew your mother," she smiled, her voice soft and, *goddamnit* somehow comforting. "When I was at St. Augustine's. She was very bright, you know...."

Nobody, nodamnbody has ever said a kind thing about Mom, not even Nan.

The teacher prattled unheard for a time until Tara rejoined her upon the words, "and you look just like her."

What else did this old thing know? Before she could ask, the first of the intermittent, ten-minute stream of arriving GED aspirants arrived. All sluts, punks, thugs, addicts, and retards. Tara felt right in her element. They all seemed to hold genuine affection for the teacher, and surprisingly for such a group of dead-end losers, were well versed at least in the rudiments of the first subject of the day. Algebra, for God's sake. After that, the teacher handed out a variety of books of various sizes, colors, and titles, one to each student. Tara came last. Only three remained in the lop-sided metal cart from which they had been distributed. "I love the term serendipity," Old Lady Smith chuckled as much to herself as to Tara. "Sometimes it appears that a divine hand or at least a blind Fate must be ordering the progress of things. Serendipity explains that in a different, and I do believe superior, fashion, however. Have you heard it?"

Tara had not, but despite herself, maybe because of the obvious affection of the class for their teacher, and the lesbo's absolute delight not just in their intellects but in who they, each of them, were, allowed herself to be suckered in just a tiny bit. "No," she said, allowing not nearly the amount of annoyance to show in her voice as she might have. "Seems kind of stupid to me."

The stupid teacher laughed right out loud, right in her face. "They told me you might be difficult. They were oh so right. What they neglected to tell me was that you only seem that way."

What the hell! Who the hell are they? And who in hell does this cow think she is anyway? Next thing you know....

As they must, next things come next; just as Tara had imagined Smitty entered her mother into the colloquy. "Your mother...Ella was it? Your mother had that same response to everything I offered her. Sadly, at the time and under the straited circumstances, I didn't have this to offer her. I tell you with no promise, yet with much hope, this book could change your life. It could have done the same for your mother. Of that I am most certain or at least somewhat so." With those words and no further attempts to communicate except the hint of a sad smile tugging at the edges of her face, Smitty laid a book before her as if it were a freaking sacrament or something. *The Bell Jar* the cover said, by that chick the teacher was so hung up on, freaking Sylvia Plath.

What the hell? The teacher was crazy, and definitely a lesbian, but the class not really that bad, and she could bag it any time she wanted. Alright, she'd take the stupid book home and read whatever it was her mother should have read before her.

Lyndi and Edward
1994

Jumpin' Juniper! Not since college, if even then, had she drunk any sort of liquor straight from a water glass, and probably never gin. To that time she had always had it mixed with something else, usually tonic and once or twice or perhaps a trifle more often, had indulged herself in a moderately dry Martini. Or two. Edward always had the bartender merely wave the Vermouth at the rim of his glass; Lyndi, on the other hand, preferred at least a thimbleful. When it comes right down to it, there's no escaping the fact that gin, neat or woefully undiluted, has a strong and unsettling taste, as well as an astringent nature which can be most unpleasant, especially to someone with sensitive membranes such as she.

Fresh from her bath, Lyndi's frosted pink Burberry robe, just the slightest bit damp, attempted at every turn to slip open, to slide up, to reveal that which she knew should not be revealed. Her own perfume offered its subtle enticement to allow things to move just a little bit further along a most dangerous way. The gin added its fragrant voice. The gin shouted louder all along the watchtowers of her reluctant defenses, "Let it go. See if you truly are willing to become the tiger. He's gay anyway.

You don't dare. Coward, coward, coward."

Self-mockery may be covert, but its pain is blatant, and Lyndi hated pain. She would not bow to her own weakness. So it came to pass that, graceful as a Siberian kitten, she gained her feet, admonitions scattering about her. "I'll be back," she almost slurred, clutching the disappointed robe back about the breast it had just then set free.

She delayed a full fifteen minutes, filling the time with minor and unobtrusive subtleties of the make-up arts and several halting passes at libidinous stimulation. By the time the time had passed, Lyndi was fully prepared for something more than innocent flirtation. Alan had just most literally been ripped from his lover's arms. He was vulnerable, and she was the tigress. A gentle predator, to be sure, but she would make her move without hesitation or inhibition. The tiger within her purred to its wicked self. *Alan,* she breathed, *Alan...Alan.* She would devour his luscious body and drink of his luminous soul.

Need it be stated that imaginations, especially those of great big cats, are wondrous faculties. That evening Lyndi supped not upon sad Alan but settled for slices of summer sausage and cold cheddar cheese along with some oddly flavored whole-grain crackers. Neither did she drink of his soul. Some most luminous substance, however, did pass between her lips. Way back in her throat...into her sinuses...her head, her heart.

Veuve Cliquot.

Some things beside music are capable of soothing the savage beast...or breast. Who in all the Hell that anyone might conjure up cares?

The tigress fell asleep curled soft about an inexplicably hardened man whose only defense against his own imaginings was to doze off himself, and dream of things more enticing than a damp woman whose husband most likely would return precisely at the most inopportune moment.

In such innocent slumber had Edward, thirteen-thousand or so dollars better off than when he departed, found them. Having become a most merry prankster from consuming his own inebriants, he took profound and sublime pleasure in short-circuiting whatever sweet dreams they pursued with a brisk shower of Stella Artois. Luckily, Lyndi, awakening to a muddle of light and familiar shadow, grasped at once the precarious nature of the situation. Reflexively, in most gentle-lady fashion, she plucked Alan's fingers from the thicket into which they were delving, and, rose in time to spare herself and Alan a warm shower of Edward's home brewed, hilarious gold.

Thankfully Ed was very drunk. Not quite so welcome was the fact that Lyndi could remember nothing of any consequence. She was certain no actual infidelity had occurred, but had no idea how far other things had gone. Now and again visions warped and wavered just beneath the fabric of her conscious reality, disjointed and completely nonsensical. Maybe nothing at all of even minor consequence had occurred. How she wished that were not so.

UNLIKE TWO YEARS previously, the evening went as planned. There was no Alan. The sex after all the preparatory entertainment turned absolutely wild; she knew Edward would be drained at least for the next few days, and Saturday, they skipped the track, instead returning home a bit sooner than planned — the track in mud time is no place to be — and belying the term "vegging" indulged themselves in an extravagant spread of Jack's sliders, dogs, shakes, and cheese fries, followed up later by a great movie from Red Box and an entire bag of Oreo Double Stuff eased on down the line by two liters of Pepsi Cola. Tomorrow would be the time for sophistication, pleasant enough to be sure, but, do we not all sometimes need fat, salt, cheese, and an overabundance of sugar, as well as an extravaganza of artificial flavorings? Is there any delight more certain to reach deep within the human gestalt and satisfy our elemental desires?

Sunday arrived with complications. The weather sucked, rain, rain, and then some more rain, but that was ideal for a day devoted to necessary social interaction. A grey day for a grayer time in the fog occluded Catskills. Saugerties may be a wondrous rural retreat for some, but Lyndi preferred the bright sophistication of Saratoga, even were she and Edward relegated to the periphery of anything seriously "in," to the Mangold's circle way down deep in the mountains where once something of great note but little consequence had transpired.

"Holy shit!" Edward slammed in the front door, Times Union Sunday edition in hand. "Holy shit, holy shit, holy shit."

He hadn't been so excited since the bombing of Baghdad. "What?" Lyndi demanded. "Somebody blow up the UN or something?" More likely, she thought, another one of his horses had come in. He had grown more excitable ever since that thirteen thousand. Not just about horses either. A new and not altogether unpleasant element to his personality, his volatility at times did have the effect of sweeping her up and carrying her along with it. Once, how he had managed it she would never know, they had, upon the fully dressed stage of Capitol Rep's production of Plaza suite, the entire building all theirs, only theirs, snacked upon truffles and piping escargot, sipped their way through two bottles of *Dom Perignon*, and sported themselves about in various states of undress, culminating their debauchery upon the perfectly laid king bed in the three-wall room, the warm caress of deep blue backlight casting its own illusions for the ghostly audience she imagined as they lay together, innocent as only fictional creatures may be.

"Woodstock '94!" he exclaimed. "They've moved Bethel to Saugerties. We're going to that imbecilic party, and do you know who's playing just a mile or so away? Do you have any idea? Where in hell could we have been? I must have seen something. Must have. How in the hell could I have missed it again? Do you have any idea who's there today?"

As if she could really care! But then, she'd better humor him or who knows what chaos might follow? "Eddie, "she blurted, surprising herself and stopping her messenger of Apocalypse dead in his unshod tracks. "Eddie," she squealed again. Does this mean the Thruway'll be closed...that we won't have to....?"

"No," he interrupted. "Traffic's no problem, unless you mean missing the concert. Bob Dylan, Lyn, Bob MF'n Dylan will be Just down the road from where we're going. It just can't be. I won't let this happen."

Sometimes the man could be so childish. Well, he would have to rid himself of any and all crazy ideas. There would be no return to the 60's, no sneaking into a muddy concert, no free love, acid, pot, and dreams of something that never would and never could happen. This thing had to stop, and she had to call the halt. How to do that?

Never, not as far back as she could remember, had God immediately answered her prayer in exactly the form she required that answer take. Sunday, 14 August, 1994 broke the string of disappointment. Even before she could form the thought let alone encode the prayer, came the deluge. The sky opened and God's answer flooded down upon them. "It's pouring," Lyndi merely stated, and Edward, a realist of some extreme degree, never one to allow a dream or an ideal to intrude upon the practical, merely sighed, farted a burbling string of anal bubbles, poured himself a coffee, and settled in upon the Sports Page.

Thank you God, even though your boon is merely temporary and its consequence might be of an unwelcome nature.

Thus did it come to pass that the fortuitous couple found themselves at a party of perhaps more than Saratogan sophistication. Some writer that everyone made much ado about named John Irving was there, and, of course, the local, Bill Kennedy, but Great God in Heaven: Bob Weir and Steve Winwood, John Sebastian, and Stephen Stills dropped in for a short time. Edward was transported, leaving Lyndi to snuggle into old times with Cher, and the two stayed well beyond their anticipated early departure time, not turning the key in the ignition until about a quarter past midnight.

At the outset, C & C as they once had taken great delight in calling themselves had chatted around any issues which might have separated them, and soon, after a very brief tour of house essentials, the two women began to rummage about their memories for laughter and the shared joy of previous days when life was simpler and today could but lead to even more happily shared tomorrows. It was truly like no one else were there. To her credit, Lyndi thought, she had felt genuine pleasure in the tour of the richly remodeled interior, so very much more extravagant yet paradoxically understated, muted actually, than would ever be their own project back in Poestenkill. Cher had neither dwelt nor sought to elaborate upon such things as a huge stone fireplace, capable, Lyndi imagined, of holding an entire Yule log. She wondered if Jewish people thought of such things for Chanukah. Again to her credit, she did not ask. The whirl through the kitchen had been vertiginous. Lyndi barely had opportunity to note the granite. Or was it soapstone? Or marble? Everywhere except those places formed of copper or stainless steel. The stove she thought must have cost ten-thousand if it cost a penny, all dark iron burners on unstained, soft-brushed stainless and shouting "Gourmet! Gourmet!"

"This is Endwell's territory," Cher had tossed back at her. "It's not to say that I can't boil water. Not at all. In fact.... Well...let it be said that I just do not like to cook. Endo, however.... Now, if I didn't insist upon eating out at least three nights a week.... There are some truly fantastic restaurants around here, and the City's.... Well you know.

After a fine catered affair, with Champagne, and light *hors de oeuvres*, the other guests drifted into their own little groups, some wandering about the outside during a brief respite from the rain, and others gathered in front of the wall-sized TV to, of all things, watch a baseball game. Of course drinks were plentiful, and a fine soft glow warmed the company as everything combined to bless the second-largest gathering of people in Saugerties that day. Lyndi, however, felt less than blessed. Edward was still sucking up to the musicians and ignoring her. He was boring them, she could tell, but he just would not stop.

She was about to insist that they leave, feigning a headache which threatened to become actual, when she felt a gentle tug at her elbow. "Come with me," Cher whispered. "I have something to show you." Down a long, dark hall they slipped, and things began to darken even more as they approached an archway into a shadowed room, its one colossal window opening onto a void which might have been a scenic vista had not the day drowned so long ago into a dank black lagoon fit only for impossible hydro-humans of some mutated amphibian nature. Cher faded into the miasma, and Lyndi felt the unstable earth beyond the fragile boundary of her safe and dry reality fall away in frightening fashion as, far off in the gloom, ghostlights flitted about in a humid universe of new and alien dimensions. Rather than enter the space, it must have been at least sixty feet long and forty more wide, Lyndi held back. Afraid. One step inside, she imagined would take her over the edge of some precipice and into a swamp from which she might never emerge.

Then there was light. A later day's creation. Streaming from over-head, up from the floor.... It spilled across walls in wide swaths, bounced in sunbursts from the windowglass, and threw easy shadows about like stray thoughts. The room, a studio really, was amazing in all the magical senses of that word. The floor was slate, the walls splotched and splattered with random shouts of multihued paint. Easels lounged about like so many bored guests at an uninspired exhibit which might, nonetheless, at any moment erupt into violence. Some supported unfinished work. Others waited empty. A myriad of carnival-colored canvases, some framed and stacked against each wall or even leaning upon the dizzying window, were strewn about in a manner apparently as careless as must have been their creator's technique.

From somewhere Cher's full throated laugh danced across the great bare room. "You ain't seen nothin' yet," boomed like Surround Sound, and all was again plunged into blackness as mechanical drapes sealed the window, and slashes, swirls and great geysers of light exploded like the sun's last end within the cavernous room. Slowly the chaos ebbed into violet, soft pink tints of radiant white, and from somewhere as obscure as nowhere, Cher's classic form, clothed in a chiton of light, grew to Olympian proportions.

Her images doubled, quadrupled, exponentially multiplied within the now boundless firmament of darkness; like comets some; others candle flames; others blue, red and green in ever shifting, ever leaping expressions of something other than human or light, more than either, yet composed of the one spirit which made them sisters and more than sisters, which is the unity we share with the true nature of ourselves. Neither particle nor wave, neither blood nor breath. Something of god as never before had Lyndi imagined. No Sunday Morning as ever had she known had ever dawned, ever stretched its warm and sundrawn arms to wrap her in a bliss as had the darkness-shattered light in this strange room.

"My favorite poet," reverberated all around, above and beneath her, "said Death is the mother of beauty. He implied that Christ is dead, not resurrected and somehow alive in some Barbie-doll Heaven where nothing ever dies and thus nothing ever happens." Rolling like thunder above the tumbling echoes, the voice concluded: "All things then must die. You, We, It all must end." Upon that most final word, the blinds parted, the multiple beings of light and form ceased to exist. In their place loomed the mundane objects of a workaday artist's studio, efficiently lit as such an atelier must be. From behind a screen and the door behind it, Cher emerged as ungoddess-like as ever she had been.

"I've abandoned acrylics, as you may have noticed. All art is light. I think I should work with that. Like it? I did this preview just for you. I'm doing a preliminary, invitation-only, showing in two months at Agora. It's in Chelsea, and my agent says Robert Hughes is sure to be there. So what do you think?"

Lyndi hated being put on the spot, and so she took the quickest route away from that uncomfortable place. "You mentioned your favorite poet," she mumbled in what she hoped would be taken as a thoughtful tone. "Do I remember right...Robert Frost?"

"Oh my, no! Once upon a time perhaps, but I've met this dear retired professor from NYU, perhaps you've heard of him, Robin Beechler...?"

Lyndi merely shrugged a "No."

Well, you'd love him! Anyway, Robin turned me on to Wallace Stevens. His work is incredibly difficult but fabulously rewarding. With Robin's help I have come not only to understand it, but to feel when I read certain things that he must have seen into my own thoughts and given voice to those very urges to insight that I have always found just beyond my grasp. I love his verse for what it is, both polished and creatively structured, but the things he says.... Oh, Lyndi, let's speak no more of this. Come on upstairs and I'll make us a cup of tea in my own private suite."

Lyndi must have shown some hesitation, and her friend continued in a rush, "You will come, won't you? I have the most elegant orange-iced scones and some excellent choices of tea. Coffee too, if you want it. Or wine."

"Of course," Lyndi smiled. "I guess that I'm still a bit overwhelmed. Are you going to do the entire thing somewhere in this area.... After New York, I mean?" she asked to fill the silence as the two women climbed the wide stairs, Cher leading the way upward toward more darkness.

"Oh, Lyndi," she exclaimed. I'm so sorry. I so much hoped you would come to Agora. Hasn't Edward told you? I mentioned it to him when you first got here. I forget where you had gone off to at the time. Anyway... I most assuredly hope the two of you will do me the honor of attending."

So awkward. So surprisingly formal, Lyndi mused as Cher opened an oaken door into, surprise, surprise, a delirious suite of rooms. The actual bedroom was small, the sitting area a trifle too large, the bathroom grand, and the galley kitchen not much smaller than was the only kitchen in the first house she and Edward had ever owned. The whole darn thing was girly right out of *Seventeen Magazine*. All pinks and whites and lavenders with, no fooling, Raggedy Anne curtains, frilly lace tablecloth and a hideous cranberry carpet, wall-to-wall, even in the bathroom. How? From where? Do they even make cherry granite for tiles and vanity tops? Mega mirrors! At least six of various sizes and locations reflecting the gleaming high-gloss colors back and forth, and across each other.

"It's my Wonderland," squeaked Cher, as from behind a brown oval hassock of incredible size she pulled a hookah. "Oh, yes, I think I forgot to mention. I sometimes am able to offer more than just tea and crumpets."

"Scones," was all Lyndi could think to say.

Tara and Smitty
1992

The teacher was crazy. Tara's mother might have been a lot like she was now. She probably was, and, just like Tara, she never would have gotten shit from any stupid book. There's no way some upper class bitch's problems could have been anything like either mother's or daughter's. Maybe it was the skirt. The stupid slut writer wore a dirndl skirt. No way Tara would wear that again. Teachers. All they know is what they read in books. Mom was a fucking addict. And a whore. And so was and so was not Tara. Sylvia Fucking Plath was a spoiled little rich girl who found her life so hard she went crazy, imagined herself in a bell jar whatever in hell that is. Then it says in the end of the book that when she was richer and famous she still found everything so impossibly confining and unbearable she offed herself.

Well, fuck her. Fuck the stupid teacher too. They wouldn't know shit if they fell in it. Probably think a stomach ache is as bad as it gets before you gotta go fucking insane. And some dude leaves you? Then you just gotta kill your pathetic self.

I ain't going back, and I'm tossing the book.

In some ether way beyond the net, Smitty's excessive concern, so real as to exist beyond reality, must have across both distance and emotional separation manifested itself in her student's awareness. Despite her best intentions, Tara found herself, *Bell Jar* in hand, boarding the #80 bus down Fifth Av. The fucking bus to school. Possibly she intended to throw the book in the teacher's face. Possibly she never would have entered the building, would have kept on keeping on down the avenue until arriving downtown. Downtown for crack, for fun, for freely-chosen sex in exchange for drugs. Even for Hydro or Oxy if Shep or Billy wasn't available. Possibly such would have been the safest course. Instead, Tara slunk into class late, her tiny skirt as un-Plathian as possible, her least-unwashed top proclaiming something unreadable, her face inscrutable. Her mind unfathomable even to herself.

What in the fuck was she doing there?

The teacher must have been doing her own chemicals that morning. No way was she the idiot drone from yesterday. She was rollin'. Her examples of all things English, including grammar, jazzed all over the place from fucking Dr. Seuss, to the newspaper, even her students' writing, and, weirdest of them all, she pulled a bunch of very strange shit right out of her own head. Who in allthefuckinhell, unless she was really ripped, would ever have asked, "If Robert be imaginary, are his concerns real?" *What the fuck?* That was followed as smoothly as subjunctive blithely flows from possible to impossible, actual to hypothetical, by a discussion of the nature of fiction and imagination. The crazy teacher actually thought you could make up your own reality. Good goddamn thing that one never heard of LSD. Or had she? That kind of shit has to come from someplace not normal. Could Smitty and Tara share something deeper than a common humanity?

Tara never asked herself that question. Smitty already had.

Later that afternoon, some ginger-bland thing of uncertain gender began droning on and on about nutrition and the body's need for very specific amounts of all kinds of things, including for fuck's sake obvious metals like iron—Tara already knew about that one—but who would have guessed Zinc, Copper, something called Manganese, and Chromium (Car Chrome?). Perhaps the biggest surprise of all, Calcium (fucking bones) and Sodium (Salt) are metals too. Damn. This dweeb of a teacher knew some crazy shit.

The guys weren't at all impressed, but Tara, never to be a metallurgist or nutritionist, in fact, never to get her GED, found herself falling under some sort of spell. Maybe this shit was what separated people like the Plath chick and the science teacher, MS. Trumbill, from people like her mom and herself. Maybe it was more than luck. Maybe not. Tara would never know, and perhaps never would Smitty, although she thought she did, nor Elizabeth Trumbill, recent Bennington College BS, nor even would have Sylvia Plath, who could not possibly have counted herself among God's most fortunate.

Luck. Lawrence's Hester claimed it was all one needed—yes, the class would read "The Rocking Horse Winner." Some, Tara learned, just have it; others seek but never find, and some, most fortunate ones, die in frantic pursuit. Luck, however, as Tara would never know, is simply one aspect of Fortune, the essential nature of a chaotic cosmos, itself most uncosmic. Random Chance. All effects result from no more than proximate causes. Chaos, forever mocking Order with its multitude of disguises, inevitably must be encountered further up every road. Logic, the great pretender, is merely the cerebrochemical, electrical Segway of fools.

As Chance never decreed, the afternoon ended with Smitty again, encouraging the class to break into groups of those with the same readings, and then turning her almost full attention to Tara, the only one with *The Bell Jar*. Not by design had this happened. They sat knee to knee, Tara in a straight, wooden chair pulled up beside the teacher's cluttered desk and Smitty, quite mobile in her wheeled chair out from behind the barrier so often necessary between *Lehrer* and *schuler*.

ONCE WHILE COLLABORATING with several nuns from other communities on creating a comprehensive mission statement as well as a definitive set of policies, procedures, and desired outcomes for Diocesan Catholic Education, Smitty had fallen under the spell of a most troubled young sister, Mary Margaret Mangold. They had shared a room at Saint Joseph's Provincial House in Latham; a lovely cell it had been, filled with sunlight during the morning, its beds comfortable and warm as the clouds of heaven ever could be. The hope and joy of flowers: Each bed had its own night stand; each stand was graced by a lamp and a small pot with the dearest little violets. So tiny they were, so vulnerable. Yet they lived, breathed the breath of God's own joy into the little room. To be sure they would not, could not last, but their beauty could only be eternal. So sad...so unutterably, beautifully, joyfully tragic....

Sister Mary Margaret must have felt much the same way. But in a different fashion. The first evening, after their minimal meal, after prayers and reflection, after the collegial interactions over light refreshments such occasions demand, Smitty had returned to her room to find Sister Mary Margaret already there, crying soft tears as she plucked the last petal from the bare stalks of her bouquet. Smitty's face must have registered her shock, for the dolorous one smiled up at her and whispered past the last sad petals smudged upon her teeth. "They mock me. So damn perfect. So serene. They mock me," at which point she lay her perfectly formed head back upon her pillow, closed her bewitching blue eyes, and allowed the classical beauty of the turmoil within her to shift the planes of her face into a troubled perfection as fleeting as the ghost of an imaginary flame, the perfect note at the perfect moment of the aria impossible for any but the most deeply human voice to attain. Then the moment of impossible loveliness passed before it had begun, and Smitty was left with sobs of violet hue and the dying stems of bygone flowers.

Smitty, sometimes to her own amazement, often in such circumstances knew exactly what to do. "What's truly wrong?" she had asked as gently as her often harsh voice would allow. "I'm no priest, but you can tell me anything, and I swear they'll never drag it out of me. Whatever it is...."

Her sister had smiled at that; her sobs quieted, but she said nothing.

"There is merit," Smitty continued, "in sharing some things. Forgive me if I appear too inquisitive, but you seem so sad."

The other smiled, a fading glimpse of something akin to despair.

"I have my own secrets, you know," Smitty offered, "and there's nothing you can say, at least I would wager not, that will shock me. I swear I won't judge."

No response disturbed the other's features from a quickly developing emptiness of expression.

Never one to be easily dissuaded from pursuing any end she found worth her efforts, Smitty reached down and stroked the back of the sad one's hand, its nails chewed, its veins standing out nearly as blue as her sweater. It was warm, not chill as Smitty had expected, the pulse leaping at her fingertips, anxious to burst its suicidal way into the graying light of the little room. She couldn't help herself. Smitty raised the warm and bloody hand to her lips, kissed its pale skin, lips trembling at the roil of blood throbbing life's medley into her own defenseless heart.

Before her nun's conscience had time to assert itself, before her so long vigilant mind could assume control, Smitty leaned down and first pecked a little tap upon the sad girl's cheek, then, before the wardens of her assumed self could act, she took that hand again to her lips and spilled her own tears upon it.

Awakened from her oppressed state, Mary Margaret, Sister for only a month or two more, sat up. "I can't do that," was all she said.

Smitty had read much and was fully aware of exactly what it was Mary Margaret was rejecting, but reading leaves much of experience to the imagination, and, despite a normal and active imaginative nature, Smitty was a nun, a true sister, born to the calling. Intellectually, she had considered several possible sexual scenarios, and those involving other women had the most, the only appeal, but then she was a nun. So too was Sister Mary Margaret. Neither of them was immediately capable of "doing it," in any of its more publicized ways.

"My dear," she blurted, "I must have given you a false impression. I meant nothing."

She had, of course imagined. Visions of the divine Mary's soft skin, her pale lips, the secrets of all her young womanhood revealed by the parting of her legs, the meeting of their hesitant breath as they lay entwined in warm embrace....

Betrayed by her own physicality, her eyes closed upon the vision of the other's arising. Smitty sank into her own bed and sighed. If she could have died or at least passed for a time from consciousness, she would have been grateful, but such denial was not to be. The season was springtime and all along the path to the dormitory grew a profusion of tulips, some of them the most gaudy brilliant red Nature has upon her palate. Smitty could feel her face ablaze beyond such muted comparison. From all about her, her neck, her chest, even her legs and feet, she blossomed with conscious humiliation in unquenchable petals. Blindly she groped for a thin, pale pillow with which to cover her shame.

Instead she found a hand, a blue-veined hand she would come to know well, and a quiet voice smiled down upon her incinerating person. "I'm sorry," the pale angel soothed. "I'm really just out of sorts this evening." With these words an almost insubstantial substantiality blessed the space beside her. Allowing her eyes to slit open just a razor's width, Smitty's vision no doubt was the proximate cause of the aura enveloping the girl, but, beyond such incidentals of perception, Mary Margaret radiated an energy indiscernible yet assertively present. Smitty knew they would not "do it," but, in some more profound way and across a span of decades, actually would do much more than "it."

Mary Margaret smiled, sad and forlorn. Smitty was fully up to the task now of mending that.

They slept together, little nun shifts covering their most taboo of places. Never did their hands betray any modicum of Catholic decency. They kissed. Women have always kissed as did they. Mostly, after just the tiniest bit of awkward fumbling, they held each other close, exulted in the commingling of their respiration, found themselves transported by the beating of their hearts, each upon each. They talked, wrapped in an intimacy each had experienced before only within herself, perhaps with her God. Mary confessed: She had begun to doubt her vocation. Questioned the Church teachings. Questioned her own worthiness. "I've even smoked pot," she revealed, her tone wavering between a sob and a giggle. "With one of my students." Finally, her voice filled with both remorse and disappointment, "I've actually done it, you know. With a carrot."

Unable to control herself, Smitty laughed aloud. "Nothing new," she giggled. "What girl hasn't wondered?" For a time the two entwined souls amused themselves by imagining all the old and aging, stern and withered Sisters of their acquaintance plying and prodding themselves with all sorts of objects both natural and decidedly not. Eventually they slipped into dreamless sleep, totally pre REM state.

There was no time. Neither had concerned herself with inconsequentialities. The establishment, however, did, and wakeup came a mere forty-seven minutes subsequent to Smitty's and thirty-three minutes following Mary's transition away from external consciousness.

Their door had no lock, privacy not only unnecessary but also unsanctioned in the nun-cell block. Luckily, most of the human beings operating within and responsible for maintaining the ancient framework of customs and regulations had progressed far beyond the Holy Sea's obsolete conception of human, especially female, rights and essential dignity. There came only a sharp rap upon the door, a spare statement of the time, 5:30, and a disappearing echo of similar arousals visited upon each cell door down the long hall.

The day proved both tiresome and tiring, but the night provided the women with one last feast of innocent physicality. Again, and in much the same fashion as before, they availed themselves of the opportunity to find another self in another person, to experience the wonders and joys of the flesh without ever straying into temptation any further than modesty and righteousness allowed. Possessed of a sure and certain invincibility, at 5:00 AM they rose from Mary's more comfortable cot, stripped away each other's minimal clothing, and for a few blessed moments allowed their eyes to drink their souls into a mellow intoxication. Mary Margaret was the most beautiful thing Smitty had ever seen, Smitty, the fulsome expression to Mary of all that being female might ever entail. They kissed, the voluptuous body of one melding for just a moment with the sparser physicality of the other. Then came the knock and the call.

The next time the two women met neither would be a Sister any more. They would, however, renew a more modern friendship, and in myriad of ways once again draw strength and comfort, one from the other.

SOMETIMES THE TEACHER could be impossibly annoying. Tara had brought her self, her stupid book and dumber notebook, three pens, and a hopeful attitude up to her desk. Right up in front of all the always distracted idiots in the class, she was left to sit, expectant, while nothing was delivered. Ms. Smith just sat, her eyes slatted like the plastic blinds at home, her rumpled face relaxing into something...something like.... *What? She get high on break? Is she getting Allhimers or senile or whatever it's called?* She sure was zoned out. *Zonked, as Billy liked to say.*

With just the most subtle wrinkle of her little bob nose Tara had since childhood been able to make herself sneeze, so wrinkle she did, the brash sound and subtle mist of her creation calling the teacher forth from whatever depths of her aging mind she had been visiting. "Sorry," she muttered as much to herself as to Tara, and gradually a smile transformed her face. Not the vacant leer of the demented fool it was an actual expression of good humor, clement

75

nature, and hope. Promise, Tara read there. Maybe her teacher, after all, had simply had one of those moments — not unlike those her mom....

Better not to go there. Her mom's moments were the brief interludes of sanity, never lasting more than a week or maybe two. Then back she went to all the evils visited upon her by the demons which dwell in such places as the teacher had just visited only momentarily, as Plath maybe had dwelt within, as had Mom, for more time than she could endure.

How had it happened? Without a word the teacher had taught. Tara knew the lesson of *The Bell Jar*, and knew it had been there for her mother — but not as cautionary fairy tale, not as dismal warning. For her it had been just one more tragic story of another lost soul who could never be found. Absolutelyfuckingnever.

"I sometimes get lost in thought at the most unexpected times," Smitty continued. "Now where were we?"

"I'm no Sylvia Plath," Tara blurted. "My mother was, and maybe I seem the same to you, but I've never been to the places Mom or that woman went. I'm not fu... crazy! I'm a lot of things, that's so. But I am not crazy! They were."

The teacher's smile sweetened to a point impossible for her weathered countenance to have achieved; her person, clad in loose and unattractive rags of the most generic sort such as The Salvation Army would have rejected as being way, way too ugly, emitted some radiation of some kind, and the teacher laughed a song of joy into the stale schoolhouse air. "You understand," was all she said.

Tara cast her eyes down upon the rough desk before her and cried dry, silent tears. She knew all right, and understood. The insane poet-woman was her mother. Her world had been their world, her state their country, unfit for human habitation. The way anyone lived made no difference at all. Their end, pathetic and meaningless was all that mattered. She too, Tara knew, would at best be remembered as a wasted life, an unfulfilled promise, and a meaningless false note in someone else's song. Shit!

Smitty's beginning to wrinkle age-spattered hand traced gentle fingers upon Tara's sunken cheek. Brushed back her unwashed hair. "I can help," she whispered.

But Tara, aware that all hope was false, the idiotic opiate, as some asshole once said, of all the fools of all the world, simply lurched to her feet and fled, never again to return. The next time Smitty would even encounter her name would be in the Troy Record Newspaper. Obituaries.

Mary Margaret

Born the only daughter of a gynecologist and his faithful nurse, Mary Margaret Mangold had spent her formative years clasped within the affluent halls of Kenwood Academy in the hinterlands of Loudonville, NY. Deprived of any of the essentials of a secular childhood, she was led to believe that Ecstasy was a spiritual state rather than a drug, that Sex was a necessary part of the holy sacrament of Matrimony, but a process best avoided by right-minded and pious girls. In other words, the girl known as Mary Margaret Mangold had no choice.

By the age of sixteen she had entered the convent – the Motherhouse. By twenty-six, both parents dead in an automobile accident, which, thank you, Jesus, was not their fault, Sister Mary Margaret, ABD, blew that joint. Literally. She had formed something of an extracurricular relationship with one Virginia Di Napoli, a lumpy, squat and utterly brilliant student in her General Psych class at Hudson Valley Community College, where she was employed in an adjunct position, and it was Ginny who first turned her on – to the evil weed, that is.

Nothing is sillier than two girls being goofy unless it is two girls getting high and goofy. Thus did Mary Margaret first come face to face with abandonment. She saw for the first time that the entire thing...the whole f'n pot of it was nothing but one huge joke. The girls looked at their knees and soaked them in the warm fifth-month sun as they sat on their books, backs against an old tree of some familiar yet absolutely mysterious kind. Sister had rolled up her sensible, charcoal, wool slacks while Virginia's Ginny's Chub-Blossoms had always been clearly visible, wobbling and bobbling below the hem of her shorts. Knees — without them we couldn't walk. Or kneel. Either for prayer or for other darker enterprises. Italian countenance red as a certain Lady's sun-assaulted proboscis, Virginia confessed. Did Sister think it a sin if a boy... you know, a very special boy puts his hand upon a girl's chubby little hinges? If he kisses them?

The incense burns hotter, its fumes rising in supplication, wafting with it the prayers, the hopes, the fears and expectations of two of God's most innocent: Two giggling and expectant girls with about to be spoken questions between them.

Why do boys want to touch girls? Why do boys need to defile the sanctity of womanhood? The sacrament of Marriage? Of God's holy temples? Do they not know that they defile themselves as well by such actions?

"I have let him put it inside me...."

"It was sweet, and we both cried afterward. The next day he bought me a golden ring. It wasn't of much value, but I keep it in my underwear drawer, and he says that he'll marry me... you know, when school is over. I love him, you know, Sister, and he loves me."

Sister Ignatius was too stoned to be serious.

"So you... You....

"You did it with your boyfriend? You actually.... Did it?" A giggle escaped like poorly hidden gas from her usually efficient, well regulated, unpainted lips, a tiny burst of helium, freed from its colorfully confining balloon. Or maybe nitrous oxide, much more fun than helium, maybe not quite so light, who knows, but no doubt a lot more fun. More flatulent giggles escaped.

"Sister, we did it! We do it all the time now. Do you mean you don't mind?" Ginny sounded almost wounded–insulted by the light-hearted response her friend had offered.

Sister Mary Margaret passed bubbly gas once more.

"Sister!"

The nun regained control. How much gas could possibly find its way past her sanctity anyway? Holy Mary, Lord Jesus Christ! Girlish giggles in the rotting face of sin, the Stephen King presence of ungodly abomination leering from red rimmed eyes, grunting from its pig-like snout, are themselves abomination. Control!

Insanity rose from the pool of her unfolding consciousness declaring an end to frivolity. Horror broke in, slowly at first, then faster and stronger. It engulfed her, a spring tide, a tsunami of evil. Sex outside of marriage is sin. Boys' doing such things to girls might be The Unforgivable Sin. Her friend's grace, her union with God, had been assaulted and defiled. She had been snatched up, a poor victim of carnal kidnap. She had been spirited away to the land of the prickly pear, and her innocent world had ended. Not with a bang but a giggle. Our Father.... Unreal as ever reality can be, the absolute depravity of her friend's rape was not too monstrous for Mary Margaret to comprehend. As an adult her duty was to remain calm, objective, not be passing judgment, not be accusatory, or cast a stone. After all, the poor child was a victim, had been deluded, had been lied to by her attacker as well as by the entire male-dominated rapist society which refused to acknowledge that even consensual sex under such circumstances is, indeed, an act of rape. Mary Margaret's mind could not refrain from picturing her friend in the mad-man's clutches, imprisoned by his bulk, assaulted by his animal phallus, deafened by his brutish cries. He is upon her. She has no will. He no mercy. She is parted, her clothing gone, her bare breasts fouled by his breath, her knees bent as he lifts them, her toes pointing up to God, her will melted, washed away in the raging currents of their desire. She willingly lifts her most sacred doorway to him. She...

"Sister. Sister!"

Ginny broke the spell, freed the sister from the grip of her own rising lust. For that day at least, the adulteress preserved the chastity of her confessor, if such a mere nun can be.

Thank you, Lord.

"Are you all right, Sister?" the harlot asked. "I thought you were going to pass out. Pretty good weed... right?"

Poor Virginia, may God have mercy on her soul. *Right now I need a little weed, a little weed, a little need, weed... need...need.* Patting her friend's hand, smiling her most understanding and all-knowing smile, Sister Mary Margaret rose into the fragrant air of a new life soon to be realized, up past the currents of cannibalistic — whatever — smoke, up into the sweetness of May — Our Lady's month.

Dance of Despair
Ruth
2013

"Baa, baa, black sheep! I suppose," I fling into the most beautiful violet irises — I *would swear they once were black* — of my angelic blue-eyed self, "that you somehow believe you (I) can fool me (myself, us?) with some Jesus babble I've long past discarded as having no relevance to the way things work in the world."

We smile and the one of us with purple freaking eyes seems about to speak. I seat myself uncomfortably—I have been left wearing only a hospital gown over a four-day worn pair of seriously tiny bikinis. Stupid Mother, thoughtless Mother, clueless Mother as well as the vegetative Flea never once considered offering me a pair of PJ's or even a change of underwear. I squirm next to the little pile of syringes, the sand unpleasant, mudding my bare skin as it mingles with a full-body sweat of proportions the like of which I have never before experienced and which, I fear, portends the inexorable progress of my illness. Cancer within, damp sand and desert air without. This is illness. Terminal. Could it be Death Herself?

My spirit, not as yet having begun her intended presentation, pipes up in a most annoying fashion — I really do not enjoy others, even should they be myself, participating in the privacy of my darker thought processes — "It could be," she pronounces. "Hence my warning."

It is not difficult to believe that the quickest and surest way out of this place is once again to submit, to offer my full attention, and pretend to care. How is it that I, alter-ego or whatever, can appear, although indescribably beautiful, so absolutely idiotic to myself?

Unaware of my thoughts, or possibly unconcerned, the spirit begins her tale. "I will make the assumption that you are familiar with the Parable of the lost sheep, and, no doubt, you understand that such as that one art thou." I *think the sarcastic bitch might just be teasing me. Mocking might be a better word, and I don't care for it.* But I only continue working my uncomfortable way deeper into the harsh — I swear it's comprised of little rocks, sharp, little rocks, sand-shark's teeth maybe — ground, offering neither recognition nor even encouragement. "Look out upon the desert," the homilist commands, "Search across the barren landscape. There is no life. This is one of the lands of the dead; it is a place of despair. It is the land you have chosen for yourself. It is the place where you must go. I am here with you because of Pamela. Three short days ago this desert would not have welcomed you, would not have tolerated you, would have spit you back into the Hell you have made for yourself on earth, and your fate would have been such that even God himself could not have looked upon you without pity, yet neither would he have shown mercy. Jesus, a good and holy man, could not bear to think of his people wandering alone without succor, without hope, but the Father has no such weakness. He will not abandon the 99 for the sake of one. That jeopardizes all of creation. The poor Israelites accepted that they were doomed to deal with this God of Justice alone, the shepherd of the flock, not the individual. Then came Jesus. He goes after the lost one without rest for himself. The Father loves that. He has found mercy in his heart for his Son whom he abandoned to the cross, and He has sent to Him and to us another. She is Pam. And you (we) are hers.

She has found you. She cannot cure you. She cannot get you into that place so innocently known as Heaven, but she can bring you peace back in the world and hope also in this not so barren place. Do not fear. The shepherdess has found you, and another awaits you here who will eventually guide you and others of your nature to the very gates of Paradise, and God will be most joyous as he opens his eternal kingdom to you.

"Bullshit!"

I wake to the hospital, dark in the night, soft voices from somewhere beyond my vision. I am very thirsty. From Mary's side of the room creaks her solicitation, "Are you alright?"

No! I am not alright! I need to shout. *I am in the motherfuckinghospital with cancer, the big C, the assassin at my back.* Instead, I merely mumble, perhaps imperceptibly, "I'm fine."

Silence ensues. The old lady is waiting for more, *a goddamn explanation.* "Just a bad dream," I add in complete submission to her will.

"The Lord is our shepherd," the crone soothes. "He does make us to lie down in green pastures, and you may be certain that goodness and mercy shall always be with you, even should you pass through the valley of the shadow, even should you find yourself face to face with Death itself."

This old idiot can't possibly know my dream. She is not just some other part of me; she is not the same sort of witch as Pam. She's my mother's old friend. And a Lesbian to boot. A married lesbian at that, to the witchy one for sure, but that means nothing. Pam is another kind of thing altogether. I am convinced that she does know things, that she may be everything the beautiful me has claimed. But Mary? She's just an old woman who's been raped and left for dead by some pig probably just looking for crack money. Or whatever. A victim who falls down her own back stairs. Just like me.

The old one stands at the foot of my bed, IV pole and dangling bags at her side. The glow from the hallway casts an aura about her diminutive frame. I don't know how I know it but she is smiling. As though she has traveled with me to the desert world and knows even more than do I of my fate, she exhales from somewhere deeper than her larynx or even her tiny lungs, "I'm slated to live to be a hundred. Now that is a burden of some proportions. We, Pam and I, both knew I would be raped; we both know the poor man's identity."

I think I'm too submissive? What the hell? What about making the bastard pay? What about the other women?

"Believe me, Ruth, I know what you're thinking. I have heard the staff around here questioning my sanity. My very morality. Of course, they have said nothing to me. I suppose they're not supposed to know the details, and should they somehow know them, never to communicate them to any others. Pam says I told them all while I was in the ER, all that is except the rapist's name. As truly as I was at Death's door for a time, I maintained my rationality. I rambled only so far, confided only so much."

Unable to contain myself, I begin to offer objection. "You must...."

"I must forgive," she cries, "and forgive every day he who has wronged me. As horribly as that man abused me, and for that time and some small time after, took from me my freedom, my individuality, my integrity as a woman...as a human being, just as surely did my husband do the same for most of our life together. Perhaps even worse. I forgave Peter every day of that eternity, and when, by the grace of God through the intercession of my Pam, he found repentance, when he begged my forgiveness, and when I unreservedly granted him absolution, he grew joyous, welcomed Pam, my one true love, into our lives, and died by his own hand as he struck out into Death's cold ocean. Really, it was in Maine. He sunk deep into the arms of Jesus, the refuge, sorry, holy mother, of all sinners and rose, Pam has assured me, into the everlasting joy of Heaven."

Bullshit. I think it but cannot bring myself to utter the word, and this one cannot read my skeptical mind. Really, I could use some sleep, but haven't the heart or perhaps simply lack the will to shoo the old lady away. So I am doomed to listen, condemned to pretend to care. Christ, where are the lobster-cold waters of Maine when you really need them?

"You cannot know," she drones, "but my Pam has suffered, has been raped by her own husband, has actually been imprisoned by him, has somehow been brought so low as to begin communicating with and eventually adopting as a pet the most disgusting cockroach you ever saw. To my discredit and everlasting shame I dispatched the thing. Pam had brought the little monster, whose name was Jennifer, for all intents and purposes to live with us in my home. I could not tolerate such vermin."

Mary's voice has added a dimension of anger to its normal placidity and I begin to wonder about the quality of her forgiveness. Could she....

"I know, I know," the sensitive one continues. I yet have not been able to forget the insult."

What a choice word, lady. You hide a lot beneath that holy exterior, don't you? Maybe you just ought to turn the creep who did you in. Have you really forgiven him or is moving a roach into your house more grievous than shoving a dick up your ass?

"Again. I know. She hasn't completely forgiven me killing the disgusting roach either. We've tried, but none of us is perfect. Surely you must know that."

What am I supposed to do now? Answer? In the affirmative?

Mary apparently was being rhetorical, "It's the little things, isn't it? Pam saw to her husband's salvation and I to my Peter's, but sometimes even imagined slights last longer than the true horrors we are subjected to. For instance, you, my dear, have also been raped. Pam has told me. She knows. Truly, tell me, do you remember them, their names, even what they looked like? Or do you remember only your own part, the helplessness, the dark despair of being nothing more than a convenient adjunct to someone else's will?"

No more bullshit. I'd like to strangle the old bitch. I used to call it getting pounded, not raped. But rape it was. I wail. My tears do not flow. They storm not from my eyes but from my very soul. "Now it's death," I shout through the gurgle of my drowning lungs. "The world. Life. Now Death. The whole fucking thing's just one rapist after another, taking me, pounding me, in ways you can't begin to understand."

"You could not be more wrong, my dear. I do understand. I most assuredly do."."

Why I do not know, but her words, possibly the tone of her voice, the bone sharp hand she lays upon my shoulder — *When did she move? When did she come so close?* — comfort me, and my lamentation — *Yes, lamentation it surely is —* ceases.

She bends and places very gently a dry kiss upon my cheek. "I'll leave you now," she whispers, and her words offer a divine promise. "You need to be alone."

She is correct. For the first time I am aware that I am no more a victim than is she, than are all the women in all the world. The thought that perhaps men as well fit into this same category slips into and out of my mind again. It is all that I can handle right now simply to accept the logical reality of the non-mystical epiphany I have just experienced. If we all are victims, is it not just as rational to believe that none of us is a victim? If we all suffer violations of our physical selves, is it not logical to assume that our physicality is not of its very nature inviolate? If our free will often is routinely subverted, then is it not probable that our will is not free? In order then to live, must we all, in some sense of that term, not be raped? Is this tragic or is it simply normal? If I could I would sleep this away. The desert was depressing. Mary's words have led me possibly to horror.

Mistah Kurtz—he dead

HOW CAN I sleep? There are flies in here. Rotten meat strings from poles set out deliberately to attract them. Is this the hospital's doing? Or Mary's or Pam's? It matters not. The antiseptic atmosphere conceals the stench from those of us known to the universe as human. But not from the flies. They gather around the pole like children on the first of May. Winged children, decay-born and filth-sustained children. All about the room they swarm, tread their gore-stain tracks across my newly clean flesh. Mary appears aglow in the sunlight from our window, green and black in her robe of flies. Falling beneath their weight she melts into the floor, and the flies follow her down the dark drain beneath us all.

It has happened for real I know it. When I awake, her bed is empty, and she is gone. So much for the lord being my shepherdess. I am alone. Even Paloma, even more so Mother (I shall soon call her Mom) would be welcome now. Even Pumpkin, even (God help me in this at least) Scarecrow. I am, however, alone. Unless that is the cancer perhaps has become **CANCER** and has come to stay with me, a constant companion, mocking me throughout the sad dribble of my remaining days, a most unwelcome addition to my newly discovered family. I wish I could remember Christ's actual last words, but English is enough. What a fool the poor man was, not knowing until he hung upon the cross that Daddy will always screw you and then desert you, that Mommy will always stand idly by, reveling in her own sadness, her own maternal guilt, as you bleed, as your screams pierce the very heart of the desert air, as your terror desiccates your very soul....

Can't help yourself, can you?

There is another. It is not the cancer, I am certain. Neither is it that other, the lovely me. It is she who was promised. It is Pam. Again, where is she? Gone. I am still alone. As experienced as I am, surely I am able to recognize a hallucination. Or am I? Her voice was so real. I hear it still. However, am I certain such as she actually exists? Ever was here? And Mary? And the shadow? How improbable is all that anyway? I have been in something of a coma, have dreamed impossible dreams, have experienced visitations of a most hallucinatory nature.

"Your fucking skin, idiot," trumpets like a thousand and one cachinnations. Oh, my, yes, it is Pam. And my skin? It is clear still. She and Mary are real. And Hope?

"Foolish, girl, you're almost as clueless as that other one. You now have more reason to hope than ever you were born for. I assure you…. God, now I'm starting to sound like you. Anyway, there's lots a shit worse than death, and, believe it, you're being spared a world of hurt. Now, just suck it up. Here comes breakfast. Eat. Drink….Ssorry, but I won't give you Mary."

The little bitch laughs herself right out of the room, or my mind or wherever the hell she has been.

Somewhere between the egg over easy and the sausage patty — *Shouldn't hospitals be health-promotional?* — I come to a simple yet overwhelming — *here I go again* — transcendent and joyous revelation: Breakfast is good. I would eat more, would, despite the cancer, grow most rotund without fear of ridicule or rejection. Who wants to fuck a cancer patient, all bald and bones anyway? Sympathy fucks! Is not that all a fat girl ever gets? I store this thought away just below the perceptive/oblivious line within the not so jumbled chaos of my psychology. I will eat, but, for certain, I want better coffee than St. Peter's offering, at least this morning.

ONCE WHILE BEING pounded by a not too disgusting John, *By the way I am no prostitute*, I found myself wandering away into a world of nearly magical possibilities. In that world women and men expressed love mutually. Neither was dominant; neither indulged himself or herself in animalistic behavior without the full cooperation, yes, desire of the other. Afterward the glow was mutual, the touches tracings of soft breezes, the ebb of intensity most deliciously followed by the gentle ripples of love, perhaps Platonic, most surely that which the Greeks termed Philos. In my short life as an adult, such states, both physical and emotional, had ever been denied me.

This once, I rocked. Not in the crass pop-idiomatic sense of that term. Rather, I awoke to myself being rocked in a most maternal fashion by the John on top of me. No flesh Pieta our embrace. Among other incidentals, I was not yet dead, and the guy was as deep as deep can get inside me. Still was he ever so gentle. At the point of our connection our selves merged without trace of friction. I could feel the pressure, the weight of him both inside and upon me, but I felt weightless as well, and he was in no way pounding. The day was bright, the windows without shades. Nonetheless, as I looked into his eyes I recognized darkness, the presence of something elemental. It posed no threat, no voracious übergravity, nothing at all so dangerous. Neither was it in any sense random or even controlled chaos. Rather, within him dwelt the darkness of one who has lost everything, even self. His face bore no expression of any kind, and even the slap and wash of our bodies upon my verminous cot was more coincidental to the dance of physical life itself than the result of passion's tics. We breathed. One in respiration. We opened and closed, thrust and withdrew as one being, yet he did not become me. Nor I him. My most yielding nature waxed hard and strong. And cold. He flowed soft and liquid all around me. Within me. His essence was the warm scented oil of Old Testament anointing. Mine the cold glint of Delilah's smile.

Ourselves Ourself. A new witness of love and salvation.

Never had and never again have I been so completely part of another human being while yet totally myself. To say that we were one would of course be a ridiculous cliché, but, while I had not dematerialized into him, I swear I might have been upon the verge of dissolution.

I have heard other women speak of "soft orgasms" as if such could possibly exist. Low-key and sweet, the "softie" is claimed by some to be an experience reserved exclusively for a woman alone or with another such as herself. Believe me I've been masturbating since I was ten or so and have had my share of girls. Never have I expressed the release of all my sexual fury in a mere sigh and a furtive tear of joy. Such is the stuff of myth or better yet comedy. For absolutely certain, anything "soft" is impossible with a man, even a gay man. And I've had my share of faggots too.

So, when I sighed and the little bitty tear tumbled down my cheek, when I looked into those great moocow eyes above me and saw their corners begin to drip, when I saw Johnnie's lips tremble with a sigh so perfectly simultaneous with mine...?

I fucking freaked!

I do believe I must have terrified the poor dweeb, for he scuttled off so fast I had to run naked into my hallway after him, and physically restrain him at the top of the stair.

"It's all there," he sobbed before I could begin my screech of accusation. "It's all on the table. I took it out of my pocket before we...before we.... You know, I really believed for a minute that you were different. That I might have found something of a soul mate. You know?"

Yeah, yeah, the hydro was back in my room, and I was naked in the hall. "Some other time, maybe," I flung back over my autonomically flirtatious behind and shut the door on his response. Funny how the hydro was soon used up, how the memory of the relief it provided has vanished. Johnnie, however, and the soft orgasms he so lovingly created for us both remain, perhaps to the end of the limited number of my days. Humorous really. I never saw the guy in person again until once upon a meeting, when I found myself coming back for perhaps the zillionth time. There he was, soft eyes and all. Eyes that looked right through me. Eyes so distant as to be from another time and place—as no doubt they were. He held my hand during the prayer at the end. His hand was cold, his wrist and fingers pale. Then he was gone. As, I guess, are all the good things.

"Finished, hon?" some no-mind chirps way too familiarly as she swoops in and scoops up my breakfast tray. I am left with only a stupid, turning just a trifle painful, memory with which to face the drizzle of the day slopping down my windowpane. Then in comes Mom.

I warned you.

MOTHER AND PUMPKIN take me home. Miraculously, my cancer is in remission. Extensive, "debulking" they call it, surgery had been scheduled, but a preliminary round of Chemo has been far more effective than anticipated. I still harbor multiple lesions, but even those on my liver have shrunk away to nonexistence. Dr. Bhatti, that, indeed, is his name, Jasvinder Bhatti, is hopeful that I may defy all the odds. Do I not, however, know better than to believe? Dr. Jaz as he encourages me, and I suppose all his other patients as well, to call him, is not at all that which his name might suggest. True, he is descended from an ancient and even storied line of royalty. Nevertheless, as he insists upon reminding me every time I attempt to refer to Vishnu, Bhattiana, or even the poet by his same name, from possibly as short a time ago as a thousand years, we all share a common ancestor, thereby indicating that, all gods and tribal fiefs aside, I am, as are Mother and Pumpkin, as related to any sixth century poet as is he who yet shares that bard's name, especially since the Sanskrit versifier in question, undoubtedly shared Bhatti as his given not his family name. Besides, as the good doctor is unable to refrain from asserting upon such occasions, his eyes are blue, unlike most Punjabi or any other denizens of the subcontinent, and so are mine. Thus, he smiles in that most inscrutable manner of his, are not the two of us almost brother and sister?

I most definitely checked this insanity out, and had no need to go further than Wikipedia. The thousand year thing is a bit of a stretch, mostly mathematical projection, and, even to this arithmilliterate, not quite convincing. The blue eyes? Everything I find suggests the improbable: All blue-eyed people share a common ancestor dating back no more than ten-thousand years. Mother loves the expression, "It's a small world." I hate it with a, *cliché I know,* passion. Still, it just might be. Thank you Dr. Jazz for confirming something which Mother and her offshoot Pumpkin seem already to have known.

All this is mere diversion. Jazzie Blue Eyes exhibits very few of the physical and cultural stereotypes one associates with his ethnicity. *Well said, Ruthie.* He is dark, but I've seen darker Scandinavians. His hair is curly. He is long of limb, svelte of physique, and speaks, as would any Jersey boy, pure east-coast American. Does he look a bit like The Boss? Sing like him too? Not at all. He does dress most casually though, and is at times most appealingly unshaven....

I really hate this cancer. My so-called life. I must admit, however, that never in a million years, were I cancer-free, at least not since my first semester at Williams, would such a man as Dr. Jasvinder Bhatti even momentarily consider such as am I anything more than.... You guessed it.

As eventualities have now composed themselves, however, I may have found someone with something of a kindred soul, a more highly educated, although possibly possessed of no greater intelligence nor enlightened spirit, Catfish John? How does one say that in Sanskrit anyway? LOL! *Pumpkin must be wearing off on me. I loathe that Facebook/Twitter crap.* I see Jazz every Tuesday at 1:30. I must admit that his office is so generic as to be discomfiting. A modicum *Mom's word* of Eastern mystery might have been called for, but nary a Palm grows tall among the plastic bouquets, and Starving-Artist prints of kittens and puppies border upon the offensive. Especially when they grace the soft plum drywalls of a man, a doctor, a human being who could be so much more than such labels might suggest. In the same vein are the idiotic magazines. *People, Sports Illustrated,* and *TV Guide.* It reminds me in something more than a supercilious, ironic fashion of *No Exit.* Eternity trapped among the dribbling idiots slumped in rows along the walls and smack down the middle of the waiting room. Death, be not proud, condescend to deliver me from this room, these people. How has life grown into something worse than death? This world become a Hell? 2200Burdett Avenue, Damnation's quotidian anteroom?

There is even a camera. I swear to Vishnu, there is an obvious eye mounted in one corner of the room and focused upon, of all things, the receptionist's glass cage. Is she under suspicion? Are her mumbled *tet a tetes* with arriving patients being recorded as well as filmed? Have mine also been? Why in all that's good and unholy have I not noticed this thing before? This is at least my seventh or seventeenth visit here. I might simply ask Inez the receptionist? But what are the odds of eliciting a truthful response? Instead, I stand and wave a *People* across the damnable thing's lidless eye. Just maybe some hidden observer, Nazi uniform and all, pseudo-police anyway, can be flushed from behind his blind and be forced to reveal this gross intrusion upon our private agonies as revealed to the one within the glass.

"Whacha doin'?" some geezer croaks from the center row.

Hallelujah, another living soul. Not only living but at least minimally aware. "Do you know what this is?" I enquire in tones requiring no answer. "It's a camera. These Fascisti are recording us as we register. Who can say how many more of these things are hidden everywhere? Even in the exam rooms?"

I would continue but Geez interrupts. "Ain't nothin' but a motion detector," he rasps. "Fer security, you know?" At which point he drops back into his Kindle, leaving me waving at nothing, feeling more than a bit foolish.

No one else has noticed. Inez remains cemented to her desk, eyes spiked onto the keyboard before her. I reseat myself and assume a proper, for me anyway, public persona, relieved that Mother has dropped me off rather than waiting with me as she is wont to do under the usual circumstances. I imagine her and Pumpkin snickering oh so genteelly behind arched fingers, pretending discretion, screeching for my notice.

It is far too easy to mock them, but better that, at least given my current state of affairs, than to slip once again into the.... It wasn't *sea* of *Despond was it?* No, it was *Slough*. That's it. Christ's Christmas Bells and all the Howls of Heaven's rejects. I hate that butt-buggering, babysucking creep Bunyan. How in anyone's hallowed halls of so-called heavenly inspiration could a human being have imagined the Horror he called God and the Misery he saw as Heaven. Damn you, Bunyan. Stay your pimpled ass in the shit-stable you imagined salvation to be. Drown in the sodden air arising from the e-colic swamp you could never move beyond. Beyond the sea, the slough, of Despond and into the Mother Pumpkin land of my own miasmic circumstances.

Perhaps I prattle on too long. Forgive my whimsy, if you would; my intention has been to indulge in a slight riff of innocent punning before moving on to more prosaic matters.

Truly, I shall best be served if I am able to slough off the hatred I naturally feel for the tubers and avoid sloughing myself away into the solitary desert from whence I have so recently returned. I'd cry if I could, but, I won't. Will not! John Steinbeck in some valley-boy tale or other obsessed over *Timschel* in a land not too far east of this one, and while I righteously deny the very concept of sin, I do sometimes give in to a most unworthy state of regret. *What if?* I cannot help but wonder. What if things had gone even the slightest bit differently? If Daddy hadn't been blown all over the godforsaken Middle Eastern desert? If Mom had had the slightest inkling of how to deal with a rebellious and, I must admit, resentful child so much different from herself or those she knew as family? If there had been nothing harder than a little blow? Oh, I not only mayest but actually mightest have found tears possible. As I readily admit, the *what if's* never were and I became she whom I had chosen to be. Lottie, the ironic addict is a very comfortable lie with whom to abide. Ruthie might find the tears. Ruthie might desire the normalcy of their release. Lottie, however, needs no permission. For anything. Steinbeck was a fine writer and his being awarded and accepting the Nobel Prize attest to same. However, in most matters I prefer another laureate. When it comes to sin and the tears it may engender, I prefer Sartre, *Je refuse!*

I wonder, mayest I hate? Just a tiny bit? An undercover bit? Just mine to hoard and nurture, and....

"Ms. Kelleher," Inez interrupts.

I look out from somewhere others may never go and directly upon a most grotesque yellow smock bulbous with belly and boobs. Shocked nearly to a gasp, I scan up the ripples of cheap cloth until the bare rolls of some creature's skin appear to form a neck supporting a tiny head round and speckled gray like the end of the turkey baster Mother kept in a drawer just in case she might wish someday to cook Thanksgiving dinner. Two dark eyes lurk behind lids with no lashes; a nose flares upon a tiny and suspiciously chafed upper lip. Her chin is lost in an avalanche of pale cheek and jowl. Her hand, fat and pink, reaches out. "Ms. Keller...? I'm Regina Fowler, Dr. Bhatti's associate. If it's acceptable to you, I will be seeing you today. Dr. Bhatti has been called away on some urgent business."

I do nothing but stare. *This? This is my doctor?*

"I assure you, Petunia continues, that I am completely familiar with your course of treatment and will follow the already established procedures you and the Doctor have agreed upon.

She's so damn calm. So fucking competent. Soothing...reassuring. Like the sacrificial lamb I have always been, I rise and follow her into the inner office. His office. Jaz's office. She wastes no time. She reads my latest blood work, draws more for next time, asks how I'm feeling, and the next thing I know I'm back in the waiting room. No old man now. Just Inez and me. Inez, as always, has an appointment card ready, offers a smile, and chirps, "Have a good one."

Fuck her. Fuck 'em all. I'd say something cutting, but I think better of it. I really am becoming just too, too nice. Girly fucking Girl. I'm through the door and in the hall. *What the hell just happened? I never even asked if Jaz — Jiz'd be a better name for that bag of depleted slime — would be back for my next appointment. I still have time before the vegetables turn up to get me. I'll march my cancerous ass right back in there and find out a few things. Miss Piggy just ain't going to be this girl's doctor. I'd rather put myself in the hands of a fraud like Paloma or even Salt Lick Kerr than that simpering excuse for a notactual doctor.*

The warthog it turns out is only a PA. Not, as one might assume, "Porky Asshole." Worse, merely Physician's Associate. Sort of an Igor to Dr. Jizbag Bhati.

Maybe I'll find a meeting somewhere. Sometimes I really need one. Wouldn't Mom be thrilled by that? At least their crap sometimes works. So long, Jiz. I'm off to find another Wizard.

I call a cab. And Mom. She'll meet me at St. Bonaventure's Church in of all places Speigletown. NA, AA and Al-Anon all in the same place at the same time. Mom will pay the fare, and Mom will wait for me. Terminal Cancer does offer a few minor perks.

"Nice day," claims the cabbie, a rotund middle-aged man with a metastasizing bald spot at the center of his head. Decidedly unattractive. Someday soon, without warning or even the slightest hint of foreshadowing, at least according to Jiz.... Then, why say it. The obvious is often best left unsaid. Perhaps, just perhaps, mind you, if I refuse to recognize it, it will not happen. Fuck you, Locks of Love! A hearty "No thank you," from this quarter. I'll tie my scalp up in a red bandana and walk my last few days without your help, your goddamn pity.

"Yeah," I mumble past my forking tongue.

When I turn my face to the glass by my shoulder, I must confess I am moved. The Hack has not at all stated the obvious. I hadn't noticed, but it looks as if the great mother of all electrical storms is about to strike the first blow of the end of all our days. Is the hacker's remaining hair rising up toward the cab's roof? Is mine? I wouldn't say nice. Absolutely one of those days of power and might that to some at least holler forth with the voice of god himself. Thor or Zeus, gods of power, and most of all, Jehovah, not the bland shepherd of all the polyester preachers but the Real Thing. Jehovah as the people of Jericho must have experienced. The God of the Four Horsemen, my favorite of whom is Death. Even, I must add, before the cancer. Don't we all ride the Pale Horse?

Our yellow-green cab blunders on toward whatever darkness awaits. Remember, Mother and Pumpkin? The driver tries again. "You goin' to a meetin'?"

A not so innocent question, I surmise, and allow my annoyance to show. "If I were, I couldn't say," I answer.

"I'm a friend of Bill's myself," he continues.

Just my luck. A loquacious alcoholic has to pick me up. It's about to rain, and I'm stuck. I have no choice. Mom has texted me. Probably Flea. Mom's not all that competent.

"Thought I'd seen ya someplace before," Mr. Sharer offers. "Ever go to McCarty? Sunday?"

I can stop this easily enough, and I will. That's AA, and I'm in another group. My father was abusive, if you must know. He was an alcoholic. I do Al-Anon. Don't drink or use drugs myself. I've seen too much already. My sobriety is probably the only good thing Papa did for me. I'll never become what he was."

"Good for you," the cabbie replies, and shuts the fuck up.

As promised, the tubers await. As we pull into the oh so very perfect lot, all freshly paved, intricately and geometrically perfectly lined, the first drops begin to fall, the thunder to grumble like an overfull stomach, and the lightning to shimmer at the periphery of the apocalyptic day. Always prepared, Mother, umbrella protecting her perfect Do from the annoyance nature is always herself prepared to inflict upon us, dashes to our cab, raps on Hackie's window and thrusts several bills into his hand. How she knows such things as the proper cab fare has always been a mystery either too profound or impossibly quotidian for me to follow. The obvious answer is that she called the company, explained our circumstances, and was given a number. Why would she bother? They even take frigging credit cards. I will never understand such compulsions. Has she nothing better to do?

Shot from the gathering gloom, right in the middle of a deep breath occasioned by the fork of Mother's ebony nails through the driver's half-cracked window, flagging two bills of indiscriminate denomination into his face, an apparition, emerges. Not at Mother's side. It is not Flea. Through the streaked windshield of the taxi I discern, sliding sideways, lurching upright and straight, and then wobbling into a handicapped space, a motorcycle topped off by the wildest rider this side of the speed-freak rabbit in some Net Flix, drug addled movie night John and I drifted through a couple of years ago.

The hare wears neither helmet nor leather jacket. Its legs show bare to its crotch, and this alien visitor from some cartoon planet or other dismounts from the brightest, sun-blast motorcycle I have ever seen. Even in the dark of the approaching storm it glares with the intensity one might associate with a blast-furnace, or so I might imagine, if such even exist anymore. I am rooted to the seat of my cab. I can but stare. The ebony tongue of nails retreats, having let the money flutter off to wherever such things go; the driver groans, and the riding-rabbit saunters rather than hops toward us.

Felicia is nowhere to be seen, and Mother is a narrow shot of black Mac, just a snippet of white boob-bloated blouse lumping out one corner of her ensemble. The biker arrives. I have already determined.... Pam.

Before she is able to shoulder Mother aside, Hackie has already fully lowered his window in anticipation. "Yo, Izzie," Pam exclaims as my vision of mother turns completely black and is replaced by a ratty hanging of Denim opening upon what must be a swimsuit bra but which could only have been purchased from a more intimate section of the Victoria's Secret catalogue. "If it ain't Kenny the Cab Man," she chortles. "How's it hangin'?"

Cabbie spits a chortle, reaches for one of the little treasures so inadequately concealed upon her chest, sighs as she backs away, and answers, "Better'n yours, I'll bet."

Pam must have thought his riposte hilarious for she backs completely from my vision, but I hear her spasms of laughter.

Quickly she turns serious and just a trifle sharp. "You might as well go on home or wherever, Missus. I can take it from here," she snaps, and wrenches open my car door. "Come on out, Ruthie. You and me got some business to do."

"J-just one minute, Missy," mother manages. "Ruth has no need of your...kind...of intervention. She called us and we are perfectly capable of meeting her.... Taking care of...." Mother is neither fumbling nor dithering. In fact her state of dudgeon has grown to such eutrophic proportions as I can only imagine Daddy once had been capable of arousing. Those nails scrape across Pam's bare front and grasp my arm. Her hand is hot, her grip intense.

She would have dragged me off to the meeting, had not Pam charmed her with a smile and a softly laid hand upon her righteous shoulder. "I'm sorry, Mrs. Kelleher. It's just that I really don't think there's anything here that can benefit Ruthie. You must understand.... Surely you do."

To my amazement, Mother's grip relaxes, and her now trembling fingers touch my cheek with an unexpectedly comforting gentleness I would not have thought possible as coming from her even a week ago. "She's my little girl," she sobs. "I just want her to get better. She's my little girl." Abruptly she twists away, her fingers now pressed to her own face.

"I only came to help," Pam soothes, touching Mom's shoulder. "I have a better place for her right now. You've met Paloma Paraclitus I understand. Well, we've arranged a new group. It meets in an hour and she specifically requested that I recruit Ruthie here."

Freaking mother! I swear she has a thing for the dove. Anyway, as she turns to placidity, no more dudgeon threatening her peaceful waters, I begin brewing up a storm. Who the fuck does this little slut think she is? Or, for that matter, who I am? And Paloma? I grew past anything that insipid little twit could offer the moment my cancer spoke its fated line. Or was that Jizbag Bhatti's cue. Whatever, Paloma has nothing but platitudes and fucking deceptions. She couldn't help me before and sure as hell she won't be able to now. My mouth films up with imprecation, "No," is all I can spit past the scum.

"Certainly, you should," Mother coos. "Ms. Paraclitus is eminently qualified. Her PhD is from Dartmouth, you know."

Good old Mom. An Ivy League education never fails to impress. Well, perhaps someday I'll let her know about some of the business I've learned that'll blow away all the shit any elite college ever taught. Like how to take three men at the same time and reach out for two more. I've done it. It's more real than some asshole's hierarchy or another's theories of human behavior based upon nothing more than pigeons and boxes. I could teach them more than they'd ever want to know about boxes and needs and just exactly what I think of Squab.

Choking through laughter of cosmic proportions, Pam commands. "Cut the shit, Ruthie. You're gonna learn a few things today that you need to know. Skinner and his box be damned, your own future has been set in concrete. You got no choice. Easy or hard, you're coming. The only question is will you go with Mommy or me."

Mother glares in her most determined fashion. Pam stands even more implacable. As always, I chose to submit.

Not Mother. The admiration I am beginning to sporadically feel for her is not at all grudging. Mother I guess never learned or even felt the need to submit to anything. Except perhaps her biological imperatives, myself and Flea exhibits A and B. After our advent? I don't think poor Dad ever had a chance. I would bet she drove him away every bit as resolutely as she now attempts to draw me in. Thank God for that. At least at times like this.

"My Ruth is not going anywhere on that motorbike of yours," she asserts, and follows with a hiss directed my way, "Not now. Not tomorrow. Not ever. Not while I live and breathe anyway."

Crazy Pam only laughs. "Look at the sky. Listen. I won't be riding that thing anytime this afternoon either. I do have resources, and here she comes now." Indeed, as if on cue a huge white truck turns into the lot and lumbers over to the motorcycle where it stops idling rough threats out two tails, I think they're called, pipes.

"That's Sis," Pam begins. Before she is able to go any further the door opens and almost unable to squeeze through its generous opening thumps a being of indeterminate species and gender, dressed as a human, and wearing the same denim wrap as does Pam. Without so much as glancing our way, the hominid, for that I am willing to assert it must be, lets fall the back gate thing, slides a metal contraption of some narrow design from out the body of the vehicle, fixes it in place so that it creates a narrow bridge between truck and ground, clumps its oversized self upon Pam's motorcycle, thrashes it into life, roars a loud circle around the lot, and, without pause or any apparent calculation of risk, rockets right up onto the back of the huge machine whereupon it bumps to an abrupt halt. Securing something or other, the hulking rider shuts the infernal thing off.

Pam laughs with delight. Mother turns pale. I gape open mouthed and speechless.

The taxi's radio crackles into life. Kenny replies. "I'm outta here," he shoots through the window. "Tell Sis she's still the **baddest** man I know," and he is off.

Dance of Destruction

Arthur

2013

Often when things trouble us we put our possible responses up for debate and indecision, but at other times, particularly when facing options too unfamiliar for meaningful discussion, we abandon thought along with its inevitable delay and reflexively roll our universe up into one ball, toss it at the decision just down the ten-pin lane and await the fall. The question before the panel: *Should we, especially as we appear to have been found out, continue into the solid-state of catatonia?* We have no way of knowing how to answer that, and so, before we dissolve into a writhing ball of indecision, itself the antithesis of immobility, I am moved to assume control and, as the one and only I, Arthur, not Mc Murphy, not Pendragon, but absolutely...for certain...truly Woolf, as in Virginia. I am descended.... Well maybe, if Dad and Mom are to be believed.

Mook here is too perceptive for my own good. I suppose for now I can let him go on...amuse me. My brother though... I do miss the freakazoid. I really do, and this Bozo had best watch his bigfooted step or he just might find I'm a great deal more than my present circumstances imply. The sense of connectedness? I know all about it. Both from over there and back here in the world I don't remember ever leaving. Or inhabiting, for that matter. The story, part of which I was going to relate to Paloma and the other Stooges — the party — that is real, even the part I cannot tell. It is remembered completely, exactly, as clear and blinding as sunlight on a thin-ice pond. More than from the Nam shit, I am ever imperiled by that one eternal moment, a solid-frozen Frug without any other partner than myself, the black Satan, the other Arthur Woolf. At any time I could fall through into the rift. Then what? Antarctic stone. That's the end, the icehard basalt I fear I may become.

All the immobility shit is really just my practicing for the inevitable day. As kids we hid beneath our desks in fear of nuclear attack, A-Bomb replaced by H, or as Dad termed it, Hell Blaster. I am still in hiding. Let us be clear. The night of the party simply confirmed something for which not even Vietnam may claim paternity. Not even Jerry Garcia, Shakespeare or the Hydrogen Bomb.

LIKE UNTO MARTIN LUTHER KING, I too had a dream. Unlike that hopeful would-be Jesus, I awoke not to the realization of some vision of universal peace, some altruistic mission. Rather, I awoke from no dream into nightmare. Nine years of age, I found myself alone in the middle of our dark, moon-hatched kitchen, cold vinyl beneath my bare feet. I have no memory of having descended the stairs, walking through one room and down a hall, but those things I had done. I stood robed in midnight, made terrible, made invincible, rendered immobile by the absolute reality of absolute evil. All of it, despite its ubiquitous nature, resided in me. I knew not from possession, but I felt the spirit, was moved beyond movement, could only stand, could not even tremble. So it was my mother found me.

I had a fever, had contracted a particularly virulent, life-threatening case of the chicken pox. For several days — in my own mind — I endured, a statue in the center of the heart of our middle class home. They say I was raced to the hospital, that I was delirious, that I took most of a month to recover. I remember only that I had died, yet lived, had been co-opted by Evil yet would always strive to overcome the void within me. That striving is due entirely to my Mother's love. Yes...yes...I know. Clichés abound. Nevertheless, as I stood a block of ice, a frigid stone, a worse than senseless thing upon the kitchen floor, she remained beside me, and I heard her prayers, smelled the incense of her devotion. Miraculously, the grasp of the abductor of my spirit loosened, failed, and I awoke in a sterile hospital room filled with balloons, flowers, and, yes, not so sterile after all, Love.

My mother's love saves and protects me still, but the Dark One has remained alive in my soul, awaiting any opportunity to reemerge.

Not one whit of this do I reveal to Lenard. Rather, I allow my eyes to roll up a bit as if in questioning mode, and allow my lashes to — not at all like a little girl — flutter. I am alive or at least mobile. I have already ascertained that he knows as much. Interesting.... Actions most someones would have taken as perhaps invitations to continue prattling, cause Mr. Cohan to go silent. He stares as directly through me as I once had done to him. Silence.

If he expects me to speak, I shan't. It was he who accosted me, who has brought me hence to this pretentious palace of pathetic poseurs. *I can't help it. I love myself in these moods when my way with words exceeds even that — impossible yet true — of most, modern at least, poets.*

A fool. I am such a fool. I have laughed aloud; my would-be interlocutor's face relaxes into a smirk of satisfaction, *simple, simian satisfaction.* Again I laugh aloud.

"What's so funny?" he slobbers over his coffee.

As always, I explain, I find my reactions and the words they spawn to be most amusing. He actually allows a fleeting shadow of something resembling annoyance...or perhaps confusion...to cloud his blunt peasant features.

"I ain't here ta muse you," he scolds. "Thought ya might jes like ta hear somethin' bout Billy. Guess not though. Ain't the first time I been wrong 'bout somebody. Won't be the last."

I can see it. The fool is preparing to stomp out, leaving me to — as they say — sit in my own shit. Thank you, whoever and wherever you might or might not be, God.

As usual, however, my spurt of gratitude is premature. Instead of leaving, the importunate bastard settles himself as rigidly into his chair, into his gross bodily attitude, as ever could I. "We'll talk about you then," he sneers.

"No," I counter. "We talk about my brother or we talk not at all."

I should have known. The bounder — thank you British Bob — has no doubt been awaiting this precise moment of opportunity all along. Without a pause or need to take a breath, he launches into an avalanche of blather such as I have never before heard. At least outside the prolix rooms of AA and its related A's. On and on out and down into caverns I have had no wish to explore, his prosaic song blunders along.

"Yer brother...he weren't no reglar kind a guy...." My look or perhaps his own sense of propriety must have warned him, for he seamlessly shifts linguistic gears and moves on in a mode more closely approaching my own.

"Am I bugging you? Don't mean to bug you," he utters with a supercilious smile gravid with the certainty that I would not recognize the allusion. Let the blighter think of me as he will. I was there. My wager is he was not.

"OK, Edge. Play the blues," I whisper into to the green and grey Starbucks clatter of coffee grinders and quotidian chatter. Whether Mooky does not hear or deliberately ignores me, matters not. I could not care less. I know much the pretentious Cretan is incapable of comprehending. Consequently, I will listen to the things he relates with more than the proverbial grain of salinity, confident that he did share my brother's last days, and, while not expecting anything to be put to rest, I do have no small degree of curiosity involving Billy's final days. After his enlistment we saw each other but twice, and, sad truth to be told, I can't remember if we ever said goodbye. I have no specific questions, but I would like to know more. This Mook could be of limited service in that respect. I shall listen.

By the time I am able to unwrap my focus from about myself, Cohan has progressed a ways into his tale. The two of them, Lenard and Billy, have found themselves together in Hong Kong about to board a flight back to Vietnam. They are drunk, stoned, and concerned they may have contracted an obnoxious little malady known appropriately as Drippy Dick. Neither one cares all that much. Instead they are submerged beyond hope of surfacing in a story, Billy in its telling, Lenny in its unfolding. The story is mine.

Mook cares not, however, that, despite my never having heard it, I have lived it. I know the details far better than ever Billy could have told them. They are mine, and I have no desire to bear up under any sort of heavy-handed, semi-fictional account. It is the story I might have once revealed to Paloma. It is the story of my darkness. My evil. My sin. It has nothing to do with some Johnny Cash/ Bobbie Brit clown. He will not tell it.

Mobile as ever Carl Lewis might have been, I leap to my feet and flash into the Men's Room before a single syllable further can slush its way past Lenard's lips. The door shut and locked, I am compelled to search for a reason to be there. Why I sometimes know invisible observers exist I am unable to explain, but they hover just beyond perception at all times, especially when I find myself in a public lavatory. Therefore, I sit. Subsequently, I move an organ or two to accomplish its designated purpose.

One such employee of my not-so-very-free will is my brain. Sitting and thinking, wondering whatever to do. I will relate the story to myself exactly as it must be expressed. I will allow Lenard to listen should he so desire. I rise, rinse my hands, dry them under the appropriately strident machine. All observers, within and without my sensory range, will be made aware that I have cleaned my hands of my own filth and am ready to be reborn pristine into the world of men.

I return to the table. Cohan awaits. I begin: "I will presume to mix two allusions as well as the attendant metaphors for you, my good fellow. Early in my mostly forgettable childhood I learned from the benighted Milton that Satan and fire have something of a thing for each other and that the Single Hitter McLean quite possibly was attempting a Miltonic reference in his line concerning Fire being the Devil's only friend. I also became aware sometime prior to Mr. Garcia's jug band epiphany that any friend of the Devil's was indeed a friend of mine as well. So you see, Fire, while not my only friend, was destined, I am confident in asserting, to become at the very least my earliest close companion. My Amigo, as time warped into Vietnamese Standard, we grew inseparable."

"I INTUIT THAT you might speak. Please do not, for my tale, a veritable river of incendiary jelly, must flow wherever it might go without interruption. Beware you who would stand in its way."

"Subsequent to a variety of inflammatory experiences as a child, my adolescent self, upon the occasion of a reluctant membership in a high-school pretense at a class in General Psychology, investigated pyromania amongst young boys, ostensibly as a research project, while actually satisfying a very personal impulse toward self-knowledge if not complete understanding.

"I see your supercilious smile, your haste to judge me negatively, your need to satisfy your unicellular organ of comprehension with superficial and simplistic explanations. I must admit, however, that even clichés have their bases in truth. I would imagine that one, a therapist for instance, just might have found me troubled. Yes, Mr. Cohan, a pyromaniac. I had set fires. Three in all. Two, rather than conflagrations, were simple dumpster events. The third.... Now that came to life, a monster of smoke and flame and something else unimaginably pure. I saw right through its externals directly into its core. Fire, Mr. Cohan is truly a spiritual being. I am not now nor ever was I a fool. Fire is of Hell, and Hell is no fatherland one should choose rashly.

"By the time my devil's spawn had spent its energy, half a dry hillside, a neighbor's garage, and their car had been consumed. Forgive me, my extinguished companion, but I must admit that something in me had been consummated... in the conjugal sense of that term. However, a fear began to burn within me even as my procreative energies spent themselves into my damp trousers.

"Had I somehow in an irrational and very adolescent moment just pledged my undying soul to the very evil force from which no mother could any longer deliver me? Thus, my inquisitive fellow, I, at least for one so conventionally reared as was I, turned wholeheartedly to the Anglican faith of my parents, sought God's forgiveness, avoided occasions of temptation, and prayed myself for a time away from the clutches of the fiery demon. For a brief span my thoughts even entertained the possibility of entering the priesthood, but, as do most adolescent boys, I eventually turned to other more desirable prospects."

"Yeah, Billy said ya was a ladies' man. Said ya had more gash'n he could even dream of gittin'."

"Careful," I caution. "Watch your tongue or watch me disappear out this door. Beside, this is my moment...my tale to tell. Your sole function is to listen. Or at least appear to.

"My grades in school were mediocre at best. No doubt due to my sterling success in other arenas such as you have just mentioned. So, much to our Mother's and Father's disappointment, I enlisted in the Army instead of matriculating in the small-town Liberal Arts college, St Michaels of Burlington

Vermont, which no doubt in an act of desperation had accepted me as a member of their freshman class. Even today I could not explain why, but from what may have been some perverse sense of irony, I boarded the bus to school, consumed the entire box of brownies and cookies Mother had packed for me, then, after an all-night colloquy with myself upon the shores of Champlain, trudged into town, cleaned up in a McDonald's washroom, and enrolled in another school altogether, located in the state of New Jersey and known far and wide as Dix. As for now, all may observe the results of my education. Here I stand, or rather remain currently seated, before you, still alive and perfectly capable of kicking should the need arise.

"So well-prepared had I become that after a minimum of AIT, also at Fort Dix, I was accepted without further qualification into the University of Vietnam, School of Death, with a minor in Holocaust Studies. No, my unlettered friend, I refer not to the European event, but, as you will soon see, to the more general and very literal meaning of the word.

"I soon became close to a mate —buddy. Everyone called him Hair. We had arrived In-Country together from separate origins. I from upstate New York by way of New Jersey and he from western Tennessee via Louisiana, Fort Puke as I recall. I, then as now, was thin as the proverbial rail with legs like a stork and the nose of a hawk, he, tattooed already with a black FTW on his right forearm which he would soon follow upon the left with the classic Death Before Dishonor dagger, snake, and Death's Head. He was ripped like a body-builder and handsome as a matinee idol, but his most treasured possession was the hair which he wore as long as Army discipline would allow and which he vowed, once discharged, to maintain forever after in the style of one Ed Kookie Byrnes.

"Sad to say, and I am quite serious, such was not to be…. As my tale shall now reveal. One dark and threatening sunless dawn...a characterization which, I am compelled to admit, is a smidge clichéd but nevertheless accurate...we set out in two M-35's for some mindless rendezvous with something other than Death. Or so we fervently hoped. The way was clear, the road paved and straight, rice paddies puddling off to either side. I sat in the rear of the lead conveyance, alone, as was often the case, in the company of others never to be my peers. Hair sat up front in the vehicle behind, no doubt regaling his driver with fanciful recapitulations of Sunset Strip episodes which existed only in his fascinating if unifocal imagination.

"Then blossomed the dark flower! The trailing Deuce-and-a-Half exploded in an absolutely beautiful burst of violent reds and yellows all etched upon the day's gray matte. Mindless as lemmings fleeing from their suicidal fate rather than toward its saltine embrace, all eleven of my mates and I abandoned with remarkable alacrity our own potential incineration. Into the excremental paddies we dove as our vehicle belched its own glory across the funereal landscape. Forgive my prolixity please, but I have revisited this moment too often not to have added a touch of parody to the inescapable magnitude of its significance.... At least to me.

"Anyway.... Back to the point. Ever curious, I could not keep my head down. Truly, we were well within a most civilized region. The only danger came from saboteurs such as those who no doubt had booby-trapped our trucks...."

"Yeah, I hear ya," my fellow Mook sighs. "Shot me a couple a them tryin' ta drop grenades wrapped in rubber bands into the tanks a some of are equipment. That what happened to you?"

"Careful," I warn, and "Yes. You are directly on the money with your forensic analysis.

"Back to the paddy. I'm looking not at the remains of my own vehicle but the wreckage of the one behind when emerging from the smoke and lingering flame, like a wraith from some updated Tolkien, stumbled a creature of Fire which I later learned was Hair. His arms, enveloped in flame, waved frantically in some horrid semaphore. The rest of his clothesless, save for jungle boots, body appeared to have turned to soot about to scatter itself into the breathless atmosphere. After one eternal moment, he fell, arms yet aflame, no sound emerging from his most elemental form. Hair was dead.

"I could only, to this day, wish! For Hair such salvation as violent death may sometimes be was not to be. You see, Mr. Cohan, he lived, a scarred and hairless mockery of both Mr. Byrnes and himself, until two years ago. That day he deployed to a jungle darker than Vietnam ever could be and never returned, dwelt mindless, a ravaged, hairless alien in the Rochester VA until the end.

As Marlon would say, *a la* Mr. Kurtz, "THE GODDAMN MOTHERFUCKING HORROR!"

The Bistro becomes silent. Even the noise of New Scotland traffic ceases its pathetic buzz. Mooky appears stunned. Not as a result of the dreariness inherent in my story but rather by my inappropriate and uncharacteristic outburst. Even I feel myself taken aback, but rage lingers in my throat. I choke upon the normalcy of their mundanely polluted air. I must remove myself from this absurd little cubby. Does not Cohan... Lenard... as if on cue, reach a steady hand across to cover my own? Does he not mumble well below the range of anyone else's audible perceptions, "It's all right, Artie. I been there too"?

Yes, I am certain he has, but not all the way. I have to make him see that.

I THINK I'LL drop the supercilious tone. This thing's gotten out of hand. The rest of the story requires a touch of authenticity... or so I believe...I think.

"There's more," I confess. "And I fear it speaks ill of me. From that moment up to the present, and, I'm sure, destined to continue on into the eternity of my perceptual existence... sorry... I've been in love with Hair. Neither as a man nor as a caricature of some fifties teen-idol, but as a spiritual presence lodged deep within me. I call him The Man on Fire.

"There, my friend, dwells the true nightmare. The Man on Fire is no simple PTSD, Vietnam memory. The Man on Fire has always been with me. He is my passion, obsession really. I believe he was sparked into existence by the demon of my childhood, emerged those three pyrotechnic times of my youth, slumbered a while, and then awakened to a dark Asian morning awash in the gasoline-glory of his brothers. A bit dramatic I suppose...but, I believe, accurate. Since then, he has led me into my current state of dysfunction."

Starbucks has returned to a normal conversational clatter. The traffic grumbles once again, Lenard settles back, his placid features set in an imperturbable smile. Only his eyes dance. "How about another coffee?" he offers.

I nod.

Soon he returns with my Venti Dark Roast, a Tazo tea for himself and two scones. I effin love scones. Thank you, Lenard Cohan. So, around mouthfuls of pastry delight I resume my bitter tale.

"First of all, allow me a brief digression. I love *Apocalypse Now*, especially the finale: The fiery destruction of Kurtz's compound, The Doors and *The End*. Even now, even here at this table, I am on the boat in the river whose current does not lead away but holds me static. The engines burn themselves toward failure; my will is frozen. Movement has become an impossible fantasy.... Then from out the holocaust stumbles Hair. He is a being composed entirely of flame. He is coming for me. Drugs, alcohol, depravity.... Even love cannot save me from his embrace. He will become me. I cannot allow that.

"To this date my efforts at denial have, for the most part, been successful. Only once have I welcomed him into myself just as some whore might allow The Ripper his way prior to the execution of his murderous intent. That moment is the subject of my secret narrative.

"Damn the drugs. Damn the booze. Damn Pink Floyd and *Time*. Damn you as well Mitch for writing and producing *Just a Sad Song*, you and your impossibly Arthurian character Mitch, based not at all upon yourself, not at all like what you had been, but more...much more...like me. Your supposed friend. Above all, damn you Kenny Merrill, you who, without ever having been in Vietnam, had the audacity to portray so well someone so much like me, and, again like me, you who too easily fell victim of hallucinogens and whisky at a party peopled with strangers and who then babbled incessantly for a good part of the afterevening, still in character, completely non-sensical, unforgivably obnoxious.

"I saw action. More than enough for any three people. And I killed for the record more than four times that number. I also have a CIB. One of my proudest possessions. At least until it became my possession no more...lost in some move or blackout month or so. I do not, and I can no longer care. Mitch though? With a name like that, Mitch Ryan, what else might he have been? Green Beret. A very special force all to his lonesome, Army of One's self.

"Never one for pictures, I have no known photographic record anywhere, don't even own a driver's license. My friend, however, for someone so absolutely clandestine has images of himself scattered about even the dustiest rooms, the darkest cubbies of his far too public private life. There's one especially with his onceuponatime fiancé I will forever remember. My internal Photoshop is state of the art. Mitch has long ago been cropped out, and only my times with Paloma can rival my erotic entanglings with Black Sonya. OH, Jesus! I could do her right here."

"You're gittin loud again," the no-mind cautions, and so I settle quietly back into my narration.

"A particular video sums up all that Mitch was, and, I do believe, a great deal of all that he has become. At first he stands alone before a background set of jungle and a hint of blue sky. Wearing Tiger Stripe BDU's with no identifying patches or rank insignia, he smiles, poses a bit with an M-25. His head is without cover, his hair too long for any man's Army. Within seconds, the camera retreats to more distant vantage, and a quick shadow falls, soon followed by the limp form of a completely nude and partially blackened young Asian female of indeterminate age and size. She lies cruciate upon the sand before him. One soon ascertains she is not completely cruciate. Yes, her arms are outstretched, one side of her torso burned past recognizable humanity, the other as clean as Venus emerging from the sea. Except, where her right breast might once have offered a man even a fleeting moment of delight or a child the sustenance of soul and body we all crave even beyond the suckling stage, gapes a shallow wound, the site of a most inexpert amputation. Her legs are not crossed in Christlike pose. Just one of said appendages remains her. The missing limb would have come from the raw side of her. One is then led, not merely by repugnance but by the camera's brief pan away from the two performers, drawing us toward a distant fire about which men of indeterminate origin, allegiance, and function are gathered as for the feast, into a most unholy vision.

"With a spasm, the camera returns to its initial subjects. Mitch has gathered the woman into his arms. She could not have stood even so much as five feet high, could not have weighed more than six or six and a half stone. He whirls her about in a drunken reel. Her foot trails behind the momentum of their swing; her dark nakedness becomes lurid, inviting. I, and I would tentatively posit, we, cannot help but become just a wee bit aroused. Then as though she weighs not so much as an ounce, he tosses her directly into the sunlight toward which the cinematographer abruptly has directed us. In a golden flash she disappears. Flies into the heart of the sun, one might say.

"All abruptly ends."

"Where we goin' here, pardner? I seen stuff like this too. Don't much care fer it. Have my way and assholes like yer Mitch'd still be locked up. Lotsa worse shit'n My Lai happened over there. Can't say as I'm right with it yet."

Oh, but can't Mooks be way too predictable?

"Hang on," I counsel. "I'm just leading into the very heart of my own darkness. Mitch is there, but merely as a precipitating factor. You'll see.

"Cohoes: The party, Pink Floyd, Mitch, Kenny, and the dance of destruction. It was, as I have previously said, the party after the afterparty. Present were at least a dozen people, among them Yours Truly and a rabble of cast, crew, and hangarounds. As one might have expected, things were fated to get at least a bit out of hand. At first it all felt quite mellow. Elton John performed some of his softer pieces for us; a couple or two disappeared into private cocoons, and the rest of us buzzed up a bit with some weed, sipped beers and settled into mellow pastels of all fruitful guises. All but Mitch and myself that is.

"Before any time had passed, Mitch discovered another woman for a dance. That she was Kenny's publicly announced pre-fiancé offered no obstacle. She could dance with whomever she chose, and anyway Kenny had become dazed by the evening's various assaults upon his consciousness. Could there have been some substance more powerful than a mere hallucinogen coursing through his veins, jittering about within his cerebral cortex, sparkling its tracks up and down his neural pathways? I know not. I would say so.

"In time others joined the dance and began stumbling their own improvised steps about the cluttered floor. Furniture removal became a priority, and soon heaps and piles of tables, a lamp or two and assorted racks as well as one straight-backed chair littered the outskirts of the painted shiplap subfloor floor. The music grew less tame. Stones, Beatles, and Zeppelin alternately assumed the stage. The party awoke to grand new life. All were on fire. All except one of us.

"Kenny Merrill slumped immobile within the enormous grasp of a moss-green, beanbag chair. Someone stuck three wooden kitchen matches in the sole of one of his shoes and lit them. With no consequence whatsoever, they weakly burned themselves out. Kenny never budged. After no little time, Mitch escorted his girl over. One of the more adventuresome young ladies present unzipped Kenny's fly, and placed his ridiculous member into his almost betrothed's shy hand. Nothing. Someone grabbed his testicles and gave a yank, whereupon he convulsed and rolled out onto the floor, eventually drawing himself up into a fetal position of hairy proportion and once again fell into his own dream. Everyone danced around and over him. He became not there.

"As such things do, things with Mitch and Bailey, Kenny's girl, got out of hand. Dancing became pelvic contact, intimate rhythmic intertwinings, and eventually deep osculation and manual explorations. Ultimately, Mitch led Bailey over to her unconscious swain, bent over the blissful inebriate and announced in his best Staff Sergeant's voice directly into an unprotected ear, 'I'm gonna fuck your girl. Got any objections?'

"Merrill moved not a nosehair.

"'Say goodbye then,' Mitch snarled, kicked the other's inert form, and the two new lovers danced their way into another room.

"Not a full minute later, the oblivious one awoke. 'I gotta puke,' he grunted, and staggered off toward the bathroom. The party resumed, but the dancing slowed while little fires of incinerating consciousness glowed furtively within the multiplying dark corners of the room. By ones and twos peripheral guests, perhaps sensing the unpleasantness to come, drifted out the door. I opened a door of my own. Tommy, a stagehand, no doubt a burnout from birth, offered me a scrap of blotter. The night grew stranger...richer than ever a night had been.

"The Man on Fire...not Hair but not I either...kept his distance, grew comfortable in his own corner of my universal mind. My mother's love held me in place, and Billy laughed off in the kitchen. All I needed was to pick my way past the seaweed shapes once human beings and wander out to where we would forever be reunited. The quick and the dead. There need be no distinction whatsoever. My mother held me still.

"My brother's laugh soon enough faded into the drunken squeaks and giggles of female substance. My mother faded too. As did The Man. Even so, I lived not alone. All around me ripened life. Ripened, and spoiled. Became the seared and obscene feast of Mitch's Vietnam video. Pink Floyd erupted *Time* from their own continuum and played a heretofore unrecognized chord within me. Somewhere a door opened. Footsteps echoed down a hall in some far away dwelling constructed not for men. Mitch appeared. In his arms, as had he the burned woman, he held a moderately sized TV. Twisting and turning in a whirligig of appearance and reality. He was and was not there. He most decidedly was a video. No such form in no such circumstances existed in anything resembling Cohoes, New York.

"'One day closer to Death,' pronounces David Gilmore, and as if on cue, Mitch raised the set above his head and dashed it to the floor. A sturdy machine, not much damage resulted. He picked the thing back up, holding it before him at arm's length, whirling like an incredibly thirsty drain. Eventually, having achieved all the potential momentum possible, he let it fly toward a window. We were on the second floor above a closed firehouse. Outside lay an asphalt apron. As if directed by radar, through the window the image machine flew, landing below upon the dark tarmac and crazing into beautiful fragmented patterns, each reflecting the scattered photons of pre-dawn light in its particular kaleidoscopic way.

"The damage done, The Dance of Destruction began.

"The result of some automatic selection of some unknown nature, Floyd's *Time* segued into *Astronomy Domine*, and I lifted airborne. Above it all, I flew into all the junked-up corners, smashing all that I saw. From some secret chest Mitch retrieved a twenty-pound sledge and began breaking through lath and plaster walls. I found a chair leg or something and broke out the rest of the windows.

"Around the periphery only two people remained, one the decidedly disheveled Bailey, the other an enthralled Tommy Blotter Boy. As must all things, when no partition stood between one room and the other, and great voids gaped between the in and outsides of things, our dance drew to a close, and, uncomfortably aware of an unwelcome and deepening chill, we built a fire of scraps to warm our rapidly cooling selves.

"Not until Bailey let out a shriek did we become aware of Merrill. Only lath-ragged, rough-cut studs separated the remains of the living room from the bathroom where for the four of us to see lay curled about the toilet the unconscious form of Kenny. Had he slept through the entire episode? Had some stray bit of debris created his present comatose state? I would never know. Perhaps no one would. For the sake of all appearance if not actuality, he was dead. Again Bailey shrieked and scrabbled through the crumbles of plaster to her once forsaken lover. Mitch and I exchanged glances. Tommy moved to his own internal music. From some depth of disassociation Mitch summoned movement and drifted across from his space and into theirs. A certified EMT he soon looked up, gave me a sign and escorted Bailey back to the land of the waking not yet dead.

"'Just passed out,' he informed us.

"'Gotta piss,' Blotter Boy answered, shuffled through the wreckage, kicked at Ken in a weak attempt to move him away from the toilet, and finally and deliberately hosed Merrill down with several hour's-worth of pent-up beer and a fistful of his mother's prescription diuretics.

"In the mood for a little release myself, I followed suit. As did Mitch. Much to her everlasting discredit, so too did Bailey who very decorously hoisted her skirt and wiggled her little butt about as she attempted to achieve as much coverage as a female of the species might. With that the evening could well have ended. Mitch had nothing to concern himself about. The building belonged to his uncle and required renovation. Now that would occur sooner rather than later. The job was to be Mitch's anyway. 'No real harm. Can't be no real foul,' he chuckled while kicking the remains of our fire out one of the open sores he had inflicted.

"'Hey,' Tommy drawled retrieving a can of charcoal starter Mitch had employed to light our fire. 'Ever see a human torch?'

"'Yes,' I calmly asserted. 'Care to see another?' At which point I lifted the can from Blotter's not so reluctant hands and with no thought, simply the beautiful illusion of Hair on fire, strode through the darkness, past my Mother's insufficient arms, and into the world prepared somewhere by someone — The Man On Fire — for me.

"Again rose female shrieks, but no Bailey appeared, and I bent to my business. The imbecilic can resisted for what could have passed for an eternity, but eventually its red lid snapped, and all the bouquet of possible immolation gurgled its petrochemical potentiality about Merrill's unconscious form.

"I do not smoke. Tobacco that is. Never did. Thus I had no means of lighting the pyre. We should have had multiple means of achieving the end, but, of course, when need is dire, no relief comes easily. Mitch had to chase down his Zippo from back in that time. Eventually, the means was in hand.

"After several false starts, I achieved a modicum of success. First a pant leg. Then a shirtsleeve. That our previous excremental offerings were interfering with the fulfillment of our sacrificial purpose became increasingly obvious. Through it all, I persevered, my mind ablaze with images of Hair. Memories of Napalm. Mitch giggled like an uncertain virgin. Tommy offered insane advice such as, 'Torch his eyebrows.' I eventually did get another sleeve to start, but the other minor sites were already smudging out.

"Then it happened. The sleeping dog awoke. Screeching in pain and horror or perhaps just surprise, it lurched to its feet, pushed past me and toward an open face staring out into the dawn.

"'God damn,' howled Tommy.

"'Holy shit,' from Mitch.

"'Kenny...Kenny!' from Bailey.

"I simply leaned back and wished the Man, whose Fire had somehow caught itself up in earnest, a nice flight. The stereo and its music long since silenced by our dance, *Set the Controls for the Heart of the Sun* flared as clearly as ever possible on any machine or even at the greatest of live performances. Into the dawn Kenny flew, his destiny soon to be fulfilled, his fate most certain. At the last ridge of fallen plaster he stumbled, a new and vibrant flame lit the tail of his shirt and traced itself up the course of his spinal column. The Anti-Phoenix, he would sail into his eternal immolation, swallowed by the morning sunrise, consumed by....

"The bitch! At the last possible moment the stupid, hormonal cunt grabbed him, brought him to the floor, and smothered out the flames with her own, apparently penitent self. As from outer reality sirens arose, apparatus returning to its old home, cries from the not really so severely burned Merrill and sobs from his returned true love blended with and became obscured by the increasing cacaphony below. The first truck arrived. The din of many saviors' voices could be heard shouting confused yet certain orders. Demanding answers from out the condensing air.

"We, as was often said at the time, beat feet outta there."

"SO YER BIG story's really nothin' much at all. I heard worse from middle class shopkeepers at meetings. You wrecked some fool's apartment and pissed all over some pathetic alcoholic, drug addict loser. Ain't that much. Really ain't."

"You yourself do not understand much," I counter. "So what if Kenny Merrill didn't burst through the window hole? So what? The point is not nor ever has been Kenny, Mitch or any other human being. This is all about me. Who and what I am. What it is I fear I may become. Can you not see that?"

"What?" the mook asks, oh so innocently. "That yer some sort of firebug or somethin'? That you almost killed somebody here rather than in Vietnam? Remember.... It ain't jes me sayin' this. It's true. Almost don't count fer nothin' an killin's killin' wherever it happens. Far's anybody round here's concerned, ain't no real harm, ain't no real foul."

The clown's eyes positively dance like blue flames with that one. I must remember that he is absolutely far more intelligent than he lets on. So I attack. Rising from my place, a glower of magnificent proportions upon my countenance, I snap: "I have warned you, cowpoke. I am finished subjecting myself to the scrutiny of someone as dense as I find you to be. Thank you so much for the nothing you shared concerning my brother. Thank you again for your muddle-headed vocalizations concerning my revelations. Go on back to the VA and expound to the addled and insane who find you so enlightening. I would rather search my own way in my own places."

Before I can take a full step he declares, "Next door ain't no place to do that. Ain't no booze can quench the fire yer flyin' from."

I truly could hate the fool. What could he know about anything I'm trying to flee from... maybe, come to think of it, fly is a good choice of verb.

"No drug neither. Not on the street. Not the Lithium neither."

"Have you heard nothing I have been telling you?" I screech into his hairy old ear. "Have you not some version of your own Man on Fire?"

"She ain't a man," he drawls. "She's all fire. An she's zackly the same thing you been flyin' away from ever since you was a kid. Billy knew. He told me all about your being a pyro. All about you being afraid."

"Billy didn't know." He could have told no one.

"Billy knew more than you do. You don't even know that Billy met his own presumed demon. You do not even know that it was no demon at all, just a presence so far beyond our primitive imaginings that from fear we all at first think it too powerful to be good. We declare it evil precisely because we fear it so irrationally. It, my sad and deluded friend, is the power within us all...and without us too. By virtue of its being an unknown, however, we assign it the same childish identity as the troll under the bridge, the monster under the bed. Son, your Man on Fire is in a limited way just you yourself.

"She is also very much more, and I have been tasked with introducing —
reintroducing — you to her. Come with me to a place you know you have to
find, and all shall not only be explained but become so clear as to be impossibly
elemental.

I must pause to wonder where the simpleton cowboy so all of a sudden
disappeared to. I suppose I should go along. I never did like mystery, although it
has ever intrigued me, and never have I been able to find clarity. Mook offers
them both, and against my better or at least saner judgment, I nod. We are off.

Dance of Oblivion
Lyndi and Edward
1994

From a shelf somewhere within the complexities of a princess-sized closet Cher produced a Holly Hobbie lunchbox provisioned with a variety of treats all neatly arranged by size, color, packaging, and herbo-chemical nature. "Oh, Cher," Lyndi exclaimed, finally emerging from the brief paralysis of will and voice no doubt occasioned by the unexpected appearance of a device she remembered from a time she had thought best forgotten when she and Cherish had experimented with simple intoxication of one of the more rebellious kinds. Such, as it often does, leads to other forms of investigation, and, thank you god, had it not been for the entry into their lives of the two best friends, Edward and William, might have lead them down a very dark path into a place from which there might have been no return. To sanity, normalcy at least.

"I can't," Lyndi whined. "I have to drive. You saw how Eddy was getting."

She had sipped but two Mimosas and was in no way feeling any adverse effects. Her will was strong, her vision clear. Yet, the millipedal thing of form, light, and shadow perched cross-legged upon the bigger than king bed before her, ignoring all protest, extracted something from Hollie's box, and soon the Hookah's Chthonic chant of burbling waters cascaded down, down into the place where dwelt her soul, and, when Cher passed the stem to her, like Eve without benefit of serpent, Lyndi partook of the forbidden, or at least illegal, ware.

No magic moment occurred. The two friends' buzzed about the complexities of the little pink chambers of their minds as they giggled themselves about the walls and furnishings of the increasingly chaotic room. Colors flared and spat about them. The sounds of music from some nowhere only to be found within each subconscious, yet shared as were they from external speakers, loosened their limbs until they began to flow like liquid light, all substance without form or purpose. "Lava lamps," Cherish cried. "We're two effing lava lamps.... I effing hate lava lamps. But I am one. And so are you. I effing hate you...and I effing hate myself too. Effing lava effing lamps," and she collapsed upon her bed all thousand arms and legs writhing in and about themselves in an already grounded death spiral.

Lyndi understood.

She never knew exactly what it was she and her friend had smoked. A "special Hash" Cherish had proclaimed somewhere amidst a forest of questions and replies, extraneous thoughts and verbal non-sequiturs, shrieks of imagined horror, panty-dampening contractions of laughter, and deep heart-wrenching seizures of sorrow accompanied by a spate of tears and ending in hiccoughs of near-terminal consequence. "Really special shit," Cherish later added, upon which utterance she wrinkled her nose in a most comic moue of near mythic quality. Or so Lyndi thought she remembered anyway.

Time, eternal as it often might be, as perhaps it actually is, moved on. Or did they simply move through the omnipresent now into another corner as yet unexplored? Whatever. In that time, the time the clocks identified as 11:45 PM, Edward, by now alone with Endwell and a half full or empty bottle of J&B, and, impelled by something beyond his ready comprehension — the two of them had just agreed that any return to Poestenkill that night would be foolish — began to blunder about the downstairs calling Lyndi's name in increasingly strident tones and ever greater volume. Endwell, himself something of a light-hearted figure, soon joined in, and the two of them might have been heard down at the concert site. Even within their Holly Hobbie womb, Lyndi and Cherish, curled together in a perfectly chaste embrace of shared abandon, half asleep and dreaming themselves as always they should have been, heard, and, wordlessly sharing the necessity of protecting their retreat from profanation, hurried with most deliberate speed to the stairway which they elegantly descended into the glare of their men's awareness. Each smiled for the other; each snuggled into her man's ribcage; each felt the void of individuality.

"We have to leave," Edward proclaimed.

Endwell nodded drunken understanding, and, without looking to her friend and evening's companion, Lyndi glittered flashing incisors up at her spouse and purred, "OK. But I'm driving."

Things might have been different had Endwell not snorted his derision, long faced horse that he was, but snort he did, and Edward could but assert his dominance. "The devil you will," he drooled. "It's my car, and I'm driving."

In her present state — whatever that was, she was no longer stoned, her mind was clear, her steps crisp across the floor, her vision acute and unwavering — Lyndi knew how to handle her child without resorting to anger, tears or intransigence. She simply agreed. In front of the audience that is; however, once in the car and down the driveway a ways, she placed her hand down where he really lived and asked that he pause a moment. The poor guy remained flaccid even within her most tender grasp, but that was only to her advantage. No need existed for awkward wrestlings and his pathetic attempts at limp-jointed entry. Lyndi knew her man.

Gently she placed his hand between her legs, guided his fingers to the nylon crotch of her panties, the very ones he had requested she wear, awkward and just a bit large as they might be, and whispered in his best ear, his left, necessitating that she slide herself across him, her breasts importunate upon his chest., "I'll drive us home naked if you want, and you can do anything you want to me as we go." He was always so predictable. Unlike his penis, his fingers responded, grew demanding, and, tugging at the elastic edge of her underwear butted their way into the swale at her female terminus.

"Anything?" he slurred, his finger's slithering toward her backdoor speaking of their usual obsession.

"Anything," Lyndi spit into his ear, biting its lobe as she withdrew from what had become an unpleasant, too fragrant intimacy with his alcoholic, garlic-snail breath. It was done.

She had really taught her Eddy well. Oh, yes, he might intimate otherwise, might threaten unwelcome explorations, but he truly knew better than to actually go there. Of course, she would accommodate his basic desire, but all other avenues would be denied him, at least until a thorough disinfecting. Men can be so absolutely casual about such things. They have no appreciation of a woman's vulnerability.

So it transpired. Just around the bend of the long drive, concealed from the almost absent traffic on Rt. 32, Lyndi did as he asked. Her cocktail dress, a comfortably loose linen, royal blue with a slightly flared skirt reaching just to the top of her knee with a daring neckline and loose short sleeves, slid easily up and over her head. As she moved to deposit it safely in the back seat, the first unpleasantness of the ride blurted from Edward's throat. "Throw it over there by the side of the road," he commanded, "where they'll find it. Your panties and bra too."

Given the right occasion and set of circumstances, Lyndi could have found such a prospect, the vulnerability of the ride home without possible recourse to any sort of cover should unforeseen circumstances arise, at least mildly exciting, and, most things considered, slightly erotic. The suggestive nature of her clothing left behind for Sonny and especially Cher to find. Now that could strike flames of a possibly intense nature. Her dress though! She loved that thing. It had cost her two-hundred-twenty-nine dollars even at Marshalls. She could not leave it behind.

At her reluctance, Edward's slouching features firmed a bit, and, unless it was simply a trick of their halogen headlights, his eyes glittered an end, or at least the beginning of an end, to his drunkenness. "OK," he gloated. "Keep it.

Only, if you do, you're gettin' it both ways. There'll be no complaints. Just obedience. The choice is yours."

She was torn. Just for a moment.

"Shoes too," he positively chortled as she lay her things by the roadside. Thus did it happen that later, upon the occasion of unforeseen circumstances, Lyndi achieved her Warholian moment.

Of course he attempted entry there upon the crushed stone. Of course, despite his desperate thrusts and lunges and her ineffective attempts at guidance, he failed, and so it was that she eventually settled herself behind the wheel just a little more than resentful, and Edward, his silence accusatory, grumbled himself into the passengers bucket. The first mile, he refused to buckle up, and the damn warning buzzer would not quit, but eventually it ceased its din, and Lyndi attempted to find some music she could stand. FM Radio Woodstock. Thank you, Lord, for these small favors. The Band played Bob Dylan, the Acura rocked along, and the night became a darker morning.

Edward's erratic passion that evening culminated in total acceptance of defeat. For not the first time, his carnal insufficiency resulted in a vague, non-focused anger, no small degree of obvious self-loathing, followed by a period of resentful silence, and eventually sleep. Within a few short miles he slumped into metaconsciousnes, and Lyndi, Bob, and the blue magic of the interior illumination rose imperceptibly above the dark Macadam freed at least for the moment from the full force of gravity and its importunate demands upon all things potential as well as kinetic, all we know as material and all at least one of us has labeled metaphysical.

WERE THEIR REALITY truly to have been as potentially meta as Lyndi might have been prone to believe, she might have, while yet behind the wheel of the dark hovercraft the Acura had become, allowed her expanding consciousness to open itself unto the enfolded sparklings of others' reality she imagined to be extant in other locations and involving other individuals not unlike herself; she might also have chosen to flutter, a crow's wing upon a dark breeze in a moonless night, past the damp little pile of her outer clothing and up the attempting to reflect the invisible aura of her passing stones of the drive, and attended upon the cozy little marital ceremony being celebrated within the opulent dwelling of Cherish and Endwell Mangold.

Sometimes, the afterparty held by a host and hostess after a grand entertainment consists of the two celebrants merely sinking gratefully into a clean and welcoming bedstead and falling down toward wherever it is the abyss of sleep desires to take us. Not so Sonny and Cher.

Had the metareality of Edward asserted itself as the reality within that mansion — and it probably would not have done so — Endwell would have taken his little slut of a whore in her backdoor. Associating closely with musicians of significant magnitude. How potentially creative it can be! In that backdoor line lies a lyric of some potential. He would have fucked her until shit and blood spewed about their opti-opulent carpet, until she screamed in the magnificent agony of a mega-orgasmic woman. Or so Edward would have constructed the scene upon the stage of his one-act mind. The reality, however, was neither his nor Lyndi's to create. The reality in the imaginary Saugerties, an entire world distant from the little town of the concert, had been elsewhere created and belonged to an artist as yet unfamiliar to them, as did the one so minimally aloft in the more than imaginary Acura.

"Good that Lyn didn't drive," observed Cherish, seductively allowing her words to rise like morning's mists up past her otherworldly eyes. "She has no conception of the nature of the beast we've just shared." In her world, unlike Lyndi's, less than an hour, less than half an hour, had been spent together with the hookah within the otherland of the Raggedy Anne parlor. As well Cher knew, the morning's entertainment had yet to begin. For both of them.

Surprisingly rational, Endwell inquired most ardently, "Does this mean...?"

"Oh yes," darling" the artist of all his dreams, as well as of his next book's cover, replied. "The game is set to begin."

Tara and Lyndi
1994

Drugs are cool and all that shit, but.... Rufies? The motherfuckin' BobsieRay twins had fucked her over good. What the fuck was she doing lying naked and alone in some kind of tent with rain shitstorming outside? She'd been had that was for sure. Just where in hell was everybody? Anybody? Vacant voices pissed about the mold-green flaps, and something like a radio voice was droning off in the distance. Where the hell had they taken her? Was she dead? In some kind of rain washed inferno? Bob and Ray.... Whereinallhell are you when I need you?

THOSE TWO! LAST she remembered they were plying her with Jagermeister, and talking about some crack-addled road-trip or other.

Jesus Christ! She was at Woodstock. They had actually done it. Who in all hell cared how?

It wasn't rufies. She'd blacked out. That's all. Hallefuckinglulah. Woodstock 94. Something of memory began to seep into her consciousness. Bobby's '85 Celebrity with NIN stickers all over the windows. Ray pouring Thunderbird gently into her brimming mouth as he held and did her in the butt-holed rear seat, Metallica blasting in some broken fashion from the Grey-Ghost's worn-out speakers. Who could care? They were off to Woodstock, and her boys were in firm control. They would drink and fuck and fuckin' drink while the music and the earth-sharing consciousnesses of a couple hundred thousand people would raise them up into a place they had never been before.

Over the rainbow some stupid song said. There is no rainbow for some people, just clouds and also rain. Goddamn it, blue sky does lay over it all. It really does. Just not for her. Rayboy poured another into her burbling mouth, and, while he fiddled about unproductively inside her, Tara came and came once more until darkness overtook her.

NO MORE DARKNESS. The radiovoice was an announcer not too far off in the distance, and the voices were not vacant. All around her shelter laughter, squeals of delight, and excited babble spoke of the rainbedamned attitude necessary for their crystal ship to launch them all into the land they had dreamed, which lay somewhere off beyond any continent accessible by mere imagination. They were gone.

So did Tara launch herself through the labial tent hangings and into a cold rain which awoke every exposed receptor on every sensory neuron of her altogether self into clamorous life. She shivered, she shuddered, she shouted with glee. She was free, she was free...was free.

No one paid her any mind at all. She was not the only naked female or male in the press, and neither was she close to being the most ecstatic. She was just another girl leaking semen into a pool of dirty water at the edge of some farmer's field. Had she remained in Smitty's class, Tara eventually would have happened upon the term *cliché*. Such had not, however, been the case, yet somewhere within the still rational depths of her left-brain lurked an unconscious recognition of the inanity, *Really, Tara?*, of certain terms such as "It's a small world," and, again without guiding principle or even recognized intent, she rarely took up the clichéd crutch. Nevertheless, at the moment, naked to the wind, rain, and chaos around her, Tara began repeating a common lost-soul mantra. *Alone in a crowd. I'm alone in a crowd. Alone in **the** crowd. I'm lost and alone. In the crowd.*

Like the shrinking violet she imagined, she sagged into the mud. It invaded every crevice and fold of her nakedness. *Alone in the crowded mud,* she chanted. *Alone. Alone. In the crowd. In the crowd. The crowded mud. The violet crowded mud!* Everywhere about her music rose above the green, green grass not yet turned to slop. She did not recognize the voice. Did not know the song or the singer. In the violet mud, it all rang true. The song was of someone's Baby Blue.

As the music rose, the chaos around her mellowed into delicate petals of a most still silence, and she sank beneath the surface of her own grotesque puddle of muck and filthy water. The singer's words entered through her ears. She knew this. She also was aware that the music came through the earth itself. Too soon the song was flown as was its singer. All the others too. She was imprisoned in some Marsh-Woman land, her tongue caught back somewhere near her tonsils. She could not move. Her eyes and ears clotted shut. Her imagination slogged brown upon brown. Her journey had come to this, her destination a cruel hoax. She had nothing, would have nothing. Never. She was some blue baby, dead at birth. It actually was all over. Had been before it even could begin. Whereinholyhell were Bob and Ray?

WHATEVER DRUGS SHE had been enjoying must have worn off. In the mud, but not within it, the sounds of new music gentle from somewhere not too far away, a familiar feel in her pelvis, a familiar form above her. "Bobby," she whispered in his ear.

"Ray, you fuckin' no-mind," her lover replied, gently bumping her brow with the heel of his hand.

Without need for further language beyond that of her sore and hotallover body as it relaxed itself beneath his ministrations, accommodating itself to his penetration and nightcrawling caresses, Tara lay back into the slime and stared up into the cloud-deep sky.

At that moment, as Ray wore himself out attempting one final ejaculation within the sweet soul he would never know, that very soul for the first time became aware of its own impossible divinity. The clouds parted for Tara, and the moon shone soft upon her. No longer was she a creature discarded and doomed by her own inadequacy and misfortune. No longer were her limbs coated, her hair caked with mud. Her ears heard beyond the last chords of some song she neither recognized nor would have ever cared to. Her mother's favorite song, the only music of her mother's Tara remembered, played about her memory as if it might be 1975 and the place Golden Gate Park. *Ripple*. The Grateful Dead. Tara's would be no simple highway, but neither would she ever again be alone. She would be guided home.

A hallucinogenic blessing, the moon descended. Artemis, Diana, Selene, and Luna scattered moonpetals about the vanishing grounds, and, as Rayboy disengaged himself from their entanglement, Tara abandoned herself to a new and impossibly comforting harsh mistresses. She did have a purpose after all. Her journey's end was near. She would be fulfilled. In a most lovely dream, Tara arose and followed Ray into the vanishing crowd. They would find Bob, would trudge, she bare as any moonchild must be, off to the car, and Tara soon would discover the multifoliate radiance of her existence.

LOST LLESSED LHELISH Ly gleely plait you name. Lie holly holy hobby lame le la long wilin lie leart. Lie lyle le la loy luv ly life. Ly lolly, lolly lace uplon la lie. Ly loll alizeth gleely lupto ly loly lace. Ly life lie live loo lou.

Had it not been for EZ Pass the Thruway would have been impossibility. Manned tollbooths even those manned by the feminine gender, are in no way a naked girl's best friend, especially one beginning to find her inability to translate into the English language even the simplest of phrases.

On top of that, she glowed like the radium dial of a cheap watch. The damned moon had done it. Three or so black miles from Sonny and Cher's the sky had broken and a ragged first-quarter lunar flood had not simply shown down upon them. The radiance had enshrouded the car, softly slipping through the cracks and ventilators of the tight little Acura. It had been seeking her, and it had found. Her arms first took on a glow, not a mere halo of moonlight, but an efflorescence as sweet and pure as any heavenly aura might possibly be. The rest of her soon came to similar light. Her legs, little round belly, and her never maternal breasts. Her face in the bedazzled mirror. All of her illuminated the interior of the car as would some twentieth-century transfigured Jesus or his virgin mother. Stealing a glance to her right, Lyndi was not surprised to see the dark lump of her husband, unaware of all which was transpiring and, no doubt, otherwise unaffected as well.

Once upon the highway, the sky no longer open, no Lady Diana to be seen, Lyndi's rationality launched an unwelcome, yet part of her recognized essential, offense upon her moonstruck perceptions. The road lay straight and well-defined; the inner light began to ebb into a mere dashboard glow, and, thank goodness of any kind, the radio began to unwind in Murakamiesque birdsong, her favorite jazzman, Harry Connick. Of all the cities of all the world, Harry's and her NOLA were *crème de la crème*, rich Praline to all the tasteless clatter of anywhere not New Orleans. Absolutely! Al Hirt would do, as would, she supposed, Jelly Roll, but Harry somehow put that pecan butter into everything he played. How better to experience this than on a warm and humid, storm-dripping nigh, naked to the world, joined with all that could possibly be real?

Always in Lyndi's life there existed room for improvement; no one thing in and of itself ever quite measured up to its own possibilities. Or might it be her extravagant expectations? Things could not have been more perfect for the trip back to Poestenkill. Except....- The solid lump of Edward sucked pleasure from her. Not in great gulps or even minor spasms, simply a fraction of a fraction of a particle at a time. She could feel her elegance dribble like spent semen into the open maw of her husband. Oh, God. Tonight would have been just perfect for Alan. He would be awake; he would have joined her within the heavenly radiance; he too would have reveled in the opulent circumstances. Most importantly, Alan would have allowed himself to become naked and vulnerable, would have united with her in a way infinitudes beyond the futile abrasions of sexual unity. Maybe that too, but in a new and strange amalgam of male and female containing the essential qualities of each yet completely eliminating all distinctions.

As Edward slept and she dreamed, Lyndi drove another twenty miles and soon found the three of them approaching the Exit- 23 ramp for Albany and home. An artificial-light sprayed a most tasteless mauve finish upon the car ahead of them in the EZ Pass lane. She fervently hoped the ugly plaza wouldn't have the same effect on her Black Pearl Acura. Without a doubt such was already happening, and Lyndi sped through the check-point, nearly hopping the light, and finding herself hard upon the rear of the impossibly puce-toned thing which had just passed through as an artificial mauve. When she swung to her left in order to pass, however, the junk-heap smoked to life and lurched ahead just fast and far enough to make passing it impossible as the choices of lane narrowed to just the one which the thing appeared to be taking as well as must she. Some teenager no doubt. Probably drunk. Or, who could know, a late-departing reveler lost in some musical drug haze. She would be wise to keep her distance. She did just that down the hill onto I-787 as it cut between the city of Albany and the river. On up toward the South Troy exit they proceeded, the other car a careful mile or two above the speed-limit, Lyndi following a discreet distance behind.

The other driver must not have been in any fashion inebriated, and quite possibly might have known something as well, for just before Menands they passed a Police car, dark and sinister in a narrow little pull-off just over a rise. Had it not been for the cautious driver of the hideous lead car, she most assuredly would have been going at least seventy. Even trolls sometimes perform a service. Maybe it was just a college kid or even a late-shift worker, a nurse or even another cop. That must have been it. How else could he have known to be so careful? She would do well to follow that car as far as their paths continued to be compatible. He would unwittingly provide safe passage for her. Her new, off-color friend would get her home safe and sound.

As though aware of his accidental responsibility, the lead driver exited at South Troy, as did she, turned up Morrison Avenue, headed south on Vandenburg, where Lyndi imagined their coincidental paths would soon separate, but then turned onto Williams, crossed Spring Avenue, and cruised at forty-plus down Whiteview. Were Lyndi in possession of a common tool of the coming century — a GPS — it could not have directed her along a more appropriate route. *Pe pust puce par pahead pa per pepame per puiding ptar.*

Almost home and that had started up again. With a different stupid letter. Lyndi attempted to speak her thoughts aloud as they slowed for a great curve set as a trap in the course of an otherwise straightforward highway, but aloud they morphed into a port puv Pig Patin: *Palmost pome,* she pronounced, *pand pat pad parted pup pagain. Put pith pa pifferent petter.* So who could hear? Her experience and even some of her education had taught her that reality could be deceptive. She had always been attracted to the Hindu concept of Maya. Perhaps she had wound a web of illusion about herself, internal as well as external. Curious as to what another might hear, she was sorely tempted to wake Edward, but then thought better of it. *Pest pu pet pleeping pogs pie.*

Experimenting a bit, but not without concern for her sanity coupled with a reluctant amusement at her mind's willful abandonment of the rational, in an annoying and sometimes perilous pursuit of its own inexplicable ends, Lyndi added quite expertly her former *L's* to her current *P's.* Surprisingly she was perfectly capable of altering her speech alteration, easily repeating with increasing rapidity and volume, *Plest plu plet plleping plogs ply,* "Best to let sleeping dogs lie." Simple, but she could not say that no matter how hard she tried. She could use just *L's* or *P's.* Nothing else. It had arrived unannounced, and it would go the same. Tomorrow would begin another day and all that might imply. Tonight it would be enough to get safely home.

Plunight plit.... Where were they going? The pucemobile had turned onto West Sand Lake road, and she had followed, all wrapped up in her LP's. Her best route would have been the extra block to 66 and then East again. Oh, well, Villa Valenti and Snyder's Corners were just a mile or so away. She'd turn off and before any time at all would be once again on the right track. Bye, bye, guiding light, she thought as the puce car gained distance before her. I guess from here on in, I'm on my own.

Tara

Tara had been staying with some friends in the Burg, a first-floor flat in an old house backed up against the river, and, as a result, Bob and Ray that early morning found themselves with just a bit too much dead fish to dispose of once they realized she either expected to be taken there or else to stay with them. For fuck's sake. They lived in Averill Park and neither alternative was in any way attractive. They'd taken her to Woodstock, had fed her...they thought, had poured more alcohol and jiz into her pig-slut body than most whores ever would have been able to take. She fuckin' stank. She was fuckin' filthy, pig-sty muddy, and now she was mumblin' fuckin' prayers or somethin'. She was best got rid of.

As often happens to most lucky boys, their deliverance issued forth from a most fortuitous set of circumstances. Tara had drunk way too much. Consequently, her bladder had become overfull. "Gotta pee," she mumbled into the tired ear of Rayboy as he drooped beside her. Really gotta pee."

Oh yeah. Them dudes, never failed not to look any kind of horse in the mouth, and thus, without hesitation, Bobbie slid off into a flat bottom of dark weed, cheerfully commanded, "Go on then. Ain't nobody gonna see ya here," as if the cunt cared who might see her. As soon as she was clear of the car, Rayboy grabbed the door shut, and the two adventurers chortled on home, free from unwanted complications. Except of course, for the persistent odors of their interminglings which just would not to fade away.

Tara would not have bothered to chase after them even had she not been deserted in mid-stream. For all she knew they were just engaging in another one of their idiotic attempts at humor. Or maybe they weren't. She could care less. The warm night held her weightless within its amniotic sac. Bright moonfeathers were beginning to drift through the energetic fluid of her awakening reality. As she pissed her old self away, she felt the tug of new life awakening, the passing of all the old into a new promise more liberating than any dream. The feathers floated all about her, caressing her ravenous skin, whispering their angelic hymns into her heart.

Her place in the weeds was sodden and slippery with beaten vegetation. The emergent Tara required more appropriate circumstances for her nativity. Above her on the roadway one particular bit of plumage perched, beckoning, alive. So out of the mire into which she had been emptying she climbed onto the warm hard surface of county route 68 and clasped the biotic amulet to her bosom. All about her in uterine eddies drifted the brightest flutters of heavenly light, struck from the moon herself, caressing all the world into the purity of an infant's smile. Tara warmed and glowed; soon she too would join with them in the holy current of their fall. Her time was at hand.

Or at her back. Down another highway altogether with the same name as Tara's, the same number, 68, and the same geographical latitudinal and longitudinal set of degrees, slithered along its sidewinding path a feathery substance of another kind, a 1994 Acura Legend GS, dark as the night about it and hungry as a sunless hole. Inside, a gravity arising from somewhere beyond any probable source, Lyndi drove into her own awakening.

Her way lay unobstructed. The road twisted, snaked round about itself, rose and fell, yet her path became evermore strait and straight toward a rising moon full beyond its astronomical quarter. There was no horizon, no distance. A radiant globe of purity awaited her immersion. Its featherlight tendrils wrapped themselves about her. At its center a brilliant star, its light too long held captive, took possession of all energy, potential and kinetic, as its terrible hunger swallowed the dark, little Acura and its passengers into the furnace of Tara's fearful creation.

THE THUMP OF collision awoke Lyndi as from a deep and dreamless unconsciousness. She must have hit something. Just her luck. Fearful, she hoped it wasn't someone's dog. There were houses strewn about this countryside. She didn't need any complications or necessary communications, especially considering her current state of *plomunications plificulties*. She would have kept on, but something dragged and tumbled about the underside of the car. Steering became difficult. *Pledward*, she shrilled, *Ply plink ply plight plave plit pla plorse...plor plumpthing plig. Plake plup! Pledward! Please.... Plake plup!*

She needn't have worried. The impact had wrenched sleep from him, and, despite some lingering effects of the evening's entertainment, Edward emerged from inert to frenetic almost immediately.

"Stop the fucking car," he commanded.

Lyndi did as she was told.

Crumpled up beneath the rear of the vehicle Tara remained conscious on at least two levels. One of these was the simple and dull monotony of life-stealing pain. The other shone brightly as any star enshrouded by feathers might. She was soon to be reborn. Above the duality hovered her birth-mother, the dove from whom the plumes of light had fallen, and Tara knew such beauty, only possible in the midst of great pain, was to be her treasured companion. The other woman, just at that moment peering uncomprehendingly at her from beyond the rigid bars of her fleeting mortality, was destined for some time to be her epic partner as well.

Smitty and Mary Margaret
1999

In the five years since hearing of the death of Tara, her inglorious Sylvia, Smitty had for the second time in her adult life abandoned one journey in order to undertake another, along perhaps a more perilous but infinitely more spiritual highway. She had acquired a sister. She and Mary Margaret had reconnected, at a Grateful Dead concert no less, and, despite Triple M's rather sinister involvement in family matters best left uninvestigated, the two of them, while not Taoists, were inclined to feel they had at last found their Way: *The Way*. The way of Lao Tzu and the East. The way of Jesus and the west. The way as well, they believed, of the Most Holy Spirit who inspires all journeys toward compassion, enlightenment, and a most spiritual elevation beyond even those two most holy estates.

IT BEGAN WITH a walk in Riverfront Park. Smitty had discovered a month previously, after a more than six month semi-volitional period of abstinence from concern for such mundane matters, that her weight had skyrocketed from a comfortably plump one hundred-fifty-five pounds into the upper reaches of the one-hundred and sixties. Holy Mother of God. How could she have let herself go so? Her clothes had begun to feel a trifle constricting, but ten-plus pounds? It could not be. She must have gained at least one size. She had forever been prone to loose fits, and now, for the first time, she admitted that loose had become more than just a mite snug. She had fooled herself into believing everything had shrunk while at the same time becoming at least a tad more fashionable. Was she ever blind!

The answer, of course, was diet and, *Ugh,* exercise. To that sad end she had begun a daily discipline of mandatory walks, a minimum of three miles, more often longer, especially on needy days such as the morning of June 20, 1995, following the previous evening's Italian feast, which had been accompanied by not just one but two bottles of *Bella Sera Chianti* and capped with a heavenly chocolate *cannoli*, as well as a side of *spumoni* just for the sake of its own sake. Weakness to be sure, but a woman alone need not be alone when woven throughout the fabric of her life exist such comforting companions as Italian *cucini*.

One must pay, however, for one's indulgences, and so this morning Smitty had embarked upon the most ambitious of her perambulations to date: the five miles down to Albany's Riverfront Park along the bike path from Watervliet and then the return. Ten miles in all, but rather pleasant her experience with more abbreviated turn-arounds had convinced her. At its southern end, the path veers away from the Hudson and skirts a car-park usually unoccupied at the time of the day and of the week. Today it had been transformed. What could be the occasion? The space, huddled beneath some highway structure or other, was absolutely crammed with all manner of gaudy, rusty, dirty, crumbly conveyances which were also serving as dormitories for all manner of odd young people, themselves in nearly the same state of disrepair as their vehicles. There was even an old city-bus...*Scranton* she could detect along its side despite an inartistic overcoat of obscene graffiti. Whatever in the world?

As she approached the bedraggled encampment, the sound of familiar unfamiliar music rose to greet her. Conflicting melodies and discordant instrumentations echoed from the concrete overhead and abutments; tom-tom percussions chunked up from the broken black-top, discoloring the very air about her. Smoke too of strange consistency thrummed through the air in conflicting wave patterns of visual, olfactory, and emotional consistency. Almost, Smitty imagined, these gypsies had created an alternative river of their own parallel too yet not at all of the cloudy waters ebbing back to the saltier body called Atlantic. Feeling akin to a discarded bit of flotsam, Smitty followed the gentle tug of the strangely compelling tides washing around her until she found herself drawn into a little eddy of two, twirling slowly in reds and oranges against a stark pillar of gray concrete. A young man, tattered and torn as a forgotten scarecrow in a field returned to weed and a crumpled young woman of little more substance than the teacher's thigh.

Tara. Could the girl be clad in dirndl? Had the news of her little Sylvia's passing been highly exaggerated? It could be. It just might be. No need to hurry, the whirl of the couple's attraction grew stronger; Smitty accelerated toward them. Tara lifted her fine gold head. Her dull eyes reflected the smoke of smothered fires. She was no Tara. But then, Smitty could tell, yes she was. Here, she intuited, was another opportunity. She would try again. This time make some difference at least of modest degree. The girl's emptiness was the heart of the disturbance tugging at her, and Smitty determined to do her best to bring, if not aid, at least some comfort to one who appeared as dispossessed as ever had her Tara, and the young man, although apparently not as disconsolate as his companion, might be in more than a modicum of need as well. Smitty entered their whirling universe.

Sometimes in the middle of the night Smitty would awaken knowing sleep was not to return. She would lie for hours amidst a senseless turbulence, crisscrossing patterns of waking visions, dreams, and visitations of stark reality such as a white moon upon whiter snow despite the season's outward manifestation. Eventually the alarm would call, and she would shuffle herself through her morning's routine never quite able to separate the merely possible from the probable, from the actual. On those nights and early mornings Tara would visit.

Never would she speak. Never would she so much as smile or even frown. No tear dampened her eye, no expression erased the blankness from her face. In the light of the moon she would hold out a feather whiter than either snow or moon...and just possibly her hand would tremble as Smitty reached across the void between them, eager to accept her gift. Always at that final second between hope and fulfillment would fall the shadow, and Tara would vanish, her feather borne away in the wind of her passing. Smitty would cry and, she feared, forever mourn.

This morning was no dream. Smitty happily found herself in one the ugliest of possible realities. No grace, no beauty anywhere to be found. Discord the only music. Forgetfulness the only hope. An ugly patch glared up at her from the youngsters' duffle, a horrific skull wearing obscene roses upon its head and the surrounding words: Grateful Dead. How could she not have known? The news was full of it, TV and newspapers. The two waifs at her feet were simply *Deadheads*, their condition no doubt due to drugs every bit as dangerous as those her Sylvia had favored. There was nothing she could do for them. Tara and her mother had made that abundantly clear. Smitty halted. She would be on her way.

To where? Had she not just seconds before been filled with the overwhelming sense that she should offer assistance? Had she not felt that somehow she might be given an opportunity to atone for past failure? Might this new Tara not be more receptive to her therapeutic intervention, her most urgent need to find some outlet for the *agape* welling to overbrimming within her?

"Hello there," she began most awkwardly like exactly what she was, an old lady unsure of how to approach some strange new breed of creature possibly impossibly similar to herself, or at least to the burden she bore upon her conscience.

"Could you help us, mam?" the young man asked with an astonishingly clear and cultured tone. "We have come upon some difficulty, and find ourselves with no transportation and very little money."

Smitty had a fanny pack in which, among other items, she always carried taxi-fare for her own emergencies, but the answer to this request would not be a twenty-dollar bill. The Tara looked up at her, gray eyes darkening, face set in an expression as empty as that of the dream. No hope could find a place in her dark soul. Of this Smitty was certain.

The easy out would cost only twenty-dollars; her charity would count for something. At least these two might eat. Smitty smiled not a bit condescendingly, and reached for the zipper of her pack.

"Thank you, mam," the boy replied before she could reach for the bill. "We need more than a hand-out. You see, something has happened to Marissa here. We need real help...or she does."

SMITTY HAD NO true memory of precisely what occurred from that point on until early the next morning. She suffered not from some insidious form of second-hand smoke or surreptitiously administered dosage of one or another of the ergoline substances favored by the home-based as well as the semi-nomadic devotees of the iconic band. Rather, her period of amnesia was the result of an extreme, nearly hallucinatory several hours brought about by the overabundance of adrenalin, endorphins, and oxytocin. Had someone been moved to suckle at her breast, that fortunate child would have found a most delicious abundance of sweet mother's milk ready to pour from Smitty's aching maternity. Had a child been present in her fundus, it most certainly would have tumbled forth onto the floor without any prompting or manipulation whatsoever. Instead, Smitty had managed through her stellar powers of circumstantial manipulation to effectuate the young woman's transport by ambulance to St. Peter's hospital, and, accompanied by the boy Joseph, to arrive soon after by cab. There her ecstasy exploded into a cosmic burst of showering brilliance. She had saved the young woman's life.

Were she to have been able to recall the events leading into her late-night reemergence into lucidity, Smitty would have gasped at the first moments of discovery. "I think Marissa's had a miscarriage...or something.... I don't know. We didn't even know for certain she was pregnant."

The young woman simply faded a bit more into the polluted atmosphere.

"Would you check her...please?"

"I'm no doctor...nor a nurse. Perhaps...."

"Look," the girl whispered with what might have been a wail or even a screech of frustration were her energies up to it. "Please...just look." Upon completion of her request, the skinny thing tugged back the hem of her skirt and revealed a red and liquid lump of something between her legs, still reaching as if for miraculous return back up inside her. The boy gagged, and Smitty felt she might faint.

"It's just a miscarriage ain't it?" the girl asked. My insides aren't falling out.... Are they?"

Smitty could not answer. She did not know. Had no way of determining the reality of the poor thing's condition other than to realize that she was bleeding profusely and required immediate medical intervention of some kind or other. "Don't worry, dear," she soothed in a voice so calm as to be sinfully contradictory of the truth both of her internal panic and the obvious peril inherent in this Sylvia's situation. Fortunately, in her pack Smitty also carried a droopy-eared miracle of the modern age, a cell phone, and she knew all about 911.

From out of the fog of non-memory came some sound as the day wound down. "You saved my life," the miscarrying girl whispered up from her pale bed, her eyes golden as the Holy Mother's halo. "How can I ever thank you?"

"A smile will be enough," Smitty replied, an unfocused gratitude suffusing her soul to a most erotic engorgement.

Her gift bestowed, little Marissa soon fell off into a comfortably sedated disassociation, and the young man waited quietly beside her as Smitty called for a cab. "Could I offer you anything more?" he asked upon her finishing. "I've heard you can't buy much with just a smile. At least in New York."

Again Smitty refused. "Believe me," she said with a sense of finality, "You have done more for me than you can ever know. Just, please, be safe and stay well." Above all," she added as she walked through the automatic doors, "be happy."

Not until the next morning did Smitty discover within her pack the only payment the boy had been able to make. Two tickets to that night's Grateful

Dead concert at the Knickerbocker Arena. After calling St. Peters and being told the youngsters had left against medical advice, she decided that she just might take the plunge. In their honor of course.

She had no friends who might in any way wish to accompany her, so off she motored alone. Luckily she took the extra ticket. Outside the arena, hordes of hangers-on milled about in a colorful pattern of aromatic questing. She could in a flash sell it, and for no small fee. The hitch, of course, was that she had no desire to find herself juxtaposed with some manner of hippie or other sort of repugnant individual. Did anyone nice attend these concerts?

As if in answer to her unspoken prayer, "Sister! I mean, Agnes...?" issued forth from within the pungent colors of the milling Gratefully Dead. Again it rose above the haze and soon Smitty could think she might possibly recognize the face behind the call. "Over here. It's Mary Margaret. Sister Mary Margaret. From the conference." With that Smitty's mind cleared the second hand smoke away from her vision, the red and tie-dyed multitudes parted, and the two former Sisters of St. Joseph stood face to face in all their secular glory. At least Mary Margaret might be called glorious. Smitty would not have said the same of herself.

As once before, Smitty recognized the primitive call of her lower nature, and this time the circumstances might prove most auspicious. Where better might one embark upon a most alternative, wild, actually, and most assuredly sinful journey then at a concert so enmeshed in all the fabled decade of the '60's once had offered and which once she had renounced? Free love? Why not? Surely they each had grown beyond such inhibitions as those previously imposed upon them by an outmoded belief system which sought to negate all that was human, especially female human. Mary Margaret had obviously shed her veil, and, Smitty happily guessed, all the repression it symbolized. Why else would she be where she was? Gotten up in such fashion?

How could such a one ever have become a nun? The mysteries of the human race, Smitty was beginning to understand, far outshine any of the so-called mysteries of the divine. Such a creature as this, and all the others, her own self included, she might have recognized were she not so smitten, were themselves divine as well as Human. There is none greater than a human being. Within that category the greatest mystery of all is Woman. Smitty felt herself rise with the liberating smoke of the multitude into a most holy place: The presence of Beauty. The unity with same.

Or so she hoped.

The corporeal vision, although clad in the same riotous hues as those cascading about her, managed to stand against them in stark relief, upon gladiator sandals which thonged their way up her ankles and around the graceful swell of her calves. Her legs were long and smooth, the white of fresh cream upon a child's lip. Girding her loins was the most minimal blood-orange skirt Smitty had ever imagined an adult could wear in public without finding herself subject to arrest. There was nothing to it. Well...it had a fly something like a pair of men's pants might and a hem. At first Smitty thought it was cotton, but it would turn out to be a soft denim. Her top was no more substantial. A sleeveless tee. Tie-died of course, the armholes affording braless views of tender breasts, its vee neck offering those same wonders escape from even such minimal restraint. Her hair! What might one say of her hair? Long and blonde, delicate and free, it rose and fell in the gentle summer breeze as did her breast with every breath, as did Smitty's heart within the osseous walls of its no longer cloistered abbey.

Around them swirled a hallucinogenic web of extravagant design within which the two once pale nuns found themselves becoming more and more entangled. The noise was overbearing, the press of the crowd too insistent for more than brief flashes of conversation. Reminiscences and news of lives' alterations would have to await another more intimate set of circumstances.

"You here with anyone?" Mary Margaret shouted in Smitty's ear as the two of them were borne along South Pearl and up a modest set of stairs toward the main entranceway of the arena.

"No. Are you?" Smitty shouted back at Mary Margaret's nose.

"Where are you sitting?"

"I don't really know," Smitty wafted into the sweet summer evening. "I just got these tickets, and...."

"Did you say tickets?"

"Why yes. I have two. I just couldn't bear to try and sell the extra. You understand. One cannot be too careful...especially in a place like this." Digging into her purse, Smitty extracted her pair of tokens.

Before she could even begin to decipher section, row, and seating assignments, Mary snatched them from her exclaiming, "My God, Sister, these are the very front, only third row back. On the floor! How'd you get them anyway? And why in all of Holy Hell couldn't you get anybody to come with you? You'll be close enough to touch my boys. My god! What I wouldn't give for one of these." at which point she waved the tickets about as if they were two prongs of some hybrid magic wand and she the beneficent Glinda.

"How about a smile?" Smitty suggested as softly as circumstances would allow.

So it came to pass that Mary Margaret sold her own nosebleed ducat for a mere forty dollars, and she and Smitty journeyed together down into a mélange which would welcome them as fellow strangers mixed into the fold for a time by music and which would become the first stage of their own long but not so strange trip together.

JERRY GARCIA DIED not two months later, and the Grateful Dead might have passed with him were it not for those among us who, always strange even among strangers, keep them still alive. A spirit cannot die; long, strange trips never end, and ripples forever ply their turbulent functions across the quantum strangeness of forever. The dead need no resurrection. They exist as do the living in the great flow of human probability, just a small part of which is a wave/particle duality of grander proportion than Einstein, Bohr, Bell or Hawking might ever have postulated. It is said by some that Jesus returned, Elvis still lives, and that rock and roll will never die. In manner more profound than these clichés express, Jerry and The Dead also go on forever. As, it is worth noting, do we all.

It may have been the LSD some gray-touched stranger offered and of which they partook. It may not have been that at all. Reasons matter not. Both Smitty and Mary Margaret emerged from Wednesday's concert possessed by compulsion beyond denial to attend Thursday's as well. But they had no tickets.

Unlike true Dead Heads, they did have local connections, especially Mary Margaret whose family possessed influence beyond anyone's average. By early afternoon via Cadillac deVille engraved back stage passes valid for pre and post-concert as well as for the performance were theirs. VIP does not begin to say it.

Arriving an hour early, they were ushered into a party of most unsettling nature. Everyone was drunk, high or possibly both. The music over some huge speakers was deafening, the profanity elaborate, and the licentiousness far too uninhibited. People of various gender combinations were all but doing it right there in the crowd of revelers. Both sisters grew sore afraid and even more painfully appalled. What on earth had Mary's brother thrust them into?

Before they could turn and hie themselves from the riot, as any sane person might, out of the jumble emerged the brightest little shepherdess any lost and fearful lamb could wish for. "Hi," she grinned, little teeth perfect behind her tiny, ebony-glossed lips. "Are you Mary and Agnes by any chance?"

The two not so separated sisters merely looked each to each, unspoken questions written across their features, warnings flaring from their eyes.

After but the briefest of pauses, the ethereal one continued. "I was told to watch for you and guide you past the insanity. Come with me. This place is not for you."

Amazed and confused, the sisters did as they were commanded, following the little thing, her narrow *derriere* not wholly concealed by a skirt designed to make Mary Margaret's seem conservative, past the tripping over their own eagerness partiers, through a guarded doorway, and into a blessed respite from the outer room. A hush prevailed disturbed but minimally by minor eddies of low key conversation. Jerry stood off in a corner by himself, and others, band members, vaguely recognized from the previous night, stood or sat, some with what appeared to be non-alcoholic beverages, some with cigarettes of various types, either alone or in small knots of people, some wearing suits and one woman in a million-dollar pencil-skirt ensemble suitable for the boardroom. Again the sisters stood bewildered. Outside, everything had been too much. Could this be too little? Should not the Grateful Dead be at least the tiniest bit flowery? Should there not be someone chanting? Another one or two wandering about in a daze of exotic origin?

Life can always be surprising, even contradictory, but the two scenarios, outside and in, evidenced a disconnect not at all obvious to any audience, at least of last night's concert. Smitty had to wonder if the whole legend of the band might not simply be an artifice, a medicine show designed solely to sell tickets and albums. To make money. Nothing more.

Jerry was to be left alone, their guide, informed them. His mental and physical states were delicately balanced, and he needed space. Anyone else, band-members or other guests, might, should the circumstances appear providential, be approached or even simply hung about. Until just before show-time that was, at which point she would show them to their privileged spots off in the wings. "Anything I can get you?" she asked.

Smitty requested white wine and Mary Margaret Champagne. Amilee smiled, darted off, and soon returned with a bottle of each and, Smitty would always swear, crystal glassware of appropriate shape and size.

"There is more. Or should I say, other?" Amilee suggested. "I can offer you anything. And I do mean anything. Any relative of Mike Ryan's is a very special person around here."

"That's my uncle," Mary Margaret proudly announced. "You mean it? Anything?"

"Anything," Amilee affirmed.

"You may just wish you hadn't been so quick," Mary Margaret laughed. "How about Blue Cheer?"

Amilee drove a spike into Smitty's heart with her response. The little girl's face twined itself about the strands of her dark hair and a sparkle of saline composition gathered about one eye. "If only I could," she lamented, her caramel legs flowing together as she pirouetted and slipped off on flat-soled sandals. Oh, how her back rose so straight above those narrow hips, and the vision of tiny *maximi* peeking from out the shelter of her skirt....

"That's one hot little number," Mary Margaret cooed. "Even I might go for that," but then she laughed in deliberate negation, and another spike, this one of a deadly nature, speared itself into Smitty's disappointed heart. She should have known better. That which cannot be never will be. She should have known.

The two friends stood silent for the brief time, each thinking her particular thoughts, neither inclined to reveal their nature, until Amilee returned with a smile and a soft-gray pouch of something certain to be exotic. "Blue Cheer is no more," the little nymph announced, "but I can offer you something guaranteed to be its equal. Certain formulae, I am sure you realize, exist for all to access, and both laboratory equipment and procedures have improved substantially since the '60's. You might say I cook some things up myself. The way a Chem. major might."

Mary Margaret's hand was eager as she reached for the sack, while Smitty's mind grew fearful. What in the world was she doing? What might she yet do?

As if in a dream everything slowed to the point of immobility while time ceased to pass at all. For ages Smitty considered the lingering effects of the previous evening, the flowers of song and rainbow cascades of feeling emanating directly from Jerry's guitar, the orgasmic chords from some machine-like thing or other, sometimes actually an organ or again a piano or again some electronic notes so synched with her own electromagnetic reality that she did not feel them but rather became them. That state had lingered into her early afternoon awakening in a strange bed in a strange room in what would turn into a fairytale house set amid a grove of woodpecking drummers and the accompanying songs of unknown birds. Scarlet Tanager came to mind, but then wouldn't Robin have been a more logical choice? Smitty had no idea what a Scarlet Tanager even looked like...except that it most likely was red. *Tanager? What in the world does that mean? Are their mauve tanagers...and violet? Yes...there simply must be violet tanagers. Such a beautiful name. A singer...Jerry Garcia...Cherry that is.*

Cherry Garcia...cool and dark, sweet and intoxicating.... All of the previous night's experience, the ineffable beauty of her transported state washed in multicolored sparkles about her mind. Someone moved, another someone spoke in dream-echo of remembered conversation. Smitty trembled, anticipating an even more profound awakening, no more Sylvia, or Tara, or Marissa. A new and updated Kate, this hundredyearslater Edna would swim out into her own ocean. Would not drown. She need not succumb to the fate thrust upon so many women for so many years, women who cry and die, who kill themselves for reasons known only to themselves and to other women, STRONG women like themselves. Nor would she lie alone and abused in the path of an automobile driven by a naked sister, herself the victim....

"Are you ok?" Amilee's concern impinged upon Smitty's reverie as her hand caressed her tensed shoulder. "Is this going to be too much for you?

Smitty had to be strong. "No way," she croaked employing an unaccustomed phraseology. Inside she feared the contents of the gray sac but outwardly she could show no such hesitancy. Amilee and Mary Margaret acted almost casual about the whole thing. The use of such substances as those of which they spoke was not at all novel to them, but she, despite her previous *good trip,* had read enough about such things to realize that one good time may easily be followed by horror. Especially considering possible residual effects.

She had read Castaneda, three of his books anyway. No further. Things too easily became strange, the light dark, the profound ludicrous, the logical absurd. Smitty needed to feel real earth under her feet, to know day from night, hallucination from reality. Dreams and visions could be fun. Last night had proven so. That way also leads to madness, a destination the Teacher found undesirable. In the extreme.

"I think... I- I...." Darn that academic stutter. "I- I'm not sure."

"Don't think you have to do anything," Amilee comforted. "Just enjoy yourself. I was only trying to...."At which she looked to Mary Margaret, held out the mushroom pouch, and smiled a confident suggestion.

Darn those two. Smitty would be left odd-girl out, a condition too often her lot throughout her entire life. Always she had held back, or arrived too late. Even in the convent the other sisters, while never overtly excluding her, had shared things, not secrets exactly...except, perhaps from her. It was happening all over again with one new and another newer friend. That simply could not be allowed to happen.

"I- it's OK," Smitty struggled. "I guess I'm just new to all of this A-a trifle confused. Whatever you girls decide...count me in."

After a cathartic laugh and something resembling a fragmentary group hug, Amilee got down to business. "It's Windowpane," she bragged. "I make it myself. Sometimes I also color it for festive occasions. These are blue in honor of Mr. Stanley. The boys say I could have been a worthy successor to the Bear if the times had remained right. But, you know how things are. I content myself with being an obscure artisan. Believe me creating and designing for this crowd is a challenge. One, I think you might soon agree, I have met with great success."

Out into her palm danced three little gels. Smitty could not say for certain, but she thought before Amilee's hand cupped them into shadow she had glimpsed angelic teddy bear faces, darker blue upon the sky of the tiny capsules. However, once one was in her hand, no such features existed. The fragile surface of the tiny ellipsoidals glowed light blue all over with no distinguishing facial imprints whatsoever. Why then did Amilee distinctly address each by name: Smitty's as *Mama*, Mary Margaret's as *Papa*, and, as she insouciantly popped it into her mouth, hers as *Baby*? Could she be feeling effects from yesterday? Or was her imagination simply overheated as a result of the stress she recognized churning about inside her?

There was no time for such thoughts. The time was upon her. *Do or....* *Oh, please.* Every bit as nonchalantly as had Amilee, Smitty popped her own capsule into her dry mouth, quickly disguising her inability to swallow it by following up with a great quaff of Champagne from Mary Margaret's bottle. After that.... Nothing happened. The concert went off as planned. Smitty found it most amazing. She would have anyway.

SHE IS SKIMMING upon the crest of sound. Sound from all around her. It is way, way, way over a key-changing rainbow of colors usually indiscernible by the human eye. They echo back at the band even before they issue from their source. Infinite violets are smeared all about the hall. A warpaint audience flares blue and red flame back. It is all too much. No distinction between sound and light, motion and immobility. Her head is full, her brain set to explode. Then comes Jerry. A fat man. Face like her mommy. Hair alight with beauty beyond color or sound. His hair...his hair is life. Yes...yes.... Jerry's hair is life...and sweet music...and comforting silence. She drifts into the shade of that vitality, into the beneficence of his occult concentration. She settles onto a soft perch at his feet. She is being borne....

He steps to the edge of the precipice. She quivers a thousand feet below. He casts his attention upon her. His eyes grow big as bouncing baby balls skipping across the generations, across the hopes and dreams of them all. Up and down they go. He leans into her, now no more than inches away, and sings. The song goes on forever changing, ever changing, and she hears with her skin. Her spirit flies into a melodic world which has always been waiting just around some corner for her but has never been found. She is walking upon the very air he...they...breathe. Double twisting, she spirals into herself, grown larger and more composed than her spirit could ever have imagined. She is the entire universe and beyond. Breaking into a sweat of chickadee down, she smooths like infant hair into focus. Upon Jerry's guitar.

The music, as innocent and pure as a child's sleeping breath comes from all around her, from the dark hollows of Jerry's eyes. But from that guitar.... Oh, God, the strings themselves shine silver and gold in the changing light. They are alive, nascent forms of energy beyond this earth's material bondage. Along their length—all six of them—trills energy becoming form, becoming life. Little pewter intimations of next to nothing begin their ballet at the silver bridge, gliding along the wires, over the saddle and pickups, growing, ever growing, changing while slipping along the fret board and neck from pure light and imagination into soft fur, no longer shapeless suggestions, until they soar into the liquid air, sweet, smiling teddy bears of most beneficent mien. Their smiles evoke long-held memories of God Himself. Their numbers tumble gaily out upon the crowd. The intoxication of their life's force sweeps her up...up and away like someone's beautiful balloon into their festival of sound and motion. No oars at all, and in a most uncommon fashion, she ventures with them to someplace she has never known she has wanted to go.

THE HORROR! JERRY let his instrument go, laid it most lovingly in some cradle or other, no more incipient little bears singing along its length. All around her dancing cubs sagged into the limp and clotted sheddings of a most vulgar ichythyotic nature. Smitty herself settled just one more scale upon the littered and malodorous floor just beyond the stage. Her head sagged, her eyes rolled up as her lids scrolled down, while all about her the clamor of goldfish burbled the air.

THERE IS AN end to everything. This is true.

A warmth enfolds her. Trickles of bright almost-meaning glitter around the edges of the dark spot behind her entopic-free eyes. It is not music. It is attractive, compelling. Smitty must open up enough to see. When she does...

The naked little bearie hanging headless upon a clothes hanger, her boobs brazen beyond her demure gown, the open hole of her pubis brown with lowland hair. She is two...

And four and so much more...

"ARE YOU OK?" the headless one, an Amileebear, if Smitty's dream state is to be reckoned as enjoying some connection with a more familiar reality, inquired from out her pelted vagina, while aiming one pinkeyed breast directly into the teacher's face.

"LITTLE BEAR...LITTLE bear...Oh, dear oh derrière.... It has become all too funny. Smitty closes back her perceptions upon themselves. The bears are gone...are gone... the song is over and all the music has stopped. Again the deep security of dark is all she apprehends.... Until....

"COME OUT... COME out, wherever you are," a voice as beauteous as the bearsound from Jerry's guitar, as musical as the tectonic flow of the arena floor called from all around her, the drifting of petaled syllables falling from the graceful hand of some goddess she has never known....

"SISTER MARY MARGARET" Smitty screams the title, howls the name. Her sister, her Mary. Headless. Headless. They never should have come to this place. Could the bears...? No. Not the bears. Who who? Who in all the Owsley strangeness her world had become? Who...who...?

THIN FINGERS WOVE their way into and through the dense fabric of her lashes. Gentle fingers urged her lids to open. Comforting fingers lay their grace upon her cheek, and Smitty saw anew. It was Amilee. She had not one but two heads. One, oh her dear God, was Mary Margaret's. The two had merged, had metamorphosed into one Siamese unification of an Unchristian order.

"Oh, God!" Smitty began to howl as though the moon above the hall might hear and thereupon bear at least a portion of her pain. Her eyes flew toward renewed blindness.

Amilee would not allow it. "Look at me, girl," she commanded, guttural as an old Ursula.

Too overcome to argue, too hyper to pass away, Smitty's only option was to comply. When she did, wonder of wonders.... The one had again become two. The band were back on stage, and Mary Margaret, looking a bit concerned, and Amilee not quite so, helped her to her feet. The rest of the concert she would experience in a fallow world behind any scenes.

IN A ROOM they called green with no bears dancing upon its surface nor beneath the veneer of gray they may have lain over it, she lounges perhaps against a soft wall of striped and rippling ashen blocks or deep within the embrace of a floating chair, dark upon the smoke of her surroundings. Music falls from somewhere above her, and Smitty would stumble into sleep were not the tendrils of something tweaking every internal nerve she possesses upon the surface of her watered-down and flowingupandover person. No windows peek in upon her, no doorway exits from herself to anywhereoranyoneelse. A plastic bubble of something suspiciously like water towers to her side. She dares not look upon its ancient face, must not contemplate the possibility of its existence. Her mouth is dry, her soul cries for relief. Smitty closes her eyes and drifts into the blue-backed clouds of a film perhaps not seen, a magnificent awareness impossible for such as she to comprehend, a beauty she must not behold.

From between her groundless feet a feather stirs, pure, white as snow before it falls. There is no breeze, no ripple at all upon the empty field of her dream. It rises, still and alive. Borne of its own intention it flirts about her wooden nose before teasing her eyes straight from her head and into the intense blue of her perfumed cloister. She is aware. As her eyes jitter along behind their angel she know all. Darkness will fall. Must fall. She will also rise. And Mary Margaret. And Amilee. And, oh, Thank You Blessed Jesus! Tara is alive. They will meet again.

As she turns disembodied eyes from the feather's radiant flight, as they slip neatly back into the encasement where they belong, the feather dances a slightly inebriated and very Irish jig across the intervening no-space and flips itself joyfully across any possibility of vision. For a brief time, Smitty sleeps in a land of no dreams where no Tara Girl or any other fancies may torment her.

SMITTY AWOKE TO a dream within a dream that she both did and did not realize she was dreaming. In a pool of dry and breathless water her embryonic substance drifted conscious of the need for transition. Currents warm and chill, quick and slow moved about her, moved her nowhere. Everywhere was anywhere, her where wherever she might go. She could not be found for she was not lost. No one could see her home, for she had never left that place.

A...*The* feather drifted past to swirl back around her to once again close her eyes upon too much confusing simplicity. The dark became her friend, sightlessness her preferred mode of vision. Her eyes fell quiet; her sleep became renewal.

Again some time other than the other time she awoke, the most beautiful of all the possible faces of beauty breathing wisps of lilac upon her, restoring her vision, reawakening her quotidian perception. Amilee. So lovely. Smitty reached her trembling hand toward the holy one who took it and clasped it in both of her own.

"You should have told me," the gentle one chided. "I never would have let you taste my bes... my strongest ware." Folding Smitty's fortunate palm warm against her breast the vision continued. "We've stayed with you. Had a doctor take a quick look and we think you're out of the woods now. How do you feel?"

Smitty had been allowing her hand to do all her feeling and as a result could only murmur with a 60's smile of profound contentment, "Wonderful. Simply...wonderful," at which juncture she burst into childish giggles as silly as ever such may be.

Another's hand touched her cheek and slipped delicate beauty along her jaw and close behind her electric ear. A wisp of hair feathered into the periphery of her awareness. Warm, soft, snowbright and Icelandic blonde. Mary Margaret. No woman such as was Smitty may experience such sensual assault, especially hard upon return from a journey so parlous as hers had been, without falling into a swoon. Her sensual being, her merely human pleasure center, overwhelmed by too much erotic data, her exhausted neurons incapable of carrying the load, Smitty would have crashed were it not for the recognition of that fact by her two companions who quickly tore themselves from comfort mode and entered full-support status. First Amilee dropped Smitty's blessed hand and gripped the teacher firmly by the shoulders while Mary Margaret's tracing fingers curled into talons which clamped themselves about her waist and jerked her to her feet.

"Oh, no!" Amilee spat into her weakness. "You ain't goin' there again," at which point the two of them propelled her across the floor and out the tiny door of her tiny room and into a curious hallway of echoing chromatics toward a destination somewhere lost in the distance of its undulating length. Then through a grander door or two and into a room most unlike the room she had once entered so long before. No one else was there. No one else that is but Jerry. The Papa Bear of all fables sat by himself picking notes from a piano while popping seeds of some percussive sort into his mouth. He looked up as they entered. He rose. He walked toward them clear air beneath his feet. His eyes told a story such as his music might have had Smitty been in his space/time at the same time. The man was walking toward them. She was certain he was fixin' to stop for just a spell. He did.

His glasses perched huge, round, and just a bit askew upon his gnarly nose. His surprisingly pale skin sagged into his white beard. Something all around him sang a dirge into Smitty's wondering mind. So much the Santa, this poor man was walking the last few miles of his life. He smiled in acknowledgment of her awareness but said not a word.

Instead, from somewhere it had not been before, he withdrew the feather of her most recent dream. Pure as was his hair, light as the graceful touch of

Mary's fingers, he held it out to her, twirling...twisting it slowly by its stem. "I do not give you this as from myself," he smiled. "It is from another, a dear friend, who has sent it. I am her messenger. You will come to know her as well as I do. Her name is Paloma. Remember that. Paloma." He dropped the tiny plume into Smitty's outstretched hand and passed beyond her sight.

"What...?" began Amilee.

Before she could finish, Jerry's voice rose from the fading light behind them, "She was born in spring," he almost sang, "but she was born too late."

Smitty knew. He spoke of her Tara. Turning to question the Papa further she could no longer find him. Her two friends jabbered questions at each other. At the empty air. Jerry had gone. Smitty had no answers for anyone save herself. "She was my twin," Smitty called after the vanished Gabriel, and only she could hear Jerry's gentle, laughing reply as the feather of the Dove spun itself in a ring about the wedding finger of her heart's holy transfiguration.

NUNS, ALMOST, ACTUAL, and active, would feign moderation in all things, but in fact theirs is a most all-or-nothing life style. Faithful to their heritage, the sisters embarked upon a strange journey not at all unlike those of Jesus or Jerry Garcia or Smitty's new favorite, Ken Kesey. Their trip was a simple humanitarian one, inspired not only by faith, drugs, and music but also by Jerry's gift. Smitty would reveal several weeks later to her Mary Margaret that the feather had been passed on by the enraptured soul of Tara who dwelt not in heaven or hell or even as a wandering spirit stricken too soon from the rolls of life. Rather, she existed a hatchling beneath the wings of the vanilla dove of peace whose bland aspect necessarily shields those called humans from an otherwise unbearable power. Tara's, the Dove's, message was a simple one: protect and serve, save if possible those like Tara who frequent the mass gatherings of souls, no small number of whom seek for hope or forgetfulness, love or at least a moment of recognition from a kindred soul.

So it came to be that Smitty and Mary Margaret began their own small ministry to drifting spirits. The Capitol District offered many opportunities. For their initial venture later in the same year, August 1, they were granted a space at the Saratoga Performing Arts Center well behind the crowded lawn for a makeshift stand. **HELP** in big, red letters printed on sheet banners hung from its front and sides. Behind it they had staked out a two-person tent both for privacy as well as shelter. Nobody came.

For more than an hour they endured Jon Bon Jovi playing songs neither of them cared for. During intermission several youngsters wandered by. Some obviously stoned, others simply curious, asked polite questions for mere seconds, ignored answers, and drifted on. Not until an older fellow, accompanied by his obviously inebriated wife, addressed them did the sisters learn one of the first lessons of selling anything — even all the good things that are free. Make certain your target audience knows what it is you have to offer.

"You're standing there," he admonished them, "behind great big '**HELP**' signs looking for all the world like you're the ones who need it. Even if somebody figured things out, what in the hell do you two middle-age housewives know about these kid's troubles anyway?" With that he guided his stumbling companion off into the chattering crowd.

That night during the second interminable encore a positively wasted young man managed to deposit himself directly in front of the stand. Of course nothing of any great moment was at issue. He had been abandoned by his friends after vomiting all over one of them and then threatening to relieve himself upon the other two. He needed a ride home to Glens Falls, directly contrary to the ladies' intended direction. Of course they took him. Of course he managed to befoul the back of their car. Of course, they both felt their efforts had been worth it. Sacrifice, after all, is the very essence of love, compassion, and spiritual communion.

At least some would say so.

All the way back home the two giggled innocent plans at each other, formed grandiose schemes for a ministry far beyond the reaches of upstate, and arrived at Mary Margaret's too exhausted to continue, too steroidal to sleep. As all things must, however, Smitty in her tiny guestroom single and Mary Margaret in her Queen's King-sized luxury, drifted into pleasant visions of their own, Smitty of the dear child so close yet so incredibly removed and Mary Margaret of another who taunted from beyond a veil of black widow's lace, "He is mine. He is yours to do with as you will," just before the thing blunt and hard as a meteor's fall dropped upon her.

Neither, however, in the ensuing weeks allowed their first order of business to become secondary. A new ministry was created with revised incidentals as well as a simple yet dynamic mission statement, a beautiful new logo, and, best of all, a new and powerful patron with a most universal if not entirely Catholic set of contacts.

The two had argued, discussed Smitty would have termed it, over the wording of their statement of purpose for more than a week when Mary Margaret, as much in a fit of *pique* as following a logical procedure, placed a call to the number Amilee had given her.

"I'm sorry," the recorded voice droned. "Amilee is not taking calls at the moment. Any inquiries should be directed to 415 555-1212." Mary Margaret followed up, and thereby did she learn that the preceding day Papa Bear had died. The harried robo-voice which somehow managed to convey great distress offered options which Mary Margaret declined to pursue. Instead, she phoned Smitty who was off on a walk and did not answer. Alone and a trifle miffed despite her better nature declaring that she should feel perhaps vulnerability and some sense of loss, Mary Margaret decided to get high.

All she had available at the time was some top-grade hash and a cap of Amilee's acid. In honor of both the departed troubadour and the most accomplished young woman, Mary Margaret chose them both. As time passes or doesn't, circumstances glide past the sometimes reflective windows of our souls, and worlds intersect and change around us as we sleep in the comfortable knowledge that we are secure and that our own music never stops and that, should we fall, it will always be into the infinitude of our own probabilities. We need find no way home since, Dear Robert, we are already there.

Darn it, a phone always rings or a crow calls through our dreaming. So it was for Mary Margaret. It may have been real. Amilee may have intuited her need, have decoded the unstated message of her hang-up call. Whichever, Mary Margaret shifted into an awareness created by the soft summons of her custom telephone. The voice was Amilee. She already knew the Sisters' need. She had an answer. No mere suggestion. Amilee dictated the entire thing. Their Mission Statement shone through miles of copper as beautiful as the morning sun through even more miles of empty space and humid atmospherics. Amilee was light herself. Her voice sprouted solar-buds, sunflowers, through the pores of Mary Margaret's receiver. Then she was gone. The space between them become dark.

Another time sometime, Smitty called and awoke her. Across the palm of her hand in beautiful blue-pen script scrolled:

YOU ARE NOT ALONE
WE WILL SEE YOU HOME

A slogan. A mission. A statement. A cause. Mary Margaret mumbled into her mouthpiece, "Get your F'n butt over here. We have been released," and hung the F up.

BOOK II
Ruth
2013

ONCE FREE OF Mother and safely on our way to only Sis and Pam know where, I emerge from the fog which has enveloped me since my moment of paranoia followed by the spell of intense disappointment at Dr. Jiz's. As the day darkens, I awaken to some very strange surroundings. First of all, I find myself cowering upon a bucket-style seat in the driver's corner of the huge, white truck, the remainder of the spacious rear compartment, accessed amazingly enough by its own doors, ceded to an immense tool-box at its center flanked at its opposite side by another leather seat occupied by some coprophagial manifestation of dog. All drool and muscle, it eyes me with little interest in its brown-smeared eyes. I told them I despise canines, but Pam just laughed, while Sis swatted the shit-eating thing on its bob-tailed butt and assured me that Billy Bull wouldn't even harm his own fleas. Ha! I'll just bet.

Anyway, the brindle shitter seems uninterested, the squish of the wipers offers no stimulation. I soon lose interest in my own awakening as well, and thus feel compelled to speak. At the sound of my voice, Coco Billy quivers and quickly retreats again into nothing dog-land. Sis remains fixated upon her driving, but Pam turns to me, her smile releasing me completely from whatever mental Sargasso has so wound my consciousness into immobility.

"We just missed you at the Doctor's," she blurts. "Got there just as you were getting into the cab. Good thing we weren't any later or we'd never have thought to look here. By the way, Dr. Bhati said to extend his apologies. He had to go to New York on business. Couldn't be avoided. You know doctors. All life and death. Anyway, he's gonna be at the session with Paloma, and he thinks some good things might just happen there for you. And for some others."

Abruptly, as Sis drives on without a hitch, Pam switches gears. "You've never met Sis, have you?" With that the big driver smiles up into the mirror and raises a fist, clenched and tattooed. Every goddamn thing somehow turns out to be a cliché. Big truck, big dog, big woman, big motorcycle, at least I would guess. Big, fat, butch, dyke. Of that I feel no need to speculate. What else in all the clichéd world could she be? Especially palling around with little, Lezzie Pam?

I keep forgetting that Ms. Lipstick is able to access my thoughts. Without much pause, she continues. "Yep, yer, right. Ole Sis is bout as butch as it gets." With a quick glance she confirms something with her sister in strangeness.

"She's married though. To a right nice.... Excuse my language. I've been spending too much time with my own cowboy. You know him. From the hospital. Lennie?"

I guess I do, but say and attempt to think nothing. Pam prattles on. "Anyway, John, Sis's old man's 'bout as gay as they come, but he hates sex, all sex, with the same passion most men feel for it. Know what I mean?"

I refuse to think anything other than *I refuse to think*, and Pam goes on. "Anyway, Sis always gets a laugh out of their relationship. As she puts it, Johnnie would have made a great woman. He cooks, cleans, gets awfully moody at least once a month, and always has a headache. Despises shopping though." Both dykes guffaw like two retardates.

I say nothing, and of course, I will not think. Not a fucking thing. These two are too much to bear. As soon as....

"Caught you," Pam crows. "Give it up. Really. You've got some heavy shit comin' your way, an' alls we're tryin' ta do is help, and I'm pretty sure we can do that."

Yeah, yeah. Everybody'd like to help. Sis cuts a corner too sharply, the truck thunks over a curb, and shit dog tumbles from his seat. Lazy as only a stupid thing like all dogs are, he just curls a bit tighter than he had been and accommodates himself to his new circumstances. Sis grunts, "Cocksucker."

Pam chuckles out a "What?" and then resumes. "Anyway, all pleasure aside, as I said, you've got some heavy shit besides cancer and death comin' at ya. An' some part of it's got to do with Sis here and her latest 'protégé. Even bigger than that's gonna be the dude you're about to meet. You and him have some things in common neither of you's on ta yet. And there's more. When we get where were goin' you'll meet him, and then you'll see. I hope so anyway.

"Mary and I've got your back. Always. Paloma and Sis here've called in more than just a couple of favors. Well.... I guess you and Arthur — that's his name, Artie. You've got some big things ahead of you. If you want them. That's a big "If." From today on — once you've been with Paloma — you're on your own with choices like that. Kind of anyway. She's got something to give you. Sort of magic, a charm or something. Anyway, you can always say no.

"But take my word for it. I do not think you should."

At that point Pam turns her attention back to the hulk beside her and mumbles something undecipherable in her shaggy ear. Butch smiles, and I am left behind with the dog.

Things might have settled back again, but I spy upon the dog's seat a leather jacket with a huge patch which had been concealed by the animal's bloated frame. It has several patches actually. The one huge one that I can only partially make out is the picture of a flower with at least the word "ROUGH" arched above it and "SISTER-" curved beneath. Just what am I mixed up in here? I recall Pam's denim, albeit vaguely. That too carried lettering of similar nature. Red and white. "ASSOCIATE" I think I remember. A freaking gang. Some kind of female Hells Angels I'd bet. I cannot help myself. I reach over the tool box, Doggie be damned, and spread the leather open.

"Don't touch it," blares from both voices in front.

"Them colors ain't yers," Sis adds.

"Sorry," I slip just the least bit ironically into the suddenly frigid air. "I was curious. That's all." The two dykes remain silent. I must add something. This is not good. "I meant no harm. I've never met a girl biker. That's all I was just...."

"Yeah, we know," Pam soothes. "You never touch anyone's colors. I'm surprised, knowing so much bout you as I do, that you ain't come across somethin' like this before."

"I ain't no girl," Sis growls and pushes the truck up a mile or two per hour.

"I can explain. If you're really interested. Sis's club...."

"That's right," comes the growl. "Club! Got it? We ain't no gang. We're a club. Rough Riding Sisters Of Sappho, if ya gotta know. A fucking club. Ain't no gang."

For the remainder of our ride, short as it turns out to be, Pam fills me in on the details, some interesting, the others, pardon my bluntness, more than a bit pathetic. First among the more noteworthy is the fact that Sis's real name is Rebecca Jordon, "Nobody calls me Becky," she asserts straight into the windscreen.

I do not suppose I would have anyway, but the implied threat serves to dissuade me from any ironic impulses which may have leapt to mind. Nevertheless, a passing reference to a sunlight brook and a sweet stretch of pastureland might get past her guard. If the right moment were ever to arise. Even more surprising is the fact that not only is she a motorcycle mamma of great stature — president of a three-year old chapter — but is also an RN employed at Albany Medical Center as something called a CNS, and she has an MSN from Drexel, and is earning her DNP from Johns Hopkins. Mostly on-line crap, but still....

Pam explains all this in great detail while Sis merely grunts now and then possibly for emphasis but just as likely as comments on the driving of the lack of driving skills exhibited all about us. "Don't matter. Rain er snow. Don't seem like nobody's able to drive anymore. Fuckin' men. Pussys. Bad as the bitches."

I think now and then I observe her ears move as if accompanying a smile, but am beginning to suspect that one should never assume anything regarding this complex being. However, I digress. Her specific area of concern at the hospital is a unit devoted to two specific patient populations, the HIV infected, and a prison ward serving the state penal system from minimum to maximum security, murderers to impossibly fragile waifs whose only crime is to have been apprehended with the wrong amount of drugs, usually Crack, at the wrong moment in New York State's erratic and ineffective war on all things resembling the pharmaceutical.

Pam drones on about other things concerning her perhaps not so unlikely role model, but I drift away, lulled by thoughts of my own experiences, my own narrow escapes, and I let my immediate surroundings, the two lesbians and the shithead dog, slip away.

Life goes on. Corners get turned. Trucks find berths in unlikely lots. We pause in front of a building for which no adequate descriptors exist. At first glance it is a typical red-brick Georgian with a chimney at either end and two third-floor dormers peering at us with deliberate unconcern. In front and all around stretches the most magnificent lawn imaginable, even on a rain dreary afternoon. Straight ahead to the rear of the building, that lawn, the earth fall away into a fog-drift valley. It is the Hudson. I can see neither the river nor any other structures, but I know where we are. Overlooking the entire Capitol District exist several such vantage points from which one may, simply by turning in her lawn chair, view the Helderbergs, the Catskills looming behind them, and scan across the cityscape clustered along the river all the way to the ominous yet seductive shadows of the Adirondacks. At this enchanted place, and such it will turn out to be, I harbor no doubts that, were I to exit the Ram, as Sis prefers to call her truck, by turning away from the house and the magnificent westward view, on a clear day I might see forever into the East, the Greens and Berkshires of ancient New England.

The shadow of a man and a wheelbarrow filled with stone gathers mist and undecided light into recognizable form. It is for him that we have halted. Through her opened window Sis summons the gardener. "Yo, my man. Where we park?"

The figure turns, but I cannot make out his features. A soggy Spanish olive cap drips about his ears. "Not your man," he grunts, and turns back to whatever it is he is tending.

"Yo!" Sis shouts into his dismissal, "we're lookin' fer...."

146

Before she can continue, Pam interrupts, stretching her feline form across the bulk of her companion. "Len," she calls. "It's me. I told you we'd be coming over. We just need to know where to park and how best to get inside."

The shadow turns. Slowly. "Didn't know it was you," he drawls, all Texas to his toenails. "'Ef I did, I'd a sure been more perlite.'"

"Cut the crap, will you? Just show us the way."

"Round back," he states. "Cain't miss it. Less that is this here girl 'hind the wheel don't know howda folla a road on to wherever it's goin'"

An angry Pam is a lovely thing to see. "Fuck you, jerk," she shoots. "Go on back to planting your pebbles. We'll find our way OK. We don't need your goddamn help doing it. Or anythin' else." She salutes him farewell with her middle finger and, before returning to her bucket, plants a most passionate kiss deep into the, I feel certain, willing and experienced oral gateway to Sis's deeper, darker nature.

With that, we are off. The road curves gently around the house before horseshoeing across the face of a terraced bank covered by lovely shrubs of some name or other I never bothered to ascertain although they are quite common to our latitude. Their green-gloss leaves are caressed by shadow-pink and white blossoms as old as evil and as beautiful as my first time within the embrace of Psilocybin. With them, in them, through them I perceive the divine history of photosynthetic reality. Much as I was able then, I waft into a most pleasant flash of renewed awareness.

Until, that is, Sis brings up short and hard against an asymptotic oaken barrier erected to prevent adventurers such as we from falling off the edge of the world. Pam further shatters my bemusement with a giggle, and Sis blows it all apart.

"I swear," she booms, "that boy's gonna shoot you or me or botha us if ya keep this kinda shit up. You tryin' fer that? I don't know. Yer crazy enough. That's fer sure."

Pam's giggles become full throated laughter. "Not afraid of little Lennie, are you? A great big biker dyke like you? I thought you were as much a man as any guy."

"Enough a that. Keep it up an' Len won't hafta pull the trigger. I'll be doin' it for 'im."

"Now, now, Becky...."

Before she can mouth another syllable, a huge hand reaches out and cuffs her so hard, *up the side of her head*, I think such people call it, that I fear for Pam's well-being. Such a blow would no doubt have rendered me senseless, have sent me back to Saint Peters with a concussion. Pam just smiles, and reaches her own delicate hand to within mere inches of the huge woman's face. Then, as if in slow motion, taps the other's cheek. Lightly, I swear. The blow, however, carries more charge than ever had that of Sis. The biker's head snaps hard against her truck window and her countenance loses all coherence. Her overstated features, especially her squat nose and big round chin flow into each other much as might heated wax, and Sis falls still and silent.

The dog sleeps. I become hypersensitive to something in the atmosphere of this suddenly very foreign vehicle. No more psychedelic fripperies. It is cold and so brittle that no longer will the air support my vision and refuses to expand within my lungs. Like glass, shards of liquid oxygen gone frozen riddle my alveoli, burning away my breath; the cold clamps its fist about my heart; my dull consciousness cringes to the squeal of all life's machinery hardening toward cessation.

Mother.... Momma. Why did I leave you behind? Have you too forsaken me?

Sis's huge laugh, threaded through and through with Pam's slivery pipings, halts all oxidation and flash-thaws me back into a July reality. Both of the bitches are laughing at me. Before I can say anything, Sis flings open her door then reaches back in and hauls, *I cannot believe I'm using such a common word; these two are contagious,* Pam across the console and tosses her sprawling into a bed of mulch piled like so much offal around the base of a great tree.

All the tiny little fool does is laugh even louder. "You won't stop trying, will you? You can't hurt me.... Unless I want you to." With the last, she simmers up from her awkward landing into a tone most coquettish.

"Little bitch," Sis counters. "That ain't gonna happen. If it did, I'd probly fall like goddamn Eve or any other weakass woman," at which point she takes in as subtle a breath as is possible for such as she, clumps over to her fallen mate, and assists her to her feet.

Again lands the little slap, but this time the large woman merely takes Pam by the wrist and draws her up close. "Yer a mess," she chuckles. "Gonna be just perfect for them inside. Best watch your colors though. Give 'em some respect. Keep 'em out of the dirt. Know what I mean?"

"I know that if they're fucked up right now it's your doing. Not mine. Now, be a good girl and brush me off. The people inside know me by now, and if they don't, they're sure as hell going to find out soon, but I might as well be a tiny bit presentable."

Sis snorts a bullnose dismissal.

Ignoring her friend's comment, she directs her attention to my face in the window, staring back at her, I suppose, like some transfixed goat at judgment, Pam commands, "Come on out and play, little girl. We won't hurt. We won't tell either." The rain commences in sheets as dark and hard as slices of granite The two clowns, surprisingly graceful, dance their way through it and into a small stone building, leaving me to follow as I will. I so will, and soon catch up with them just as an elevator door whispers open. We enter. And ascend.

We emerge into the largest room outside of the Grand Concourse that I have ever been in. My sense of distance and dimension is suspect and has often been proven faulty, but I am compelled to try a description. From outside, the main house appeared to be at least two hundred feet from end to end with a smaller addition at either extremity. The room we enter stretches from fireplace to fireplace along this length and is at least half that dimension deep. Fucking overwhelming... if I must say so myself.

All good things, as I am certain my escorts, Loonette and Molly, would say, must end. So too did the transcendent wings provided my imagination by the room soon fail, but in this life nothing can possibly by any greater than that of which it is a part. Can it? Whatever, the sad, eroding nature of all reality quickly asserts itself, and creaks, cracks, peelings, drips, and gaps compete everywhere for notice. The place must have been built by Henry Hudson himself. It trumpets its age at every leaking pore, especially the half-glassed front entry. A July gale gusts sheets of rain over the tiles and sweeps across the dull wooden floor half the way our way.

"This is not at all like I expected," breathes Sis into the turbulence. I'm not sure my friend's going to be OK with it."

As she speaks, I am accosted by a vomit yellow ribbon of some vinyl sort and for the first time become aware that the room is divided roughly into lateral thirds by this tape and another just like it further toward the front of the room, both of which appear dedicated to segregating the entire central length of the cavity. Marching between them are sporadically spaced posts, some solitary, a few clumped two-together and, in one case, three. My surmise is that their function is to support support beams and exist in order to prevent the entire building from caving in upon its miserable self.

"Duck under the tape and come on down," calls a vaguely familiar and depressingly vacuous woman's voice from a throng of mostly female figures, eight or ten in number, off to our right, gathered, it would appear, around the dark hearth of an imposing stone fireplace. "Hi there, Rebecca, the voice continues. "Lyndi's already here. We've been having a nice little chat while we waited."

The freaking squab! Oh, my everlasting cruel Jesus. She's worse than ever. I can just tell. Whatever Pam thinks I'll get from her I can't imagine. Whatever prompted me to spend one of my last summer afternoons allowing myself to be wallowed up in her bullshit, I'll never understand. Fucking Pam.

I think I can pick out the Lyndi flapper, but my attention is immediately drawn from the at least superficially intriguing figure so rigid beside the counselor as to be perhaps a most pale and emaciated mannequin by an even greater mystery. Most gruesome Jesus Christ, it's Doctor Jizbag Jaz. I had forgotten Pam said he would be here. I guess the delicate little pigeon needs you more than I do? Just wait cumbag.... Wait 'till I tell Mother this. Today's the last you'll see of me. I'll bet your trim little ass on that.

To top it all off, Pam, a smudge like day-old shit wiggling across her butt, jiggles toward them amid a scattering of "Oh's" and "Ah's." Even some soft applause. These assholes were expecting her. Sis too. The Dike lumbers away, clobbering to catch up. I stand alone.

As always.

Oh, Hell, I'll follow. This is way too strange.

A waif, a Smaug chasing Pierrot by my best estimate, slides in beside me all crooked teeth and pocked skin, its long knobbed legs paling from the hems of camouflage shorts. Rat skin sandals flop upon its pale feet. His breath, although I cannot differentiate it from the cacophony of malodors competing for primacy, given the state of his teeth and the dirt — actual soil — covering his hands and freckled arms, is certain to be atrocious. Go away you sad outdated clown and I will refrain from adding to the woes you must already be toting around upon those scrawny, slumped shoulders of yours.

"Hi," he chirps in the manner of a fledgling not yet aware of its imminent demise. "I'm Arthur Woolf, and I have been sent to greet you. It appears our destinies are in some fashion bound together from this moment on."

Here I thought Paloma would be the worst of it.

Lyndi
1995
Plilty, plour plonor.

Judge Ceriseo, cooked cherry cheeks over pie crust lips, sparkling blueberry eyes alight with malice, picked up the tome of New York State Justice and flung its maximum weight upon the plubbering plorm of poor, remorseful Lyndi. Edward stifled a cry laid upon a curse while Cherish slunk off to SoHo to drink and smoke her way into a more comfortable and realistic dispensation. She had done all any friend might be expected to do. She would visit. As would Edward. Cherish twice. Edward once, unless one count his farewell appearance subsequent to the divorce he had so understandably obtained.

Pli'm plall plalone.

SLIDING DOWN THE shadows of narrow Manhattan lanes, flung around the rim of each gliding light as it approached from uptown or further down, Cherish eventually mothed her way up the flights to her Spartan *pied a terre* and, without bothering to wash, brush or disrobe, fell into her single bed and drifted into the radiance of her own inspiration.

A magnificent flowering of light and life was that night conceived. At its heart was a single bloom from the field of sunflowers she and Endwell had wandered through one sweltering Kansas day, the meadow alive in the beating sun, the immediate world encircled by storm clouds, crashing hints of forked lightning below the horizon. Everywhere stretched infinity. All about them dwelt occult danger.

She and Endwell were younger then. And free. So it was that both of them halted before a tiny flower, half the size of the others, and Lyndi chanced upon something profound. Not until the night of Lyndi's sentencing did she understand what that was.

We are all flowers she told herself. *The delicate little one, Lyndi, is you.* Thus was created Cherish's greatest work. Two walls of the too small cubicles of the gallery would be removed to fit it all in. Not a field of sun flowers, but real grass in real Kansas earth would be spread upon the floor. The walls would reflect and emit, would flash and glow. Would grow dark. Sunlight would stream from above. Wings of shadow as if from larger flowers would be projected upon the earth. At the center would grow the smallest fully-formed sunflower the world has ever seen. Its name, were it to have a name, would be Lyndi. Each day it would live — its dark center emitting bright yellow petals of hope and joy. Each night a great weight would drop from the cloudless firmament above.

The Lyndiflower would die so that it might be reborn.

IN TRUTH, THE weight of all the darkest matter of the infinitely dark universe did fall upon Lyndi. Immediately after sentencing she was led back to holding, trucked to Albany County, and within two days' time had been deposited down-state in the medium security Taconic Correctional Facility for a term of no fewer than five and no more than ten years. Her life was over.

Miraculously enough, her new life was just beginning. Much is made of the penal-imposed situations involving large women and their smaller sisters, who, despite their default heterosexuality, find themselves without the comfort and protection of a man, and who find in a mature and caring woman of substantial physicality a champion and a lover. Isabelle was such.

Lyndi's family, her distant sister, even her non-existent brother, provided her prison account with money sufficient for a bit more than mere amenities. As they should have known — athough, how could they have? — others were likely to find this out, and within six weeks some Latina girls had made Lyndi's good fortune their own. The fools in administration provided her with a print out of her available funds. She couldn't even lie. The Latin Queens glommed onto it the day it was issued. For a time afterward, Lyndi fell down into the bottom tier of the bottom tier of New York State Prison Society. She couldn't even keep a touch of shampoo or tooth paste or, God help her, a snack or two to chase away the aftertaste of the insipid inmate food.

Into the witches brew waded the magnificent Isabelle. Like the majority of the inmates, Izzy was a person of color, but there all similarities ended. Iz stood six foot three, barefooted. Her chest measured forty-five inches around, and very little of that was breast tissue, although she often bragged that she had "borned three girls and breast fed them all." Despite those minimal mammaries, Her entire upper body could have qualified her as Mr. America with the merest touch of a surgeon's blade. Her legs were long and not at all lanky, her thighs a full twenty-three inches in diameter. Her calves, proportional, nevertheless added a grace to her fame which could only be described as ultra *femme*. Her abdomen would make most male body builders cringe in shame. And her face. Ah, her face. Framed by the most natural blonde hair any black woman ever boasted, her features peered out at the world, huge, overstated, yet as delicate as even some *über* buildings may be. Her eyes were blue, blue as ever could have been any most-white woman's. Icelandic, they engaged all about them, the very air itself. These eyes set the Queens back from their prey. Her voice, soft as an angel's whisper, followed with words of salvation.

"She's mine."

The queens disappeared in search of more tractable subjects.

"Pl-plank plou," gasped Lyndi, pressed to the nervous limit of her expressive abilities.

"You ain't gotta thank me," Isabelle replied. "Now let's find a quieter place and see if we can talk."

Plieving plat plomunication plof plany plubstantive plature plould plove plimplossible, plo pler plurprise, Plindi plound plerself plearning ple pludiments plof Plamerican Plign Planguage plalmost plimediately. Plisabelle plas ple pluflilment plof pla plomise plever plade ply plany plone. Plut ple plecame Plyndi's Place plof Plod.

Isabelle had been a teacher. Of the deaf. Her incarceration was the result of her over-fondness for pain killers such as Oxycodone or Hydro in a pinch. The prescribed accompanist of surgery on her left knee, the substance proved malevolent, depriving Isabelle of her will and capacity for rational behavior. Soon she was depleting her children's college fund and betraying her husband's trusting nature. The poor soul was a pharmacist for Walgreen's. Against store policy and what should have been his better judgment, the uxorious little Dominican allowed his beloved free access behind his counter whenever no one of any consequence was in the place.

Isabelle stole. Then she stole some more. Until the hammer of God dropped upon her poor Leonel. He was arrested, threatened with deportation and held without bail. Isabelle, addict and wayward spouse in all but the erotic sense of such prodigality, found her center in the frightened brown eyes of her little ones and, as would any person of virtue, confessed.

For her trouble and reluctant honesty, she found herself serving one and one half to three years in Taconic while Leonel awaited his deportation hearing in the Metropolitan Correctional Center and her babies were scattered across the boroughs in foster care. The sadness behind those blue eyes must have been staggering, yet her lips smiled cerise comfort upon her newest friend, and kindness haloed all around them. "I'm Isabelle," she said, "and I know who you are. Lyndi Lapida-Vita, I presume."

With that they were off.

Only a week or fourteen days into the relationship — for such it truly was — Lyndi awoke to an epiphany of a most electric nature. As her roomie slept soundly on her tight cot across the floor, thunder from the hidden clouds of a

Cherish dream barreled through Lyndi's skull in waves of purest moonlight. Tumbling in multiple forks of ambient lightning, the feathers of that mystical night of death fell upon her. Lyndi knew that she would know, and Lyndi understood that she would....

The words of her favorite hymn rode upon the pennae all about her: "I once was lost, but now am found/Was blind, but now I see." They were not expressed as passing waves of probability. Neither was the music anything more than a soundless presence deep within her, all possibility, lacking any and all actuality. She had been blind while she could see. Deaf while able to hear. The cacophony of the prison, Edward and Alan, Endwell and Cher, and so much more. All had drowned the truth alive in her soul.

Lyndi awoke to the sounding night. Inside her, deep down in a place she had never ventured, had not known existed, from out a Dodson/Carroll mushroom grew a Lotus flower of tender proportion and exquisite color. The petals opened to reveal their treasure. Alive within the sunlight center, the radiant heart of the flower, stood her daughter. No Alice, not even Gracie Slick, the child she once had killed smiled up and down upon her. How she knew, Lyndi could not know, but she knew. The child was Tara.

> *Lead   Us*
> *From   the*
> *Unreal   To*
> *the   Real*
> *Lead   Us*
> *From*
> *Darkness*
> *To Light*
> *Lead   Us*
> *From Death*
> *To*
> *Immortality,*
> *Let   There*
> *Be   Peace*
> *Peace Peace.*

The child's benediction, uttered so solemnly, with so much power was no more Tara's than Lyndi's own. The words as she subsequently remembered them had not been words at all. Neither had they been some mysterious unity with some center of peace and understanding either within or without her. Should one attempt to discern the origin and exact composition of the air she breathes or the water she drinks, should she seek the birthplace of love and hate, the place within her where life dwells, she would find no satisfaction unless she were willing to accept that such may or may not exist at all, that, if she experience them, they may exist for her alone, and dead girls deep down the rabbit hole of oneself, seated upon *padma* of one thousand or merely two petals, may not be alive or present at all. Lyndi knew these things. All is mystery. All is an aquatic plant of brilliant hue. All is unexplainable. All is so very real.

The voice in Lyndi's darkness continued with indecipherable verse:

> *Is a dreamer dreamed or*
> *Dreaming?*
> *If the dream is she, who*
> *Then dreams*
>
> *Her?*
>
> *Is one alone within*
> *Herself?*
> *If so, what may there be*
> *Without*
>
> *Her?*
>
> *Can one be everything*
> *That is?*
> *If one is all, then all*
> *May be*
>
> *One?*

Pler plind plabuzz plith ple plubbering plyllables plof pler plaffliction, Plindy pelt pla plurge plof planic. Ple plas plreaming plut ple plould plot plake plup. Plut plas plappening plo pler?

"Plut ple pluck plup plorrrr.... Plo pluck! PPPPPliiiiiii...." Tara's Lyndispeak skidded completely off the slick highway of her mockadem and the girl resumed standard English telepathy. "As I was attempting to say before I so rudely

155

interrupted myself, if you don't shut up and listen you're never getting out of here. Alive or dead. As things stand, you're no Sisyphus. There's no hill before you, no rock to roll. If bland were gold, you'd be priceless. But even then, you'd probably just turn somebody's finger green.

"Forgive me, Lyndi. I love my new ability with words, and I can't stop trying to sound like more than I ever was. You broke me free from that you know. If I want to I can talk like Colette in French, even de Beauvoir. But I prefer that English speaking witch Sylvia Plath. I could write like them too. That is, if I had hands. If I were alive.

"Anyway, enough of me. Except as much as I am here to affect you. Now why don't you stop hanging up there in the corner of this chamber you call a mind and settle yourself down beside me? I have saved a lily pad just for you."

No sooner was Lyndi invited than she complied. Without so much as a ripple of current within the still water of herself, she drifted feather-dark across the infinite space of no-distance and found herself seated in full lotus position beside the girl she had killed. "Are you of the Earth?" she oh so clearly inquired.

The girl laughed most inoffensively, understanding softening her words. "Once upon a misbegotten time, I might have wondered the same. That is if I had been equipped to do so. The fact is, I was named after a movie my mother remembered from her own childhood. Tara was...."

"I know," Lyndi interrupted, not at all surprised by her reacquired verbal facility. "'Gone With the Wind.' The plantation. I should have known. Tara not Terra. I suppose you could say I'm not exactly myself these days."

"Wouldn't say that I am either," the apparition quipped before breaking into loud and most inappropriate laughter. "You made certain of that about a year ago."

Once upon a Chinese restaurant in some dry city Lyndi and Edward had been passing through in their search for pleasure neither alone was able to provide the other, Lyndi had sat upon the hard rock ledge of a koi pond awaiting her husband's return from a trip to the MEN'S. The place was generic: red and gold, scalloped and scrolled, but a most pleasant gurgle softened the glare and Lyndi dwelt for the moment in her own little garden of serenity. The plants were real, the water clear and clean. Gliding silent as memories of dreams, multicolored fish sang a holy song.

Lyndi fell. Deep into two feet of filtered water she tumbled. Her clothing drifted away. Her limbs assimilated into her torso; her hair became a translucent mane. As water passed through her, as it enveloped her, as it became the medium of her emergent life, Edward returned. He called her up from the depths of serenity back to the surface of need and desire, hunger and disappointment. Had she been a shark rather than a beached carp, she would have torn the life from him, the flesh from his bones, the air from his weakling lungs. Instead, she was only Lyndi. So she rose to meet him, take his hand, and exit the restaurant into the desert afternoon.

Not unlike that time, Lyndi's present circumstances were both dreamlike and real. Not unlike then, Lyndi found herself immersed in an environment both foreign and comfortable. Since that particular koi pond experience, she had taken pains to investigate any such installations she happened across. Never again did she experience a similar moment of transcendence — if that were the proper term — but she often felt the stirrings of possibility beyond the surface world she found herself inhabiting. If only for a too brief time. She was no Cherish Mangold after all.

Always she found herself disappointed. Goldfish — koi — are just decorative and of no more distinction than hair ribbons or cheap scarves, pretty, superficially attractive, but not even worth a return trip to the restaurant where one or another may have inadvertently been left behind. The same is true of moments of enlightenment, transcendence or epiphany, whatever one might desire to call them. At least for Lyndi, they were never any more than fleeting flashes of water sparked grease in the soiled and shallow pan of her awareness.

"You're not you, I know," she spluttered at Tara. "You might as well fade back into whatever clump of misfiring synapses you came from. As they say here, I'm fucked. As for you? You're part of the whole fucking mess.

"Just disappear, will you?"

"Now, now, my gleamish girl, just sheathe your vorpal tongue for a minute and listen. I make no sense because I am not of the sensate world, and you are on your own way to your own removal. Not nearly so dramatic as mine, but of no small consequence to some you know nothing of as yet.

"Me. I simply became the I you see here before you. A whole lot more than anyone might have expected. Except the foolish teacher. She saw through me. And, the new Lyndi about to emerge from the common sludge of the old, you will find common cause with her. Others as well. You may not believe it now, but you are going to be of great significance in the lives of many such as I was. You, the teacher, and a couple others. Anyway, I'm getting ahead of things. Settle down on that pad and I'll fill you in."

When a person is stuck in her own dream, she has no choice but to obey the dictates of that autochthonic reality. Lyndi settled, and, if another, some objective observer had chanced upon the scene, that one might have found the storybook Tara conversing with a creature constructed of a thousand ears.

The ghost had a most disturbing sense of humor and an even more disturbing message. *I will awake*, Lyndi assured herself. *Prison, confining as it may be to the spirit as well as the body, is preferable to the preordained freedom this thing holds out to me. I will wake up, I will wake up, I will....*

Without transition other than an ironic — possibly rueful? — chuckle, Lyndi's unwelcome companion began. "Plefore pli plet plo ple plart plove ple platter, plet ple plemind plu plere plu plare pland plere plu plill plontinue plo ple. Pli pleak plour planguage plow plor plat pleast ple plext plive plears. Playbe plore. Plere plis plonly plone plope, plut pli plan't plee plit plearly. Plif plat plall. Plo plesign plourself. Plou plare plin plis plor pla plood plong plime.

"I speak plainly now. Ignore what I tell you, and you'd best resign yourself to pleaking pls play plorever. I think I'd better warn you of something else too. You're really going to need that American Sign Language what's her name's trying to teach you. As of this minute, you're deaf. You can't hear, and you might as well not be able to talk. No way in hell's anybody able to understand the gibberish comes outta your mouth.

"This is the deep down unenlightened mud girl Tara talkin'. You fell into a world of shit maybe worse than the one you knocked me out of. As the song goes, you're gonna be so goddamn far down it'll look like up to you. The exact same place I've been.

"Anyhow, you see me sitting on this flower, pretty as it pleases, content and happy as I can be? Let me tell you. You've been lugging around a ton of guilt over what you've done. No reason to. I got what people like me usually get. Live hard. Die young. But I got more as well. Remember the feathers?"

Lyndi may have. She may not have. At least until that moment. Of course! How could she have forgotten? The night just before the fatal moment had been Christmas-bright with drift upon drift of snowflakes. In July. Of course! They were feathers. Or the drugs. There had been no Christmas, no snow, no real feathers. Just a dead muddy girl and her own undoing.

Real or unreal, illusion or true vision, were matters of no consequence now. That night, she had seen feathers. White and pure.

"Yes," she whispered. "Yes, I do."

"I'm going to tell you something," Tara pronounced in a most uffish fashion. "It is the secret to you, the mystery of me, and the key to one door which should be opened and one which should not. I'm pretty certain that this one I'm about to unlock for you opens to a good and necessary room. Not all pink and cotton candy. Very, very much more. You will want to think it the key to forgiveness or understanding or some trivial exercise like reconciliation, but, believe it, those things don't come close to the treasures about to be revealed. They all can be yours if you'll let them.

"If you want them.

"I'll tell you my story, and maybe it will show you what I mean. How it works. It don't come easy, as the song says, but, if you follow the path to its end you will return to a world set right side up and your time of trial will result in triumph. So listen carefully. Take heed of my words and allow them past the things you think you know. I offer neither tricks nor riddles, yet the things I say may puzzle you. When that happens, you must let yourself go. You have already plunged into the void, my dear, Lyndi. You have already fallen and there is no one can catch you. No one to bear you up. Except yourself.

"I am telling you things I never was told. Yet here I am. You are still descending to the place from which I began. You must allow yourself to die so that you may be reborn. The feathers dear one were our own. We had shed them all. They blew about us in the winds of night while we huddled naked in the wreckage of our lives.

"I fell upon the road before you covered in all the mud of a foul summer. You rushed pleadlong plo ploin plith ple."

Slowly Tara faded into something too dazzling to be endured, and Lyndi's soul filled with a blizzard of words delivered in a burst.

"I squatted in a ditch, coarse brambles scratching my arms and legs, filth squishing up between my toes. I was sore from the things the boys had done to me. My urine stung and my head thumped like the drumbeat of some heavy metal anthem. I felt my heart race, my breath quicken even before I heard the guys take off. I couldn't so much as care. I'd always gotten by. Anyway, at first I figured they were just trying to scare me. A real couple of jerks, those two. Then I saw the first feather. Falling to the ditch in front of me, it soon got soaked and began to clot and sink. Then came another. Then another. From the moon, I thought. The night was soft and white with them. Shadows and wisps of ivory with just the slightest hint of gold. Then came one more. It landed on the roadside above me. I had to reach it. Something was compelling me. Touching it meant everything I thought.

"It did.

"I myself became a ray of light and the particular world fell away. No longer was I trapped inside the dreary biology of the one known as Tara although I remained Tara in all her possibilities. I became aware that the human entity was about to die, but it was of no consequence. Every probability even of minor degree available to that Tara was bound to the mud from which she sprang. I was the flower you see here and you were the instrument of my bursting forth from the muck, opening the shell of one state and rising free into the cosmic possibilities of the no longer imprisoned spirit.

"Forgive my prolixity. I told you I could probably surpass Sylvia Plath. What I am simply saying is that I am here to give you knowledge and to trigger a bit of understanding of what looms ahead for you as you lie dormant in this infested swamp of your life, and I hope to give you courage and hope that you too will rise. Most of all, I have come to thank you with all my nonexistent heart and from the depths of my soul. That night you set me free and by doing so condemned yourself to the darkness.

"You are still able to see. I suggest that you turn to the New Testament. Three out of four gospels tell of Jesus' admonition to the rich man to sell what he has and give it to the poor, and then to follow him. You haven't been offered that choice, Lyndi. All you once had has been taken from you. Me, I started at the bottom. Was as low as anybody could go. Sorry to say, but from what I understand, you've got a ways more to fall.

"Anyhow. You'll know when you touch down. When you do, bear me in mind.

"When that happens, look for the woman with the feather like those of our sacred dance. She was my teacher. She loved me. Too late, I realized I could have loved her back. She once tried to help my mother. Then me. Both times she failed. There is another like me in her future. Another lost soul. Another child fated to die in order to live.

"You must tell the teacher who you are, even if you can only sign. Let her know what happened that night on the road and what is happening here and now. It is up to you to save her and others too. Left on her own she will lead Tricia to the place she hoped to take me. It is a place of love and of easy grace and salvation. However, by easing the way for that one poor soul, she risks destroying the lives and altering the spiritual realities of at least three others and possibly more. In fact, most certainly more. Tricia must go her own way. She comes from the same kind of place I did. Just like me, she will find her spiritual liberation through death. For Tricia, life, even when fully realized, will only diminish her.

"So study your signing well. You are going to need it.

"Again. Thank You."

At that point, Lyndi awoke to the dead air of one who cannot hear. Pland ple plill plould plot pleak plithout ple PL plefixes.

FOR THE NEXT year and four months certain incidences of synchronicity meshed into a fabric of unexpected comfort and a new kind of satisfaction. Lyndi's cellmate disappeared — into witness protection, it was rumored — and Isabelle's room suffered severe damage from both a leaky roof and a mold of proven toxicity. Within two days of her dream of Tara, Lyndi was blessed. Isabelle was to be her roomie for the duration.

For that entire time Lyndi managed to hide her new-found deafness from anyone in authority. As well, she gained many new and, while unexciting, potentially profound insights into both herself, the world around her, and another world altogether. At the most basic level those lessons involved human social and biological needs. One might not expect that interaction with convicted criminals of any stripe, even those not so terrible specimens found within the modest keep of a medium security facility, might present opportunity for a college educated associate and confidant of artists, musicians, and literary lights to gain any appreciably significant awareness of the world in which we live or any awareness of her own true nature. Nonetheless, in Lyndi's case, those very things occurred.

Cherish had a saying, *We all put our bra's on, one cup at a time, and we all bleed from the same hole.* Never could Lyndi feel comfortable with that, and Cher knew it. So of course, every time they changed at the Y, very publically if someone's period was upon her, she literally sang the thing. Even one of her earliest paintings of any note featured a bloody thighed young woman placidly frozen in the process of fumbling for the loose end of an errant bra strap.

Lyndi just didn't get it. Even with Edward she had remained modest. *"Ma petite prude,"* he sometimes called her. He was right. As was she. Women could be so incredibly gross. Men talked like pigs and sometimes acted like pigs. But women…. Women were filthier than any man could imagine being.

In a very little time, Taconic taught her differently. Her first lesson from the other inmates was not one of necessary humility, but rather of sublime unity. The fact of her hearing loss became known among the general population, and, even the baddest of the bad girls soon felt free to express their most illicit thoughts within her presence. What Lyndi couldn't hear could not come back upon them. Despite her condition, however, knowledge of illegal goings on and revelations of a profoundly immoral nature found their way into her awareness. Her fellow prisoners would never know that Lyndi, deaf as the

Shakespearean stone, could apprehend much of who and what they were, everything that they hoped to achieve, to become. She fully understood their pain, their regret more completely than ever a therapist of most acute ears and altruistic impulses ever could. They shared something that allowed her to understand. They, even the worst of them, were all human with needs and fears, hopes and disappointments. They were all in the strictest sense of the word sisters.

THE REC ROOM as usual is busy with multiple tongues, agendas, glares, leers, and the shrill brilliance of excited female voices. Of only the first and last of these is Lyndi unaware. She has, however, already discovered that if she only remain still, safe within the shelter of Isabelle's presence, she will know more than anyone listening could comprehend concerning any of the affairs being shrieked into the overburdened atmosphere. Should she wish, she has found that she can apprehend even the unspoken, the unconscious thought. This day, a cold diet soda before her, Isabelle at her side with a cold tea and bag of corn chips, she opts to listen with her soul.

Two of the Queens sit at an adjoining table. From the corner of her vision, she is able to discern their stoic faces, the black smudges of eye beneath the ropes of thick hair. Lyndi knows they will remain silent. She also knows she very much desires to discover what the one they call Empi is thinking. It will be the first time she has attempted with anyone other than Isabelle more than a casual peek into the immediate impulses and minor psychic disturbances made evident by facial expression and bodily attitude. No more hit and run incursions. This afternoon, Lyndi will invade, without warning or justification. It impinges upon the erotic.

Lyndi is aware that Empi is serving time for grand theft auto and drug possession, and that this was a totally trumped up charge. Her boyfriend or someone had stolen the car, crashed at the crib she shared with her sister, and then disappeared leaving the year-old BMW prominently displayed in the driveway of their almost middle class Yonkers dwelling just a hack and a spit from the authentic Westchester county town of Dobbs Ferry.

Empi had slept through Alejandro's coming and leaving. She had slept right up until the 6 am arrival of Yonkers' finest. Three cars, six officers and a late arriving DSP sergeant. All for a stolen BMW? Three hours later Alejandro reappeared, a rueful smile upon his strangely pallid face. He would testify to Empi's having taken the car and to his own innocence as well.

"Man, I thought Emps had hit the LOTTO or somethin'," he explained right in front of her. "When I figured shit out, I split man. Slick as shit, you know. I don't need none a that kinda trouble." He looked directly at her. Smiled his lie directly into her brain. "I'm sorry, momma. I gotta tell the truth," at which point they hustled him from the room, leaving Empi to squirm within her manacles as she awaited the arrival of a public defender.

No water. No bathroom break. One silent whiteboy sat for a while chewing gum, but he soon deserted his station. Probably had to take a dump or somethin'.

The best news her Jack Shit pretender had for her was that she could make a deal. It had been offered before she had been officially charged and would be withdrawn should she insist on delaying even so much as overnight. The deal was simple. She would plead guilty to Grand Theft Auto and to possession with intent to sell of the more than ten kilos of pure cocaine in the Beemer's tires. For her cooperation she would be sentenced to twenty-five years and her sister would be granted immunity to prosecution. Otherwise they both would go down.

What could she do? Empinada, once Alejandro's spicy little dumpling, folded. Her sister was safe. Alejandro would pay even if she had to wait twenty-five years, and Empi allowed the prison to cook her up a fine thick shell. Not that she wasn't already one badass *cholita*, but no reason she couldn't get badder.

She was innocent of the auto theft and the drugs which never appeared anywhere as anything other than allegations. In truth, Empinada pled guilty to possession of substances for which another citizen from the neighboring state of Connecticut had already been prosecuted. As if knowing such things could be of any significance! Did the trooper who coincidentally appeared at the raid on her house? He the main man of a cousin. He knew he could do nothing. In fact, unless he desired to see duty in some hellhole like Plattsburg, his best course of action was to allege, to whisper and to deny. Anyway. In no way was Empi innocent.

She had gained some renown as the girl to go to for all manner of club drugs. Her newest and finest being the prosaic little Molly as she named her finest version of X, but surely a minor dabbler in hallucinogens does not deserve the railroad ride Empi had been ticketed for. There just had to be more, and Lyndi, upon first entry into her intended's womb of consciousness finds the answer right up front in lobes clamoring to burst their intended violence upon all this miserable world.

Memories of impotence and humiliation, laughter turned to sorrow, tears of joy dried away before they could be shed. Cut, burn, hack and slash. Empi had felt it all. She was thirteen, charged with ransacking a suburban home and stealing an unspecified amount of cash. Following a plea to misdemeanor malicious mischief, Empinada was spared confinement. But then.... The motherfucking probation officer, just like in that fucking movie! He did her every which way, even ways approaching the impossible. For her fourteenth birthday he had body-painted her in psychedelic colors and, as he so cheerfully put it, rolled her up into his little three-holed bowling ball. At fifteen, he mixed her urine and ouzo cocktails, and when she was drunk enough pissed directly down her throat.

The woman Empi became could not forget, could not forgive. She knew nothing of Lizbeth Salander, had neither seen the movies nor read the books. She did take the same route, however. Five years after completion of her sentence, Mr. Whitefuck Whitford was found with his penis stuck in his mouth and his severed thumb stuck up his dead ass. Everyone knew Empi did it. Even the cops. They just could never make a case. Rumors of difficulties has circulated during the first months of her probationary period and these had led investigators to her. However, no official records of anything extraordinary existed. In fact, Mr. Whitford's reports could be viewed as nothing more than the smooth progress of a typical situation. There was nothing substantial, and the little hard-ass was admitting nothing other than the fact that she and Whitford had established a fine and mutually satisfactory professional/client relationship.

Whitford's family extended deep into the hard rock of New York law enforcement politics. His father had been NYPD. His brother was a city court judge in Ossining, and his cousin Michael was Sherriff of Putnam County. Such atrocities as the poor guy's death and disfigurement cry out for vengeance. Such action is not exclusive to any Lord. Empinada had been set up most effectively, and were it not for the protection of her sister Latin Queens and their uneasy allies the Latin Kings, Empi would not have survived her first week in prison.

All this Lyndi gathers in a flash, not unlike data transfer. It consists not of words nor even sensual memory. It simply once was not and then it was. Something more of a most disturbing nature also dwells there in the buzzing hive of Empi's consciousness. Loud and angry currents strive everywhere for dominance, but a softer melody plays behind it all and is not drowned out.

Sometimes when listening to artists from her past, Pink Floyd primarily, Lyndi would be surprised by the fact that she had been experiencing instruments and a melody to which her ears had been deaf. Now, actually unaware of all auditory prompts, Lyndi hears the unheard again. This time most clearly. The goodnight songs of drowsy birds to their fledgling chicks, the call of the ocean waves hidden inside a castaway shell. Lyndi hears love and is struck by pain and terror no bowling-ball pervert could ever engender.

More than Empi loved her freedom, her life, her immortal soul, she loved her sister. She was willing to give them anything to save Paloma. She would protect her against God himself. To the death, with her last breath she would speak her name. Paloma lives because of her sacrifice. They would have sentenced her too for the same bogus shit, and her little sister would have turned from a dove into a crow or a fuckin' turkey buzzard living with death and off death for her way too short life. Empi had made that all go away.

Who would have thought — Love?

That emotion lies deep within the obfuscations of her deliberately unconscious mind, but even deeper crouches a presence both mute and felt but invisible. No one but Lyndi, not even Empi herself, could have detected its presence, yet it lies clear to Lyndi's perceptions. Buried beneath the dribblings of the multitude of tormented, angry, and violent thoughts inhabiting the other's mind, exists a seed. Mud-choked and unnourished, it manages to live. To wait. Perhaps to grow up to the surface and into an impossible light.

My good God, Lyndi's heart exclaims. *It's Tara*. Immediately, she is disabused of that notion. Tara is her own dead, most inward child. This child is Empi's. This unborn creature is Empi herself. She has no need to carry the burden of any Tara. Empi has crushed the life from her own self.

Somewhere, however, that life still exists. The child awaits her moment. She too can be reborn. The question is, how, given present circumstances can that occur? Hopelessness overcomes Lyndi. Drains her resolve to know more, causes the vision to fade, the unity to fall apart. She finds herself back at the prison table, her eyes filling with tears, her hands clasped to her breast. Something moves beside her. It is Isabelle blotting up something spilled on the toxic surface. Lyndi looks away.

Right into the hostile glare of Empinada who has half risen from her chair. Lyndi feels Isabelle's awareness. Catches her own start. "Plon't," she cautions. "Pli've plot plo plue plis," at which she scoots up from her seat and over to the hostile Queen before anyone can make a further move. Taking the startled Empi's shoulders in her hands, she gently pushes her back into her chair. A brief look at the other halts any intervention, and, without so much as a "please" or "play pli" buries her face in the coarse strands of hair atop Empi's head and breathes a kiss down into the soft juncture of bone which is an essential feature of any newborn infant.

Without any "P" she whispers three times into that darkness, "Love." That is enough. Stepping back she looks down into Empi's upturned face. "Love," she says again, and before her friend can utter, "You better move it, mama," Empi's brief smile tells her everything she can ever hope to know.

"Pli'm ploing," she states and returns to Isabelle who, by this time inured to her friend's oddities, grunts and takes a drink, leaving Lyndi to drop into herself where she can wonder just what it is she has just done.

AS TIME FLOWED around them, Isabelle found Lyndi to be a brilliant student of Sign. Within mere weeks she had become fluent. In fact she developed the knack of anticipating the flow of her mentor's thoughts and responding to questions as yet unasked. In so little time as to seem no time, she could read lips. Within two months, Lyndi was suggesting subtleties of signing never before imagined by the über competent Isabelle, who was wont to inwardly speculate concerning her pupil's having developed some as yet unrecognized form of ESP. Not only could she read her mind, but, Isabelle began to wonder, might just be directing its flow, altering its utilitarian focus.

One moment of weakness six months or so into their relationship, Isabelle, a bit mellow from two hits of PCP laced weed and, as she said, "totally good with it, if that's what you're doin'," asked the pertinent question, and only a most altered consciousness could have accepted the answer with equanimity.

"Pli plon't plow," her friend replied through a peach fuzz jumble of something other than light. "Plut, Pli plink plo."

When it came to Isabelle's horrific pain, that of loss of freedom, of spouse, but most of all of children, Lyndi found that *empathy* was too mild for the rush of despair she felt whenever she chose to look into the soul of her mate. Behind the veined irises and beneath the dark surfaces of Isabelle's lifeless pupils Lyndi traveled at will. However, just as she who chooses to descend into the volcano must eventually succumb to the devil's breath of the two-faced earth and find herself consumed by the magma at her molten core, Lyndi found torment beyond anything she had ever imagined. Thank you Tara, boiling up to the last vision of her bubbling eyes would always float the feather. The child's feather becoming more and more her own.

After one such experience, as the two women lay together, their need for comfort as well as for the deception of pleasure momentarily satisfied, Lyndi felt a tickle upon her cheek lift her from the pit. It happened to be the featherlite touch of Isabelle's blunt fingers tracing the path of an imagined tear. "I was with you," she whispered. "I was you within myself. I felt my own pain like I was you. I saw the whole thing. The lava, the black smoke. I felt the pain. Felt all the heat of my own torment, but I did those things like I was you.

"I don't know what to do, Lyn. I want to open up and let all that hatred, that anger bust out and at least take a few of them with me. I wanna die, and I want a goddamn couple dozen of all them assholes going down with me. Know what I mean?"

That Lyndi did, and she knew Isabelle had it within herself to take a couple of others if not a dozen or more. "I don't blame you," she said. What else was there? If she had all that agony roiling up inside her, wouldn't she feel the same? "But, I'm not sure...."

"Don't give me any shit. I know you've seen the real me. I've got no hope. No fucking possibility of anything other than gettin' old, gettin' sick, and dyin' alone."

Where her response originated, Lyndi could never say, but it must have been Tara. Maybe Isabelle's caress. Reaching up to her giant lover's face, she allowed her fingers to trace the actual trace of warm tears along the course of Isabelle's cheek, across the hard mandible, down her neck, and along the inside of her left arm until their hands met and joined dry and cool. "I love you," Lyndi murmured.

"Oh, my God," Isabelle sobbed. "I love you too." With those words, even before they could be spoken, a ripple disturbed the air of the cell, and ghostly feathers danced about them. No one saw as each woman fell into the other and into the spirit haunted moment. They breathed the magic; their pores, their worldly orifices opened and the truth of human circumstances calmed the fires within Isabelle, while offering Lyndi a moment's respite from her own headlong fall toward grace.

TIME DRIFTED THROUGH their lives as would tufts of dandelion through spring air. Around them the world raged, children cried, lovers quarreled and made up, mommies tended to abraded knees, and the seasons died only to return as though they had never departed. In prison these things are only rumors spread by CO's change of uniform, new inmates' aura of something resembling connection to a world of wind and rain, sunlight sinking into violet night. In a world of artificial light and regimented recreation, trips to a yard unlike any yard known to the outside, all crying babies are painful memories best stowed away somewhere, mommies are mythological figures, and the seasons are not for sewing or reaping nor for vacationing on the Gulf of anywhere. They are irrelevant things marking the swirling nature of infinite time.

Lyndi and Isabelle, however, found in the dandelion fuzz whirl a brief time for love. For their own meta-season each knew the other as she did herself, and each found the injured child's comfort only to be found in the embrace of another conscious being who suffers, has suffered or is sure to suffer the same afflictions as has she. Their time did not pass X-ed out on a ratty wall hanging. In truth, and contrary to outsider assumptions concerning the nature of prison time, their two years may as well have been a day. As some singer once lamented, it "was done too soon."

Arthur
2013

As difficult to admit, even self to self, as it is, I should be more appreciative of the VA. At the very least, and no doubt on an essential level of necessity somewhere in the never was ago, imposed from shared experience upon our very D or at least R NA, the members of this group and I have some actual event, calamity or at the very least unwilling observation to hang our troubles upon. Fire and Monsoon, shit and the sweet smell of Napalm, agents of darkness and orange sunshine, we are all changed. Forever the outsiders in a kingdom made for the fat and contented, the fit and ambitious. Citizens all. All the same. We do not belong. Perhaps we never did.

I would return to Holland Avenue, even were it for an indefinite stay, without complaint or hint of snark, but Lenard is determined that such will never be. Now that his promise of some form of confrontation with or at least introduction to my Man on Fire has been proven as empty as his head, why I remain attendant upon him should be of more concern than it is. That the stubble-face has an agenda is clear. I cannot help but wonder what it is. For the current time within the scope of my short-timer existence, that remains a question of mysterious substance.

Perhaps I should say I have questions. First, what in all that is holy, unholy and vanilla-pudding harmless did I do to warrant this self-important asshole's attention? Second, Since I am so obviously aware of the asinine nature of the too humorous to be tragic clown's persona, why do I insist upon casting rational perspective aside and allowing his continued parasitic presence upon the fabric of my own existence? Finally, How is it that not only do I entertain his braying comments upon every aspect of my life both former and present but also have submitted myself to be guided into my own future by this being of less than comic proportions?

More persistent, so as to be nagging, interrogatives continue to trump those above despite my growing sense of annoyance both with the idiotic round of meetings I am subjected to as well as my growing awareness of the adjunct nature of Lenard's guruvian pose. He communicates with someone—or might better be *thing* at night while, haplessly homeless, I lie awake upon the mattress he has laid upon the floor for my use. From his room, paper-thin door no obstacle, come the mumbles and extended long silences of what must be cell-phone conversations. The morning after, he reveals new plans and objectives which were nowhere in the neighborhood the previous evening.

Except for the meetings.

Always the fucking meetings.

HERE I STAND not alco ho lick. Call me DeNile but I am not sick. Not like you losers anyway, and, yes, Lennie, that includes you. I am NOT an alcoholic. Although I attest to the contrary each and every time I am called upon to do so. Life holds little reward for those whose adherence to the truth prompts them to speak it in inhospitable circumstances. Look to Socrates, Jesus, and King. There is nothing I have found to be worth martyring myself for. Nothing. Except my self that is. Polonius was even more of an asshole than Lennie, but some of what he said rings true. I will always be a borrower, but, wealthy as I might never become, I shall never lend out a dime. Unless the interest.... Usurer thy name could easily be Arthur. Take away the "ur" combo, and my default status is accurately characterized. Anyway, back to the point, "To thine own self be true," rings most valid to me. However, I ask how does one remain true to a self which that same person abandons to some absolute and external ideal of truth, possibly resulting in lethal consequence?

"Hi, I'm Arthur, and I am an alcoholic." Len beams his sooty smile, and the group of six or so turn their milksop eyes my way. A cornerstone of AA as well as NA and as far as I know all recovery programs is Truth. I have opted to begin with a lie. I wonder if Mooky Len suspects. I suspect not. Thus do I continue into my favorite land of all, Make Believe.

"I have been to war," I continue. "I have killed my fellow human beings." This part is true. Something like Wendy and Peter I need a real window ledge from which to launch myself above the rooftops of communal comfort. From here the adventure begins.

"While in Vietnam I discovered the allure of drugs, including heroin, *true enough I guess,* but once back in the world I found Alcohol as well. I quickly became aware that smack was a dead end and that the other varieties of chemical non-enlightenment were equally, or almost so, dangerous. I must confess to a continuing romance with marijuana and an on again off again flirtation with cousin Coke, but very soon after Vietnam I turned to alcohol with a passion I might have best applied to getting clean and sober. 'Do not forget,' I would tell myself, 'you have killed, you have seen your friends, comrades, and, yes, clichéd as it may sound, brothers disfigured, decapitated, burned to ashes, and killed in some most gruesome manners.'

"I have been splattered with the fragmented skull, the slime of brain, and still living blood of the man boarding a Huey just ahead of me, his head neatly removed from the rest of him as the chopper lurched within the concussion from its neighbor's RPG induced frisson."

Part of.... The only enjoyment possible for me to extract from these ostensibly communal yet actually solipsistic, self-pitying gatherings is the confusion I am able to sow with just a few phrases of the language the fools claim to speak and to understand yet which on any level beyond the most basic befuddles their simple thought processes to the point of producing blank stares and panicked flights to the coffee urn or the bathroom. Usually, only a few remain with me, and those, I surmise, lack the comprehension of their own confusion or tremble within the darkness of fear induced withdrawal.

Many, maybe most of the drunks confess to feelings of inferiority, bouts of panic, and a need for the comfort only booze, a diseased liver, and, the ultimate prize, a pureed brain may be depended upon to deliver. Some of same work to escape the inevitable. Again, most find themselves unworthy of salvation. I do belong in that company — the unsaved, the never to be so. I, however, am not unworthy. No. I reject anyone's or any deity's hegemony over me. My mother saved me. She has passed on to, she hoped, and I doubt, a better place. I need no place other than the one in which I might find myself were I to break free of Mookey's spell and this group of detoxified whiners.

I shall continue. I shall soon be finished. Sharing, listening, sitting. When this hour has passed, I shall pass myself away from Lenard's company and find myself a place to get a drink. Who might say... perhaps a moment or two of more potent acquaintance.

I am this time, thanks to Lenard, always thanks to the Mook when it comes to such onerous duties, the speaker, first of two this afternoon. I am already before the downcast eyes, drooping heads, sagging chins, and trembling hands. I swear one middle-aged biker type is twisting his head about in a way reminiscent of the Tourette guy who for a time shared a spot in Paloma's non-recovery type session at the VA; thus I must continue. I fear I have already paused for too long. No one has left for any other pastures yet. Give me time.

I have begun my Vietnam Veteran as victim rant. I will drive these timid souls before me like so many wind-blown herbs out into the hallways...away onto the clotted streets of the irrelevant city in which they presume to dwell.

Someone enters from the rear. I know him. Who might it be?

He slides, some hangnail to Lenard's side, and sits, his lips already to the Mook's ear. Lenard nods and listens. My rant segues into the bland pap the assembly "needs to hear." No one moves from their chairs. Heads nod, but I cannot be bothered to note them further. The words slither out. "I took my first drink from my father's coffee cup at ten. Years that is. Not AM." They chuckle mirthless response. I am no comedian. I do not care.

Who in all the living hell is the strange memory communicating with Len. I know they are speaking of me. Laying plans.

Well, my chickens, don't start counting just yet.

"My bottom came. That is if it has actually come yet. I hope it has. I can't go through all the crap and self-inflicted pain...." That one, the combination of pain and its auto application gets them every time.

He's from long ago. That much I know. I can tell by the way they keep looking up at me that I'll be unable to escape their clutches when this travesty is concluded. I can, however, zone out. I shall become motile stone.

"All I know, all I can say," I conclude, "is that I am sober," *extended caesura,* "Today." Oh, yes. That one always gets them. No one has left. A few actually applaud as I take my seat in the front row, just beneath the lectern where Jerry Jellohead immediately begins his dreary tale of weakness, dependency, and hopeless inability to manage even the most basic of his affairs. I have heard him request the group's permission to use the dentist's mouthwash.

They determined that for his first time he should take his own — just in case — but that for subsequent appointments they were certain his dentist would provide a non-alcoholic rinse. Lo and Blessed Billy behold! He reported back that the entire group-practice employed only alcohol-free substances. He remained insecure on another front, however. The preliminary examination revealed a need for extensive repair perhaps involving root canals and crowns. Pressing question: should he subject himself to the insidious wiles of pain-killing drugs? To this, at least one of the alcoholics warned against any and all such foolishness, opining that sometimes such incidentals as dental health must be forgone at least for a year while the alcoholic concentrates upon his number one, his only priority. Sobriety.

Until Jello crows the watchword, "Today," I have been lost in memory. I have even forgotten the two conspirators. Prayer time is here, and, as soon as I stand and reach for the hand of the man beside me, Lenard blunders in, Familiar Stranger beside him. "God grant me..." I begin for all to follow.

"Gotta little surprise," Len inserts into my serenity. "Remember Kenny?"

Jesus AlmightyfuckingChrist, it's Merrill. The almost man on fire. How the hell do I get out of here? This is some shit I do not need. Not Today. Not ever.

As the drones buzzing their unhappy little secrets about the room might have been vocalizing at the same moment I was attempting it, "Escape leads only to entanglement, dependence, and, if the fugitive is fortunate, to recovery."

Feigning an overinflated bladder, I flee the two ambuscaders into a place of temporary sanctuary. Am I to experience any luck at all, the dummy duet will remain in the hall of nonalcoholic prattle, and I will be free to sneak away undetected. Sadly, even Mortimers such as these Snerds at times guess aright. On station just outside the Men's Room door, they await my exit. I am wrapped up in Lenard's ill-considered plan of some form or other of redemption and off they whisk me to a dull, little coffee shop three doors along Central or Madison where we order....You guessed it. Two coffees and one Tazo tea. Why cannot some people, possibly all or most people, leave other people alone? Or at least me?

God, I could use a drink.

The stink of coffee permeates the atmosphere, billows visibly from Kenny's mouth, staining his words as brown as his teeth. "It's good to see you again," he lies. We have not spoken at all during the short walk to this dive, not even Lenard. Now, here it comes.

No doubt I am to be offered the opportunity to make amends. I shall be required to admit — to own — my misdeed and find solace in Mr. Merrill's forgiveness, accompanied by a self-congratulatory tone and poorly concealed smile of superiority.

They can wait until Hell freezes over and thaws back out again. I will not provide them the satisfaction. I will not crawl. This might even turn out to be enjoyable... observing from a safe hard place as their confidence turns to jelly, their serenity to consternation.

Let us proceed. "Likewise," I assure the imbecile sitting across from me, his too high-waisted Walmart slacks contrasting their chocolate mess to an ecru shirt of most feminine tone. His abdomen is bloated and soft looking. His arms piping from out the folds of his girlie blouse are thin and pale. He affects sixties' long hair behind made ludicrous by the comb-over up front. I would refuse to speak to such were it not for my semi-dependence upon Lenard's good graces. I must remember not only his bread but board as well. I shall remain engaged; I shall respond. Offer nothing. Like most of his kind, Lenard can accommodate disappointment. Such is a constant factor in their compulsive ministrations to the unwilling and ungrateful such as I who inexplicably attract their altruistic natures.

True to that nature, Len, possibly sensing a certain stiffening of the ether about us, leaps right in where no wise man should venture. "Kenny's a friend of several friends," he informs, "When you mentioned him that time I was interested in finding out if he might be the very Kenny M. we knew," at which point he gestures toward Merrill before continuing. "As you might have expected, he remembers you well." As if passing a microphone to a featured speaker, the clown nods solemnly toward Merrill and intimates that he should carry on.

God help me.

Despite myself, despite the assistance of any deity either, the tale draws me in, and I soon sit enthralled. Merrill has come neither to accuse nor to forgive. He is bent upon offering his most heartfelt expression of gratitude. Strange things, Horatio, most unbelievably strange. Kenny, Dr. Merrill, is a staff psychologist at the Capitol District Psychiatric Center, having earned a Bachelor's and Master's degree from SUNY Albany and a PhD from, for Christ's sake, Johns Hopkins. What the bloody Hell! He claims to owe it all to me and the night we each danced to our own destructive rhythms. The morning he might have become the Man on Fire. On top of all that, real as Lenard attests, education, he is married with two children, two little girls. To Baily no less. I would surmise that I might remain closed-mouthed concerning that one's little adventure with Mitch.

Remaining closed-mouthed requires no effort. Merrill's next revelation dumbfounds me. "I humbly beg your forgiveness," he pleads. It is real. It cannot be mistaken. His lips quiver. The sleeves of his pale shirt tremble about his nervous arms. I look into his eyes. They plead.

"Yeah," I blurt, more no-comment than question. "For what exactly?"

"Things have not gone well for you," Mr. Cohan informs me. All the while you were suffering, drifting in and out of addiction, recovery, relapse, etc., all that while I pursued my own ends, my own satisfaction, and pleasures without once attempting to find out about you even were it simply to offer a sincere 'thank you' and then move on my way.

"Not once.

"I must tell you that I found myself sore and depressed and in Leonard Hospital the morning after our little party. Suicide most certainly was not far from the most acceptable response to the degradation I had suffered. I remember your friend and Bailey, you know. As in a dream… but real. Nothing further could have come of our relationship were it not for her confessing everything and begging my understanding. It was then in the little psych section of the facility that I learned the most important lesson of my life. To forgive may be divine, but it is also among the human possibilities. I may have been wronged, but I did not care. I took her hand, looked into her eyes and said the magic words, 'I love you.' From that moment on we grew together until now, as the ritual decrees, we stand together until Death shall us part.

"Furthermore, I remembered the last part of my, as I like to call it, trial by fire, and Bailey has told me the rest. Arthur, without that moment in my life, without your literally lighting a fire underneath me, I might have ended up... ah...."

"Just like me," I finish for him. "Go for it Kenny. You forgive me. You're glad to be you and just a little sorry I'm me. 'But for the grace of God,' I suppose."

"Not at all," he pronounces in his best professional voice. "Indeed, I did stumble at the end. I did begin to reference yourself. But allow me to add. In no fashion am I prone to feeling superior. Yes, I could have ended up poorly, but I am not as strong as you. I never would have... could have... survived. Without your fire, without Bailey's honesty, and, yes, without the Twelve Steps of AA, I would now be dead.

"I owe you my very life."

My coffee has grown cold. Lenard's scruffy lips are closed against something other than each other, and Kenny looks down at his tea. Am I expected to respond? How?

"I gather then that I am to suppose you have forgiven me."

"There is nothing to forgive," Kenny drops upon the table. "Can you forgive me?"

I nod. Kenny smiles bleakly and Lenard suggests we call it an afternoon.

THE RIDE HOME is silent if one excuses a few brief comments on weather, dinner, and evening meeting possibilities. "I got personal business tonight," Len communicates to the drone of his terminal automobile. "You oughta go to RPI at seven."

I nod, in no way sincere in my affirmation.

Lenard nods back. We arrive at his apartment. The sun disappears into the dying sky. An April chill descends. Inside, he reads and I look out toward Pawling Avenue imagining the pigeons homing back from their jobs, visions of cold beer and even mellow weed dancing in their fairy-tale imaginations....

TWO HOURS PASS before I awake. Mooky is gone and I guess I should attend the ridiculous meeting. The denizens of the Polytechnic Purgatory at least are a cut above those in most such circumstances, and they don't mind your bringing up addictions other than alcohol. Conceivably I could have a bit of fun.

Again, maybe I won't. Ever since the asshole asked me to forgive him, something has been gnawing a hole in my serenity blanket. Is Merrill so imbecilic as to think being, literally I must add, set on fire could somehow be misinterpreted as a corporal work of mercy? Could he imagine me as his very own *Deus* from some offstage *machina,* unknowable and beneficent? Truly, for long I have viewed myself as above average, even exceptional. But godlike? Not even I go that far. Not even when higher than the almighty's heavens above. I do now, however, feel prompted to consider the nature as well as the scope of my influence, to ask a simple question. Is my life's purpose to bring death or at least the possibility of, the fear of same to those who offer themselves vulnerable about me? To burn their bridges, cities, and towns, to ignite the fires of immolation latent within them?

I watched Hair burn. I would not now cause such physical agony, not to anyone. I have, however, metaphorically, psychologically done exactly that to those around me for years. I enjoy it. It is my only remaining pleasure — except for Paloma that is. A story I once read by a woman most infatuated with blood contains a line I shall never forget. "No pleasure but meanness," her character pronounces just before shooting someone's grandmother. Later, however, he concludes — The Misfit I believe he is called — "Ain't no pleasure in life."

Some teacher I was subjected to at some time, in a most self-assured and egotistical fashion, proclaimed this criminal as the second coming of Christ, the Christ of Justice without Mercy. *Bullshit*, I knew then. Now, I am beginning to wonder. Is such not at least a remote probability? Have I become an unwitting redeemer? Has the evil I have done, if not all at least in part, not been evil at all? Have my misdeeds been directed toward a greater good? A good, I must assert, I will eventually despise if it continues along the same misbegotten path as the incident with Merrill indicates it might. I despise all the little drones, the sexless, passionless nodules, and turnip-brained non-entities such as he who crowd our streets and drown our thoughts in their senseless chatter.

Kenny might have been a ball of flame bursting from out the side of a derelict fire station, plunging to the asphalt below with a meteor crash to the consternation turned horror of the first-responders arriving with naught but salvation upon their trivial minds. Most assuredly the lesson taught in such fashion would have been more profound than the cumulative effect of all the prescriptions and clichéd profundities of his current practice. Whatever that is.

AGAIN I AWAKE. Sometimes a lethargy descends upon me the only cure for which is one of the depressants such as Hydro, Oxy, or even alcohol. Of course, heroin is the first choice of those such as I possessed of a discriminating taste, but I have always feared the Dragon Lady, and, exclusive of one or two minor aspirations, have successfully eschewed her polar seduction. Marijuana, on the other hand, serves passably in such cases as mine as does alcohol. However, given my present circumstances, I fear I am left without succor. Except a meeting. Talk and coffee put me to sleep, but such are my only options. Perhaps the walk will quell the waves of introspection threatening once more to send me off into dreamland, the blathering fools to awaken the cold anger which is my strength.

My salvation? I almost thought salvation. I wonder....

Was anger at me the root cause of Kenny's so-called awakening? No doubt it was. While my anger has served at best to save me from dropping into immobility, extended sleep, catatonia even, has Dr. Kenneth Merrill's, at work upon so much dross as is he, stripped him of any pretense at being anything other than himself and plunked him into the common pool to swim with all the other puppies of the mud? I may not know myself, may never become anything resembling genuine, but at least I am no Kenny Merrill in my ecru lady shirt, my jolly-baby belly jiggling as I walk. So true that I have no answers. So true as well, is it not, that no answers exist?

I smile. I am pleased. Happy. I would laugh out loud if in the company of one as sophisticated as am I, such crude behavior were not presumed to be unseemly. I shall trek down the grade and roll my rocky self up the hill to the college. I shall sit and listen. Will decline to share. I shall glut myself with cookies and pastries, prime my midnight bladder with bitter caffeine, and expand my consciousness into nullity.

As anyone such as I should come to expect, the happiest of possible circumstances—even the happier of same — fail to materialize. I step outside, a sweater my only protection against the evening.

Where has April gone? March, even February, has returned. The temperature must have dropped twenty degrees while I napped. It's nasty. A cold rain, pellets actually, scrapes across my unprotected face driving me back indoors. I shall trek nowhere tonight. Exhaustion slides warm fingers about me. Whatever had I been thinking?

SINCE BLACK IS something, it cannot, therefore, also be nothing, and so, with that easy and logical assumption of mutual exclusivity, I find I awaken not from nothing but from something extant within my unconscious perceptions. It hangs about the lighter darkness of my newfound estate. In the room no light exists other than that leaking through the door to Lenard's kitchen. The sound of someone's pacing slips dimly along and past its dying presence. The Mook must have returned.

Perhaps it was an unremembered start or just a catch of breath, but Mook has heard, and his shadow precedes his form into my space. As that form grows into someone decidedly not any sort of Lenard, the shadow flattens into the dark floor. Backlit like one of Mitch's starlets, a female figure glides toward me across the space where her shade lies. I swear she is naked. Except that is for some sort or other of vest inked upon her torso. She is coming for me, and despite the rigidity of my awakened sex, I wilt back in fear. This sort of thing does not happen. Not to me anyway.

She is the darkness to my mother's light. I am about to be subsumed. No hope for deliverance. Except Lenard.

"Fear not, my son," a gentle voice whispers. "I have not come to harm you."

These momentarily comforting words are followed by great gusts of nearly inaudible laughter and a tight little pirouette more that of a Bruce Lee than some twenty-first century incarnation of Anna Pavlova. "I've come to fuck you," Brucette crows.

I knew it. I'm about to get.... You get it.

SEX WITH ANYONE while alone with one's self is always far more adventuresome, kinky if you will, and deep-down satisfying than it ever can be with the too-much other any other partner may turn out to be. Even Paloma in the flesh would fall far short of the little dove in my imagination. I create the Paloma I spend my biological essence into while someone else is responsible for the one I find so pedestrian even as she sits, slim calves twined about each other, before us during sessions. I unwind those defenders of her virtue until her smooth thighs open in welcome, the dark cavern of her vagina glistening through her fluent labia....

"Cut the shit," the shadow snarls, and a physical being of actual mass and human structure climbs aboard my helpless form. My boxers have disappeared, and a most actual vagina is slurping my penis up into its greedy maw. My awareness follows. I think I have been sucked into some event and removed forever from the comforts of Lenard's home.

Within a sack as black as a Melanomic womb, I twist forever backside-to, upside down, and inside out. A push, a shove, a contraction within the fundus of she who has pirated my being, within the impossible uterus of my own self-creation propels me down a chute, up into a cosmos devoid of stars out into the darkness of my borrowed room.

"Hey, Speedy Gonzales," the dark one exclaims. "I think you're my fastest yet. When's the last time you got any? Huh?"

Her face is shadow, her mouth her teeth darkness within that lightless place wherever it is she dwells. Then she smiles. Great white teeth, feline lips, a Cheshire....

"Really," the thing mocks. "Alice in Wonderland's the best you can do? Anne Rice or Stephen King, maybe. Fucking Dodgson? He was clever, I'll admit, but on a very adolescent scale. He wrote some unforgettable characters and situations, but, without the addition of a psychedelic perspective such as the *Airplane's,* it's all a bunch of schoolgirl drivel."

"I forget. You, Mr. psychotropic, psychedelic, and just plain psycho, you just might find yourself having fallen down the same rabbit hole. I hope not. I like to think of the hole I just sent you through as more to the wormy side of things.

"Get what I mean? Oh, fuck.... Of course you don't. Just commeer an' I'll do you a bit more conventionally."

She mocks me. I am in my late sixties, and, hot as the little succubus might be, I am fortunate to have performed even the once. Her lips whisper contradiction. Soft breath, warm labial flesh, and a teasing tickle of fingertips. Eureka! She has awakened the dead. I would gasp in wonder were not those saltine lips already smothering my cry, her lower parts once again descending upon me. *Hallelujah,* I would shout were not my throat already filled with tongue.

I may die, and should that be her desire, I shall comply. Willingly. Gratefully.

Such is not to be. Her tongue returns to its proper station, her lips free my own, and the heavenly creature speaks. Her hair falls black from back about her face and brushes my cheeks with locks of flame. Her voice crackles between us, electric in the air.

"Roll me over," she grates. "I'm fucking tired of being the aggressor. Roll me over and fuck me old man until I beg you to stop. Then fuck me some more."

I do not believe that even at eighteen I could have performed the acts I manage that early morning. I must admit, I can be magnificent. I fail, however, to elicit the response she has requested and which I devotedly seek to produce. Never once does she beg me to stop.

Eventually, each of us sated in the particular and peculiar ways our current genders most enjoy, we drift apart. The shadow slips from beneath me and rematerializes on a shared pillow. Without conversation or, at least on my part, volition, we waft our individual ways into another place, one to which I have never before journeyed, and, despite our separate conveyances and incidentals of departure, she, her name I know to be Pam, fully clothed and no-longer a bottom, stands beside me as we observe the sleeping form of someone who might be female, whom I might have encountered somewhere previously in that other light we consider immediate reality.

With a gesture I cannot see but follow to its objective, Pam pronounces. "She is Ruthie. Or Lottie. You will honor her preference even should it shift often and indiscriminately," at which point she laughs. "Shit, dude, I think I'm startin' to talk like you. What in hell'd you do to me back there anyway?"

Without affording me opportunity to respond, the succubus bulls on, "She's a special project of mine. Thanks to my old lady."

Before any two or more fragments of thought might join themselves together and metamorphose into speech, or even manifest themselves as a brief gulp of surprise, she interrupts.

"Relax, Ace, I'm nothing at all like you think. OK, I prefer women, but I bet I'm still the best piece of ass you've ever had. Or ever will have. I'm bi, asshole, and you're one lucky heterosexual son of a something or other to have gone where you've just been. And to go where you're about to go. So keep your thoughts to yourself or I might hafta change my mind about includin' you in on this."

I have no doubt that she possesses the ability to intuit my innermost processes, but neither have I any concern that I stand in danger of being replaced in whatever role she thinks she has created for me in her drama. I have no need to be employed in any fashion by any one. I receive a disability check every month from the VA which buys me food, drugs, and alcohol. That is until now. Now Lenard claims three-hundred of my paltry five-hundred and seventy-seven. Goddamn good thing I no longer smoke. Strange as everything is turning out to be, I probably should give this thing a chance. If I get free from Lenard, I might actually be doing better than I have in a long time.

Lead on Pammie.

"Don't call me that," she hisses. "Just shut up and listen."

I told you, she is able to read my mind.

Without the experience of transition of any sort, not from place to place or sleep to waking, we return to my mattress, Pam's pheromones hinting at something I am certain to find impossible, she buries her face in my armpit. Licks the sweat from my....

Jumping Jesus H. Christ Almighty! I gotta get outta here. Jesus F'n Christ!

Another shadow slouches along the kitchen's pathway of light. A most menacing form is soon to follow. I fucking forgot about Lenard. There is no doubt; this Pamela chick is the one who has been occupying his attention of late. Jesus, she came out of the same room naked. She's Lenard's woman. I am most righteously fucked.

I might be able to make the door, but I cannot untangle myself. We have become inseparable, and with the approaching danger comes further insanity. I am growing hard again.

"Don't mind him," the lunatic assures me. "He's not even aware we're here. Call it somnambulism as you probably will. To me it's just Lenny sleepwalking again."

I cannot contain my trembling, but the threat passes into another room, Lenard's private sanctuary, and Pam takes my hunger between her thighs. "You've made me too sore for anything else, buster," she laughs. "Try to be quick will you. We still need to talk."

Were I a trembling fourteen-year-old, I could have been no quicker. Pam laughs too loud for my comfort as she wipes herself with my sheet. "Better get this to the laundry before Lenny gets wind of it. Wouldn't want him suspecting things now would we?"

Lenard does in fact discover my forgotten ejaculate, but, as one might assume, only surmises that I have been amusing myself. Is not innocence invincibly dense?

Upon completion of her most unsanitary task, the witchy woman speaks of things to come. I can hear, can listen. Only later do I realize that I do not understand.

"The girl we just visited is more lost than you can imagine. More than you even. As I said, her name is Ruth and Lottie. She has nowhere to go but death. You, my former lover, will be her companion."

How can I not object? No matter how brilliant sex with this Pamela might have been, no sex any time with anyone is worth dying for. I think I shall simply turn....

"You'll do nothing of the sort, Arthur. You're gonna listen and listen good. Lenny told me about you. He knew I was lookin' for somebody to help out with Ruthie, and he tracked you down. Why in hell else would a guy like him bother with a loser like you?"

I am pissed. "He knew my brother," I counter. "In Vietnam."

"What does that mean exactly? Lots of guys knew your brother. How many've come looking for you. As a matter of fact, where's shithead Mitch been the last couple of years? Face it Artie."

"No one calls...."

"Shut the hell up, Artie, and hear me out. The others in your so-called life have moved on. Even Mitchell. You've not just stayed behind, but have proven yourself incorrigible. You're in and out of programs like they were revolving doors. You got no friends. Except Lenard. The idiot tells me he's grown fond of you.

"Don't think it!

"You're full of high sentence and empty of substance. OK, I gotta admit, you've rubbed off on me some. But I tell you, it won't last with me either. Anywho, to make matters impossible, you're a liar. Of the worst kind. You lie to yourself every bit as much as you do to those you feel so superior to. And you're a user of people as well as drugs. In a word, Artie. Pathetic."

Unaccustomed as I am to such abuse, I find myself frozen. Unwillingly so. No pretense even at *fybrodysplasia* of the *ossificiant* complexion. The *Naiade* has stolen my tongue, my breath, and, I fear, whatever might have been left of my soul. I will myself to move. Am unable. I will myself to breathe. I am still. Yet I suffer no symptoms of.... Could that be it? Has death, perhaps exclusively from the deceased's perspective, no symptoms? Shall I lie immobile watching myself decay? At least until the coffin is closed and the earth laid upon me?

"Exactly," the evil one chortles. "What in all the hell do you think you've been doing these last fifty years? Your mother did her best; she brought you from dark to light. Her love gave you a new life, but you, you pathetic little fool, chose death all over again. Hair didn't do it. Kenneth had no hand in it either."

She has no knowledge of me. How could...? Lenard! He must have told her all. The two of them conspiring against me. Why?

"You're only part right, Artie boy."

I hate her.

"Can it, imbecile. I might just be tempted to find somebody else for the job. You're damn near perfect for it, but there's other trout in the Hudson. All I gotta do is look. Anyway, I don't have all decade or even half of that. So, keep your thoughts to yourself unless I ask for 'em, and follow me."

THERE IS NO following. One moment we are in the apartment and the next I find myself upon a rocky ledge overlooking some wasteland of global proportions. Hypos and a pink flip-flop lie scattered across the stone of my perch. I am all alone with no way either up or down. I can breathe. Am able to move. But there is nowhere to go.

Sputtering flares of something akin to burning magnesium sparkle bright tones about me, from within me. I am to be consumed. A halo of whiter, brighter, yellow, gold, and orange signifies my impending immolation. The witch, Pamela, has set the Man inside me free. I have evolved. I am the Man on Fire.

There is no pain. I do not oxidize away. No consummation awaits. I burn. I grow. I am the sun.

"Enough," a familiar voice intrudes. "I can take it from here."

"Mind if I watch?" This voice is Pam. Her significance, anymore, is negligible.

The new voice is familiar, but I simply am unable to focus enough to place it. My consciousness spatters about me in jubilant bands of flame. I have become too large, have become one with the cosmos, have....

The entire illusion, yes illusion, collapses upon the dead stick of myself. I stand charred and cold.

"OK," the new one answers. Just don't interfere. These things can be delicate. By the way, thank you for cooling the pyrotechnics."

"Yeah," is all Pam replies.

Something is inside of me. It is other than I and yet is I. I am possessed. I far prefer the Man on Fire to this. This infestation — parasitical presence — has not completely erased me, but has made of my singularity a duality. Some psychic tapeworm curls about my cerebral cortex and fires its messages into my consciousness.

"Relax," the well-modulated and professional voice of Paloma admonishes. "I'm just visiting. I'll leave you to your own devices far sooner than you might wish. First, however, we must talk."

If perhaps I have begun to accept these incredible conditions as real, I am now disabused of that notion. Paloma inside me. The Man on Fire. Marathon sex. Hallucinations. I shall wake soon from this opium dream, emerge from my Asian den enlightened and amused. For the present, I shall entertain the vision of my little dove as she sat directly opposed to me in the round little circle of my first-ever group session. Her attire screamed *Professional,* a black dress of the type called sheath. Oh, God, and what a well-honed piece of cutlery that garment cradled. Black it glistened, aristocratic fabrics soft in the candlelight glow of her outer office. Her black hair hung to her pale shoulders, and a simple silver chain suspended something precious into the darkness between her breasts. Her legs were folded under her. She wore stockings I am certain, and one black sandal lay abandoned upon the carpet while the other swung most fetchingly from her toes. I think I might have blacked out. I remember nothing else. But, *ei chihuahua* and hot-hot *chili* peppers, I was forever hooked.

And now? If Paloma is inside of me, is not turnabout fair play? Pam can....

"Your time with Pam," my little dove chides, "was designed to remove such images from your mind, to free your thoughts for communication of another kind."

Their stratagem does appear to have been effective. I am actually more than a bit sore, and Pinocchio has become mere flesh and too-little blood. I suppose I might be able to just listen. At least for a time.

Paloma's communication begins on a mellifluous note. Her voice softens and caresses whatever my internal auditory sensitivity might be.

What can be her purpose? Her words amount to nothing more than a sad farewell or as she states, *adieu.* I am not left with Pam either. She has disappeared no doubt for more hospitable environs. Alone, I face the desert outside and an emptiness within. Along with them they have absconded with the elusive awareness some might choose to term "self-concept." I have read and casually debated the probability of the existence of said psychological construct and find myself coming down on the side of those who claim that consciousness does indeed exist outside of the biological nature of human beings and thus, when one observes his image in a mirror or his behavior in the plane of existence we term reality, he is in actuality observing not himself but rather a separate entity altogether in much the same manner an amputee might view his prosthesis. Therefore, I suppose Paloma could not have stolen my concept of my physicality away since I am able to observe my hand, and neither could she have purloined my conscious self. I think; also I am yet a part of my biological modality. She has robbed me of something else. I observe, I feel, I am aware of an absence. I have no idea what is missing.

She reappears. A small jet as from the behind of a cartoon rocket announcing her presence. She wavers in no female or avian form I recognize. She has become adjunct to Buzz Lightyear or some other crass appeal to childhood's penchant for credulity. Alighting upon her own invisible ledge above the void once the missing element of myself, she speaks, her voice as rough and dry as the wind from the dunes. "Your soul, you poor sad fool. I have taken a piece of your soul."

She has.

I am bereft.

"Cut the drama," she sneers, "and get your sorry behind into this," at which point the cartoon jet explodes into a fusion reaction rivaling a nova of greater than super magnitude. I am unharmed. Indeed I find myself alive within a corona of the first order and observing my novel circumstances much as must any human animal observing his own body and actions while speculating about the nature of same. I am a star.

No longer a mere man **on** fire, I have become the Man **OF** Fire. Accidents and substance need not be separate estates, despite the most unholy ravings of the magisterial imperium in Rome, and neither am I any longer both observer and observed. I am one. In the flawless illumination of myself I perceive that I am who am. I am I, *nee* Arthur William Woolf. I am light and life, the undying flame of all eternity....

"I knew it. I knew it'd end like this. That he'd go too, pardon my Sanskrit, fucking far. The asshole thinks he's God."

I am about to dismiss the dreary little whore with a waggle of my blazing central digit when the cultured alto of Paloma intrudes. "So he always has."

To which the suck-breath replies, "Then why'd you let Lenard pick him for something as delicate as helping Ruthie. She needs love and comfort, not the posturing of some freakazoid about to turn Schizophrenic. Her mother and sister'd be a whole lot better at keeping her comfortable. Odd as they might be, they do love her. In their own way."

"They would be unwilling, and, indeed, would be emotionally incapable, of providing the life she needs until her time. They would smother her with imagined kindness and torment her with incessant care. As well, Pamela, and I know that you know this to be true, only someone such as the ball of fire, or whatever it is he likes to imagine himself, will be able to provide for her the death she needs."

I might be tempted to intrude at this point. These two birdbrained witches have no business interfering with my autonomy as a human being endowed by God Himself with certain unalienable rights.... Or is that "in"? However, I find myself intrigued. Paloma most certainly, in this situation at least, has transcended her cooing support-pigeon role in the greater script of my life's dramatic unfolding. I have become the Man Of Fire directly as a result of her most irregular intervention. No doubt, if I remain silent, I shall learn more. Thus do I dampen the internal flames of my resentment as well as the external manifestations of my conflagrant nature. For a time I shall conceal my light beneath a bushel of my own creation. I am become a dark corner who hears that which it wants to hear.

I do hear. My flame burns low to the point of extinguishment.

"HE BELIEVES HE is fire, and in a most essential way he is correct," Paloma explains to a Pamela only she can apprehend. "Fire will become the closing statement of his existence. Our Arthur is destined to become that which he has imagined himself to be, that which his Hair never was, and that which he once hoped to create of Kenneth.

"For the present, as he huddles in his little nook listening in on adult conversations, this boy, despite his illusions to the contrary, is to become more like a drop of water. One all surface-tensioned into an individual unit until it is slid up next to another much like itself. Observe it on your kitchen counter...well, Mary Elizabeth's maybe. Anyway, as one drop approaches the other, they both become agitated, yearn for unity. Then, all at once. Blip! They are joined. Have become one, a single drop of water born of two. That, Pam, is the necessary union of this sad clown and the most tragic Ruth. Until now their lives have been nothing more than pathetic Harlequinades. My role is, through the melding of two lost souls, to create more than the mere illusion of transcendence. Each will die happy. Neither will die alone. One will die in peace in her lover's arms. The other, more than ever he has ever been, a falling star for all the world to see."

What the fuck? My natural supercilious attitude, my linguistic facility desert me. What the fuck?

"Sounds a bit like you, don't you think?" Paloma remarks. "I'd say it's time we sent him on home."

She is laughing at me, and I have no response. Fuck her.

The Dove continues. "Stay out of the way when that happens. I have one more chore after he wakes up. He has to be alone. You'd just mess it all up. You'll see what I mean when it happens."

"I hear you," I yell as the gloom around me begins to glow, and light supplants darkness. I open my eyes. Smell smoke. Over against the far wall, bright red against its bile green, a trash basket burns cheerily, filling the room with the odor of conflagration. I smell a burning Kotex. I swear it. There is blood, fresh blood, boiling up and shouting its presence across the streaked floor.

What the fuck! The bitch planning to fight fire with fire? Mine is stronger than some trashcan can produce. Maybe, I should just let it go. For certain I don't feel threatened. That is until the goddamn thing speaks, its voice spitting sanguineous tones about the fluttering room.

"You have been changed. Forever," the thing pronounces. "Witness your own reactions, your newly acquired ability to care, as well as the alteration of your language, both that of your tongue and your mind. You have not become the man of fire you imagine. Neither are you the man on fire. You will someday become both, but for now, this present and the next few months, you are to become one of those beings you have so often scorned.

We, both Pam and I, are mere agents for a power greater than any of us. Yes, A Higher Power. Notice, Arthur, you are neither laughing nor feeling any impulse to do so. Neither are you scornful. Again lacking impulse. You have become that which you never wanted to be. As a result, you will be afforded both the pleasure of actual humanity and the grace of God. With Lenard's help, you will seek out the woman we have shown you. Her name is Ruth although you...."

"I know," I interject, my vocabulary not completely debased. "Pam told me."

"Of course. I forgot. Sorry. Anyway, Pam has her own reasons for championing that one's cause, and I have been charged by your Higher Power with seeing you both through the proverbial shadow valley and onto a precipice from which point you will decide upon the course of your further existence. You will do this together. On your own. Oxymoronic as that may be."

Damn it. "Oxymoronic?" I failed to see it until she pointed it out. Damn it. I wouldn't like the new me if I were still the old me. Maybe....

"Quiet, Arthur. I'm in danger of burning out before I'm finished. Just listen."

Nowhere am I able to discern the slightest hint of derision within myself. Sometimes listening is the best course.

"So anyway, for a time, we have taken from you, that which is not but which you might believe to be your soul, and to some extent you would be correct, since your autonomy is the essence of your actuality, and that is what we have removed. You are fated, Arthur. You have no choice. You are to fulfill the purposes of a will far greater than you can imagine. That will will eventually become your own. Our brother, is said to have quipped freely, 'Thy will, not mine, be done.' Don't believe it. By that time he had no freedom left him. His will had already been subsumed, his choices exhausted. Lucky you. Your end is in no way so gruesome. In fact, only those who are too blind to see the truth beyond the end of their snub little noses could think so.

"As did Jesus, you both will make your final choice convinced of the reality of the illusion. However you fly, it will be good.

"I leave you now in Lenard's care.

By the way... I want no more of your fantastic imaginings. I would burn you up and spit you out nothing but a cinder smudge on the pillow. That's why I sent Pam to you first.

"Remember. Fair warning."

At this point Lenard emerges from his room stretching toward the new day. There is no fire. There never was.

Smitty and Mary Margaret
1999

1999 MIGHT HAVE been called a watershed year for the two former sisters of avowed Mercy had the weather those July days in Rome, NY been as washed out as once upon another two festivals in Bethel and Saugerties had been the case. However, the sun was blistering, the wind a mislocated Simoon, the vibes dry as a cicada's song. Topping it all off, the cluster cluck had ended in violence. "Police riot," Smitty pronounced.

Mary Margaret was not so sure. Anyway, their struggling little '90 Lumina and the black rust, borrowed landscaper's trailer were safely ensconced in a nice long truck-space outside the Travel Plaza toward which the two discouraged ministers to the deliberately needy slumped in their tired shoes. The weekend had been a true Hell. Or as close as one might imagine that impossible place to be. If only it were possible to get a drink along Dewey's asphalt ditch. "We could exit, and then get back on," Mary Margaret had offered from behind the shimmying wheel. But that would be impractical. A diet soda would have to do.

Given the estimated two-hundred thousand or so homeward bound revelers just west of the plaza, Smitty would have been surprised by the lack of any crowd in the plaza, were it not for the fact that the highway also resembled its usual sleepy central New York Sunday self much more than she would have expected. Whatever, she was pleased to be removed from anything resembling the maddened crowd within which she had so recently been forced to operate. For Jesus' holy sake, they hadn't even had time to set up before the casualties began to flow. "Gush," was Mary Margaret's take. Girls and boys, ladies and far from gentle men had come tumbling in before one bit of music, even a warm-up rehearsal, had begun. The lunatics had arrived in no condition for anything except maybe a long nap, a frantic trip to the local ER. Or death. Don Henley's title track, "The End of the Innocence," had been most prophetic. As well as itself innocent. Naive.

A favorite song of hers, from her own so clueless time, while she still thought of herself as sister, "Where Have All the Flowers Gone?" hummed through her mind, its words mixed into incoherent yet pleasant memory. She knew. The flowers had died with Tara as had the music died this very weekend. Not in some Mr. Clean nineteen fifties' lament, but in smoke and violence and chaos. The best she and Mary Margaret would ever be able to do would be to salve the self-inflicted wounds of the new generation so many more than two-hundred miles removed from all that Woodstock had hoped to create.

The Two Sisters might save some of them from themselves, but, what would be the use? The cycle had been established. "Peace and Love" were words as irrelevant as any other of the slogans from a long past era blissfully forgotten by a world unwilling to see beyond its immediate needs. They might as well hang it up and join the crowd, focus on themselves, look out for number one, and, should all else fail, find their own mountaintop, possibly join an order of contemplatives and get to know their own and each other's navels on intimate terms.

Holy Mary mother of God, look down upon your namesake here beside me along this simple highway we travel and marvel at her wonton abandon. As Smitty picked through the GMO greenery in her salad bowl, setting aside steroidal plum tomatoes, counting the six slivers of onion, two cucumber slices, and three spotted black olives, the sounds of Mary Margaret's consumption joined the bitter *vinaigrette* in the acid swamp of her depression. Roy Rogers had been unable to act or sing with anything resembling even minimal accomplishment. Neither could this eponymous eatery offer anything resembling nourishment. Her salad was a disgrace, and her friend's mess was disgusting. She had ordered a burger, not a simple hamburger and bun, not even a cheeseburger and fries. The thing was huge with dribbly lettuce, nearly liquid tomatoes, a redolent pickle or two, all topped off with Mayo. The thing had to be as lethal. Yet she slurped, chewed and slobbered it all down with such gusto as would indicate something akin to starvation.

The second she finished, licking the last stray trickle of obscene mayonnaise from the corner of her mouth, she cheerily hopped up and had slipped half way across the room before turning and asking, "How about you, Smitty? Want anything? Another Sprite maybe?"

Smitty shook her head and returned her eyes to the salad she could not help but eat.

The ride home she knew would be long and silent. Mary Margaret had the annoying habit of sleeping many things away, among them her moments of substance and alcohol abuse but also her piggish overeating. Smitty would be left to drive the horrid contraption all the way along the creepy nighttime streets of South Troy, past the menacing wire of the jail, and into the broken tarmac of their garage and equipment warehouse. She would be left to unlock the gate around their property, open the reluctant doors, and navigate their rig into the dark cavern. Only then would her spoiled little sister awaken.

Words of less than amicable tonality formed in her mind, sounded pure in her ear, rose with her refreshened breath. "I think," she leveled directly into the other's glittery eyes, "that we need to get something straight. I am not capable of driving us all the way home. You know that."

"So?" Mary acted surprised. Even nonplussed? "Who's asking you to?" The last accompanied by a small dribble of some dead hopper juice down her chin. All communication halted while she wiped her chin, and Smitty could see that as far as her friend was concerned no more need for discussion existed.

She would not let it happen. "I know you," she croaked. "You're tired...We both are. On top of that, you've over indulged yourself in this food. All you're going to be good for is falling asleep. I can't have you driving like that. You could kill us both."

"So then you drive. I don't care."

In all her days Smitty had never met anyone as impossible as this one. In some fashion, Mary Margaret, who was happily munching at a tangle of cheese fries, had allowed her to turn the argument back upon herself.

That was not about to happen. "I told you," Smitty pronounced as she would to a deliberately obdurate student, "I cannot do that. I am as tired as you are, and, my driving skills are poor even when I am at my best. P-perhaps we should get off the Thruway and take a room. Preferably one with a big tub, maybe even a spa."

Always too quick for at least Smitty's own good, Mary Margaret leapt upon the notion. "Well OK. We'll do it. Two king beds if possible. And cable TV. Oh, yeah, a bar."

So it was that they exited the interstate, found a nice room with a Philips flat-screen TV, two double beds and a large but standard tub. As Mary Margaret had deemed necessary, the motel also boasted a most upscale — by central New York standards — bar, and Smitty's pique was soon washed away by two fine glasses of pink Chablis. Mary Margaret ventured more audaciously into the smoky land of Scotland and its aged spirit of Glenlivet. As anyone might expect, any chill between the two women warmed, and the evening slipped most pleasantly away into a soft July fog of comfort and most easeful fatigue.

Morning found them fully clad atop their respective beds, the bedstand clock reading 10:37. A sound from somewhere outside, a lawn mower. Traffic. A sound from inside. What might it be? Unrecognized music of some horrid sort jangled into their retreat. What?

"Damn," spouted from Mary's side of the room. "Goddamn phone. Where is it?" At that point she lurched to her feet and stumbled to the table near the foot of her bed where she reached the thing just as the caller must have hung up. Not without resources, however, Mary tapped a few buttons and peered into the gadget's memory. "Oh, My God," she exclaimed. "Guess who that was."

Smitty had no idea, and was in no mood for games. Her head hurt and trouble was beginning to rumble about her insides. "Why don't you tell me?" she answered. "I've got to use the ladies' room."

"Remember Amilee?" Mary Margaret beamed.

Another question. Was the little monster being deliberately annoying? Smitty squirmed, shot a poison dart her friend's way, and turned toward the bathroom without replying.

"She wants us to meet her downstate. Port Chester."

Smitty closed the door upon her words. Some things are more important than memories of fairytale princesses. Even if they are as real as the Divine Miss A. Just in time her pants were down and so was she. Water moves according to its own pact with various gravities, and Smitty's proved no exception. She just made it. It felt so good,

From outside came a timid rap. "Did you hear what I said?" Mary's muffled voice asked.

By that time Smitty was washing her hands and heard only a jumble of incoherent sounds. "I'll be out in a minute," she called. "You can tell me then."

The minute became fifteen, the quick washup a shower, and by the time Smitty returned to the main room, the only words awaiting her were neatly penned upon a pale piece of hotel stationery.

I must go. Couldn't wait. My grandfather's in the hospital. I've called a cab. The keys are on the dresser.

Ps. Call Amilee back. Here's her number. (323) 661-5464.

PPs. I'll call you later on.

The note was signed with Mary Margaret's elaborate triple-M signature.

After checking out and once more on her way home, Smitty chased anxiety away by assuring herself that Mary's grandfather's hospitalization was undoubtedly just a routine precaution such as are often taken for old men. As a former nun would, she said a series of Hail Marys, prayed to Jesus for healing, and with forty some miles to go decided to make the call to Amilee.

Marry Margaret

Sometimes a sullen redneck jerk of a driver can be a blessing, especially if a girl needs time alone to think things out. Grandpa Ned had been her salvation, had found her leaving the convent to be understandable, had insisted that her uncle Mike pass the bail business on to her, and had even staked her to seed money for her other ventures such as the issuing of non-traditional loans. Added to that, whenever possible he bragged about her Psychology degree as well as her being the Goddamn best perfesser at the little community college which, he never failed to assert, was unworthy of her brilliance. More than anything else, Mary Margaret, orphaned as a young girl, knew he loved her beyond reason as might a father. As would a daughter, she loved him back.

Grandpa was Irish and emotionally reticent as were most of the men who comprised his crew, as she liked to call them when he could not hear. To him they were friends, some even brothers. "We're a family," he would insist. "Even your mother's brother in law, Mangold the Jew. Blood's blood, but brotherhood's a hell of a lot more than that." The former nun could not disagree despite having misgivings about Grandpa's all-male perspective. Could not women in that particular sense be brothers too? Grandpa would never admit the term fellowship into his world view, however, and so Mary felt herself blessedly unique. Grandpa did think of her as something more than "just a girl." He loved her with all his heart. Also, she was fully aware, he respected her every bit as much as he did his own son. *God, don't let him die before I get there.*

Thank God, he hadn't. In fact, more than a minor spike of current pulsed in his snow-blue eyes when she bent over his eroded face. "Mary," was all he said past the tubes crowding down his throat.

Mary smiled. her Madonna's smile. "Papa," she replied. It was done.

MARY MARGARET WAS tasked with the arrangements. Mike uncharacteristically lost himself in a great deal of Irish Whisky and leftover Hydrocodone from his knee surgery. His response to all questions was, "Ask Mary."

Mary found herself not only willing, merely equal to the task, but, if she had to say so herself, which she didn't, outstanding. Thus it came to pass that Wednesday morning the little group of family and crew members, including a pale and trembling Michael, gathered around Ned's grave to bid him farewell. Mary Margaret had the final words to say.

The priest stood aside as she took her place at the head of the flower bare coffin. "We do not come to bury Edward Ryan," she asserted. "Nor do we come to praise him." No one got the allusion, but Mary felt its strength anyway. She knew. That was all that mattered. "I insist that you recognize that we are not gathered here to say farewell to my Papa. Grandpa Ned is not in this coffin.

He is in my heart. In my memory. Uncle Mike...and all of you. In your hearts too.

"I do not come to put you in the ground. You are not dead. My sweet grandpa, you will live forever."

Brushing aside a tear, she moved closer to the casket and placed a trembling hand above the spot where his head might have been. "I have a poem. Short, I promise. I would like to recite it now. I am no poet. It is no doubt flawed, but I call it *Papa* and I make no apologies."

Again a tear. A wipe. The requisite clearing of her throat:

"Grandpa Ned, out in my memory
I still see your bright light shine
Always here you'll be with me
Through all the days of all my time.

"Amen," she added, although that had not been her original intent.

No tears followed. Instead from a hideous laurel carryall slumped on the ground beside her elegant patent heels she extracted a quart of Bushmills Irish Whisky, broke the seal, unscrewed the top, and took a hearty swallow before passing it off to Uncle Billy Mangold who took his own comfort and passed the chalice on.

It soon returned to her at which juncture Mary helped herself to another swallow and then in a most ceremonious fashion sprinkled the remnants upon the walnut bier. "As we Irish are wont to say," she intoned, 'May the road rise up to meet you, May the wind be at your back.' You will walk forever the fields of my memory. And upon the road we will still travel together, if I fall behind, I know you'll wait for me.

"And I will come to you."

With that, a disapproving priest sprinkled some holiness upon the Irish waters of life, and Mary Margaret fell into a hole deeper than the one from which her uncle was beginning to emerge.

OFTEN LOSS CREATES a need for replacement even when such is certain to prove inadequate. With such motivation Mary Margaret took herself across the ebbing Hudson and into the asphalt heat of State Street Albany. The temperature according to the bank clock/thermometer was 101 degree and the time 4:46, neither, by her own reckoning even close to accurate, Her radio told 90 even, and the time had just changed to 2:00 PM. Jack's would be nearly empty and she would be way ahead of any Early Birds. She might be able to sit at a bar table and have her lunch as well as a few drinks in the cool, mostly male atmosphere of soft green, glittering ice and the golden song of cold drawn ale. She would order a Guinness in honor of Grandpa Ned. A Harp too. This hump day as the DJ had called it was best kept Kosher, not as her father might have observed it, but in the Irish way: Stout drink and a Reuben. That was her in a shot glass, Kosher Irish, Catholic Jew. Thank the lord for such possibilities. We can be ever more than just one thing. We can go through both doorways at once. We actually are capable of being more than physical circumstances dictate. Our possibilities are infinite only our probabilities of quantifiable nature.

With that thought, Mary entered through the one available door, veered left into the bar, and shivered in the sudden chill of a first-rate air conditioning system.

A bartender clad in white shirt, black bow tie, and black trousers greeted her with a smile as she passed behind the two men at the bar and took a seat at a table about half way into the room. No sooner did she get herself arranged than the barman called politely over. "Sorry, mam, but there's no service at the tables. If you're thinking of something to eat, you'll have to order up here."

"I can do that," she responded. "Will someone bring it in to me?"

"Of course," came the smiling reply. "That'll be Susan's job."

"How about a menu then?" Mary inquired.

"Do you want bar food or are you looking for a meal?

"Just a drink and a Ruben sandwich. I don't need a menu."

"Coming up. What's to drink?"

The two pints foaming their bouquets into the crisp air, the man called over. "Sorry, but you'll have to come get them. Policy. Sorry."

Mary cared not a bit, but before she could stir herself, one of the seated men turned toward her. His hair was jet black, his skin tanned dark brown, and from the sleeves of his Izod emerged two firm and most ungodly buff arms.

"I'm Stephen," the divine one offered, setting the two drinks before her with something of a flourish. "Might I be so bold as to add these to my tab as well?"

As experientially inexperienced as a former nun might be expected to be, Mary Margaret nevertheless had the boundless lessons of television and motion pictures upon which to draw for appropriate responses in circumstances such as this. "Only if you...and your friend of course...will agree to join me," she smiled, allowing her words to originate from back in her throat.

Casting an exaggerated glance at the table setting, Stephen commented, "There seems to only be room for one more. How about you join us at the bar? That is if a lady such as yourself should find it acceptable."

"Lead on, Mac Whoeveryouare," Mary replied, gathering her purse and keys, leaving the potables to her new friend. Without complication all was accomplished and Mary Margaret found herself seated on a comfortable low-backed bar stool between the two exceptionally presentable men. Although one of them, Stephen she surmised, had used just a bit too much cologne, the arrangements were pleasant and the possibilities intriguing. These two seemed harmless enough, and this sad day might possibly end on a lighter note than she had imagined.

Of course nothing is ever exactly as one imagines nor is reality subject to the rules of humanity's favorite games. Stephen introduced her to his friend, Vincent, "Vinnie," Romaine and explained that they had just stopped in after a round of golf, "eschewing," as he put it, "the drab little nineteenth hole at the public course" for more sophisticated accommodations. "Besides," he joked, "Vinnie's wife never thinks to look for him here," at which point both men engaged in a second of tentative laughter.

"Anyway," Stephen continued, "how about you? If you will forgive the cliché, haven't I seen you somewhere before? Where are you from? Troy by any chance?"

Without a second's thought, Mary replied, "Not exactly. I live in Pond Hill, have an office in Cohoes. You haven't been arrested lately have you?"

Stephen appeared puzzled. "No. Why would it matter? I usually don't find myself subjected to a background check after maybe ten minutes of chit-chat."

Feeling a bit foolish, Mary Margaret hastened to explain. "No.... No. You misunderstand. I run a bail bonding operation for my.... For myself now, I guess. Anyway, I was just joking. You certainly in no manner remind me of my clientele."

Both men laughed heartily before cutting themselves short with samplings of their jiggling drinks. Feeling foolish and common, Mary followed suit with her Guinness. Each man had one drink, Scotch. Neat, no doubt, while she sat before two pints of ethnic banality. "I also teach part time at Hudson Valley," she blurted. "Psychology."

"That's it." I knew I had seen you before. I'm employed there too. English. Stephen Bruno?"

If Mary had seen him before, she would have remembered. She might have heard the name, but she wasn't certain. Anyway, best make the best of it, "Of course," she sang in her most sincere voice. "I know you too. From the Association Christmas party. Or was it the end of the year thing?"

"I would guess neither," Stephen frowned. "If I'd spied you at a party, especially one of those bashes, this would not be the first time we had spoken." His eyes left much to Mary's imagination.

Somewhere lost in a mist behind her, Vinnie laughed softly. Footsteps approached. Her Reuben. Just what she needed. Seated between two men of some finesse, she was not about to begin chomping and slopping on some greasy sandwich, forking fries into her mouth at every pause and gobbling a dill like some you know what. "I'm sorry," she apologized to the bartender. "Could you please wrap these? I seem to have lost my appetite."

"Of course," the man replied pleasantly enough but not without tossing a knowing glance at her two companions. What he, they, thought they knew, Mary Margaret could not say, but she would guess it was not merely judgmental. She could feel something off-color in her companion's subdued responses. For one of the few times since she had left the SSJ's Mary Mangold felt completely out of her league.

Retreat was her best option, but two not even half empty glasses waited accusingly before her, and the barman had not returned with her takeout. Well, she could lay the groundwork. Prepare for flight at the first acceptable moment.

Silence had dragged into embarrassment before Stephen spoke. "Is anything the matter?" he asked in a hesitant voice. "I mean...you haven't heard negative things about me at school or anything have you? I'm not the most beloved professor on campus. In fact...."

Mary could not help herself. She laughed, ruefully enough, she hoped, so as not to be offensive. "Not at all," she finally offered. My problem is that I'm sorry but.... Well, I've never even heard of you."

At that point Vinnie nearly snorted his drink all over her as well as himself. "Gotcha!"

Judging by that reaction and Stephen's drawn-up lips, Mary knew she had struck a chord, an unpleasant disharmony. "I'm sorry," she added. "I'm only on campus Wednesday and Thursday mornings. I don't even know most of the people in my own department. Sorry."

"Don't be," Vinnie laughed. Mr. Ego needs a good kick in the Id at times. Know what I mean?"

"Shut up, Vinnie," Stephen snapped. "You're not so terrific yourself."

"Please," Mary interrupted. "I didn't intend to cause any hard feelings. I'm just a little out of it today. I'm sorry. I just came from a funeral. My grandfather, and I'm a bit out of sorts. Sorry."

Both men, forever gentlemen, toned down all but their sympathetic notes and sang their empathetic songs for just long enough. In less time than it took to raise a fresh glass of Bushmills, Stephen's choice, to the departed, the air cleared. Mary felt the warmth of sunlight ribbon through the front windows, and she felt the fetters of grief slip from her shoulders. Her heart began to sing a fresh and hopeful song. She was alive. She would survive.

Her renewal was in no small way influenced by the spirits she had consumed, but in much greater magnitude was it enlivened by the presence of the beautiful man to her left. She began to experience an unfamiliar quickening of her pulse, a lightness of being. Despite the certain heaviness developing in a place so intimate as to be taboo, she was constrained, at least in her own mind, by her vow of chastity. No matter that she had already abandoned both poverty and obedience. The last thing she intended to become was some romance infected girl. Beautiful Stephen or no.

Nevertheless, she could not leave. Having finished her two Irish brews, Mary ordered a glass of Chardonnay and turned her attention to Vinnie. All she really needed was to refocus; everything would be fine. So things might have been, but for the beeping of her cell phone.

The call was urgent. A young man was in need of making bail. He had assaulted two cops, and the price for his release had been set high. Opportunity beckoned. She had no choice. Mary took a parting sip from her glass and hustled her unsatisfied self out the door.

TRACING LINES IN the spill from his drink upon the smooth bar top, Stephen turns to his companion, something akin to enlightenment aglow in the dim atmosphere. Vincent, who has, he would wager, caught a glimpse of something deep, bright, and secret up past Mary's knees, smiles a private smile. Stephen has for some time been entertaining a woodie of major proportions. Never has a woman so excited this readily excitable man, and Vin has followed his lead. His khaki golf pants have begun to grow full upon the stool. "I'd fuck that in a second," he mutters before his friend can say exactly the same thing.

"Me too," Stephen replies, and in some time longer than a second, he will. They order another round and drink in silence, each consumed by something each fully understands.

THE BAIL CONSULT had not gone well. The perp's family were never going to come up with the money, even if they cashed in everything they owned and mortgaged their house. The two parents were nice enough. Not nice enough, however, to warrant charity. Soft hearted as one part of her might be, Mary Margaret knew her business. Even as aid to the drunken and drug addled she remained separated from their distress and found her dispassionate approach an effective foil to Smitty's empathetic impulses.

As she reached into the bottom drawer of her cluttered desk for the bottle she kept to ease such empty moments back into more optimistic patterns, a sharp rap came upon the door followed by the burly figure of a man, hooded and ominous in the shadowed office. The intruder had all the marks of an alcoholic. His belly protruded its navel from beneath his bulged up tee, and, as she focused upon his darkened face, she recognized the signs of desperation. The loser dropped a delicate yellow gold band set with diamond chips in front of her.

"Yers fer fifty bucks," he slurred, his breath vomiting before him. That the piece was not his was obvious. Its origin was no business of hers, but fifty dollars was not to be.

"Maybe ten," Mary countered.

That he expected her to be intimidated by his attitude was apparent. The threat implied by his tone hung rancid in the air. Looming over her, his face in shadows, his eyes lifeless as they caught stray intrusions of sunlight leaking into the room despite the smothering brown curtains drawn against the scrutiny of the outside world, he croaked, "Gimmie the fifty. It's worth at least five hundred."

"I don't think so," she retorted, her eyes boring into the emptiness of his person.

"I said, gimmie the fifty. You ain't callin' me no liar are ya?"

A fleeting smile lit her face and kindled fire behind her guarded eyes. "I think I am," she said. "No! I take that back. I know I am."

He leaned across the piles of paper, knocking over an old Dunkin Donuts coffee container, soaking pages twenty-nine and thirty of *Notes From Underground* which lay open beside it. He would have reached for her, would possibly have throttled her had she not been quicker than he. The barrel of the thirty-eight, which she had lain in her lap undetected by her visitor, jabbed brutally into his slack jaw, breaking loose two of his twenty-one remaining teeth.

"God damn," he howled, faltering for just a second before once again turning to the attack, only to find her standing back too far to reach, leveling her pistol coolly at his dribbling mouth. She had never before pointed that thing at anyone, not even the mouse which shared her professional quarters. But this moron did not know that.

No fool he, just an alkie, he immediately became conciliatory. "Hey, let's start over, huh? I can deal. How about twenty-five?"

His smile made her think of Halloween. "How about you put the ring on my desk? How about you take those napkins and wipe up the coffee? Then how about you get your ass out of here?" she countered.

"Who the fuck do you...?"

The building was unoccupied except for her office, so she pulled the trigger. To her credit she hoped she wouldn't hit him. To her discredit she missed, punching a hole instead into the desktop thereby injuring him slightly with a splinter or two of finest MDF.

"What the fuck?" he exploded, and lunged for her, but there was a desk between them, and, instead of the satisfaction of feeling her throat between his hands, of tearing the bitch's pants off and fucking her up the ass before he strangled the fucking whore, he found himself beached like a stranded whale totally at her mercy.

Possibly the result of her gentlenun nature or maybe simply due to her amateur status at this game, Mary grimly ordered him out of her office, reminding him of something before he lumbered down the worn grey stairs, "If you don't know who I am," she tossed at him, "ask around. Ask about Ned and Mike Ryan. Then get the hell...get the fuck outta town, you piece of dog crap." Slamming her door on his mumbled response, she barely made her swivel chair before collapsing. Shaking, atremble with the after-effects of a first rate adrenaline rush, fighting the mounting need to void, to empty both bladder and colon, she dialed Mike and told him the story.

A week later both the T.U. and the *Record* carried a piece about the man found dead in the bathtub of his River Street, Troy apartment, apparent victim of an overdose of too-pure heroin.

Their beloved Keith James had never used heroin in his life claimed his family. He was a simple drunk.

In another three days, as his mother and non-alcoholic sister attended to the scattering of his ashes upon the languid Hudson from the Green Island Bridge, Mary Margaret's phone rang. In no mood for idle chatter, she almost allowed it to go to the answering service. As Fate — at times known as Pamela — would have it, however, Mary read the ID of the incoming caller and found herself unable not to pick up.

"Why, hello, Mr. Bruno. To what do I owe the honor?"

Smitty and Tricia

SMITTY HATED SOUTH Troy. The entire neighborhood, not just the narrow, ill-paved one-way streets. In order to get to their garage she was required to drive north on either Second or Fourth, recognize the right corner at which to make her left turn, cross to First, make another left, then make the right turn into the alley-sized, ironically named Main Street which shunted her to a desolate stretch of mixed up Macadam and stone, the completely bereft of all manufacturing East Industrial Parkway. Only then would she arrive at the double gates of their three acre lot complete with brownfield turf and the hold-over from the nineteenth century building Mary euphemistically called a garage. The walls of the surprisingly sturdy structure were ancient brick and had been topped by a new roof of some historically accurate nature. Inside, it bore the scars of the years when Troy made steel as well as shirt collars. Sometimes Smitty imagined she could hear off in the immense interior's far corners the faint clatter of metal upon metal mixed with the hiss and roar of whatever a blast furnace might have been. At present, all around was desolation. She was reminded of Dylan's song. East Industrial had surely become a Desolation Row.

As if by prearrangement, a large pickup truck raced its dust toward her from an impossible origin. The road dead-ended just a short straight distance beyond the property. The truck definitely had not been there as she drove in. Neither had anything passed by as she paused outside the drawn and secured gates. Black with something silver in streaks along its sides, the machine rumbled to a stop beside her, and the round red face of Jerry Llamellca smiled through a lowering window. "Thought I seen ya," he twerped. "Gimmie a sec an' I'll let ya in," at which point he slewed into a backward approach, halted just short of the chain-link, and dismounted.

The gates could be difficult, even for Mary Margaret. Not for Jerry. Kicking one back upon itself, he steered the other wide and beckoned Smitty to pull through. Once safely inside the enclosure she approached the double doors of the building, Again Jerry cleared the way, and in no time at all the rig was safely docked, the perishables, of which there were but a few, secured in the industrial sized "refrigeration unit," as both Jerry and Mary called it, and Smitty was free to pursue her own ends. That is if those ends involved arriving in Port Chester by one the following afternoon.

Home for Smitty was across the river in an upstairs flat in a secluded, dead ended section of Menands. Her back yard abutted the Albany Rural cemetery. Her landlord and downstairs neighbor, Emily Feinstein, kept the property properly groomed, the house well attended. Best of all, despite the proximity of the sometimes raucous I-787, it was quiet. She would not term it a pall exactly, but Albany Rural cast something about its environs which, if it were not exactly peace, was of similar nature. In no time at all, once home, Smitty slept.

She awoke to difficult circumstances. The day had faded into evening; her bedside alarm read 7:37. Since she had not set ahead whenever that spring time thing was, it was an hour later than that even. She would most certainly be awake half the night and, as a result, be worthless when she most needed to be otherwise. She probably should cancel with Amilee. To that end she dialed the number she had been given. It went to something called "Voicemail," and, intimidated by the unfamiliar, Smitty hung up. Whatever was she going to do?

With the passing of time, shedding its veil of illusion, the day's light assumed the guise of darkness and Smitty passed from confusion into desperate certainty. A person need not sleep exclusively during appointed hours of any sort. The night was warm, the hillocks of the cemetery alive within the moon's fulsome grace. Her mind awoke to possibility and eventually certainty. She would drive into the haloed nighttime. There would be minimal traffic, even in Westchester County. She would book a room near by her meeting place, Amilee called it the Texas Lunch, but cautioned, like everything else in her favorite little town, hard times had come and much had changed. "I think it's called Hubba Hubba's or something," she had complained, "but it's on North Main. Whatever it's called now, you can't miss it. If all else fails, ask anybody. It's famous. They'll get you there."

Amilee needn't have been concerned. Smitty had driven through Port Chester on several occasions and had relatives in Stamford. The area held no mystery at all. Wouldn't you know, the sweet little deadhead would choose to meet at some hole in the wall dive rather than anything grand. So much like someone else might have been. If she....

No need for that. She'd take the Taconic and then cross over on 287 to 1. The trip would be a cool night breeze. She would arrive about two, rent a room, sleep until ten or even ten thirty, have a Starbucks, if she could find one, and easily meet her friend by one. It was a plan.

As plans go, it was simple, easily followed, and should have been successful, but does not always the ploughman happen along at the most inopportune times? The first leg of the journey went without a hitch. I-90 East to the Taconic and then a truckless, traffic-free glide south along the mountainsides deep into the forests of Putnam and Westchester. Or so it should have been.

The first jarring note was her being passed just five or so miles into the Parkway by a BMW or some similar vehicle all high beams and ninety miles an hour. Smitty had not been puttering along. She had been keeping her speed around seventy, sometimes allowing it to creep a bit faster, but Mr. Ego had shushed by her as though she had not even been moving. As always, the good sister shed a prayer for the one behind the wheel and for those his carelessness might endanger. About ten miles further along she saw the car again. This time attended by two police cruisers strobing their bloody alarm about the highway. Again, she uttered a brief prayer. She could never imagine what it must be like to find oneself in such a predicament. She hoped never to have to learn.

Another two miles and the simple plan assumed complexity. Two red eyes flashed on and off and on and off again and again from out a depression alongside the roadway. Upon the pavement a grey mist within the forest darkness waved into her headlamps. It was a human figure. A woman. Smitty slowed to a stop on the shoulder just past what appeared to be a car fallen well off the highway, and quickly the young woman was at her window. "Thank you," she gasped through the slit Smitty had allowed for guarded conversation. "Please, can you help me?"

The alcohol on her breath was overwhelming, and Smitty became aware of a slur in her speech. The little fool was way far gone. The Concert Angel knew all the signs. Another adolescent tragedy. Exactly what she needed to usher out this crazy twisted Monday. The little waif kept stumbling out into the road almost as if she were being repelled by two incompatible forces, one her own and one either Smitty's or the car's. Eventually another driver would happen by, and the police were just up the road. If Smitty did not act quickly, she feared the tiny thing would soon be facing the most dire of consequences, and she could not allow that to happen.

Zooming her window all the way down, the savior of all such lost souls, or at least as many as she might, called to the wavering figure. "Please, Miss, why don't you get in the car? It's not safe out there. We need to see what we can do about this."

"Who the hell are you?" the creature slurred as defiantly as such a one might be able. "You gonna get my car outta this ditch?"

No expert, Smitty was nonetheless fully aware that the girl's car was stuck in something more substantial than a mere ditch and that they were not about to miraculously extract it from its snare. "Please," she repeated. "Just get in, and we'll figure something out."

"Whatever," the girl tossed over her shoulder as she felt her way toward the rear of Smitty's vehicle and then dropped out of sight.

When, after a full minute or more, she did not reappear at the other side, Smitty lowered that window and, stretching across the console and other seat, extended her head to the outdoors and, seeing no one, called into the darkness. "Miss? Miss? Where have you gone?"

"Where the fuck am I?" came drifting up from somewhere below. "What...? What the fuck's happenin'?"

The signs obvious, Smitty scrunched herself over, opened the door, and nearly took her own step off the ledge of the roadway and into the same pit as had fallen the girl. "Thank you, God," the good onceanun breathed. "Thank you, Holy Mother." The best she could hope to do would be to guide the girl vocally. "Up here," she shouted down. "Can you hear my voice?"

"What the Hell? Where...?" answered back, at which point the figure of the lost one began to emerge from the depths like some cartoonish character Smitty had once been required to endure as a result of Mary Margaret's indiscriminate and often juvenile tastes in film. The young woman must have climbed up on her car's trunk or something, for the upper half of her torso soon loomed above the rim of the embankment. Further, as Smitty's eyes acclimated themselves to the moonlit chiaroscuro of the midnight hour, she was able to determine that the abyss into which the girl had fallen was no abyss at all. Instead, she had tumbled into a simple roadside ditch.

Scrambling as cautiously as one may scramble, Smitty reached out to the girl and soon succeeded in settling her into the passenger's seat of the car. Once settled herself, Smitty turned to her newfound charge and asked, "Can you tell me your name?"

"Tricia," the other replied and fell silent.

There was no time for extended go-rounds of question and reluctant answer, so Smitty started her engine, turned to Tricia and announced. "If anyone comes along...and I saw two police cars a mile back, you could be in very serious trouble. So...."

Tricia mumbled and allowed her chin to droop to her chest, her shoulders to slump bony wings forward.

Smitty continued without further pause. "So what I'm going to do is, as they say, get us the heck out of here. I'll find a safe and comfortable place. You could use some coffee... and so could I. Then, when you've had a moment or two we can talk things over. See what it is we might do." With the last she swung her car into the travel lane, and the two strangers fled down the highway toward lights and possible rational action.

At the first exchange, Smitty exited the Parkway and with almost no thought to possible destinations drove east on route 217, soon finding them in the drawn-down town of Claverack. Nothing was open. No Dunkin Donuts even, and so the two fugitives pushed on, Smitty's mind ablaze with the possible consequences of what she had just done, Tricia apparently slipping to and from consciousness or at least rational awareness.

Eventually they arrived at the approaches to the city of Hudson, yet nothing at all offered itself as a possible way station. So Smitty continued on until she found them approaching the Rip Van Winkle Bridge, at which point a plan began to form. She would cross and by so doing lessen the risk of their being associated with the Parkway mishap; she would take the Thruway north toward home, pull into the first service area, find a secluded corner, and decide upon the best course of action. Not a perfect plan by any means, but a plan just the same.

An experienced traveler, Smitty had her car equipped with E-Z Pass and so tolls were no problem. Soon the two were headed toward Albany and home. Just a few miles into this leg of the journey they came to the New Baltimore service area which boasted a Roy Rogers and the offer of late-night privacy. Even were there a Trooper in attendance, Smitty knew the two of them would appear as generic mother and her over indulged daughter. She would order two coffees and things would work out as best such things might.

Tricia had regained a semblance of stability, there was no obvious police presence, and soon the daring duo was seated across from each other, the steam of coffee fragrant between them, the off-hours shadows most conducive to privacy. The girl was young, perhaps not even twenty, with a smear of broken acne across her left cheek. Her arms were thin and skeletal. Small breasts barely disturbed the fabric of her top, itself too white. But her lips, oh, her lips were soft and sad, wordlessly speaking of despair beyond a mere minor accident.

"What's the matter," Smitty asked. "Whatever has happened to you?"

"It's nothin'," Tricia mumbled into the coffee she had not yet attempted to drink. "I-it's just that nothin' ever works out. You know?" She lifted her eyes to Smitty's own, and sadness spoke in tones beyond a single voice. As if a tragedy such as Shakespeare might write were he alive at the present time could be contained in a pair of green eyes and expressed by their eloquent nullity, Tricia's gaze evoked the whole of Romeo, Juliette, Desdemona, Lear, Ophelia, and Macbeth without need of words written or spoken. No tears fell.

Smitty began to feel true pity for her little charge, and along with that arose an almost paralyzing fear for her safety. What could have happened to her?

Where had she been? Where was she heading? What could she, Smitty, do to avert the inevitable outcome of her situation?

Stumbling upon the possibilities within her trembling consciousness, Smitty was absolved of the responsibility of asking importunate questions, demanding unwilling response. Perhaps Smitty's own eyes told a story. Perhaps Tricia simply needed to vent. Whichever, the girl opened the gates and the full tale fell to her lips and into words.

The tale was so far beneath tragedy as to be comic, were it not so sad. Tricia was barely sixteen and already neither a sexual nor controlled substance innocent. "It's my mother's car," she blurted. "She's such a bitch...sorry. If it was up to her, I'd have no life at all. She chased my first boyfriend away. Just to get away from her, he joined the Army. Now he's going to Afghanistan or one of those places. I've had too much of all of it. I was just going down to Georgia where my cousin lives. It's Macon, Bacon, or something like that. Anyhow he's stationed down there. You know?"

Smitty was beginning to understand that she didn't know much of what she needed to know. "Sixteen?" she asked. "You're not even legal driving at night are you?"

"Who cares?" the girl wailed. "Who in the Hell except Fio ever gave a big messy shit? Even him? He hasn't written in more than two months. I found out about him being sent away by his trashy sister. I think my mom's stealin' his letters. You know, throwin' em away." With that the poor thing let escape a delicate belch and allowed her chin once more to sag and her eyes to slit almost shut.

Smitty needed more. "Don't go away just yet," she admonished. You say the car is your mother's?"

"Yeah," Tricia mumbled. "So?"

"Well then, maybe.... Just maybe, you're in the clear." Didn't she sound just like a TV detective though? "Does your mom know you had it?"

"I don't guess so. She was dead asleep when I left. I sure as hell didn't wake her up leavin'."

A sudden chill gripped Smitty. "Do you have a purse?"

"What? Why?"

"Well, if you did, it's probably still in the car and the police will find it."

"Not to worry" the girl smiled up from her cup. "I never carry one of them." Fumbling in her pockets she drew forth a cell phone, some assorted small bills, and a tissue. This is all I need. I did leave the rum behind, but I don't suppose that'll be any help to anybody. Even cops. Betcha mom'll just say somebody stole it. She's gonna be hopin' to get something outta it. It was kinda new and I think had all kinds of insurance. Mom's going to think she's won some kind of lottery or something." Once again her chin sunk, but no eructation accompanied the action.

They were in the clear. Almost joyously, Smitty shepherded her lost lamb back to the car and soon the two of them were on their way to Menands and the safety of Smitty's home. Further and necessary arrangements could wait until later in the morning.

"Thank you," Tricia whispered as Smitty settled her into the passenger's seat. However, almost immediately she freed herself from the shoulder harness, and, laying her sweet head on Smitty's welcoming shoulder, made the now moonless night glow with the soft illumination of a most chaste eroticism.

As anyone of Smitty's age and persuasion would know, even a ginger haired moon goddess can be a harsh mistress, especially when a lonely drive to the soft strains of Tchaikovsky' *Elegia Something* followed by more of the same Russian soul frees her mind from the shackles of ordinary time, her conscience from petty constraints, her consciousness from all worlds but those of the dreamer. As she prepared to turn onto her street from route 32, Smitty abandoned the new Bach just beginning to unfold from her stereo and fell into the profundity of "Not Fade Away." Humming to her own irregular beat, she obsessed over the lines especially Jerry's voice as clear in her head as was the love, the "for real love" in her heart.

Wakening Tricia for the trip into the house and up the stairs also woke Smitty from her moonshine daydream. At least for a time. Once inside, however, the world safely locked without her chamber door, the reality of love again filled her soul. The bleary little girl truly stank. Her sweat, indigestion, stale alcohol, and dried-up terror posed a most difficult barrier to anyone's hopes for physical intimacy, even of the most discrete and tentative nature. She could not help herself. "Would you like a shower?" the libidinous ex-nun inquired.

The little thing looked up into Smitty's brown eyes with her own so fragile green ones and smiled along with a tiny nod of acceptance. Having no shower as such, Smitty escorted her charge into the small but adequate bathroom. To the right of a narrow center aisle lay a tub of some plastic substance adorned with a curtain depicting the skyline of New York behind which lay the fixtures necessary for bathing as well as showering. Unwrapping her arm from around Tara's waist and fingering a white and blue towel draped over the tub's edge, Smitty offered, "I'll get you some fresh towels and a clean washcloth. The linen closet's in the hall. I'll be right back. OK?"

Without awaiting an answer, she hurried out the door and quickly secured the necessary accoutrements, including fresh bottles of conditioner, shampoo and body wash, as well as a new bar of Irish Spring. Upon her return, she found Tricia sitting back against the outside wall, one hand in her lap, the other dangling lifeless fingers onto the floor. Her eyes were closed, her lips slightly parted. "Are you all right?" Smitty blurted, dropping her burdens and hurrying to the girl's pathetic slump.

"I'm just too tired," Tricia murmured. "I don't have the energy to do anything. Even shower.... Even though...I know I need it."

Nothing if not resourceful, perhaps just a wee bit opportunistic, Smitty bustled the girl up into a disjointed state of erection and quickly, before she might reconsider, hustled the clothing from the girl's bone hard form. Before her in the dim light of the vanity lamps stood revealed a vulnerability such as Smitty had never before perceived. The skin of Tricia's shoulders was so pale as to allow the shadows of darker bone beneath to assert their fragile tracings upon its surface. Her ribs numbered themselves down her sides, and her nipples were blossomed pink flowers upon ripples of ivory flesh. Her hips were narrow as a boy's, her legs thin and trembling against Smitty's more substantial underpinnings. This wisp could weigh no more than eighty-five or maybe ninety pounds. She was no more than five feet tall—4'11" even.

It must have been impulse, for Smitty was no less surprised than Tricia when in a whirl of arms, legs, and feet the tiny girl was lifted and set secure within the vinyl tub with Smitty already at the controls. She would bathe the child. Make her clean and bright. Fold her into clean towels and eventually lay her down to sleep between the cool linens of her own queen bed. To that end, Smitty carefully drew warm and warmer water up around the little one's bottom, up between her spindle legs until her flat little belly was covered to the navel.

Not until Smitty had thoroughly and modestly scrubbed her, twice shampooed and conditioned her hair, did Tricia regain some life. As Smitty attempted to raise her up preparatory to lifting her from the tub, the girl laughed a rueful little laugh and scrambled out herself, in the process wetting her attending angel down the front of her not too damp blouse. Then Smitty saw for the first time past her fascinations. The sweet thing carried marks. Some the result of the accident, for certain. Not the others. Both of her wrists were bruised suggesting she once had been restrained, and along the edge of her fine little jaw raged not just another acne stain. A dark purple and harsher red stretched from just below her right ear almost to the midpoint of her mandible.

"What the...?" Smitty gasped.

"What?" the other answered.

"Is that it? How could I not have seen? Who has been doing this to you? Not your mother?"

"What are you talking about?" Tricia whined. "Whadda you want?"

"Your bruises," Smitty asserted in her most schoolmistress manner. "Someone has been hurting you.... Is that why you ran away?"

"It's none of your business," the little one snapped, but continued in a softer voice. "It was Jay. My new boyfriend. We were both drunk. You know how that is."

Smitty merely stood uncomprehending.

"Well.... Well.... Last night. You know. Uh...we were both, you know...drunk. We did it once. You know. Sex?"

Smitty stood speechless.

"Well, anyway.... You know. Anyway, he kept wanting something else. Know what I mean?"

"No, I do not!" Smitty pronounced. "I most certainly do not."

"Whatever. What I'm sayin' is that he wanted something and I didn't want to do it. He kept pawin' at me. An' tryin' to force me. So I hit him in the face with my beer bottle. Made him bleed too."

The crazy little demon actually straightened, nonexistent breasts jutting before her. "So I guess I kinda got what was coming. Know what I mean? Anyhow, he didn't get no BJ. Just went home to Mama for all I know. An' that's when I decided just fuck it all. So here I am. All clean and sober." The imp began laughing those nipples into the most beautiful of patterns.

All Smitty could do was shut her eyes and repeat over and over the penultimate line of the Lord's Prayer. It was, however, too late. She had been led, and Temptation was standing wet and bare before her.

All must resist temptation; the cost of not so doing might be her immortal soul. So did Smitty keep her head turned away, her eyes downcast as much as possible. To the same end did she secure a long and very large tee shirt a friend had given her once upon return from Disney's Wonderful World. So too did the chaste one secure Tricia in her bed and prepare to establish herself in a most comfortable recliner in a wholly other room.

Temptation, thou most fickle of maidens.... "Where are you goin,?" Tricia called from somewhere within the folds of an oversized pillow. "You're not gonna leave me, are you?"

Of course, Smitty did not leave. Instead, she attired herself in a too flannel for summer pair of pajamas and slipped into the womb her bed had become.

"I sometimes get lonely," Tricia whispered, her breath tickling into Smitty's ear as she spooned up to her backside. Thus they slept away the half hour until dawn and the next three until the sounds of thoughtless existence intruded through the open windows and woke them, first Smitty who remained immobile in Tricia's embrace until the girl, perhaps sensing something, stirred and broke contact leaving Smitty feeling bereft.

"Mind if I go first?" the girl trilled as she scampered toward the bathroom.

Of course she had no objection and so Smitty waited, her own needs easily put on hold, and indulged herself in a bout of sensual memory most dangerous and yet most essential. Most sad. The girl was only sixteen and she was about to turn forty-seven. Not only would hope for anything further be futile, but its consummation illegal. *Abandon All Hope* the inscription warned, a caution Smitty knew she had best take to heart.

Logic, you fool. Smitty, you pathetic dupe of the seduction of rationality. From out the passageway between rooms emerged the blithe spirit of transcendence in the guise of a dancing child. Tricia wafted into the bedchamber to the rhythms of unheard music and pirouetted before the stunned woman whose defenses crumbled as did those of the ancient city before the trumpet song of God. A trembling Baptist she shook before the naked dance devoid of veils. Tricia tossed the used tee shirt onto the bed, following with her own ascension, naked, her raspberry nipples calling to all the sisterhood of Smitty's blood.

"Anything for breakfast?" the little cuckoo chirped.

Of course Smitty did not lose her head. "I'll see," she cried, and fled the room.

As she searched among whole grains, tofu, and yogurt for something a teenager might like, Smitty began to count the ways of gracefully shepherding the girl back to her mother or at least out of her life. In total there were none. Every way was graceless: crude, thoughtless, or impossibly cruel. Her only hope would be the girl's own expressed desire to move. Rather than fervently hope, which she was unable to do, Smitty turned to desperate prayer.

"Most Holy Mother and Lord Jesus Christ, my.... Our Lord and Savior, please take this burden from me. May thy will be done; may I remain free from the stain of sin; may your innocent child be set upon the proper path. May I do what is right. May I do not merely what is good but what is best for your lost lamb. Please Most Holy Mother, my beloved Jesus Christ...."

She would have continued but....

"Where in the hell are we anyway? This don't look like anywhere I've ever been. We in New York or something?"

There would be no easy way.

As she prepared her answer, Smitty was denied any respite from her torment. Through the shadowed doorway emerged the bare naked angel, and before all resistance might fall to the assault of her senses, Smitty could only blurt. "Please...shouldn't you get dressed? Please."

Tricia casually scanned down her ripening body then bored those gimlet eyes directly into Smitty's browns. "Don't like what you see?" she joked. "So how about another shirt or something. No way am I getting back into those filthy things I was wearin' last night."

Of course, Smitty, who for a brief moment had imagined the girl's intentions to be wanton, realized, the poor little thing had nothing. "Just look in the bottom drawer of my dresser. There's bound to be something there you can use. If you want, we can wash your things while we eat. I have a washer and dryer in the basement. Shouldn't take too long, and when they're through? Well...when they're through maybe we can get you home. Or whatever."

"Sounds OK," Tricia replied. "Still, where are we?"

"Menands. Now hop in there and get yourself decent. I'll make some eggs and pancakes. That seem all right to you?"

"Any coffee?" the girl called from Smitty's room. "How about aspirin or Motrin or something?"

"Yes To both your questions," Smitty answered, and humming a song of hope, addressed the essentials of hospitality.

HALFWAY THROUGH BREAKFAST something broke inside the little thing. Without preliminary she began to cry. One minute she was commenting brightly on the virtues of the real maple syrup Smitty served, contrasting it most trenchantly to the varieties of artificial substitutes served by her mother and all her aunts. The strange little creature actually knew the process of tapping trees, the boiling and the attendant loss of volume during the transformation of watery sap into sweet viscous syrup, "Worth every penny of the extra cost."

At that point came the tears. Without words or any other sound, Tricia fled back into the bedroom from where Smitty heard the slight creak of her springs. This was unexpected. This could be a major setback. Things had been going smoothly toward Tricia's moving forward. Or at least on. Now? They would have to start all over again. Now....

Oh, my God. Amilee!

Smitty's thoughts had just leapt directly from the griddle onto the red-hot ring of burner beneath. *Oh, my God!*

Thank goodness she had kept Amilee's number. She had to call at once. Where had it gotten to? Had she called from the car? Where was her cellphone? Her mind was a jumble of unsortable data. Every event, each minute piece of sensual input, all the tumult of her heart and libido-dominated mind jumbled together in the mixing-bowl of awareness which threatened to blend them into a homogeneity from which no particulars could any longer be gleaned. Smitty had long before learned of the cliché that trite was often true, and the venerable "in a fog" asserted its virtuous nature past all her education. She was soo deep and lost.

Not really. Her Sinopia purse stood open on the countertop. Her phone was inside, and even if she could not find the paper with Amilee's number, the phone's memory would have stored it. Technology, art thou not divine? She needn't have worried. Crumpled alongside her cell was the paper, and, despite the cell's battery being dead, she could call from her house phone.

What to say? For the first time since awakening, Smitty checked the time. The stove clock read 9:14. No time. No time. Amilee had been insistent. Port Chester at 12:00. It was vital. For all of them. What to say?

So, her troubles not merely doubled but exponentially multiplied, Smitty resigned herself to the inevitable and punched in the numbers, first of course forgetting the 1, but succeeding upon a second attempt. Sometimes Fate smiles upon even the most unlucky of us. The call went directly to voice-mail, and Smitty began a long and apologetic dissertation. That smile is fleeting, however, and as she wound down, relief beginning to flow along the strings of her heart, Amilee broke in.

"What are you saying?" she demanded, uncharacteristically abrupt...even harsh. "You're not going to get here by noon? What time then? I have to be in the city by three. I was hoping we could take care of business before then. I need to know. I need to have some certainty before I meet with the people this afternoon. I was going to introduce you to a couple of someones who I think might change more than your mission. If that's what you call it? They just might alter an entire chunk of the rest of both your lives. Can you get here by one? Maybe I can hang around that long."

Given her circumstances, Smitty knew one or even two o'clock would be impossible. How to tell the insistent one? How to reconcile her failure with her own sense of purpose? How to explain to Mary Margaret?

As her mind raced about fleeting possibilities, the phone hissed dead in her ear.

Not nearly as dejected as she should have been, Smitty returned the piece to its cradle, and surprisingly more clear-headed, addressed the immediate problem of Tricia's removal. A scenario began to evolve. She would claim an unavoidable appointment, outfit the girl in some of her own workout clothes, too large as they might be, and either take her 'home or leave her anywhere her fickle heart might decide. In less than an hour it could be finished.

The phone rang, and confusion resumed its reign. Amilee spoke briefly, "I'm sorry to have been so abrupt," she apologized, "but you wouldn't believe the stress I'm under. This morning I'm meeting some people here to arrange a memorial show for Bobby and the boys, and then there's Pam and her friends. That one could mess up God himself. And I have it on some good authority that she actually has. Anyway, she wants to talk to you and says she'll go with me to New York and you can meet at the Plaza around four-thirty if that suits your situation."

Smitty could not refuse. "I'll be there," she promised.

"Just go in the main entrance across from FAO Schwartz. We'll recognize you," Amilee hastened to say as she rang off without so much as a good bye.

Some element in Amilee's voice more than her words conveyed a sense of urgency Smitty could not ignore. She would dress as elegantly as possible. She was meeting Amilee and this Pam at the Plaza Hotel of all places. So much for the Texas Lunch! She had no time for all the proper preparations, but at least a shower, makeup, attention to her very manageable hair, and her best business suit, a wool-polyester blend, black with ghostly stripes. And her pearl silk blouse. Her black pumps. She could do it in an hour. The drive would take three or four and parking would possibly be a problem. Time was of the....

Gagging. The flush of the toilet. Creak of the bed.

Oh, God. Tricia! What was she going to do?

Only one answer presented itself. She would have to leave the girl behind. In her apartment alone. Oh, God. What if? Something told her the girl could be trusted, but then just exactly what sort of credibility should she ascribe to some vague sense of very convenient trustworthiness? She didn't know the girl from a thousand others she passed every day on the street. She might steal her blind.

Then, what did she have? Three hundred dollars in the freezer. She would need to take that. What else? Her clothes were too large. Her furniture too old and used. The convent had taught her many things, among them a disdain for money and the things it could buy. The line goes, "Freedom's just another word

213

for nothing left to lose," and Smitty had diligently seen to maintaining her freedom. At least as it was relevant to material possessions. She could... she would risk it.

So it occurred that as Tricia wallowed in alcoholic detoxification, buried deep in the comfort of sweet scented sheets and soft mattress, Smitty rattled off her tale as well as her intentions of leaving her alone for perhaps the entire night. "I have a spare key in the silverware drawer," she informed her new housemate, "and I'll leave you twenty-dollars should you want food. There's a Burger King and a diner just down a block or two. I'll leave you a little note explaining things should Mrs. Feinstein say anything. You just sleep now, and when I get back, we'll do something about your circumstances."

Possibly the girl was asleep before she had finished, so Smitty resolved to write out the essentials and leave them on the table. She could then indulge herself in the pleasures of preparing for a special occasion. Whatever Pam proposed, she would see. The meeting! The Plaza Hotel. 5th Avenue. New York City! Such was enough. Even if otherwise it came to nothing, she would wine and dine, perhaps take a room. Life was full of surprises. Not all of them pleasant. When they were? Thank you, God in heaven.

Smitty sat at her table scribbling as legibly as haste would allow the promised note. The money, twenty-five dollars instead of the measly twenty lay off to the side. As she penned the last words of her message to Emily, the breath of something sweet whispered across her cheek, and, turning, she nearly jabbed her elbow into Tricia's hip.

"D-Don't go," she sobbed. Please. Don't leave me alone."

"I-I have to," Smitty stammered. "I have no choice, and gently laying her fingers upon the other's hip, continued, "You'll be OK. Look. I've even left you twenty-five dollars. If you need more...."

"I could go with you," the girl cried, her voice quivering, her eyes begging.

She had no time to argue. Perhaps?

It was impossible! The little refugee from something Smitty did not yet recognize had no clothing, and one does not arrive at the Plaza in an overlarge undershirt and nothing else. She could not take her.

Refusal upon her tongue, Smitty was arrested by the touch of two delicate fingers upon her tense lips. As she looked again into the girl's eyes, a desperation born of circumstances somehow familiar took Smitty up into its whirlwind and deposited her on the other side of anxiety in a land which knew not caution.

"Of course you can," Smitty found her voice saying. "We can stop in New Jersey, Paramus, and I'll get you an outfit. Then we'll put the car up," she observed herself joyously pronouncing. "We'll take the train into Manhattan. Then a taxi ride.

"Yes, it'll be fun"

Sis and Lyndi
1996

TWO DAYS. POSSIBLY as few as thirty-six hours and Isabelle will be gone. All time must end. So too will the sweet hours Lyndi will always remember, her only regret their inevitable conclusion. "I'm getting' out in a week," Belle had exclaimed as soon as she cleared the entrance to the dayroom. "My lawyer just told me. I'm outta here. I've been granted parole."

She might have continued with further details had she not been cut off by the stricken look on her lover's face. "My, God, I'm sorry! I'm just so damn excited. I'm sorry. Don't worry. I'll come see you. It may be a while. I've gotta go to a halfway house and daytime rehab, but I can write. After a while, I'm sure they'll let me come see you. Eventually. I'll just be in Queens. I'll call whenever I can I'll…."

Lyndi simply smiled and nodded her head. "I know. It'll work out."

"It will, it will. I promise. I just know we're not gonna lose everything. You just wait and see." She laid one gentle hand on Lyndi's shoulder and brushed her cheek with the other. "You're all I have, you know. My husband's already gone, and I'm not getting' my kids back. At least not right away, and, I'll bet, not without a fight. I'll need you Lyndi. I'm not goin' away. You can depend on that."

Lyndi's fixed smile and reflexive nod spoke her doubts. Isabelle understood. They both knew.

PROBABLY FEWER THAN thirty two hours now. They settle together into Isabelle's inadequate cot. As with everything in the place, a prison's cell offers few amenities. The bedding is coarse, the springs hard and stiff through an inadequate mattress upon a woman's delicate surfaces. There is no carpet to sooth a girl's tender soles, and animal sounds grunt along the unit floor, intruding upon everyone's never too pleasant dreams. Lyndi lies as would a bride beneath the bulk of her partner. Isabelle usually prefers to be the woman, but this night Lyndi needs to be taken. Surrender has become her default response to the inevitable. With the assistance of an inadequate section of plastic-wrapped sausage, Isabelle takes her as would a man, and Lyndi mourns the premature loss of a childhood come upon her so late in life.

Not in months has she thought of Edward with anything more than resentment. This night is to be different. Lyndi remembers moments repressed but not forgotten. How they sometimes fell asleep joined in love, how he sometimes played a liquid song upon her labia with his own rough tongue. How he sometimes took her as he might a whore, how he loved to hold her down and rut about like a hog. She despised him for that. Hated those times. She loved them too.

"I can't help it, Lyn" he would mumble as inadequate apology. "You're just too damn hot. Too fucking beautiful."

She would not admit it, but she found more than a little satisfaction in precisely that knowledge. Never, while completely at his mercy, was she more dominant. Everything he had — everything he was — poured from him through the pathetic little instrument of his sex. In to her. She took it. Mocked it as he sweated above her even during subzero nights, and cherished it as one might the eviscerated rodent a proud cat presents its mistress. Edward too was simply the plaything of his own basic impulses and drives. Unlike Felix or whatever the cat's name might be, he bought her things she could use, took her to dine at wonderful restaurants, and fed her to satiation with guilt and apology.

Isabelle is no Edward. She is attempting to manipulate her foreign instrument with some degree of skill — Lyndi had mastered its various applications — but is too soft, too loving. Wrapping her legs around the solid form atop her, Lyndi growls in her ear, "Pluck ple, Plelle. Pluck ple plas plard plas plou plan." When she doesn't, the desperate Lyndi snarls, "Pli plaid pluck ple plard. Plin ple plutt, plif plou plan."

Isabelle does not just pause. She halts, the moldering sausage left drooping from Lyndi's vagina. "I can't do that," she cries. This could be our last time together. I don't want it to end this way."

"Pli plo," Lyndi snaps. "Plow plo plas Pli play plor pli'm plotta plere."

"I don't think…."

"Plop lit plor plelse," Lyndi orders, and, reluctantly, Isabelle rolls her over, draws her up upon hands and knees, and complies.

When it is finished, when they lie entangled upon the sheetless palate, Isabelle attempts an Edwardian apology.

"Plave plit plor ple pluts plat ple plalf-play plouse," Lyndi jets into her ear. "Plow ploll plover. Plou're plonna plet plours plow."

Thus ended the brief but intense sexual relationship of Lyndi and her Isabelle.

THIS IS NOT to say they spend none of the remaining hours subsequent to their awakening together. In fact an event occurs during the noon meal which sets Lyndi upon a course of greater significance than ever a most uncomfortable moment of sex play could have been. Empi once again intrudes her disturbing presence into the actual final moments of their imprisoned cohabitation, and eternal vectors of more than four dimensions describe Lyndi's turn away from Isabelle and all she once has considered essential. Normal.

Her annunciator is no angel, not even a blinding flash of unbearable radiance. Instead, Lyndi's moment comes at the end of a shiv. Before Isabelle can move to defend her beloved, Empinada has crowded herself up to the careless Lyndi and pricked a sharp point of deadly design into her throat. Just a small prick. Perhaps not a prick at all. Certainly no blood has been drawn. The threat is real. "Don't!" she cautions the uncharacteristically uncertain Isabelle. "Sit the hell down, and shut the fuck up. One move, one word and this kid dies.

"And you, fishie, you too. Just shut up and listen. Then you'd better got the right things to say."

Lyndi feels no fear. Empi's motives are clear. She is accomplishing a task set before her by one whom she cannot refuse.

"Ploloma," is all she needs to say, and Empi's mind falls open to her. The intended message comes strong and clear, but, perhaps unintended, so too does knowledge of a more personal — at least to Empinada — kind. As she has done on more than one occasion with Isabelle, Lyndi strolls the winding pathways of Empi's perceptions and memories, of her hopes and irrational expectations. Overhead a dim light shines. All around dwells darkness while from a long way off and impossibly far away comes a song of familiar yet otherworldly nature.

"It's *Black Muddy River*, announces Empinada. Thought you might know it. Can't get it outta my own head. Ever since I heard it. My Moms. She loved them. Thought Jerry Garcia was like us. You know, Garcia and all. Anyhow, I think maybe she was kind of right. He sure did like his own kind a white girl, know what I mean? It weren't cool, you know. I moved on in all kinds a ways, but that song stayed with me. I still know all the lyrics. Right now, I couldn't tell you if that's Jerry Garcia or me singin'. Even the music. Maybe I'm the whole freakin' band. It's true, you know. Whatever kinda stars and moon shit I walkin' through. I'm always gonna' be alone."

"You're not," Lyndi comforts. "You know that. The whole reason I'm here is Paloma. Your sister is with you. And something else. You know this too. She has always been with you. From the very day of her birth, maybe even her conception, she has been with you. You are not alone. You know it. You always have"

The shiv draws a taste of blood. Lyndi feels nothing. Empinada's face twists into a tragi-comedic mask. Lyndi continues along her twisted way. The trail grows dim. Tangled briars and bowed sumac threaten to interdict her progress. The track ends at a steep, clay dripped bank. The music beckons. Her highway, no longer simple, perhaps no longer exists at all. Lyndi turns; the path which has led her to this place is gone. All is blackberry, redberry, sumac and poison. As she stands, her mind reaching for possibility, thorned tentacles seek to wind about her ankles. She must move or she will become so entangled as to be denied any possibility of escape. There is no way out. She is trapped.

As the vines claw their ragged way up her calves, the drifting music shifts into a British tone. Familiar. Unknown. The words are lost but the tune, the rhythm — it's something about dandelions… blowing them away. A voice, far away grows clearer. Of course! It's The Stones. One of Edward's favorites. Mick's words separate themselves from themselves and drift about her. It's all a dream. She can fly. The dandelion has made her wise. Or at least a bit less blind. As bright seeds lift back toward their origin, so does she. How could she not be lighter than air? Laughing, she allows a nonexistent breeze to play her about toward a lovely rising sun. Eventually, she finds herself above a wide clearing, around the perimeter of which travels a black-paved highway. Toward this she is borne. An encampment of sorts grows toward her from the field, but Lyndi is enraptured by the dark spiders scuttling across the darker pavement beneath her. They all stream toward the same end. As does she. Her descent will deposit her within their venomous midst. Closer and closer she falls until it becomes obvious that she is targeted upon one particular member of the scattering arachnids. Closer, ever closer, until her feet touch pavement as does another seed at her side. Both of them merge with their individual shadows. That is all the spiders are. Their own shadows.

Bright red, the memories of the briars are bloody scrawls upon her legs, but she is insubstantial and feels no pain. Another concern arises. The sound of revelry grows stronger than the music. *Dandelion's* tones are soon painted black. Loud guffaws, masculine yet obviously issuing from a female set of lungs, swell toward her. A large figure separates from the blacksootfire about which a group of four others stand. Chromelit shafts knife from leaning motorcycles, themselves grouped in an irregular row. The creature emerging from the smog becomes distinct. It is a woman, large, but not like Isabelle. Lumbering.

"Yo, Lyndi," it calls. "C'mon over. We ain't going to hurt you. Somebody here's got somethin' to say."

Paloma! Lyndi has known it all along, and not just because this is Empi's mind. Paloma is the key to both their futures, their lives. Empi's sister has an obvious responsibility, debt actually, to her sibling, but Lyndi fails to make any connection to herself. Nevertheless, she joins the huge biker, and, immediately, connections manifest themselves. The biker is called Sis. Rebecca Jordon, not Becky, nor Becka. Neither is she Paloma. She is, however, among that one's most trusted confidants. Slipping her strong arm around Lyndi's insubstantial waist, she guides her to the silent group waiting by the fire.

"Better watch out for Sis, Lyn," a dark and scantily clad girl in black Doc Martin boots, a tie-dyed tee shirt, leather vest, and only possibly — hopefully — shorts of some description mocks. Her legs are shapely, her breasts ample and free beneath their sweat-blotched covering. Her eyes blaze with an intensity more than ever could an earthly fire, and her smoky hair moves across her cheeks of its own volition. The girl is totally still. No breeze moves even the settling seed. Still every strand of her hair is alive dancing upon the verge of turbulence.

Gathering her courage and her for-certain assumptions up into one great ball, Lyndi addresses her underwhelming question to the kinetic vision, "You are Paloma, I presume," at which point the dark one nearly suffocates herself with spasms of laughter.

"Best not let her hear you say that," Sis finally croaks from out her own mirth. "This here's Pam, and though they're related they ain't got all that much in common."

"Don't worry, my dear," a soft voice flows from somewhere beyond her vision. "We're all sisters here, and nothing you might say could possibly be as offensive as some of the things I've been forced by these two to endure." Out from behind Sis a slight and elegant figure emerges. Absolutely the most beautiful, most radiant, and, yes, most perfect woman Lyndi has ever seen. This time, Lyndi is certain. Paloma extends her right hand. It holds a pure white feather. As Tara promised. Her moment of decision of blessed possibility is upon her.

Or is it? This is Empinada's world, the dwelling place of Empi's sister and all the promise of her salvation. Is not she, Lyndi, merely an observer? Is not the feather, some form of salvation or at least forgiveness, Empi's?

Paloma's answer calms any fear, erases possible doubt or misunderstanding. "My sister's future course has long ago been decided, and she is fully aware of its nature. Part of that is exactly what you are experiencing now. I must say I regret the crude means she took to get you here, but, they were necessary. Anyway, this is for you." Without ceremony she lays the feather across Lyndi's welcoming palm, and everything makes perfect sense. The hidden is revealed, and the future exists in the present. Lyndi realizes this is not the teacher of whom Tara spoke, but the feather she has given her is most potent and will serve as a bond when she and the teacher, Agnes Smith, finally meet. It will also be a source of comfort and strength during the years of hardship awaiting her. She still has a ways down to go, but the feather will offer the promise of her eventual rising.

Lyndi also grows to know so much more. Isabelle, will never regain custody of her children. Her husband will find another woman and another life in the Republic, leaving her to her own imaginings and midnight visions of bloodshed, until one dark morning, rising before the sun, Izabelle will step out into the darkness and put an end to hopelessness by dropping herself from the Brooklyn Bridge into the ebbing tide of the East River. Never will her body be found. Never will she be missed. Except by Lyndi who will not forget her great warm arms and the unexpected vulnerability of her heart.

At this point within the whirl of Lyndi's awareness, Paloma's voice intrudes. "Before you follow your lover over the edge and into the sewer of guilt, remember that many people jump off bridges and most others, even those so motivated, can do nothing to save them. Isabelle's fate is her own as is the case with the majority of those called human. Should you know all that I know, you might be inclined to affirm the validity of the old cliché, 'We make our own beds, and then we lie in them.' You, on the other hand, are of a different breed, and it is necessary that you shed the false skin and common perceptions of the ordinary. Isabelle cannot exist without human love, without her children, without comfort, and certainty. You must realize that they are deceptions. I cannot say that love is a bad thing. Just that as it is practiced — embraced — by those such as Isabelle, it is merely a necessary comfort for such who can never become — another cliché — 'all that We can be.'

You have the potential of becoming that which Jesus promised in John's gospel — one of those who will do everything he did... and more. Jesus was — is — so much cooler than our priests make him out to be. Before Nietzsche, he spoke of the *übermensch*, she who will take the next evolutionary step. It's been two-thousand years, and it hasn't happened yet, but believe your elementary Biology. Evolution is a slow process. Hear me, the most recent Quantum discoveries will hasten the process. You, for example, are both here in this Empinada world and in the other place called Taconic. You know you are here, and everyone in the facility knows you are there — as you are. Non locality, Lyndi. That's one of the names of your new game. I've known about that one for a long time. I also have been aware that Time runs backward and that, if I so desire, I can turn sunlight into actual gold. Hang on to the feather you have been given, and stay true to the path laid before you. Someday, you will be able to too.

"It's time now for me to go, but one more thought. That big thing with her arm still around you… Sis. You two haven't met yet. You will. I'm trusting Empi to fill you in a bit on that, but understand, despite what I just said about human love, inadequate as it is in the face of infinity, for a time and relegated to its proper ancillary position, it's a fine distraction. Your love for Isabelle was of the illusionary kind. You are going to discover whole new worlds of emotion with this one, and as ever you may become a couple, so too will you each everyday become more your individual selves."

For the first time wholly aware of the strong arm encircling her, Lyndi looked up into the rough-hewn face of her….

The briars scrabble further up her thighs. So too do they loom above her where once sang the sun. There is no campfire, no sound of music or of human expression. There is no road, not the slightest indication of a path, and even the sky above is locked away behind a toxic wall of brambles. The wilderness tangles itself about her, its thorns digging deeper. Lyndi is to be grown into an inescapable thicket. There is no Paloma, no Sis, not even a group of disinterested bikers, one of them so elegantly dark.

"YO, LYN," RINGS a cheerful voice. ""Just givin' you a little thrill."

It is Empi, and the way behind her is clear. The grasping tentacles fall away, the sky is visible through a heavenly arch of Maple. Lyndi has been rescued by the mind responsible for her peril.

"Come on, Lyns. I don't got prickers like that. They's all your doin'. Now let's get outta here before you call up somethin' else to cause us trouble. You're somethin', that's for sure."

Empi leads her along a path carpeted with mulched yellow, brown and dark chocolate leaves, twisting between tall, dry oaks stretching foliated branches toward the distant sun. Light the color of autumn grain dapples the way before them until they reach a place open to the sky. At its center stands a rough-hewn pergola draped with graceful leaves of a broad and teasingly familiar design. Their generous hands and prominent fingers beckon the travelers to the shaded grotto they have created. "That's my hidin' hole," Empi announces. "We gonna be stoppin' here for just a while. I got some extra shit I gotta tell you. Anyway Paloma thinks so. Says you're gonna need to know enough to keep you goin', and once we back to Taconic, ain't no way you're gonna be hearin' anything I'm saying.

"So, come on. Won't take but a minute. Or so."

Once within the shadow of the natural canopy, Lyndi is surprised by the lush grass soft beneath her bare feet. "Set yosef down a while," Empi suggests while lowering herself into a most regal pose upon the friendly contours of the soft surface. It's better than the fucking Ritz here. I know. Used to work there. The Plaza too. Those beds are like prison cots compared to this."

Abandoning herself to her companion's whim, Lyndi complies, and, surprise… surprise. Her guide is correct. Lyndi had spent a weekend at the Ritz once upon a happily married time, and Empi's assessment, if anything, is an understatement. No hotel, no matter how swank, offers bedding not only soft but also so caressing. The best mattress, unless of a feathered kind, is only able to hint at intimate embrace. In Empi's private space the long grass and the soft forest earth beneath wrap themselves up and around Lyndi as might the love of God.

"Told ya," Empi chuckles.

What she has neglected to tell, however, is the fact that Lyndi is naked. She knows she has been fully clothed upon their approach to the refuge. So what is happening to her now?

"Relax," her guide comforts. "It's just naked's the only way to get the full effect. Know what I'm sayin'?"

Surely Lyndi does. Clothes are sometimes a barrier to the full experience of the things around us, and, most assuredly, they would have been in these circumstances.

"Just let yasef go," Empi suggests. "Then we'll talk a bit. Lyndi does just that, allowing the grass to weave a magic spell about her, experiencing the deep connection between her own spirit and the soul of Empinada's earth beneath her. So it is that Empi's summons back into the world of human interaction is at first unwelcome.

"Just a little longer," Lyndi murmurs as would a sleepy child. "Give me another minute…. Please."

Empi is not to be denied. "Come on," she asserts. "Shit's startin' to happen back inside, and I gotta get this done. We got no more time."

Reluctantly but with little more prodding, Lyndi returns to her return to the world of ordinary people.

The lone sign of Empinada's physical presence remaining in the beginning to vanish refuge is her voice. Her words are clear, their import unmistakable.

"You are deaf," she pronounces. "You are also unable to make it inside without Isabelle or someone like her. I am not the one. There is no one in Taconic Hills who can take her place. The Queens are my girls. I can't turn on them, and so we have, as Paloma puts it, a dilemma. But there is a solution. None of the CO's know about you being deaf. Alls we gotta do is use that to your advantage. It can only be done one way.

"When you get back to the inside outside world, they're already gonna be comin' to your rescue. I've still got my pick to your throat, but don't worry, I ain't gonna stick ya. I am gonna hafta thump you up side a the head pretty hard though. Enough to put you down and out for a while. I'm pretty good with my fists. Could a been a boxer if I'd been able to stay straight and train, but that ain't of no account. Just know. It's for your own good. The Queens hate you, and they're just waitin' for Izzy to be gone. Your life ain't gonna be worth shit by tomorrow. If you know what I mean? So what we gotta do is get you into the infirm. Once they find out you can't hear and then try to make sense outta the gibberish you talk, they're gonna be sure certain you need serious attention. Get ready for it Lyn. If Paloma knows what she's tellin' me, you're headed for a psycho ward someplace. And that big biker queen too."

Before the last psychic ripple of these words can die away, Lyndi awakes to Empi's face bright with laughter, her eyes alight with something akin to joy.

The curtain falls.

PALOMA SURMISED WELL and Empi has acted her part to perfection. Lyndi awakens in the infirmary, unable to speak plainly or to hear at all. Confusion speaks volumes from the attendant nurse's face as it continues to do from the entire mien of the doctor called over from Bedford Hills. The next day a neurologist is called, and she immediately suggests transfer to the nearest hospital. It comes to pass that Lyndi first visits Mount Kisco which is not equipped to handle a prisoner in a confused mental state as well as with a life-threatening condition such as Lyndi's might be. Not at all coincidentally, she is transferred upstate to Albany Medical Center, a facility possessed of a first-rate neurological department, and, while its inmate floor is male only, adjustments are easily made, and Lyndi soon is ensconced in a private room, granted, one with window bars, but a welcome upgrade from basic prison accommodations. Everyone is so nice. Especially the big nursing student named Rebecca who visits her every day.

Loosely affiliated with the Albany College of medicine, the hospital boasts a stellar array of medical specialists and diagnostic tools, but no physical factors emerge as likely causes for her sudden-onset deafness or the persistent apraxia. No tumors, no evidence of stroke are apparent, and the concussion, if ever there were one, was most minor. Eventually, the inevitable Psych consult directs everyone to a diagnosis. Her problems are psychological, probably not schizophrenia, but hints do exist. This clinical evidence in hand, after a month's maneuvering with the court, her legal team is able to arrange transfer up the avenue to the Capital District Psychiatric Center where her life settles into a pleasant routine of therapy, psychoactive drugs, and frequent visits from that persistent student.

Mary Margaret and Stephen

Mary Margaret could be cold, was cold most of the time, at least internally. Her constant, normal temperature was 96.7, and even in a warm tub she could feel the endemic chill of the world. Her mind and heart reflected in arctic purity her body's blazing chill. Her thoughts this evening had not been warmed by a luxurious bath; neither had they been purified by her prayers. The memory of Stephen's call swung its endless loop through her consciousness while a clearer voice, her very own, urged her to the obvious logical action.

Mary Margaret was a woman who, once having made a decision, refused to trouble herself with second thoughts, visions or revisions. She did what needed to be done, accepted the consequences of her actions, whatever they might be, and continued on with a clear conscience, even in a matter so fraught with moral, social and personal peril as adultery, the taking, if such be the proper term, of another woman's husband. It was clear to her that Stephen was interested. In fact, his marital situation never more than flitted through her mind as she firmed up her strategy. Obviously, the illicit arrangement would require secrecy—no need to embarrass anyone unnecessarily, especially herself. Surely something must be amiss in a marriage when a lovely, little number like Stephen's wife Patty — *Matty? Whatever!* — was unable to keep him interested enough to prevent his roving. Culpability for such infidelity is at least a fifty-fifty proposition. Luckily for Mary Margaret, and, of course, for Stephen, and, who knows, maybe for Patty herself, this interlude would be discrete, short-lived and dispassionate.

The former nun simply wished to lose her virginity, and she was certain that all Stephen really wanted was a little adventure and, perhaps, an affirmation of his masculinity, his status as Alpha Male. No one need know the details or even the existence of their relationship. All would be adult, mutually satisfactory, and most of all, no one would be hurt.

Thus, with clear conscience and the purest of souls, Mary Margaret emerged from her virginal bath, dried herself vigorously, coaxing blood to her soft, butter-cream skin, warming herself with the rough texture, the vigorous massage of the oversized, mauve Egyptian towel with which she wrapped her torso before scampering into her room where she would select an appropriate outfit for an evening meal at The Old Daley, alone with her thoughts and, as she couldn't resist terming them, her "schemes."

She wore her hair up, spent a quick five minutes with her makeup, slipped into her pale linen dress, slid into a pair of new sandals, and was off.

Emerging into the breeze of early evening, she was stricken by the panorama of approaching night. Treetops swayed like graceful girls, pink licked low clouds stretched across the distant mountains, and behind it all, the setting sun struck the world aflame with its departing song. If Stephen — *Stevie?* — were present, she too might be borne away.

Prime rib. Rare. Half-eaten, the rest put in a bag to grow cold. Baked potato. An overload of butter with a generous scoop of sour cream. A taste of iceberg, a chill tomato, and twice as much vinegar as oil. No wine. Two Margaritas. Two Drambuies and a twelve-mile ride home. To sleep. To dream.

Too much alcohol. Mary Margaret slept as soundly as a dreamless baby. Awaking cold and fully dressed into four AM darkness, she shuddered some equilibrium into her slewing world, shambled into the bathroom, shed her sandals, and returned to her place of refuge. She would greet the morning five hours later, her mind unclear, her intentions crystal. She would set it all in motion that very day.

9:06 AM
No answer.
11:02

The same *Please leave a message* nonsense. Mary Margaret will have none of that.

4:37

Stephen calls. "Sorry," he explains. "I have a summer class. Short Story. I just saw your number on my missed call list." He allows a long pause to grow tedious.

What is she supposed to say? That morning's inspiration has become this afternoon's uncertainty? She has been about her business, has dealt with criminals and hopeless seekers after release, however temporary. What does he expect her to say?

"Well...?" Stephen suggests.

""Well yourself," Mary Margaret replies. Too quickly. *Way too glib.*

"Well..." he laughs, "besides being a deep subject, can it not also offer a suggestion of something valuable?"

Mary Margaret's mind snaps back into full function and her response is to the point. "Well..." she purrs, "this morning I was going to suggest lunch. Any plans for dinner?"

Stephen has planned an evening on the prowl with Vinnie. He will have to modify those plans. Fortunately, Pam isn't expecting him home at any given time. Vinnie will understand. Stephen's mind races through myriad possibilities. He is slow to reply, struck mute by his own imagination.

For a full minute Mary Margaret stands at her granite-topped island listening to something someone has christened "Dead Air." She is accustomed to surprise reactions from felons and other seekers who find themselves hard against the realities of her particular world of finance. She has also observed certain students' reactions to extreme grades. Human beings are a strange lot. She returns her own receiver to its cradle.

At once it trills again.

"Hello."

Stephen offers a pure white lie by way of explanation, and goes on to suggest seven-thirty at Villa Imbroglio.

Mary's queasy stomach rejects the idea of heavy, home-style Italian, and her mind prompts the suggestion of Turkish Delights. Their sweet lamb and rice.

"The bar sucks," Stephen complains.

As compromise they settle on Pablo O'Reiley's, a Mexican/Irish meld of some sophistication. It can be spicy, but they have terrific lamb chops as well as a bar worthy of the place's ethnic roots. Pablo O's is located in central Troy, on the west side of River Street, snuggled comfortably between a brew pub and a college-centric bistro. The clientele is a mix of people from professors to professionals of a shadier degree. The large room is sectioned off into three small dining areas by nineteenth century dark wooden rails and bannisters, and the smoky ochre walls mingle scenes of old-Troy, rural Ireland, ancient Mexican towns, and an ink-drawn Emiliano Zapata looking much like an early Marlon Brando. The ambient music is a tasteful mixture of Celtic, Country, Son, Corrido, and Ranchera. There is no juke box, but the bar is way too intimate for any of the drinkers to mind. Along the wall across from the bar stand three tall tables each hosting two compatible stools. One setting is unoccupied. Mary and Stephen, after a nod from the fiftyish bartender, seat themselves and are quickly addressed by a small young woman, her black hair twisted into a bun, her white blouse and black trousers crisp, her skin pale as vanilla cream.

"Welcome to Pablo O'Reiley's," she offers in *Chicana* tones. "My name is Dolores, and I'll be your server." She brings drinks, then more drinks, then more. Mary Margaret's are of a dual nature—a shot of Jameson's chased with a severely cold Harp draft. Stephen is less traditional but more single minded. He orders double shots of Jim Beam on one ice cube in an Old Fashion glass. He drinks with gusto bordering upon reckless abandon.

Eventually they order meals. Mary insists upon her chops along with a delicious scoop of potato, mashed and infused with garlic and cheese. She adds butter. Her asparagus spears are also cheese and garlic graced. Were she a bit more sober, she would have found the same mixture in the small iceberg, tomato, and cucumber salad with, of course, the house dressing. As the evening develops, however, she never touches the salad, tastes a forkful of the potatoes, and manages only one chop. On the other side of the round table, Stephen consumes his "Mexican" corned beef and cabbage, eats his salad, and finishes Mary Margaret's potatoes.

Then comes the time for Irish coffee, Lusca Cabernet, and a final tip of the sombrero with tequila, salt, and lemon. Their next step would have been across the narrow way to the bar, had not Dolores offered to call a taxi when delivering the bill. "We'd best *vamoose*" Stephen jokes while signing the slip, "Next thing you know, she'll refer us to an AA meeting. Spare us, I say, from sober people…. As Alfred Doolittle quoth, we're 'up agin middle class morality' here. Let us be off to seek our collective fortune in a setting more conducive to such as ourselves who dwell in circumstances at a far remove from the common herd."

"I used to be a nun," Mary Margaret smiles. "For most of my life I not only dwelt in such precincts, but actually attempted to impose 'morality' upon others." Both find these words more amusing than their sober selves might have.

Mary Margaret would have continued, but Dolores appears, sweeps the folder with the payment from the table, smiles a condescending farewell, and stalks off without so much as a "thank you." Regretting his thirty-percent tip, Stephen would have made some sarcastic comment loud enough for everyone to hear, but Mary Margaret is already on the move, and, anyway, for the life of him, he is unable to think of anything trenchant enough for the occasion.

Despite a minor struggle with the door, they make their exit as gracefully as possible and find themselves on the street, a fine mist beginning to turn everything unpleasantly damp.

A BLACK BRUSHFULL of hair stuffs Mary Margaret's mouth and cuts at the corner of her lips. An unpleasant swish from off somewhere speaks of laundry water, grit, and, heaven help her, the leavings of a large dog. The smell invades the sanctity of her dark cell. She aches in an unfamiliar place.

"Jesus Christ, her lord and savior! They did it. She knows they did. She remembers little. Drunkenness. Wet and alcoholic pawings and osculations. His head. Down where it had no place being. She thinks she liked that.

Pushing up on her elbows, Mary Margaret opens her eyes to a dull day oozing in through her windows, turning all it touches a dispiriting shade of too-brown taupe. She had stockings that shade once. They made her legs look dirty. Now everything is stained. Her walls, hardwood floor, bed clothes… her hands and arms. At least Stephen has gone. God help her if he ever were to see her like this.

The sound of running water asserts itself from the direction of her bath. The door is shamelessly open. She senses grey steam in the discolored air. The sound of the shower stops. The frosted door bangs. *Oh, my God, he's here.*

Overwhelmingly. He drifts through the doorway accompanied by tendrils of infernal smoke. Greyer than the steam, a cloud gusts from his mouth and nose and twists from the pipe he holds before him in a Santa's wreath. His maraschino lips are pursed in a Cupid's bow as he exhales, and his hawk nose flares. For the first time Mary Margaret is aware of a roundness to the abdomen she had imagined hard and flat.

Most striking is the erection leading him on. The towel wrapped around his waist parts above his left thigh, and his penis is slithering through. Mary Margaret is not unaware of the probabilities. She must do something. This cannot happen. Not yet.

The bed is filthy, and so is she. Sticky and soiled, her sheets and her newly undone body are repellent. The dog poop odor is not dissipating. Has she been flatulent? Has she or he done worse than pass gas. She must stop him before he gets close enough to smell her. To that end she attempts a humorous parry. "Not yet, Stephen, she giggles. Can't a girl get a shower herself? Or at least brush her teeth? And, really, this is a no smoking home."

Stephen is no fool. Halting two paces removed, he scowls down upon her. "You had no problems getting high last night. In fact, it was your idea. Your weed. Your pipe."

The man lacks any sense of decorum. Any saving grace at all. Not even humor. Nor embarrassment. The towel falls. He sets the hot clay pipe on her antique nightstand, and before Mary Margaret can realize all that is happening, he is upon her and inside her. It hurts.

She should not be allowing this. She can smell the pipe, the dog. Beside their entangled forms she spots a stain, yellow and gross. This is rape. The man is forcing himself upon her and she does nothing but clench her jaw and, God forgive her, wrap her arms about him, caressing his back and sides as he lays waste her body and soul. Her will is frozen. Her mind screams foul. Demands resistance. Instead her traitorous physicality relaxes its pelvic muscles. Of their own volition her legs open wider, and she allows his tongue into her mouth as his hand squeezes her left breast and rolls the nipple between its thumb and forefinger. Too hard! She cries out in pleasure and pain. Pain…pain…pain.

Her mind abandons her. She is thrust hard against the granite of herself. The penetrations and pressures threaten to break her into driftwood splinters. She cannot comprehend this. She will not hold together. She wails.

Abandoned, lost upon a shoreless ocean, she has come apart and never shall she be reassembled.

His shouts return a bit of her mind, reattach her limbs, reestablish the necessary mind/body, neuron/brain connections. She is thrown about, a rubber ducky in an excitable boy's tub. She has survived, butwill she be the same?

Stephen extracts himself from their embrace and casually retrieves the pipe which smolders still. Offering it her way, he smiles the most charming, little boy smile any grown man has ever managed. "You, my amazing little goddess, are beyond description. I swear I was almost lost. No pun intended, but you, Mary Margaret Mangold, are a black hole of immeasurable attraction. It's called coming when a male ejaculates…. Well Mary, I came and came inside you, and for a moment I thought I might expire. I'm going to have to be very careful in the future. Perhaps hold off with the drugs or something…. Anyway," he offers the pipe again, "it can't hurt now."

They smoke, eat waffles, drink coffee, and make love again. Eventually, Stephen takes his leave, and Mary Margaret is left, bloated, sore, and confused. She now understands why Ginny allowed herself to be used in such fashion. It was indeed rape. It was, but as with much evil, sex with a man, especially one of such splendid physicality as Stephen, is horribly attractive. She will see this through. At least for a time.

Sis

Rebecca Jordon was born in Saint Mary's Hospital, Troy New York on a bright blue morning in May, the twenty-third day of a month of promise and beauty. Her mother and father had hoped to be the proudest parents of the most beautiful child with whom God had ever blessed their earth. Instead, they produced a cranky, chubby daughter with a cleft palate and the most god-awful harelip any nonleporidae ever sported. Thank God, her ears were round and close to her huge head, and her eyes were brown, her nose flat but recognizably human. Still she seemed more some disfigured Harvey than Mom and Daddy's Little Ray of Happy Sunshine. Bob and Nancy cried and prayed, averted their gazes from the unnamed child's great dark eyes until Nancy's father, a theretofore semi-worthless chunk of bilious decay, imposed his thoughtless will upon them. "You gotta name the little shit," he ordered full of spirited import. "If you can't think of one yourself, your mom always loved Rebecca." So it came to pass that on the twenty sixth day of May in the year of someone's lord, the birth certificate was drawn and subsequently registered. Rebecca Jordon officially entered the population, and her parents turned their attention to planning for a child more worthy to continue their proud name as well as give evidence of their superior genetic makeup in the accepted fashion that only a beautiful face and culturally perfect body can do.

To that end, no more that seventeen months intervened between the emergence of Rebecca into the world and the premature ejaculation of her sister Susan, the perfectly formed, delicate child the Jordons felt they deserved. Parenthood can be a joy after all, especially when one is one of the proud progenitors of a model-quality child of sunny disposition and most considerate impulses even from the first dawning of awareness in her black and soul-deep eyes.

Nancy would tell to her fatal day of the time she woke to her Su Su's sweet face drawn up into a most serene — loving — expression so close to her own in the twilit dawning of another brilliant day that she could feel her soft respirations, experience the muted oboe essence of the hunger undetectable by any but the most maternal senses. Bob slept on. The child's eyes traveled past Nancy to his innocent form and quickly back to her mother. Nancy knew. SuSu was starving yet had remained quiet out of concern for her parent's comfort. Quickly baring her swollen breast, Nancy offered her life to the holy child. Only fourteen months old, Su was a child of God. His gift not only to her parents but, both would assert, eventually to the world as well.

Alongside Susan, Rebecca grew a noxious weed, tall and spreading into bulldog configurations of muscle, sinew, and heavy bone. Her eyes were light blue. Her skin pale. Of course, unlike the distinctive countenance of the feline, her face was most resolutely that of a snarling rabbit, cleft off to the left, until long into her eighteenth year. "Bugs," her hilarious relatives often called her. Once upon her fifteenth Christmas an older and most inspired cousin had boxed and wrapped a carrot as a surprise gift. Having fled the kitchen where the family had gathered, Rebecca took her first scalp when Wilbur, having been sent to apologize by his snickering parents, walked directly into a well-directed Doc Martin. At that point, a profound truth revealed itself. For the different, the outsider, and unaccepted a snarl is more potent than a smile, a curse more effective than a prayer, and, if those fail, a boot to anywhere vulnerable wins the day.

The family soon gave Bugs a rest, and the kids at Robert Packer School quickly accepted that "Cat Face" brought about a most unwelcome painful response. Bugs and Cat Face, Rebecca and Becky soon became Sis. Even to Mama and Pa. Nobody fucked with Sis. She was different, outside of it all, and had no wish to be accepted. She would make her own way. She needed no one.

Except Susan, that is. That one Sis absolutely adored.

TIME PASSES DIFFERENTLY for us all, especially children. During the infinite present of their childhood Sis and Susan grew closer with each passing season until first Sis and shortly thereafter SuSu found themselves faced with the budding thornbushes of womanhood. Somewhere in sixth or seventh grade, Sis realized that she admired men but hated boys and that she also loved most women but despised bitchy, little girls. Always trailing, yet ever halving the distance between them, SuSu discovered just the opposite. To her, men, except Daddy of course, were an ever looming danger while boys were so easy to manipulate that her attraction threatened to become contempt. As for girls, SuSu flowered into the cutest, the nicest, and the most despised of her feline classmates. She soon found herself almost as lonely as her sister, and thus did their connection wax stronger and more intense. Together they made their way alone.

Let it not be assumed that they had much in common except for radically different expressions of common DNA, but just as opposites are said to attract, blood and genetics are bonds which often need possess no significant commonality. Each girl had a sister and each was a sister. The world be damned, they would make it through. They would be happy. They would be proud. They would love and be forever loved.

Dad manifested all the once proud stature of the once vital "working class." Spring through summer, through fall he devoted his time and energy, seven days a week ten to twelve hours each day to his landscaping business. He seeded, sodded, repaired, mowed and tended to lawns. Planted trees and flowers, mulched extravagant plantations around houses great and small. He taught himself the art of setting pavers, pouring and stamping concrete, installing watering systems, and designing absolutely whimsical gardens for those inclined to imagine themselves dwelling within a storybook setting.

In the winter he plowed and hauled snow from several private and municipal lots, cleared driveways and sidewalks, and in his spare time began chiseling trails for a cross-country ski facility he had planned for the not too distant future.

Mom was no stay at home housewife either. She was a paralegal with a great job at a prestigious Albany firm, Wilcox, Healey and Farrar, brought home a sizeable paycheck, and steadfastly resisted her husband's suggestions that she ease into part time or even early retirement. It cannot be stated that Nancy had it all, but it would not be invalid to assert that she gave all she had. To her job. To her family, and, in the close moments of her nighttime awakenings, she realized, to herself as well.

WHEN THE CYCLONE struck, Sis had been working after school and summers with Dad for two years. She had learned to shovel and spread, wheel and dig, had graduated to commanding her own Ford F-350 with stick shift, and she could haul a trailer, a tri-axle capable of hauling both the Bobcat and small backhoe. True, she later graduated to loving the Hemi but at the age of seventeen, Sis was madly in love with the Triton. She could freakin' drive too. Handled the rig better'n any of the guys. Except Dad, obviously.

SuSu used her spare time for dreaming and designing. Addicted to the fripperies of her childhood Disney fantasies, she had become enthralled by fashion magazines and catalogues by the time she reached eleven. Her childhood's favorite pastime was sketching elegant women wearing extravagant outfits and posing in sophisticated settings. Daddy's little jewel and Mommy's precious "Precious," she soon began outfitting herself in like manner, and by the age of fifteen had purchased a professional quality sewing machine, and treasured her artist's collection of sketch pads, easels, and colored pencils. Mom touted Fashion Institute as her future. SuSu was holding out for Parsons. Donna Karan's school. FIT, after all, is a state college.

That fifteenth year the winds shifted, their direction changed velocity. The cyclone twisted death into them all, striking SuSu before her fashion bud could become a flower. Dad worked too many hours and relevant to most things health related was as clueless as a child, while Mom spent too much time expending all she was beginning to run out of ever to notice mild and minute progressions of temperature, lethargy, and general malaise in her second and most treasured daughter. Discovery of Meningitis was thereby delayed far too long for much more than prayer to offer a hopeful prognosis. One September Tuesday around or about 6:45 AM, both Mom and Dad off to work, Sis, concerned that her sister had been acting strangely and was now sleeping through another day of school slipped — as well as she might be expected to accomplish an act or such delicacy — into SuSu's dark room and found her all but completely unresponsive. Her eyes refused to open; nothing but mumbled groans resulted from Sis' shakes and demands.

911, frantic cell calls to both parents, a ride along within the siren-sound of the ambulance, and six hours later, SuSu was no more.

Sis, having just turned eighteen and unable to feel anything but confusion, left her parents to the details of mortal disposal, looted her savings account — six thousand dollars hoarded toward an impossible acceptance at college — and by seven the next evening sat atop her first Harley Davidson. A four year old Sportster, 1200, peanut tank, blacked out even to the wire wheels, the Death Machine became her chosen ride.

Within the passing of a year's time, all the love and companionship once treasured by Bob and Nancy Jordon dribbled away. First, Mom turned to prayer, the Virgin, and complete removal from all she once held dear. Then Sis discovered her father's entanglement with a youngster slightly less than half his age.

The change in mom, her oppressive piety, her day-long bouts of prayer and self-denial altered the family structure almost as radically as has Susan's death: No more job, no more Pizza Thursdays, no more frantic-cleaning Fridays. No hope. Except in the resurrection. Sis could not help but wonder if this had driven Bob away.

The girlfriend? Pam? She was wicked cute.

Whatever, Sis never blamed either of them. She came both to like and admire the little witch, even after, after less than four months, she and Dad went on their separate ways. As far as Sis was concerned, the girl was way too cool. Anyway, somewhere along the roads they had begun to ride together, Pam had confided. "I know what you are," she asserted as the two of them sat underneath some kind of widespread elm or something and shared a joint. "I like girls, too, you know."

Having never officially admitted her proclivities to anyone, not even completely to herself, at that moment Sis emerged from the oppressive cloud in which she had been enveloped ever since SuSu's passing. Except for Mom and Dad, Susan was the only other human being she had ever loved, and, while many of their sensual moments of sororitous intimacy may have sparked acute physical reactions on her part, never had they been anything more than flashes of a *pyractomena lucifera's* tail in the outer darkness of her repressed awareness. There had, indeed, been times, but they were sisters. Their love for each other could never go into any of those forbidden places. For all others Sis felt nothing at all, had never romanticized, fantasized, or masturbated. Not about anyone of any sex. She had slowly accepted herself as one of those sexless maidens one reads about — at least mother did — but never really believes in.

Her dad held no love for faggots of any sort...even very hot Lesbos. Sis had embraced denial.

First, beneath the horse chestnut tree, not any weepy elm, with Pam's encouragement, she allowed her grief to rise: All the poison of all the days and nights, the interminable weeks and months of riding away from the tragedy of

SuSu's senseless death. Rebecca sobbed, then silently wept herself into a full-throated, marijuana scented roar of anguish allowing the spiral winds of agony to spend themselves upon her.

Her arms too weak, her toes too numb to ride, Sis sagged against the tree's stout trunk until two small arms lifted her head, brushed the snaggled arborage from her hair. Until two lips of power took her own into their chamber and drew forth new life from deep within her. Until she felt Pam's light fingers draw songs upon her breasts. Until she fell into grace.

Everyone must have seen it. Sis was a man in all ways except anatomically. Once aroused, she became Alpha. Pam, most comfortable with either male or female, found herself amused by the big woman's inexpert simulations. It took Sis not three seconds to completely denude her, not even three half seconds to insert herself between the little thing's willing legs, at which point the real fun began. Pam had often snickered beneath the drunken bulk of her Stephen as he attempted wiggly entry, whispered her own inebriated encouragement into his ear as his "magic wand" bent and twisted into nothing more than an invertebrate parody of anything masculine. How he would howl.

How she would laugh. Until she had driven him either to slink away or, even better, to attempt a digital assault. Usually into her back door. She loved that, whining and begging for mercy, all the while reveling in her own pleasure, as much the result of her amusement at his increasing frustration as it was of her own neurological response to the asinine stimulation. He could be a trip.

Well, Sis was no Stephen, although she did eventually resort to digital exploration of several dark places. The yowling was all hers. For the first time — at least as well as memory was able to serve her given the circumstances — Pam discovered a capacity for experiencing a pleasure so mingled with compassion and ineffable sorrow that as Sis worked them both into several effusive orgasms, her only possible response was to throw her arms wide and allow tears, gentle and unaffected, to sing the sad music of her heart.

This poor girl would never belong, was destined never to be happy. Sis was fated to die way before any normal stretch of years. Pam could not allow that to happen. So, as Sis grappled about inside her, Pam resolved, as might the mother of a grievously afflicted child, to make everything all right. To see her newborn through the danger, to alleviate the pain. Sex, she realized was not the means to do so, but since everything was way beyond recall…a few more minutes wouldn't hurt.

"Give it to me, Bear," she growled into the big girl's ear. Gimmie all you got."

NOTHING SIMILAR HAPPENED between them again. A long and emotionally rewarding friendship did, however, and the rewards were not restricted to the interior landscapes of the two women. Sis encouraged Pam to buy her Sportster while the larger of the two women became the proud owner of a brand new Fat Boy, quickly renamed Big Mama. How the two did love to ride. The following spring, Sis having engineered replacement of Sporty's peanut with a four gallon tank, painted black with violet ghosts and just the hint of a red eyed cat somewhere behind the flames, they took a trip all the way to Key West, the next summer to Seattle, Vancouver, and then back home by way of Calgary, Winnipeg, Ottawa, and Montreal. The next year would have seen them attempting the Alcan Highway, but Sis had over the same course of years finished her RN at Hudson Valley, and opted for a program at Drexel shuttling her directly through BSN to MSN. There would be no time for adventures. Pam bid her farewell as the big woman, her new Ram crammed to a bulging tonneau, set off for Philadelphia and a further step into the strange fulfilment of a promise never made.

SOON AFTER SUSAN'S death and the dissolution of his marriage, Bob had begun losing interest in his business and became increasingly enthralled by alcohol. At the same time, Sis found herself developing academic inclinations, especially as concerned matters of diseases, their manifestations, and the care of those afflicted. So it was that father and daughter both lost interest in landscaping and lawn sculpting at the same time, resulting from the same cause, but for different incidental reasons.

She might have chosen medical school or pursued any number of health care options, but her pediatric caregiver had been a nurse practitioner. Ms. Spencer was tall, thin, sharp-faced as a KA-BAR, and her no nonsense, take no prisoners approach to Susan's and Rebecca's girlish phobias, imagined bacterial peril, dietary sensitivities, and hyper-critical self-centricities eloquently demonstrated to Sis the power of a confident, competent, accomplished woman. Mom served men at the pleasure of men. Ms. Spencer strode independently through the life she chose to lead, doing as she chose to do. Had she seen Susan even a day prior to her collapse, possibly had she been at the hospital upon her admittance, things would have turned out differently. Regrettably, as it actually turned out, Ms. Spencer, FNP did, after all, serve at the whim of another. Doctor Romney, William Romney, the man, who assumed Susan's care in the face of its critical nature.

Such was the law. Always must women be kept in their place. Someday…. Sis intended to carry on the work those such as Ms. Spencer had begun. Someday, nursing would be recognized as the primary and essential component of any health care team. Sis would damn well see to that. First, she had to do the time, get her credentials, and become part of the leadership of that indispensable profession. So, off to the City of Brotherly Love, leaving Pam and Mary Elizabeth to their ongoing mission to change at least a little bit of the world.

Of course she would return as often as possible. Ple plust pluldn't pleep plat Plyndi plout plof pler plind.

AS LENARD COHAN, Pam's not-yet lover and awkward proponent of Chaos Theory, might have asserted, "Changin' the world ain't no big thing. We all do it. Asleep at night, awake and snortin' exhaust outta are diesel exhausts. Even dreamin' we influence the universe. The flappin' Japanese butterfly's jest a simple-minded bit a metaphor — parbly could be called a parable, but the truth it illustrates is profound. Stamp yer foot, drop a bottle into a can sommers in Maine or Afghanistan, and Boom. Yev caused the Big One. Shifted all the tectonic plates just that infinitesimal fraction of a fraction of a fraction of an inch. California's the Lost Continent of future legend. Utah's a latter day Santa Barbara.

Pam as she might have become, but never did
May 23, 2003

FRIDAY MORNING INTO THE NON-OCEANIC and decidedly Unislamic world of Troy New York, into the dark clutter of an upstairs room, a can of sorts was dropped — a cellphone call — and, as a result, a shoe was dropped. Thus came about the unhappiness of multitudes of the disenfranchised and the loss of several key players in the unknowable scheme of God. Of Fate? The name matters not. The significance of the chaotic interference of the planned wave of higher probability is that Pam was brushed back from the necessary chance for her own enlightenment by the slightest of changing winds.

She had made certain both the humid and deliciously sweaty, unairconditioned evening before to ply Stephen with his favorite summer ale from the Troy Brew Pub as well as extravagant oral and vaginal manifestations of her wife's arsenal. Then again at seven AM on the lovely May morning of her planned departure for Philadelphia. Tomorrow was graduation day. Sis was being awarded her MSN, and Pam felt almost as proud as would have been the ill-fated Susan. She and the big lunk had become in some ways closer than sisters ever could be. She was riding the Sportster all the way. It would be a test. She had heard evil stories about Philly's traffic, and had decided to take a room in a Jersey hotel close to public transportation so that, should she feel the need, she could just bus or train over and avoid unnecessary risk altogether. She had ridden by most big cities not through them, and, in truth, avoided even Albany during rush hour.

A wimp for sure, but she was good at covering up her fears, and as long as Sis didn't suspect anything, she was golden.

When the call came, she was packing her toiletries. Lurching for the stupid little thing, she succeeded only in knocking it to the floor. Some items like cell phones have become necessities for modern Americans, especially American women, but Pam was not average by anyone's estimation. She hated the idiotic thing, and, were it not for her need to talk privately, even while at home, she might have forsworn the entire universe of electronic communications, and a girl — especially one like Pam — does need her privacy. Even from... no, especially from, her husband. She might not have answered had she seen Stephen's name on her screen, but fumbling for the thing before the caller, probably Sis, was sent off to voice mail caused her to open the line without ascertaining who was on the other end.

241

She might have known. The asshole was jealous, and after a brief flurry of accusations ranging from the homo to the hetero erotic possibilities of her weekend away, he demanded she meet him in his office for a reminder of the consequences of any misbehavior.

Pam often loved such situations, reveled in them actually. If he did things that really hurt her, he would weep and plead, buy, and buy, and buy. If all that happened was a little kink of a mildly perverted nature? Not only could she handle it, but actually adored it. Of course she would meet him. Of course she would promise to be a good girl. She was his, his wife, his whore. She would be right over.

She rode the sportster and parked in the nearly vacant lot just a building away from the library which housed the English Department faculty offices. Climbing the concrete stairwell, bare of paint or decorative impulse, always depressed her, sent her mind into prisons where she had never served and ghettos misconstructed for such as she might have become were it not for Stephen. He had lifted her from a world of poverty and ignorance and, despite her lack of any academic credentials, actually enjoyed showing her off to his colleagues and their hair-legged little mates. Yes, she owed him.

She loved him.

In her own way.

So it was that, with a smile and a happy heart conjured into existence by the oppressive surroundings, Pam let herself into the windowless cubicle Stephen generously termed his "office." Directly opposed to the heavy, grey metal door sat his coffee-brown desk, directly behind which sat Stephen himself. Hard against her right elbow rose a grey-specked, green block wall, and to her left, up against its own wall, lurked another desk, its resident computer dumped beside it on the floor. A grey metal chair had been shoved to the other side. Stephen's desk lamp shadowed evil intent upon the entire setting. Pam knew her duty.

Her main problem was that she had worn jeans not her usual short skirt, her new Harley Davidson belt, black Doc Martins, and a pale sunshine widowmaker topped by a worn but righteous black-leather jacket. She could tell Stephen was not well-pleased.

"Shed the jacket, shirt and pants," he growled. Save the panties and boots. Unless you're wearing socks. You'd better not be. You'd better be wearing underwear though."

She hadn't wanted to wear panties, but had thought the ride might be made more comfortable were she to have a bit of extra protection. Good thing.

Damn it! Such thinking also suggested socks? Long, white, cotton. Stephen was sure to make her pay.

Disrobing as efficiently as possible, she stood before him. No bra, goose-bumps from the full bore AC, nipples erect, little blue panties, untied, partially laced boots. And white socks.

"Off with the fucking socks," her husband ordered.

When she had complied, had inserted bare feet into the Doc Martins, and made to lay the socks on the desk, he stood. He decreed. "Not there!"

Pam knew what was coming. Hoped not.

"One goes in your cock-sucking mouth."

She had worn them all morning, had sweated into them. They were gross. Mutely she complied, fully aware that even a questioning look would bring retribution.

"The other in your cunt."

At first she tried just sneaking it beneath the cover of the crotch of her panties.

"Oh, no you don't," her husband interrupted. "Panties to your knees. Sock all the fucking way up your snatch. You know the drill."

She did. Again she complied.

"You know what's next."

As he never tired of, she assumed the position. Bent over the computer stand, legs as far apart as her panties would allow, all she could do was attempt not to choke on her gag and console herself with the hope that, despite the excesses of the previous twelve or so hours, his importunity would be brief. Unlucky Pam. She was to be given a glimpse into the fevered imagination of a man most profoundly disturbed.

His thorough lubrication of her anus and lower digestive tract came as no surprise, but his next move was unexpected and unwelcome.

"I have a little surprise for you," he chuckled. "A little gift. Here. You unwrap it."

A lesser woman might have cried, begged and pleaded. A braver woman might have torn his eyes from their sockets. A stronger woman never would have found herself in such circumstances. Pam simply gasped and tore at the plastic protecting the most hideous piece of equipment ever devised for another's imagined pleasure. *Red Devil Butt Plug* was its name. The damn thing tapered abruptly along its silicone length from tiny point to two-inch thick base which then lengthened into a finger-hold tab, she imagined, for ease of extraction.

Stephen took it from her and, without preliminaries, jammed the thing into her further and further until she feared she might tear. Finally, he took away the hand, which had been pressing her flat, let go of the little devil, stepped away and retreated behind his desk.

Pam turned, sock stuffed with her cries of pain, movement disrupted by her panties as well as the unrelenting, synthetic invader, but before she could focus upon her tormentor, Stephen commanded, "Eyes down. Don't look at me. Gather up your things and put yourself right out in the hall. If anybody sees you, too bad. School's over. It'll probably only be a janitor. Whatever. You tell them I'm responsible and things'll get a lot worse. That's a promise."

As some of his games went, this one wasn't so bad. When she had come in, there had been only two cars in the lot. No one, she would bet, would be in the hall. Eyes down, hair damp against her cheek, insides screeching for relief, throat on the verge of spasm, she reached for the door handle, but before she could exit, Stephen issued his ultimate sentence. "It's not difficult to deduce that you've ridden your stupid motorbike. Have fun riding back to Winter Street. The plug stays in until I get back. I've about an hour's work to finish up. Then I'll take care of you, and you can be on your way.

"I've my own opportunities, you know. Perhaps you should consider that. I'll call you while you're gone. Do not call me. I won't answer, and each attempt will result in an additional hour's ride upon Big Red."

As expected, the hall was deserted. Pam felt nervous anyway, jittering herself together as quickly as possible. Stephen's head popped from out the office before she could make the stairwell. "Have a nice ride," he called in his most candy-spun tonality.

THE TRIP HOME, although less than a mile, becomes an eternity of pain. Her bike has rear springs but is no "soft tail." Even without something jammed up her ass, it can be a painful ride. Every patch, every goddamn manhole she thumps into stabs the fucking demon deeper into her swelling colon. She has to shit. Or at least fart, but the plug-devil won't allow it, and the battering ram her saddle has become keeps driving everything back into places to which they have no business returning. She feels like a character on *South Park*, Martha Stewart with a turkey up her ass.

Across the line. Into Troy the bike once again drops down into the hard well of broken asphalt in front of Holy Spirit. She belches. Swears she can taste the shit. Feels something liquid trickle past the device. Thank God, she's made it home. She creeps across the broken interface of her drive with the street and only then notices the Firebird pulled up to the akilter black and white shed Stephen thinks of as a garage.

It's Dan, Dan the Dreaming man. Just what she needs. A visitor, a cute male at that, and she with a stick up her butt and shit oozing down her leg. Probably right up the tract and into her breath. Nice guy and all. Lousy timing.

He is behind the wheel. She pulls to his passenger side and dismounts, lessening the pain to some minor extent. Way cool! His windows are automatic, and the one on her side slides effortlessly into the door's dark crease. "I'as jus' leavin'," he rumbles over the muted bass of exhaust. "Stevie said to meet 'im here at ten. You know where he's at?"

Of course she does, but is not about to say. He'd drop everything for Danny Boy. She really doesn't want him home. At least not so soon. "He told me you were coming," she answers. "But he thought it was tomorrow."

"Na, it weren't," Dan grumbles, thumbing through a very neat and professional-looking appointment book. "Says right here," and he offers the entry her way, but only briefly, "Yep. Says right here 'Friday, May 23. 10 o'clock.' Wrote it down's we was talkin'. What I think's the nutty professor can't git his days straight. Probly never wrote it down. Anyways, I got other people looking fer what I got. Tell 'im next month or maybe six weeks. Don't know. Shit I deal with don't come 'round regular, ya know."

Pam does know. Pam is not happy with waiting. Danny has dynamite hash, windowpane of the finest quality on the right coast, and mushrooms or maybe psilocybin. All at a reasonable, if not bargain, price. She knows where Stephen's stash money is and begins to feel within her congested bowels a further congestion demanding retribution. Comes an inspiration. Fully formed, a plan springs to life way up into her lower digestive system. She will make Stephen pay. He will be none the wiser. She will know, and Stevie boy will be the fool. Forever.

Her discomfort has become a secondary aspect of her renewed self. It must be dealt with. But first. "I can handle things," she breathes into the new-plastic interior. "Come on in and have a beer. Stevie's got the cash already put away and I know exactly what he ordered." With that and without even a glance backward, Pam glides across the crabbed up grass and shale-chip yard, and, by the time Danny sticks his mop-top mullet through the doorway into the kitchen, she is snapping the tab of a Budweiser and welcoming him into her newly woven web.

"Be right back," she sings over her shoulder, once he is seated at the unusually clear and clean metal table. "Gotta get your money. Got some girl stuff to take care of too." The contented look on his batchy face tells it all. He likes the money, but "girl stuff" has him wrapped and ready.

Pam climbs the stairs, and by the time she reaches the top is once again inspired. Her butt hurts, is on fire actually, her colon is due to explode at any moment, and something akin to the first rush of a fever chill is generating beneath her still untroubled exterior. A wave has gathered. Has not yet broken. Soon…it must.

Then arises a tsunami of another sort. She has known for some while that she is strange. At one time a short time ago she cradled a fragile little bird in her hands, certain that it would fly no more, only to feel it revive, its heart grow strong and quick. Then it flew away. It could not have been dead. She has always been certain that it was.

Next came her little nephew, Jake, her sister's firstborn. They said he suffered from Multiple Sclerosis. She had seen, had held him close, had felt the jumbled patterns crossed up within him. That day she kissed his cheek, laid her hand upon his pale forehead. Jake had cried. Screamed would be more accurate. The next tests showed no sign of the condition. The present Jake is a star fifth-grade soccer player. She knows it is her doing. There are others. Just not as dramatic.

Eventually, Pam accepted that she possessed a strangeness beyond anything scientifically explainable or experimentally demonstrable. Made perhaps over confident by the Jake experience, she attempted healing her mother of the diabetes and the COPD which eventually killed her. She might as well have tried to catch the wind. Her mother's soul grew dim; her life ebbed into stillness, and her spirit went the way of its kind. Pam had been left defeated and certain that hers was a case of unwarranted egotism. She was no Jesus. No Holy Mary. Not even a Pentecostal tent revivalist. She was gentle — at times. She was kind — again.... She also believed in synchronicity. She and apparent miracles happened at times to occupy the same time and space. She did not, however, cause them to happen. Her observation presence serve some useful purpose, but, truly, she couldn't even be sure of that.

At the top of the stair this day, however, stands the truth. She **did** raise the bird up from death. She **was** the agent of Jake's cure. Is the message in the sunlight streaming through the bedroom door out into the hall, directly into her dazzled eyes? Or is it from within? Her own light shining upon her own self? Who is it from?

Whatever. She might never know. This she does know. She may sometimes fail, as with her mother, but most often she will succeed, especially as she learns to distinguish those whose conditions are merely the chance events of human existence from those who suffer as a result of some purpose beyond even her advancing awareness. There is more. She is capable of far more than healing. This day is the moonrise of that darker power. Were she Hindu, she would recognize within her the archetypical figure of Kali. As a fallen away Baptist reborn into Stephen's particular brand of Roman Catholicism, she has no idea who the potent Lady within her might be named. She does, however, recognize vengeance and retribution as her playthings. Knows that death as well as life is hers to command. Before this day is done she will embrace the symbol of all that she is to become which is no more than that which she has always been.

No doubt Danny can hear her exclamation, "Hallelujah!" A song lyric. Not a prayer to anyone he would recognize, but she knows: the two are often one and the same. Her butt no longer screams, her colon is placid, and "ague" is both a word and a condition she need not concern herself with. A simple mental or spiritual, at least conscious tic into a place she knows she has visited before, and the intrusion into her digestive extremity is of no consequence. "I still need the toilet," she cautions herself with a giggle, and to that end expels the artificial devil into the soon to be foul water. Then she flushes it all away, at least as far as it will go. Unconsciously, she has clogged the waste line. Accidently on purpose too. Another thing Stephen will end up paying for. Oh, yeah, the price of perversion. The price tag set upon abuse.

"Vengeance is mine," sayeth the Lady Pamela.

No Lady, not even a newly incarnate goddess, is comfortable with the odors, effusions, and stains associated with her biological manifestation. Pam reeks; the mirror tells a crimson tale of blood and brown down her thighs and no doubt caking its crusty self up into her crack. She needs a bath. A shower will have to do.

Fearful that she may lose Danny, she calls down in her most light-hearted tones. "Sorry, Dan. This is gonna take a bit longer than I thought. Help yourself to another beer. There's gin in the cupboard. Tonic somewhere too, if you like. I won't be long. I promise. Ten minutes. OK?"

"Yeah. Take yer time," the stoner returns after the briefest of pauses. Just long enough to hold onto something fine for just an extra second or two.

The guy can amuse himself. She needn't have worried. Thus does Pam spend extra moments upon her preparations, even trimming just a little down where too much hair tends to grow. Adds a little scent too. Just above the clit. Between her breasts. And lipstick. Most guys she knows don't even notice a woman's eyes or her blush. They do, however, respond eagerly to lips drawn and colored as if they had tasted blood and were open to being themselves a whole lot more than sampled. Stephen loves it when she leaves lipstick smudged up and down the length of his penis. Claims to dream about them. She'll see how the Dreamin' Man himself will respond.

Slipping a sundress over her still damp and naked body, Pam sails down the stairs and floats upon a wave of her new energy into the kitchen where Dan sits contemplating a spider which has chosen to share the table with a human of strange vibration.

"Fuckin' thing's tryin' ta talk ta me," he shushes out. "Don't say nothin'. Don...."

Pam works the life from the brown thing into a mess upon the laminate top. "I hate spiders," she states. "But I love mushrooms," at which point she drops the agreed-upon cash onto the spider smudge. "There's something I bet you like better than a fucking spider too. Give me the goods and maybe I'll let you send another thing or two my way.... If you know what I mean."

He does. Obviously. From the moment his eyes found her form upon entry they never once strayed from her breasts, unbound and nipple erect beneath the thin fabric of her dress. Until the cash buried the arachnid's remains, that is. Nobody's fool, Dan's first act is to count it. Only when satisfied does he push the soft bag of goodies from his place across to her. "Check it out. It's all there. And just a touch of something Stevie was askin' about. Thought I'd let him give it a try. On the house. Ever heard a Ecstasy?"

Pam knows that in no way is he referring to the word Stephen's colleagues would immediately think of. This has to be some kind of new drug. Interesting name. Conjures up images of orgies and wild abandon. Also of spiritual elevation and mystical enlightenment. And fat old Mother at a tent revival, struck by the Spirit and writhing upon the floor, a bloated arachnid missing half her legs shouting "Praise Jesus!" as loudly as her failing lungs will allow.

Ecstasy. Transcendence or spiritual gluttony? No matter which road one may choose, "ecstasy" involves loss of autonomy. Pam will have none of that. For Stephen, Ecstasy is the ideal drug.

"Whatever," she responds. "I know nothing and don't care to learn anything. This is quite alright with me," whereupon she reaches into the bag withdraws a sample of the acid and, assuring herself that the pane is not too much, pops it down into the kiln of her digestive system which will soon transform it into visions and pleasures she knows she can manage.

Dan sits placidly, even when she approaches him, kneels, and unzips his fly. She knows it. He has probably been hard since first seeing her. Men are so fucking easy.

Bending to her purpose, Pam manages to draw little, red rings upon different extensions of his uncircumcised penis. About an inch apart. "Nice and big," she gobbles at him, successful at marking her territory way down at its base. Expelling his business back into the humid air, she cajoles as would a mother to a child, "Wanna put that in a better place?"

Without another word, she rises, spins about, and, flashing a quick glimpse of her clean butt his way, skips from the room and has nearly reached the top of the stairs when Danny catches up. Without words but accompanied by grumbles resembling something a nervous dog might utter, he pushes her down so that her elbow strikes hard upon the edge of the floor above them, and begins attempting some form of rear entry but butting impotently between the two possible accommodations. "God damn," he moans in his dogfright voice. "I can't git it in."

"You ain't gonna either. Not out here anyway," Pam snarls over her shoulder. Something more akin to killer wolf than nervous poodle coloring her voice. Then, in subdued and friendlier tones, "The bedroom's just across the hall. It'll be more comfortable for both of us."

Thus it comes to pass. Dan is well into his second wind when the phone sings. Pam answers, mumbles something unintelligible, pops Dan twice upon the ass, and chortles, "Better get it done, Danny Boy. The old man's on his way home."

Some men might have shrunk away, other men might have bolted from the house without even grabbing their boots from the kitchen floor. To his credit, if so you wish it to be, Dan smoothly dumps a second load of potency into Pamela's vagina — as she knew he would — unhurriedly gathers his things from both floors, checks to see if the cash is still in his pocket, and calls up to his onceandneveragain lover. "See ya, darling."

Hearing the cuckoo bird fire up, Pam smiles. Nearly an hour later Stephen finds her, demurely clad in her sundress, hips elevated upon two pillows, a very acidic smile upon her dark lady's face.

Without a word, he parts her knees, his face registering a close approximation of disbelief. "I told you to leave it in," he snaps.

"You said you'd be home in an hour," Pam crackles right back. "It's been at least two."

"That makes not a whit of difference," the faux cad declares in something of an accent. "You'll have to pay."

"Stephen," Pamela pronounces directly into his twisted little smile, "I'll pay if I decide to do so. Try and force me, and you'll wish to your almighty Jesus you hadn't."

A further wrench applies itself to the expression about his lips. Confusion begins to twist itself beneath the humor of his eyes. "Exactly what might you mean by that?" the wilting roué questions, uncertainty evident in his New York tone.

"What I mean is, Cuckoo Bird, I get my own pleasure or you get nothin'. I'm not in the mood for a spanking. Still, I'll play the bad girl if you're willing to play the good man."

"At what precisely could you be hinting?" The twisting winds of confusion visibly clear from Stephen's face. He loves these games. Pam knows her asshole well.

"Take a look at what you've left me with," she demands as he lifts the hem of her dress and allows his vision followed by his imagination to visit her holy grotto. Pam cautions, "Don't touch. You've made a slimy mess of me... all last night and then again this morning. Be happy I couldn't stand the shit was leaking outta my butt. Had to wipe my behind. The other mess from my other hole? That's yours, nutty bird. All yours. And I expect a thorough licking. First whale away on my butt. I'm gonna love it the way you know I can. Then, even better, work your cunning linguistic charm upon the mess you've made of me. Afterwards maybe we can work up another long, strange trip from the goodies your boy Dan left us."

For the first time ever, Pam crashes to a halt. Wherever did she get the language she has just used? You might think she'd gone to college or something.

She's starting to sound like Stephen. Well, whatever. She guesses it is a change for the better, especially if she is to judge by Stephen's reaction.

As he rummages around the top drawer of her dresser searching for his fraternity paddle, he too jerks to a halt before whirling about as she positions herself for his ministrations, her skirt gathered around her waist, her thighs shiny in the brilliant sun pouring over them like the spirit of God. "Why are you calling me cuckoo" he demands. "Do you have any idea what that implies?"

"Crazy," Pam snickers into her pillow. "Now, My Lord, give me that which I require."

He does. Twenty-five smart ones. Pam is red and beginning to blister. She only comes once.

Rolling back upon her back, her wounds already healed, her pain a fading memory, Pam's thighs part as they should, and as Stephen settles between them, she experiences the moment of implantation of the zygote resulting from the fortuitous union of Dan's sperm with the ovum she had so hastily produced just prior to their coupling.

As her newfound mastery of her physicality allows, Pam hastens along the slow crawl of her vagina's cleansing process, delivering to her vulva and exterior labia two full doses of Daniel's ejaculata. Stephen can't tell the difference, but Pam knows.

Barely able to conceal her laughter as her husband roots about in another man's leavings, Pam dwells in a land of magical probability. The child will be a boy. She will see to that. He will be named Stephen Edward. He will be her champion.

Will grow strong and dark.

Will understand the chaotic nature of the world around them.

Will right all of the wrongs his father has imposed upon her.

PAM NEVER MAKES it to Philly, in a slow erosive manner loses touch with her overlarge friend. Sis continues on, and encounters Pam only as a profile in random passing cars on the streets of Philadelphia, her adopted home town. She dies of kidney failure at the age of forty-seven, on her own unit of her own hospital with no one there to more than perfunctorily regret her passing. Her parents are dead. Her colleagues shed some tears. Two NP's attend her funeral, as does the Pam who has not forgotten her but never reestablished contact. She just never had the time. Friendships often pass before the friends.

FOR THE FIRST four or five years of little Stephen's existence, Big Steve, his proud father, doted upon him. The *übervater*, initiated college savings accounts, invested in an IRA, purchased balls, soccer, of course, and made a show — or is that a *point?* — of taking his child everywhere he was able, including: office hours, an occasional class, department meetings, play rehearsals, prayer groups and Bible studies. At Mass, every Sunday and at least twice weekly, he would carry his son with him to receive Communion, both species, requiring that the Priest deposit the host upon his tongue in the old and superior fashion and that the Eucharistic Minister hold the chalice to his lips while he sipped a bit more of the precious blood than that functionary deemed appropriate.

Of course, he then shared just a tab of the body and drop of the blood from his own mouth to that of his child. Did not Jesus decree, ""Suffer the little children to come unto me"? Did not God, himself, approve?

Pam did. She breast fed Stevie until he was four, rejoiced as Stephen shouldered her aside at changing time. Inhaled the glory of his baby scent, felt her soul bond with his as he curled into the profound sleep only a baby knows. Sadly, most of the chores of motherhood are so quotidian as to deaden the mind, fatigue the body, and eventually drain one's energy until she has nothing left of all that once had been herself. She is MOM. Men, fathers, rarely go there. Stephen might have. To be certain, his early obsession left Pam with the necessary freedom to create a Pamela who could be both Mom and autonomous human being. Little Stevie did not become her life. She could love him as a separate individual. She did no other than that even when Stephen's paternal ardor began to cool until it eventually froze.

The chill took its time developing. Hastened to the freeze.

Somewhere into Stevie's fourth year, Stephen could be observed holding the squirming toddler at arm's length, staring intently into the little one's puckering face. "I can't see it," he might be heard to say. "He hasn't your eyes. Nor does he have mine." The child's eyes were brown, more akin to ochre than Stephen's blue-coal or Pam's deep-earth mystery. Sometimes Stephen would mutter to himself as he jogged on a Saturday morning prior to Prayer Breakfast, "His face. It's not from my side of things." Other times, he would demand of Pam, "What did your father really look like? All I've ever seen are bad pictures of him. Could Little Stevie perhaps look like him?"

Eventually, three months prior to Stevie's sixth birthday, the no longer *übervater* arrived at 111 Winter Street in possession of his ticket to the land of the dead. Rampaging into the kitchen where Pam sat awaiting her kindergartener's hour of release from the church-school two properties over, his first act was to tip the table upon her, spattering coffee and the leavings of the previous evening's meal across the spotted floor.

"Here, cunt," he shouted, waving a paper about, then throwing it toward her stunned form. "You think you could fool me forever? Read this, you fucking whore."

Without any rational thought, perhaps just a bit dizzy from a modest toke of some blonde, Pam could only chirp. "Cuckoo! Cuckoo!"

With murderous intent, Stephen dragged her from beneath the table, kicked her jaw into several misaligned sections, and caved in three ribs on her right side, puncturing a lung in the process. He left her gasping and bleeding on the dirty floor then walked out the same back door through which Danny had once entered. Little Stephen discovered his senseless mother forty minutes later.

Were it not for the kind, beautiful, and closeted-lesbian minister who had walked Stephen Edward home, the future might have found itself without a Pamela Bruno. Hard as she had tried, healing herself would not happen. She lay close to death and inching closer with each bloody, tortured gasp. The Reverend Sally McKenna saw to her removal to St. Mary's Hospital, tended to the boy until she was released three days later, soon became a regular fixture in the shabby little household at 111, and soon Stevie could proudly proclaim to an awakening America that he had two mommies.

Pam as she turns out to be
May 23, 2003

INTO THE NON-OCEANIC and decidedly Unislamic world of Troy New York, into the dark clutter of an upstairs room, a can of sorts is dropped — a cellphone call. A more insecure and more fearful — a weaker — woman might have responded, fumbled for the cell and been summoned to a dark office where an abusive husband lurked within the deeper well of his own imaginings. Pam is not that woman.

She knows it. Stephen is attempting to sabotage her trip. That is not going to happen. She depresses the "off" tab, cuts herself loose from all interference. The bike's two saddlebags and her backpack are stuffed with her things; she has just inhaled no more than two or maybe five or six draughts of prime weed. The weekend awaits.

The Sportster flaunts straight pipes and a tail hard as Pam's is soft. She's loud. She's light, and she loves to share each dip, hump, and pothole thump with her rider. A thoughtful mate, she also soothes her mistress' jangled nerves, humming her into a paradoxical disassociation from the oppressive particularity around them. It is more than a remote possibility that a lesser rider than Pam, her mind pleasantly clouded by Sinsemilla and her physicality atingle with the Stir's Milwaukee vibrations, might fail upon some moments of traffic irregularities or waft over a hill's infinite crest into a great wide open beyond the petty bonds of mortality, but Pam is no mere putterer. Straight and true she rides — except on curves and turns — away from the estuarial towns of the Capital District, descending toward sea-level, through the apple tree valley, off to the city of sisterly love.

For such a little chick, Sporty really guzzles gas, and the crazy think keeps her secrets. No gas gauge. Except in Pam's mind that is. So it is that four gallons, at somewhere around fifty-five miles per, necessitates a refill along the pike. Why she does such things, why she always would do them, Pam cannot say, but again, waving her middle finger in the stern face of Mathematical Probability, she bypasses the Richard Stockton Service Area and thunders straight on toward Cherry Hill, New Jersey. About four miles worth of Pike. Then a sputter, a buck, and a kick into exhausted silence. She has already been running on Reserve. She is screwed. She is not stranded.

She has a fork lock. Her ignition takes a key. Securing a note to her seat, Pam hefts her pack across her shoulders and treks back up the highway toward gas. After a good and sweaty hour and a half or so she reaches Richard

Stockton. The guy at the pumps tells her he has no means of selling her fuel unless she has a legitimate container. "Maybe inside," he suggests. "Be sure you get one's DOT approved. I can't fill no milk carton or nothin'"

Muttering something uncomplimentary under her breath, she turns to the squat building indicated by the pump jockey.

"Aincha got triple A or something?" Jock calls after her.

No, she thinks but doesn't bother saying.

The jerk inside is no better than the asshole outside. "Got nothing like that," the flat-faced, outtie bellied lout grumbles up from the racing form. "You gonna have ta call for somebody. That's if the cops don't tow ya first. Where yall from anyways?"

Before she can help herself, the Pam always waiting behind the little woman smile lunges, "From Hell, you red-neck asshole, and you're gonna wish you'd helped me. I'll make it worth your while if you do. If you don't...? Well, that's a chance you take."

The idiot's laughing. Not cruel, not sarcastic. Ironic? Must be. Genuine? Certainly is.

"Red neck, sweetheart?" he spits through his mirth. "You blind or something? When's the last time you seen a red neck on a dude black as me?"

Laughter forces its way through her anger. "I never have she admits, but you don't sound like no boy from the hood neither."

"Alabama all the way," the man states more than a little proudly. "Talk like Bama and love the Crimson Tide. My Mama even named me Paul, and jus ta make sure everybody knew her intentions, always called me Bear. Last name's Briant, just an i off from the Man's full name. Went to Alabama too. Graduated with a BS in Business Management.

"See how far that's got me, doncha? Alls I do is set here each and all livelong day dealing with the State of New Jersey, suppliers, cops, deadbeats, and more often than I should have to, citizens. Whole lotta 'em just like yourself."

"Yea, yea," Pam retorts. "I'm stranded on the Jersey Turnpike, and I should feel sorry for you?"

"Yer a real charmer, aincha. Most women in your shoes...really most women wouldn't be in your shoes...wouldn't wanna be...." He pauses long and looks hard into her eyes. "As I was about to say, most women in your shoes would be in here turnin' on the tears, playin' the helpless routine. Not you though. Anyway, all ya has to do is come up with a little gratuity...."

"Ain't got an extra twenty do ya? That'd fix things up just fine, make me happy as a yellowhammer on an infested pine tree. You catchin' my drift?"

"An' what's the twenty buy me, anyway?"

"Two gallon can fulla gas."

That's all Pam needs. The walk back to Sporty'll take its toll both in time and fatigue, but you gotta live with what you got. "Yeah, OK" she answers. "One thing, I wanna see the can and see the gas before you get the cash."

A Yogi smile lights Bear's face. "Hold your water, and I'll have it for you in nothin' flat."

The Bear is almost true to his word. Pam spies him outside his office window in little under a minute and a half by her cellphone's clock. Tapping on the glass, Bear beckons her outside. "Can't bring this stuff inside," he explains once she has joined him. "Open 'er up and take a whiff. Good old 87 octane'll have your car purrin' like a kitten 'till you can drive 'er back down here. Can't imagine you're more'n a couple miles up the road. You know…you walkin' an' all."

Pam smiles to herself while presenting the Yogi with her most severe face. "I'm down south of here. Maybe four or five miles."

"You'd best get a move on. You leave a note or anything? Trooper's er likely to tow ya if yer there too long."

Shit! That's all she needs. Get all the ways back down and find her bike gone. So, she quickly shoves a bill in the man's long hand, controls as best she can a grimace, shoulders her pack, hooks her fingers around the can's plastic handle, and smiles farewell as ironically as she is able.

Not two steps away, however, Paul interferes. "I get off in lessen an hour. Goin' that way on home anyway. Nother twenty'll buy you a ride."

Pam finds her response so amusing that she laughs out loud. Is this backwoods anti-hip hop thug best called a brigand? Or highwayman? "'Tlot, tlot,'" she spits his way. "You got a sweetheart waiting by her window for you?"

Surprise…surprise. Really. "Rememberin' ninth grade English?" he mocks. "Like the Barrel Organ better myself." The imbecile becomes positively lyrical, "'Yes," he chants far away from the asphalt world in which he usually dwells, his voice as lovely and musical as the Garden's in springtime.

"…as the music changes
Like a prismatic glass,
It takes the light and ranges
Through all the moods that pass;
Dissects the common carnival

Of passions and regrets,
And gives the world a glimpse of all
The colors it forgets.

Paul's face falls empty as the lyrics die into the Turnpike chaos. His eyes turn up and inward, and Pam fears he may swoon — the only appropriate word — but he recovers, smiles a bit shyly, and mutter more to himself than to Pam. "Sorry. Don't know where that came from."

"Where did you come from?" Pam responds. "Where's the highwayman who's been sounding like a backwoods hillbilly who somehow fudged his way through a southern college. What in hell they teach business students down there anyway?"

Bear grins in a most unmirthful way. "Should a been an Arts major. Wanted to, but, I lived home, and Mom wasn't about to support me through four years of an education with extremely limited prospects for employment of any substantial nature. At least that's how she put it." Light, refracted by droplets of sweat begins to shine through his face. Pam spies energy either reaching toward the heavens or flowing from them. Whichever it is, she realizes she knows nothing of what this Pirate truly is. She wonders does he? How does she inquire without disrupting the dazzling eruption of energy reaching into infinity from his crown and beginning to envelop his entire physical being? This is not some randomly energized chakra, not a trick of sun and heat. Paul Bear Briant is becoming light. He will soon blaze brighter than the sun....

Business at the pumps goes on as usual. Traffic passes at turnpike speed. Paul, meanwhile has become a face, blacker than those of his original Ancestors, at the core of molten flowing rivers of photons never quite dissociating themselves from the great wave of their origin. The eyes are blacker than black and burn with energy as yet unleashed.

Again, she asks, "Who are you?"

"I am your father," the burning man answers. "I do believe it's about time we met."

Pamela Bruno is not easily frightened. She is the daughter of The Most High, sister — half — of Jesus. This thing before her is nothing like her brother's description of their Dad. Sometimes the guy is powerful and all. But a hydrogen fireball of some sort? Black at its heart to boot? She does begin to tremble. Just a bit.

"No, you're not," she quavers. "My father died long ago. In New York. He was a county worker not a gas station attendant. He most definitely wasn't some black dude from Alabama." Know what I think, don't you? You're the Devil. That's who. Thanks for the gas and all, but, I'm outta here."

"Yeah, that's right, girl. God can't be a black guy. We all know, Jesus was white. Maybe a little tanned... but white through and through. Black! Now that be bad!"

Something in the fireman's tone stops her. She would swear he is mocking her.

"So? You trying to tell me you're who? God."

"Damn right," the Great Wave flares. "I'm God, and I'm blacker than the cinders I won't reduce yall to. Or should I have said, 'to which I shall not reduce, yall?'" At this point the rioting tongues of firelight embrace her with a warmth much cooler than is possible, and Pam finds herself become a being of light, someone she has always known herself to be. Just not until this moment.

*I am no longer human. Why do I not burn? Is there nothing **to** burn? Are the nerve endings, the flesh in which they lie, the marrow of my many numbered bones consumed? Am I born into some heaven or hell not dreamt of in any sane person's philosophy?*

"I am the great I Am," enfolds her within the rich embrace of a dark vocalization. "You, my pretty little girl, have yet to be. Quiet now! Listen. Observe. You are about to learn more than you ever supposed you might. As well, you should realize several things and recognize the truer natures of several people you think you already know."

But.... How...?

"Be still. More will be answered than you could ever think to ask.

"First, my sweet little yet to be, look to the one you call brother. You think you know him. You mock him. You try to avoid him. However, from this moment on, understand that you continue to do so at your own peril. Now, I'm not meaning to suggest you treat him with reverence or anything even resembling that. He can be a bit of supercilious prig at times. At others annoyingly mischievous, but, overall, he's the real deal. And you're going to have to get past his annoying qualities, especially his more outlandish personae. When it comes right down to it, even more than my Man Ali, he's The Greatest.

"Come on over, son."

From somewhere so far off as to be right beside her appears a black-giant of a man, arrayed as an Egyptian king with the sharp eyes of an obsidian eagle, their volcanic fire still alive beneath their surface shine. A golden helmet clasps his shaven head, and twin cobras flare rampant from its polished surface.

"Cool it a bit, boy," commands I Am. "Can't you just be yourself at least for this cubit of time?"

"Dad..., you, yourself said I should be all things to all men...at least all good things," the regal figure whines. "Then, when I try.... You reprimand me."

"Just bring it down a notch," the smooth voice croons. "Into the twenty-first century. Or at least the twentieth. No need for robes and sandals. How about jeans and a tee shirt? Tie died, if you want. Running shoes'd go good with that. Try New Balance."

Immediately the king segues into a very tan Elton John, a trifle pudgy, going a bit bald with an incongruous sprouting of very sparse dreds. "Goin' Rasta," the black Brit pipes as from the fire he draws forth a joint of tremendous magnitude upon which he feasts as would a proper queen upon his lover's biological number.

"Jesus Christ," the smooth I Am rasps. "Only...."

"Here, Father," Elton Marley sings, his native rhythm beginning to assert itself at the very outset. "We be jamming," whereupon he exhales a cloud of potent vapors substantial enough to reduce I Am to a dreadful fit of deep throat coughing, and to create in Pamela the most delightful lightness of being anyone as insubstantial as a wave of pure light might find herself elevated unto.

As the Great One recovers himself, Elton reassembles into a very recognizable twenty-first century neo-hippie. Long black hair, crooked front teeth, scraggly beard, and s-curved spine. His legs poke all curly-fried from his shorts. His eyes are glazed, concealing an inward acuity Pam has begun to realize is characteristic either of the righteously stoned or the even more righteously self-aware, those who have become observed and observer, who have realized their inward Word and have emerged from the first moment of that recognition into the infinite possibility of their own oneness with the infinity Mr. Harrison realized was within and without them.

"I said it first," the unshaven one chirps, his face twisted into something resembling a light black Alfred E Newman. He does not worry, but, his insecurity demands this defense of his own Word. "Remember? The kingdom...?"

"Zip it, J H," The Light commands. "We need to get your sister up and running. By the way, as we do that, you might consider why it is I need a new spokesperson for this new millennium. As I know you know, times have moved way beyond the year zero, but your crowd remains dedicated to keeping the old ways alive. Now, I am aware this one has a lot to learn, and, my good son, I'm putting you in charge of that education. Her well-being as well. You might also try to learn a little from her too. "According to ancient wisdom, as the current idiom would have it, she's fucked-up to the max, but, you'd best believe it, for these times she is the Max. She's already done things to offend you and those who claim to follow you. Her style is decidedly un-Christian. Still, she's my little girl. My hope as well as my joy.

"For you, my First Commandment is: Honor her.

"The second follows: Through her, honor Me.

"Third, and final: Through her, honor yourself.

"All else will follow."

"So, I'm now become merely an adjunct — a footnote to the new dispensation?" Jesus wails, grabbing another super-blunt from the fire as he so does. "Then what? Off to another of your crazy worlds? Another crucifixion? Is that all I am? The sacrificial Lamb of God, my task menial at best, merely to ease the way for such as this one?

"Now I get it. You made me give up my little Jennifer to her, and she immediately wrapped her up in excrement, wrote a nasty word using that particular medium upon her bedroom wall. Then you had me take her...."

"Jesus Fucking Christ," a stricken Pamela explodes. "That creep. Fucking Gerry. He was dead. Killed himself. Was on his way to Hell when you had me save him. What a fucking salvation that was. I got him away from the demons sent to collect him, somehow brought him back into my room. The room with the shit writing on the wall, the room where fucking Stephen had imprisoned me. Then....

"Then you let him rape me. In the ass. While he called me Hansel.

"Who the fuck are you? What the fuck...?"

A suddenly very normal human being, brown to black, the apple from his father's ancient tree, Jesus, as he is too bored to forever remain, in the tones of an Oxford Don explains. "It was necessary, Pamela. It is written that upon Calvary I took unto myself the sins of the world so that they might be forgiven. To a great extent, that claim is nonsense, but a hint of truth glimmers there. I have forgiven many wrongs. Understand me. We condemn ourselves to Hell. We elevate ourselves into the Heaven of our own imagining. That sad man, Gerry Faustino, needed to empty himself of the greatest part of that which he had become. His life was a foul deposit into a septic well. He needed to rid himself of that. He needed someone greater than he, someone more than most human beings may ever be. He needed you. He found his salvation the moment you allowed him into yourself and accepted his spectral member, embraced the darkness within his soul.

"Pamela, as his ghost came into you, his spirit was cleansed, and Gerry moved on. Into his own pink little house, alongside an interworld highway, with his own sweet Glad, next door to Hansel, the child he never killed."

That makes no sense to Pam and she says so. She is remembering this episode for the very first time in its disgusting entirety. It happened. She knows this without a doubt. In fact, she has been visited by little flashes at random times over the past several years, particularly when she and Jennifer, Stephen mercifully off somewhere, shared a drink or two as well as a pipe of something rocket strong. For a roach, that little one can party with the Pros.

Jesus explains further. "You've seen me. At your window. Usually in disguise, I'll admit. Your association with *Ladies of Mary* and the resultant association with you know who? That was my doing. I've been watching you for quite some time... from the moment of your birth actually. Now, my little sister, I guess our Big Pappy's turning some of my function over to you. I'm not really as surprised — as pissed—as I've seemed. Dad explained as much as he cared to—no more than was absolutely necessary, I might opine — long ago. Look at our situation this way. You're the intern, and I'm your mentor. You know all you need to know...no doubt intuitively...and my job is to guide you in the performance of your craft. To polish your skills, so to speak."

"My craft?" Pam scoffs. "Just what in bloody hell—where in bloody hell did this CS Lewis via Elton John expression come from? — might my sodding craft be? *Bloody Hell!*

"Just the second coming. It's absolutely simple," crackles the Father's voice. "You were promised. The world's been waiting. As everyone except the growing ranks of atheists acknowledges, I am a man of my word.

"Now, son, if it is not overly harsh of me to ask, would you step aside? Another awaits her audience."

The very normal Christ sifts away into the roiling McNeil interactions as another intensifies at first forming an impressionistic wraith, vaguely human, but soon forming into a classic van Gogh self-portrait—that is if Vincent had been a beautiful young woman.

"I know you," Pam asserts. "You're that doctor. Psychiatrist maybe? Amilee's friend.... Paloma?"

"Guilty," Paloma smiles through the Dutchman's firestrokes. "We really have too much to talk about for this limited situation to handle. So, if you don't object, I shall briefly speak my piece and then we can all move on. Don't worry.

We now are in this together and I intend for us to become as close as sisters. To share like sisters too."

Paloma's words lick into the corners of Pam's consciousness as would lingual flame. Paloma becomes her words, enters and entangles herself with the divinity at Pam's core. The two become one while remaining two. Then comes Jesus. No more disguises. No more parody. His light modulates that of Paloma, and together they call forth from Pam the most beautiful radiance the initiate has ever experienced. The gold of sunlight through bare dark branches, the whisper of moonlight upon springtime grass, the dance of starlight upon calm water. She is all of these. They are all of these. And they are more. Pam would have died of fatal ecstasy were that not impossible in such company.

The Father speaks. "Well said, Paloma. You've....We've made our point. Now, let's set her on her way."

Upon his words, a high octane explosion shreds the fabric of her tympanic membranes, sears the sclera of her eyes into crisp and brittle husks, and Pam finds herself blown across infinity much as had her companion roach's mother that fatal morning of Jennifer's birth. As had the cockroach become possessed of a very human intellect when her mother rode upon the nuclear exchange of Bikini Atoll, Pam awakes to a transcendent state. Unlike Jennifer, however, she has not exchanged consciousness and intellect with one of another species. Simply, she has found her entire spiritual reality open to her as she becomes one with her father, her brother, and the most extraordinary young woman named for a dove. She and they have become one while each continues separate and distinct from the others. Pam is also aware that such has always been her condition, and that the increasingly persistent intimations of her exceptionality have been mere lead-ins to complete understanding and acceptance of who and what she is and has always been.

She is consumed. Such is consummation.

A million, a trillion, a googol to the thousandth power, Pam scatters across New Jersey. Pale, airborne spiders, the propagating feathers of her blowball self soar and climb, gather and regather before returning to the earth from which they came. Cars slush along soft asphalt. Trucks wail into distance. Pam begins to awaken from her own fulfillment into a familiar state, the aftermath of dissolution.

Really, this has been one radical flashback. Short, maybe, but almost as good as any trip she has ever taken. Must have been the, sun, the walk. She's probably dehydrated. Paul's brown face and soft eyes look through her as though she isn't there. "Pam," he calls, and her mind returns from wherever it has gone.

She is still alone dealing with the highwayman. She needs a ride. There is much more she thinks but is forgetting the flash as one would a dream. She feels things, among them the certainty that her life has just slipped into another dimension hidden like a shadow within shadows, more real than the light which has created it. Or thus she thinks.

Until Paul chuckles out a warning. "I wouldn't go there if I was you."

She doesn't. Does not even remember exactly what it was she was thinking. Wiping sweat from off her cheeks and setting the gas can down, she allows a sigh to escape her, "I think I need to sit in the shade a minute. Have a drink of something." The feeling is strange. She is not sick, doesn't feel the slightest bit woozy. Does feel a need to regroup. To think clearly, if that is possible. "Any chance you've got some water?"

"Better'n that," Briant answers. "C'mon inside. I got a fan and jes a little bit a sumpin gonna do ya a whole lot better'n water."

How can this rednecked blackman have done it? Rather, how has she so altered him from thief to savior, or at least Samaritan of some degree of goodness? He turns the fan on her. The breeze chills her face and arms, slides up under her clothing and inflames her every nerve ending, pumps her respiration into gasps of insane pleasure. Then he brings a big and only vaguely discolored glass choked up with ice and she soon recognizes, root beer.

"A & W" Paul boasts. "Drive a long ways for it. It's the greatest."

She takes it all in two gulps, and without being asked, Paul refreshes the potion. Again, until, with a grand and grateful belch, she indicates she has had enough.

For several moments Pam is content to revel in the chill blessing of ice and a cool breeze. Despite her teeth's jittering toward full blown chatter, she closes her eyes and remains still. Something strange has just happened to her. A sunstroke of some kind — *a very orang sunshine* — she muses, and would have allowed herself to drift off into another place other than her present circumstances had not Paul broken the spell.

"You a strange one, alright," he rattles through his own mouthful of cubes. "Ain't got nothin' to say? Nothin' to ask me?"

"I just need a ride…. You said for twenty bucks," she allows the words to drift from her lips like long held smoke.

"Don't mean 'bout that. Hell, little missy, I give you the ride for nothin'. I mean bout what you just seen."

Pam's reverie has become turnpike real. "Whadda you mean? Did I say anything?" *Shit.* She thought it had been just a few seconds of almost remembered psychedelia.

Paul's face begins to glow. Tendrils of flame creep up and down his neck, and Pam remembers. At least some of it.

"Jesus," she exclaims. "You're God? My father?"

The ignition is scrubbed, and Mr. Briant assumes his chosen manifestation.

"Now were getting there," he rumbles. "Again I ask. Any questions?"

For the most part, Pam has remained computer illiterate. She can barely operate the functions other than call and receive of her cell phone. This state is now in flux. The previous year, after an occasion at the college, Stephen, already with a bit of a bag on, brought the evening's presenter, Phil Katz, inventor of the Zip File, home with him, and by the next early morning she had become intrigued by the compression of data as he explained it, as he projected the future of technology into something she thought he had termed quantum memory. To be honest with herself, she is compelled to admit they both were very drunk and stoned. Even Jennifer had disappeared, and Stephen had long before succumbed to the soporific qualities of a major bundling of primo weed and peppermint schnapps. The projection also had become more the biological extension of one bit of Mr. Katz into her own POP 3 box.

Nonetheless, Pam is becoming increasingly aware that once she experiences something in any of the possible manifestations she never truly forgets it. Even should it sink for a time beneath the surface of her consciousness, should necessity offer its prompt, her recall is total. Therefore, with no sense of venturing into any territory remotely foreign, she unzips her nuclear awakening and remembers it all. As the compressed memory unfolds, and again unfolds into its unquantifiable whole, she finds herself remembering, indeed knowing, but in most cases not at all understanding.

She is the actual daughter of God the Father himself, half-sister to Jesus. At the same time she knows with all her divine soul that she is Pamela Bruno, child of completely human parents and through them sister to a fully biological woman. Stephen often discourses, especially when they are at some function related to his Catholic activism, concerning the dual nature of the Christ as well as the probability, contrary as that might be to accepted Catholic doctrine, that Jesus actually had brothers, and that Mary was not the eternal virgin the church claimed her to be. How in all reality could such things be so?

"You got heaps on your plate," chuckles Papa Bear. "Might be best if you save that kinda shit up for a sleepless night or a rainy day. Yall might even ask yer brother if yall ever get sos you can just talk with each other 'stead of playin' all your little ego games." Then after a pause so extended as to cause Pam to wonder if Bear has spoken his final words, at least to her, he continues. "Let's move on outta here. I pretty much come and go as I please. Wouldn't want Sporty getting' towed or sumpin now, would we?"

Pam knows she has not told him she was riding. Most certainly has not mentioned her ride's name. *What the hell?*

"Heaven, might be a better term," Paulie Bear chides. "Remember who I am."

Of course he is right. Isn't he always? A memory from before her infernal awakening arises. Dad is nothing if not inscrutable. Annoying even. He has probably known about Sporty since before there was a Sporty. Cool as that may be, it raises troubling thoughts.

"Rainy day," Dad chides. "Now buckle up, and we'll be on our way."

Pam never experiences leaving the little office. Nor does the day's temperature impose upon her chill. She had been sitting in a ratty metal chair. She is sitting in beautiful leather in an automobile of considerable appointment.

"Sweet chariot," Dad sings. "Got an image to uphold, you know. " She's a Benz. E63 AMG. Custom built. Sit yourself back and enjoy. We'll talk as we go."

Enjoy she does. For all of thirty seconds. As soon as they reach the highway, Dad sweeps her up and away from the perfect temperature, gentle ride, and black leather. As his instruments hover about the subliminal, as their speed reaches one hundred, Mr. Briant takes control. "Just listen up," he states as might a judge imposing a life sentence. "You'll always have questions. There must always be things you do not understand. There are, however, several things it is necessary for you to grasp right now. So, settle back while I tell you.

"By way of preface, I feel compelled to say that you are my daughter and I love you. As risky as this next is, I fear it must be said. I am about to lay before you a twelve-step program not at all akin to those followed by several of your future colleagues and clients." For some mysterious reason Dad nearly chokes on his own humor at this point.

Pam doesn't get it, but the ride is smooth, and the uncharacteristically deserted turnpike slides beneath them as they pass like sunlight through featureless landscape and faceless signs. They must have passed Sporty already. Where is Dad taking her? Will she ever ride again?

"Don't worry, sweetheart," he comforts. "All will soon be much as you once might have expected. Now, I continue. As I was about to declare: Because of my love for you, and despite my fervent hope that you will embrace the destiny I have set before you, should you reject all you have experienced this day, I will never stop loving you. Neither will I ever be disappointed. The choices are yours. The necessary actions are yours to accept or reject. Your ministry to the incurably fucked up of this world is yours to embrace. Or to shun. However you choose, wherever you go, whatever you do, remember, Pamela, I love you.

"Nonetheless...." Dad is no longer Paulie Bear and neither is he Daddy. The man beside her burns beneath his charcoal skin and his eyes warn of horizons best not approached. "My commandments are," he intones.

First, I Am Who Am. I am Father, Brother, and Holy Spirit. And I Am Everything Else. Think not to limit me. Your brain is animal. Your language capable only of obscuring the truth. Once upon a time I decreed that my name should not be spoken. For good reason. Thou shalt not limit me. At this point he mellows. "Of course, my little girl, you may always call me 'Daddy.' Except with Jesus and Paloma, however, you might best keep such expression to yourself. I can be 'Father' to selected others, but for practical purposes, 'Daddy' is unique to you and Josh. Now, where were we?"

"Oh, yeah.

"*Second, Find yourself and you will find me.*

"*Third, Find love. I am there.*

"*Fourth, The universe is you.*

"*Fifth, You are the universe.*

"*Sixth,* "*Seek and thou shalt not find.*

"*Seventh, Seek not and thou shalt find.*

"*Eighth, All that is, is*

"*Ninth, All is infinite.*

"*Tenth, All is one.*

"*Eleventh, Ignore one through ten.*

"*Twelfth, Do as you think right.*

Feeling a child in the land of grownup aliens, Pam is left with no appropriate response. "I don't get it," she complains. "Any chance you could write that down? With translations or something. It's cool and all. Stephen talks a lot about paradox. I don't think he really gets it though Me...? I've never had a problem with taking things as they come. Love and hate, hot and cold, male, female, good, bad, ugly, and beautiful.... The list goes on and who cares? I love winter and adore the summer too. I never worry about opposites or contradictions. 'One for all and all for one,' matters not just sos the candy's good."

Dad laughs a hearty baritone, spitting drops of glory about the AMG. "That's my girl," he rejoices. "Just do it, Pammie. Look in your pack. They're written out on a piece of red paper in blue ink. Holy Writ." His photon exhalations are contagious. Pam needs no script. She knows. She knows she understands.

"Of course you do," Dad says. "But try explainin'. That ain't so easy. You got a ton a work ahead a you.

"Yer first chore...? Well, that's tonight."

The words are in her ears. The smooth voice of her Dad lingers much as would the sweet aftertaste of a rich chocolate mousse. She wonders. She will accept....

Except. Dad is not even in the car. She is alone. Stationary. Across the hood of the Benz impossibly black shadows of unreal white seabirds streak into air then return, crissing and crossing in complex patterns until they threaten to weave a curtain across her vision. Pam must look away.

Beside her leans her ride. Dad must have gotten out to refuel her. Pam cracks her door and slides one foot into the raucous atmosphere. Sporty glitters and reflects her colors. Where is Dad?

A set of red and blue lights flash. No more than two or three car-lengths before them an unmarked vehicle of an official nature flares a warning through its rear window. Dad and a severe young man, a badge hanging from a lanyard, a pistol at his belt are deep in conversation. They haven't noticed her.

Eventually the officer looks her way. So does Dad. The pass a few more words, the young man returns to his vehicle and is off. Dad walks toward her. "I'll take care of things," he tells her. "Why don't you get back in the car 'till I'm through. Got a couple more words to say. Then you can be off."

"What the cop want?" Pam asks before making a move. "He wanna tow my bike or somethin'?"

"Just checkin'," Dad replies. "It's his job, you know. You got no worries. These guys'r my buds."

Pam returns to the car and in short order her father is beside her.

"Didn't wanna wake you," he explains. "You zoned out almost soon's you got buckled in. Took me a while before I noticed. Interesting how everything I was sayin' still got through. You're full a surprises. Awake and asleep, aware and gone. All at the same time. Didn't know you had it in you."

"Was I dreaming?" Pam asks.

"You might say that. Anyway you got the essential parts of what I had to say all stored up. You won't forget, but, Just in case I wrote it all down.

"Now, one more thing. Tonight your buddy Sis is gonna want you goin' out with her and a couple of her biker girlfriends. She's gonna start a new chapter back up in Troy. Sisters of Sappho they calls 'emselves. She's gonna want you ridin' with 'em. You should. But....

"This is real important. Don't go too far or stay too late."

Pam chuckles at the implication. Typical Father!

"No. It's not that at all. You need to be straight, and you need to be alone by ten or so. Don't screw this up. You may or may not ever earn your patch with the Sisters. It doesn't really matter much. This night you're going to earn your bones in an organization of much greater significance. Or not.

"Pammie darlin', you best not fuck it up.

"Now, let's move yall outta here."

He is out the door, stands aside as she secures her pack, dons her helmet, adjusts her glasses, and snaps Sporty into unmuffled life. The noise is overpowering, but Pam hears her Father's farewell words as if spoken directly into her ear in the midst of a warm Alabama glade. "Remember," he commands. "Ten o'clock."

She is down the highway without a glance into her mirrors. He won't be there even though he is.

Sisters of Sappho

SIS, ROSIE, AND Tricia sit on the curb of the Cherry Hill Weston lot smoking their second fattie. Pam is late. She answers neither a call nor a text. They'll wait another ten minutes and then leave. At least Rosie, club president, and Tricia will. Sis, despite any possible repercussions, is not sure she can go with them. *Damn it, Pam!*

The mellow weed plays its game. Ten minutes become an hour. The sun is sounding into Philly. A third joint has been shared. Pam arrives, spies them, and idles up. Recriminations are few although heartfelt, and soon the ladies are traipsing into the lobby, three imposing biker women wearing colors of a decidedly outlaw nature, featuring an image of a lotus, black against dark water, encircled by a sky of fire. Arched over them is one word *Anactoria*. Rockered below, black as Pam's hair, SISTERS OF SAPPHO PHILADELPHIA. The clerk keeps his timid eyes down. Confirms Pam's reservation, handles her registration with a minimum of discourse, and soon Pam, key-card in hand, is leading her companions to the elevator.

"There's no smoking," the clerk finds voice to call after them. Rosie turns and offers an unspoken invitation which returns the attendant to his pile of nonexistent paperwork. The girls laugh their way to the sixth floor. Everyone is in the mood to party. Pam sucks in her first lungful, and resigns herself to the flow of energy around them. Sis is psyched about her graduation. The other two are tripping on their sister's vibes. Or so they say. Dad is soon forgotten.

By eight thirty, Pam is addressing her second Black Russian, the music in the Camden bar is loud, and clumps of desirable leather-clad flesh whisper temptations. This place is too much. MAMA's KITCHEN it's called, but nothing's cooking here except a bitches' brew of drugs, alcohol, and good old female lust. A slight young blonde maybe named Luna traces her fingers across Pam's tingling knee. Sis bulks across the room. Rosie and Tricia are nowhere to be seen. Chrissie Hynde sings *Hymn to Her*, and all is wonderful in the world.

A man more imposing than Sis blunts through the door. Red, green, orange, and violet lights paradrop about his face. The song is over. The party has been sung. The man with barlight for eyes is raven black.

Sober and compelled, Pam scoots back to Cherry Hill, the sixth floor, and Destiny.

DEEP AND DREAMLESS, Pam's sleep fouls itself upon tendrils of consciousness. No sound. No light. Not so much as a red dot where the television should be. Or on the nightstand phone. Her shades are not drawn, but no moonshine, no startwinkle, streetglow of passing traffic, not so much as a darker shade of pale. No sound. No AC. No late night or early morning traffic. No rustle of passing souls. No suggestive bumps in the emptiness.

The odor. Pam has never smelled blood in great quantities, but she recognizes its stench from deep within her biological subconscious. Her throat constricts. Her stomach makes ready for reaction. There's shit behind the blood. Pam has smelled this upon more than one occasion and in copious amounts. Her hotel room opens upon the failed septic system of long ago Hoosick Falls. Dad has opened the tank, has attempted to replace the leche lines or whatever disgusting name they are called. All is failure. The yard wallows in saturated, excrement. Flatulent bubbles bubble back into the house and up the bathtub drain. The toilet cannot flush and the basement fills with sewage. Blood and shit. All upon her this Cherry Hill Night. She must puke. Begins to gag.

"Not now, Sis," Jesus murmurs from the nowhere of a far corner. There's something you must do. He allows a glimmer of his light to shine, and by so doing manifests himself in robe and sandals, long hair and seriously sorrowful countenance. His blood glows dark upon background radiance. Beside him slumps a clotted presence. "I bring your husband," the Lord announces. "I give you Stephen Bruno. His soul's fate is yours to decide."

Pam recognizes the shirt. Stephen's face is a smudge of flesh, bone, blood, and… shit. "What the…?"

"Need I say it? State the pathetically obvious?" Her brother asks. "You can see for yourself. The man is dead."

Despair and Destruction
Ruth and Arthur
2013

The Arthur, the obsidian monolith of just these few weeks gone would have scorned this match. Never would he have allowed himself to become so debased, so turned over as to put his will and his life so willingly in thrall to the likes of a higher power such as Mooky Cohan. Forgive me Pam and Paloma my spirit love, the power behind us all, for this uncharitable outburst. Really! Of my own volition I have resigned my right of self-determination, or more correctly spoken, have submitted to the excision of, as you, my precious Dove have termed it, "a piece of my very soul."

I am permitted no second thoughts, no time for misgivings. Like one unjustly condemned to ignominious slaughter, I lam lain upon a hard altar and sacrificed to some purpose I neither know nor comprehend. Another purpose, one not my own, moves me. You, Pam, claim I serve the will of someone called Mary, not the supposed Holy Mother, however, just some mortal love of yours. What of Paloma? This thing who shuffles beside me? Her fate is your concern as well? I fail to see the light here. I am indentured to Lenard, reduced to wheeling stones about the endless yard of an abandoned mansion, all for the incomprehensible sake of a broken old lesbian. And the reward, the courtly *merci*? This thing beside me, both the subject of my will's coercion and, it would appear, my new life's companion? My soul mate? If you will?

Excuse ma Francais, the bitch is *tres* freaking ugly. I can see it in her. No doubt once she possessed a modicum of youth and beauty. At present, however, she looks more the pale, walking corpse in one of the positively dreadful anti-smoking spots Lenard's excuse for a TV has begun to hack about his living room. One of the ladies' high school picture — her "before" self — has captured not only youthful female pulchritude, but the essential goodness and purity of — forgive my insipid piety as well as befuddled Romanticism — the essence of a veritable child of God. So possibly may this one have been. While I bear up under the onus of my current state of affairs, including such base emotional responses as the aforementioned, I am unable to refrain from speculating. Why? Why are so many, if not all, of us born with such promise only to end as horrors, drooling out platitudes intended merely to warn others away from the same practices which, were we to be Karmically set upon the same path once more, we would find as compelling as ever and which we would not hesitate to embrace all over again?

I have been informed that she is sick unto death. That cancer not heroin will kill her. My task? I am to be her nurse? God, have mercy upon us both.

THIS SUCKS THE big bamboo! Old chocolate tooth turns me away from the fire and my companions. Leads me toward the far end of this stone canyon. I refuse to take another step. At least until he offers something more than a sickly smile and a grimy guiding hand. This has to end. Now.

"We can run but we can't...." sifts my way both from ahead and behind. The voice is Garcia's, its purity could only be of Pam's modulation.

"Ruthie," rasps within the melodic wrappings of The Dead at their best. "Over here."

"I should have seen it coming. My Intuition is shot all to hell. Freaking Pam only plays at discombobulation — *sometimes, Mom, your words are perfect.* It's the old lady. Mary Elsbeth or whatever the hell her name is. She's looking better than she did in Saint Peter's. Maybe, she's.... No. Not a Marine's chance in Beirut. I'm stuck with pockface here.

Just her head and shoulders appear, thrust up from an opening in the floor. Judging by the makeshift, unfinished railing framing her, I would guess it must be a rude stairway of sorts. She rises further although not completely from out of her den and makes that squiggly little finger-flicker so many women employ when beckoning to another, be that other child, adult, or even dog. It also means "bye, bye." I am tempted.

As I knew I would, I obey her old lady summons. Has the disease done this to me? The meds? I know it has always been my lot to accept, comply, submit myself to the whims of the multitude of substances, Johns, Moms, Dads, vegetables and passing fancies tumbling along the riptidal course of my life. At least, I was able to maintain an ironic attitude. To revolt with all my interior self even as I opened my exterior to the many ministries of the flotsam around me. The ability has abandoned me.

As we approach, I see more clearly what it is, that indescribable something Pam sees in her. Mary Elizabeth's eyes are the black flame of those of a woman some hopelessly befuddled weakling once described at a meeting. According to the delusional one, she had been graced by a vision of the veritable mother of Jesus. "Of us all." She said more. Extreme delusion, I was certain. Of the sort one such as myself, and I would wager, this deathbreath at my side, might happily pay a substantial price to experience. Anyway, she claimed the woman spoke to her, that she spoke not in words but in flowers, roses and asters, tulips of spring and chrysanthemums, orchids, and something she called "the flowers of the sun." No one laughed. Neither did anyone express surprise several weeks later to discover she had been "checked into" CDPC. Such visions, even such deluded beliefs, are cool, even enviable…. Also, best kept to one's self.

Her skin is dark, not tan, Mediterranean. Her hair is black. Natural Thick. I could hate her.

I LOOK INTO the goodwitch's eyes, and my vision is altered. Again, I am changed against my will and possibly my own best interests. I look away, I hope in time. Not. The ogre beside me has been altered through my alteration. The troll is now a creature of divine beauty. A flower…. A soft feather, multihued as one tie-dyed by an artist of supernatural vision might be. Her colors are those of a light from places unknown to such as me. Yet she is in no fashion supernatural. The colors, the impossible translucence of her being are qualities we may all someday or somewhere or when find within ourselves and in each and all of us other. I might be struck dumb. Or blind. Instead, a tear, a single bitter drop of regret, wells from out my eye and carves a prisoner's tattoo upon my cheek. This once ugly one, this hopeless addict, this cancer riddled walking corpse has returned my soul intact to me.

WHERE HAS ALL the shit brindle gone? My most corrupted guide has looked into my eyes while smiling fine white, pearly, teeth at me. As for the slow blaze of resentment so obvious in his face? I saw it disappear. Presto! Change-o! It was gone. Beside me now stands the straight and vital figure of a most comely older gentleman. Poorly dressed, I must admit, but clothing is merely a disguise, rat's coat, straw in a nonexistent wind. His hand reaches to mine. At the moment before our final meeting, I am overcome. That calloused palm, those swollen knuckles were never meant to be so, and they change. His touch is the touch of Mr. Softie. I find comfort before our skin makes contact.

I feel my cancer tear itself free from restraint. Feel its rage upon all that sustains me.

This man, this Arthur, my life's final gift, my newfound love, comforts me.

A MAN'S HEAD pops from out the old lady's hidey hole. Not totally my worst nightmare, but part of same. Were I not unalterably tethered by an adamant leash to charity, I would employ the term "fool" in relation to it. However, since such judgment, other than when accurate, and not always then, has been forbidden me or better, since my more than spiritual castration, I am reduced to a surprised exclamation to self. *It's Kenny!*"

He waves between the old one's cheek and shoulder and mouths words I am unable to read. Nothing resembling "sorry" as one might expect when taking note of my extraordinary circumstances. What' could his part in this be anyway? No doubt I'll soon find the answer.

MARY ELIZABETH'S EYES radiate an angelic kindness. Without opening her arms she gathers me to her bosom. I feel the disease setting Death free to rampage within me. I am not afraid.

WE DRAW CLOSER. I am able to discern Merrill's faint whisper. "It's going to be OK," he croons. As if I need soothing. "Come with us, and we'll make it all clear."

I hear a truck grumble into life. Lenard is off for rock or topsoil or the festering heap he calls mulch. The storm must have been brief. Not so much as an hour ago, Igor to his Lawn Doctor, I found myself humped up into a pathetic troll, scuttling about, a reluctant manservant resentful of the entire process. At this time, I am inclined to wish I were in the seat beside him, a no longer reluctant assistant, breathing in the new life of the post deluge earth. Instead, I follow the old lady and Merrill into the hole, steadying myself upon the splintery rail while attempting to add stability to the most unhesitant one behind me. Perhaps, no doubt, our roles should be reversed. I would return to the thunder. I miss the most potent rain.

I have become unsubstantial. Should I relinquish my hold upon the rail, should I stumble, I would waft away with the updraft back to the world I once imagined I despised. I may not allow that. She must not be abandoned. I must assure she is not alone.

No longer a block. No more of stone. I am mere uncertain flesh? Sadly, however uncertain my uncertain particularity may be, I am real.

I STILL HEAR the song. Intoxicating as Mary's perfume, it rises from somewhere below. Its direction, however, is still not certain. Nor is its origin. Above, it emanated from the walls, the ceiling, the floor and below. In the basement now, I know its presence. I breathe the truth. A's, E's, and D's. Some folkie once sang that music could soothe his very soul. Clichéd, I know. Again, how very true. I am no longer Lottie. I can feel it. I have seen it in the other one's eyes. I am Ruth forever, cliché again, forever is most LOL eternal. Anyway, I know nothing about this guy who is to be mine, but I cannot help but wonder if he might be an equal part of the "We" referenced in the Dead's song. I suppose I might extend the embrace of the pronoun to all humanity, but, for the life of me, I have rarely been capable of seeing beyond the moment or embracing more than one or two others during that limited scope. Interesting. Despite the fact that I find love or even caring most foreign to my — Or was that Lottie's? — basic nature, I am unable not to wonder about my dire Wolfe. Could he also be fated to a destiny neither of us as of this moment is able to understand?

I discover that I care. I find a genuine tear rise into my left eye.

Thank god for the basement floor. The raucous caged and swinging incandescents. Thank god for the new guy's voice, a pussycat whine larding all one might be tempted to term transcendent with the slime of mundane mediocrity.

Hey, Baby Ruth, I may be gone, but I'm not forgotten. You, my nutty little bar, have every right to such outbursts of exaggerated response whether emotional or verbal. Let it out, Baby. Let it all out."

I am sure to miss this part of me, the Lottie who is so capable of interjecting irony and sarcasm into the otherwise most quotidian circumstances. *Don't go, girl. I may need you again.*

The pussycat talks, attractive/repellant as the odor from a just visited vagina. His words seep like coital slime into my awareness. I am to follow him. Into another room along a worklit corridor. I want Mary. He takes my elbow. I desire the gentle caress of the sad old woman.

He leads.

I follow.

THE CRONE SETS me down in a comfortable overstuffed chair crouched upon a huge carpet of some discardant origin. She perches upon the arm of a recliner, constantly risking a tumble into its worn spinach embrace. I find myself hoping such will occur. Despite her age and rough-edged voice, she is most attractive. This one could be Paloma's mother.

I begin to imagine….

She allows her knees to open a bit. She is no child. She knows what she does. Her black cherry lips part, their surfaces clinging for a moment each to each, into a smile. Come hither, I determine. I rise.

"Sit," she barks, those moist labia now sliding across the surface of brilliant teeth. Sharp and pointed, deadly and cruel as those of a panther. "Pam and Paloma warned me about you. Sad, my friend, how predictable you are. How disobedient. Couldn't you hear the processional? You cannot hide. And, Arthur,

275

my reluctant pupil, you are unable to run as well. Both my ladies know everything you do. They always will. You've come far, and I understand you have been made spiritually whole. But! Do not presume upon my good graces. Or theirs either. Ruthie is now yours to keep and care for. Forsake all others. I give you fair warning. Otherwise, those who count will forsake you."

Sucks, doesn't it! A woman —I want to say "bitch" but can't — can open her legs wide and slide her fingers up....

MORÉRE!

The voice is both Pam's and the Dove's. It is the crone's as well. I am warned. I am saddened to admit that I should have known better. I shall behave. I have no choice.

How am I still an autonomous human being? Has my soul truly been restored? Whatever....

"Zip it!" springs from the tired recliner across from me.

I do as I am told, denied the release of unanswerable questions.

The old lady smiles again.

I settle back. I need to listen.

HE SITS IN a brand new, shiny-lacquered wire lawn-chair that could be from a surplus sale at some MOST COMMON GROUNDS coffee shop. I am left a collapsible outdoor concert-style folding abomination, olive as never was an olive with smooth tubular, not quite black framework. He crosses his legs revealing cornsilk stockings which match his tie while repudiating his choice of trousers. Were they not so obviously almost green, one would be tempted to call them blue. He wears a wrinkly orange and gray and white striped shirt. He must have been a frat boy. An accounting major. Or computer science.

"Hello, Ruth," he says so confidentially, so intimately that I am nearly reassured that, at least at this time, no one else exists in this world. Just the two of us. I can see myself developing gratitude for the cancer. Just imagine! Our progeny.

In less than a minute's existence I have been disabused of my stereotypical notions. He is no geek. He is a psychiatrist, Dr. Kenneth Merrill, and upon further than first impressions, I find him possibly insightful, even brilliant.

"I have been told quite a bit about you," he commences. "Nonetheless, no one truly knows another human being more completely than does the particular human in question. What say you?

"Care to share?" He laughs.

I am led to follow his lead.

Without prelude, with no thought whatsoever, I blurt, as if in some Episcopal confessional, High-Church all the way, "I seduced my father."

"No, you did not. Nor, as I am certain you were about to tell me, is your name Lottie." Try again. If you would be so kind."

I have no choice. "My name is Ruth...."

FOR AT LEAST half an hour.... Perhaps ten minutes.... Almost that anyway. For some interminable time of short duration we sit and stare. I studiously avoid the old lady's perfect calves, the faint promise of nurture beneath the folds of the black and snow-gray knit of her summerwear, winter weight sweater. Wool, I would swear. For a time her skirt slips ever closer to revelation until she resettles herself, legs crossed most adamantly forbidding. Her eyes seek only mine. Eventually, I am forced to yield. I drown.

Her croak become a summer night's fantastic symphony of harmonious instrumentation. One voice composed of many, reeds, brass, even an occasional drum, but atop it all sing the divine strings of Amati and Stradivarius as only the hands and heart of Perlman and Heifetz and a handful of others, including the blistering Janine Jansen whose performance with the Boston Symphony at Tanglewood quite literally caused me to do you know what upon the romantic greensward. Oh, Janine, your music, your skill, your divine.... I find myself rising to the occasion.

Mary looks my way. She is stern. Isaac perhaps.

"Calm down, Arthur," the ancient one warns. "Although... I must admit to feelings of a similar sort for another of the great women. Do you by any chance know Diana Yukawa? In many ways she reminds me of my Pamela."

My smile tells all. As have I done with Paloma and Janine, so too have I experienced the more than sonic wonders of sweet Diana, the most fecund eternal virgin ever to stroll beneath the huntress moon. This is becoming hard!

"We must stop," Mary interjects into my Greco-Japanese fantasy. "Leave it at the door. We're about to enter into the mythical world of your own perception of your own history as it now reveals itself in you as you are today."

That fucking word!

"Sorry," Mary soothes. "I only meant your present self.

Now shall we begin?

I nod.

Mary opens. "They, specifically Paloma and Pam, have told me a great deal about you, but I have always found that personal connections with the one in question are necessary for proper, or at least useful, understanding. Can you tell me a little bit about yourself?"

For some unknowable reason I start with the dark night and my Mother. "I awoke from no dream into nightmare. Nine years of age, I found myself alone in the middle of our dark kitchen. I have no memory of having descended the stairs, walking through one room and down a hall, but I had. I was alone, immobile in the grip of absolute evil. Moved beyond movement, I could only stand, could not even tremble.

"So it was my mother found me...."

AS FROM A dream of someone else's imagining, I refocus into waking, my ears conducting tones, then chords, harmonies and eventually familiar lyrics to my unfolding consciousness. "We can run, but we can't hide" embraces my awareness. Have I been singing along? Have I listened silently? I know I have been sharing. I have retold the dreary story of my empty life without the disguises of invention. The music takes me nowhere, the lyrics mumble and jumble into meaningless phrases of nothing resembling poetry. My inquisitor smiles. His eyes grow sad.

Irrationally jogged by the given illogic of humor in the face of confusion especially when one finds herself in such dire straits as are mine, I gasp, "Where am...?"

"Don't," the shrink counsels. "You know full well both where you are and what it is we are about."

He is direct. Also very wrong. Indeed, I do know where I am...within certain necessary elements of uncertainty, but, aside from the revelation of my impending relationship with the old man, I have not the faintest clue as to our purpose here. The dawning of that enhanced awareness might be peeping over the Taconics when.... The god-awful dog slumps into the room, takes a sniff of my rotting crotch, and plops itself at the inquisitor's side.

"Sorry," he says. "Dogs will be dogs," at which point he scratches the thing behind its ears before turning once again to me.

The song ends. Begins again. What is that line anyway? "The song remains the same"? *Zeppelin*, I think. Maybe a movie or something. I usually don't like them and never watch the hyped up filming of idiotic concerts. Maybe Catfish... I did see *The Wall* at the old Delaware Theatre. I have always felt a kinship with *Floyd*. Wonder if this one's seen it. Or heard the album? *Ummagumma!* Wonder if he's ever set the controls for the heart of the sun." I wonder....

"In answer to the last. Yes I have. Long ago and further away than you might imagine. Our present concern must be attending to the business which is at the heart of this colloquy."

He must have seen my quickly concealed smile. Perhaps I chirped just a bit.

"You're not the only one, my dear, with a vocabulary in excess of the common fifty thousand or so words, most of them two syllables or shorter. You might be surprised to learn that there are many others all around you with equivalent verbal skills, superior math and science knowledge, and, yes, a higher degree of native intelligence as well. I must admit to your being advanced, superior even, in many aspects of human existence, education and intelligence among them, but, my dear girl, you are far from Hypatia of Alexandria. My thinking is that the proof of superiority in any field is the result of doing not assuming. In that regard you have achieved nothing. I'll admit you once had the necessary tools. No longer do you. Under realistic circumstances, this would most likely be something of an exit interview.

You have failed all the tests, and the natural result of said failure is death and oblivion. You have been found wanting. Truly, if not for Pam and her intercession, your death is destined to be long and cruel, ending in nothing, not even happy memory. Your mother and sister love you, but the ordeal of your dying while in their care can only make of your last breath their own collective sigh of relief. For others, naught but a fading photograph, all memory of your presence on this earth is soon to be erased. You will have ended lower than you began, and more pathetic. Nothing from nothing. Passed beyond any hope or possibility."

Hardly the babble of a professional. This jerk's a real downer. I know I'm a goner. Is it necessary for the asshole to rub it in?

Screw him. I'm getting the hell outta here. Pronto. The last thing I need's this kinda shit.

Pammie's a real fuck too. This is what all that shit in the hospital, all the promise is about?

The dog groans, stretches its obscene length my way, then settles back into its mindless observations. I begin to rise.

"We're not through," the jerkoff warns. "Walk away and everything I've just said comes true."

Returning my weight to my tired butt, I settle back. I'll just sit and await the next onslaught. Instead, Merrill smiles as the stupid Dead begin their stupid song anew. I deliberately make a face, twisted lips, rolled eyes and all.

The doctor offers a small tone of agreement and continues. "The Grateful Dead and this particular song are wholly Pam's idea. She loves them. Claims to have known the lead singer. She also is certain the lyrics may have some appeal to you…perhaps aid you in an understanding of your situation. I don't pretend to understand

"The band's name is perhaps the key. Or might it not be the adjective? We all, Ruth, are doomed, fated you might say to die, but then might not such knowledge lead to salvation of sorts? I have always treasured Meursault's situation in…."

"Please, Doctor, don't bore me with tired old existential clichés. I've read Camus too. Really, and I mean really, old hat. Just wait 'till they drop the hammer on you…or should I say the blade. None of us really knows shit about dying. Not 'till were in its clutches at least. Say what you will. I know, and you absolutely fucking do not. So cut all the bullshit, as a sign in one of my professor's office read, 'eschew obfuscation' and deliver the message or pronounce the sentence or whatever it is you've been sent to do. One thing the Algerian asshole did get right was that as one condemned, I'm free. Especially from any kind of lies and deceptions deliberate or otherwise.

"You can take this to wherever it is you bank, We can run. I have been running. You are running. We all will be running, but, whereas I won't hide, the rest of you can and do. The meaning of the song is perfectly simple. I'm shocked by my density up to now."

I printed out the lyrics, you know. It's a simpleton's environmental song. I had no idea how it could relate but just now, just as the dog over there began lapping away at his privates, something like the left handed god's hammer struck. Pam's intentions!

I, Ruth Kelleher, am not simply going to die. Not, as are all my fellow human beings, antiseptically, philosophically, or inevitably going to pass on in some future time, but never the present. The right now.

I, Ruth Kelleher, have a purpose. A function. In a deep and unknowable sense darker than any tragic poet could ever imagine. The reason for my existence, my purpose if you like, Is To Die.

Merrill remains silent. Glances at the dog, at me, his shoes. He clears his throat. The dog begins to snore. I sit mute, staring the empty purpose of my existence in its snake framed face. I am alone. I cannot help it. Something clutches at my throat. I swallow it back. It will not stay down. It is a sob. Heartfelt and forlorn.

Merrill has heard. A sad — I am tempted to term it ironic — smile tugs at his cheeks, trembles his pale lips. The dog blows again. The therapist speaks.

"My accustomed role as a psychotherapist — the term I use to distinguish myself from the pill-pushers who have hijacked the professional identity once known as psychiatrist — is to listen, nod encouragingly, jot random notes, and be supportive. In other words, allow the patient — client, if you so please — to heal her or himself. Such is not to be the case with you. You have been chosen for two principle reasons. First, is the simple fact that Mary Elizabeth loves you beyond conventional understanding of that term and the emotional possibilities it attempts to identify. Second, and a consequence of the first, is to effect the salvation of another's immortality, his soul if you would allow, and by so doing to achieve your own immortality as well.

"The other person is Arthur, the one who accompanied you into our little recovery nest, and he is being informed of his responsibility for you and the necessary function that plays in his own continuation."

My face or bodily attitude or both together must be spouting their own involuntary tales.

"I know that may be a bit much to handle, but Ruth, if you are not sick unto death, and if you do not come to the edge of the abyss with someone there to guide you, there is no hope. The darkness will swallow and digest you. Make of you itself."

Damned inadvertent comments.

"Of course," the patient one answers. "Arthur must teeter upon the edge also. Only together may either of you fly across the chasm, escape the grasp of zero. Absolute, frozen, from which light itself may not escape."

I have given nothing away. Of that I am certain, but the blathering psycho raves on.

"I am required to keep much from you, but have also been encouraged to reveal certain circumstances of your situation so that you may understand the pure and vital energy at the heart of the situation.

"First of all, both you and Arthur have been selected as candidates for eternal life by the cosmic power of the universe itself…."

Tell! Big one.

"I see you scoff. Do not be so quick to judge. Call that power God if you wish. Or Father. Allah or a wave of infinite probability. Names, Lottie, are of no significance. Even Death. That too is different for everyone.

"I digress. I must fill you in on important background. By the time I'm finished, you should have all you need to do the necessary thing.

"First, without Mary Elizabeth's intercession with Pam, you would have been just another promising seed lost among the stones. Or possibly not. One must question, must he or she not, from whence originated the coincidence of your and her hospital stays such as dates, room numbers, and relative situation? Mary claims that she felt your presence even before she awoke. She asserts that you and she were 'meant' to be together.

"Pam laughs at her. Behind her back at least, and truth be told, Mary sometimes does act a little batty. Nevertheless, in the time I have been privileged to be of Pam's association, I have found her to be right about such things far more often than she is wrong. Pam herself, at least in her more serious moments, is prone to an often grudging admission that Mary Elizabeth Bruno is s beyond the scope of the most enlightened analysis. In simpler terms, she is a mystery. Even to the very daughter of....

"I think I had best allow that one to pass.

"Back to Mary's intense interest in you. First of all, I am speaking with you now, because she felt herself incapable of correctly dealing with the pain you must suffer. Fortunately, as a friend of Arthur's I preferred not to deal with him on these issues either. We two are far too close and personal for anything approaching objectivity to exist. Therefore, here am I and in another room Mary and Arthur in their individual fashions repeat our scenario as it must occur.

"As I say, Mary Elizabeth is your putative salvation because of a series of coincidences, such as I have just mentioned, dating from your earliest childhood. To say she loves you might be both an exaggeration and an absolute. In no sense has she expressed any hope for you other than the change your death will bring, and she is convinced your only hope lies there. This can in no way be interpreted as love for the person you have become...that you are. Yet....

"Mary has asked me to express the following sentiments if, in my opinion, they might assist you in the decision you will be asked to make. I do so think.

"So please listen carefully and with an open mind.

"I will attempt to relay her exact message as faithfully as my memory will allow. She wishes you to know that from their teens your mother and she were friends...perhaps even good friends...and, as Mary Elizabeth put it, 'you were the cutest, most mischievous, and saddest little girl' she had ever met. As well, she held you as dear as if you were her own.

"As it must, however, life moved on, circumstances changed, and your mother and Mary grew apart. Soon you became, again Mary's very words, 'a barely recognized form passing on the sidewalk, a name in the high school graduation program. Finally a brief thought in fleeting moments of reflection.' She lost touch. Until the hospital that is. Then it all came back. The concern, and, absolutely, Ruthie, the love.

"Mary's message to you, verbatim, 'A parent can never forget her child, even a child not biologically her own. Never. So I sent my Pam, to you. If you will allow her, she will see you through.'

"We sit here now, Ruthie, at her bidding. You must choose. Be aware, however, the choices are limited and lead to the very same end. Death is absolute. Certain and imminent. Yours is to decide which path you will take. That of anger, denial, and eventual hopeless surrender? Or an equally painful, way, but one made more bearable by love. Either will take you through rather than to the end. Either way is the...."

I hear no more. The obvious answer is "let it be," but what exactly does that mean anyway? More profound for sure than "We can run," but again is it profound only because it seems to mean nothing? "There will be an answer?" Bullshit!

Especially if that answer is death. Even with love, Arthur, Pam, Mary, Merrill, Mom and the pumpkin. Fuck you Dylan. Death is too the end. I'll make my choice all right. If death is inevitable. I'm not dead yet. Eat my infected pussy, Psychobabble. May the old lesbian clean me up after you have jazzed inside me.

I need a fucking fix. Now.

I turn to Merrill and laugh.

THE DEAD SONG drones on. Familiar words. Nothing behind them that applies to me. The thing must be stuck in an infinite loop of some sort. I am led to believe that perhaps I have been conducted into one of the subbasements of Hades. There is no fire. No howls of despair. Just the dead over and over. The words I once may have thought profound lose their sway and buzz into an annoying drone. Repeated. Over and over and over. Where is Dante when I need him? Or any poet? Even Joyce Kilmer. I offer up sulfurous incense.

The ghost of long past laughter drifts like sunlight through dying leaves.

My nose hairs curl.

What does the witch notice? Nothing it would appear. She crosses and then recrosses her nylon legs.

I am beyond further notice. Minutes drift like flakes of lysergic blotter upon a nonexistent breeze. All about me the still world devolves into further immobile chaos. I am a stone, unmoving and unmovable. My restored soul opens to the demise of possibility. I am no man of fire. There is no fire. Flame is energy. Motion. Transformation of base matter into energy. I sink beneath the uneasy river of no crossing, swim upon the arid sand of the eternal desert....

The lady coughs. I return to her world. She smiles the smile of Mother Mary and all the angels of all the imaginings of all the saints and pseudo holy women of all of human time.

"Earth to Arthur," she mocks. "Do you copy?" Her laughter, her mockery, moves me. Once again I roil in this incoherent sea of someone else's creation. I am sated. No more. No Paloma, no Pam, no Lenard, no Mary Make A Wish or who or whatever this newest imposition upon my sanity may be called. I shall vacate these tenebrific donjons. Lenard awaits. He truly is committed. He will never abandon me to my own dysfunctional devices. Even the meetings and Lenard's rebarbative platitudes are preferable to this. At least they make sense. At least I choose to ignore or ridicule them at my leisure.

I am feeling the old, the authentic Arthur begin to stir. The crazy bitch of my dream was correct. My soul is whole. I am MacArthur! No mere Mc Murphy. No, however dramatically presented, mere fictional character. I am the conqueror. I have returned and I shall rain destruction down upon...

The ancient one interposes. "Yes indeed, sweet Arthur. You shall rain fire. You shall become all you have imagined yourself to be. In order to help you see that, Paloma asked me to remind you of a story you once read. She said you used to mention it at your sessions when you two first became associated. Whatever...she asked me to remind you of Garcia Lorca's, I think it was called *The Dreaming Man.*"

This one sure as all Hell is a real know-nothing when it comes to literature. I cannot refrain from speculation. Of how many other things is she ignorant? Even the simplest transmission of possibly essential messages such as this apparently are beyond her capabilities. "Borges," I assert, the awakening of a most cutting expression accompanying my acerbic tone. "The title is *Circular Ruins,* not as you so erroneously claim *Dreaming Man.*

"I have read the story," she asserts. It is one of Pamela's favorites. It is also one of your characteristics — your love of so many artistic things she is attracted to also — that originally caused her to approve you for this role you are being offered. Forgive me if I have the incidentals wrong, but the dreaming? Is that not essential? And fire...?

"Ask yourself. How wrong can I really be?"

The bitch is a witch. Once I would have responded with acidic gusto. This day I smile and consider. I will hear her out. For a time.

Garcia's voice and the band's incessant strumming obscure her words. Her expression, however, conveys her own sense of disquiet. Eventually the swell of Muzak ebbs, and her voice reasserts itself. "I myself," she carps, "never much cared for the sixties and seventies. Nor have I any fondness for music such as this from that era."

Her voice, despite its conspicuous edge, is significantly less grating than I first thought it. In itself, this is blessed relief.

She rattles on. "Forgive me for being what I am, an old Italian lady from the era just prior to that one. Oh, indeed, I do remember the Hippies and the immorality. Free Love and all. Thank the good lord I was able to shield my little ones from that. I fear my friend Isadora, Ruth's mother, fared not so well."

On and on *ad infinitum*. Old lady. Old Italian lady. Old Italian Catholic lady. I had imagined that I had passed beyond *Fibrodysplasia Ossificans Progressiva*, but I begin to imagine that a return engagement with catatonia would be a blessing.

Nonetheless, even as I conjure up the blessed possibilities, my altered self betrays the old. The percipient old lady apologizes.

"I'm sorry, my dear. Sometimes it takes me far too long to reach my point. In no way do I mean to bore you. It is just that I have been given a dual role to play and am not completely sure how to begin. I was supposed to be conferring with Ruth. You know, Ruthie Kelleher. The one you came here with?"

"I am afraid you are mistaken, Mrs. Bruno," I reply as sweet and smooth as a *crème brulée*. I came here with Lenard Cohan, my friend and sponsor. Perhaps you were to meet with someone who remained upstairs."

"I'm sorry," she groans, a very believable expression of remorse upon her too smooth even for surgery face. "I simply meant the young lady you came downstairs with. My Ruthie. You might say she is my third daughter. I cannot help but love the little girl I remember her as and who I still see inside her. In a certain maternal and therefore probably very illogical way you might say that the wellbeing of the little one hiding so deep inside her is more important or at least of more immediate concern to me than that of my own children. They are mothers themselves now and have fine homes and husbands to care for them. They have no need to be found, for they were never lost. Were I to pass beyond tomorrow, their lives would remain substantially the same. A bit sadder perhaps, but soon that sense of loss would fade, and they would do as most of us do. They would carry on.

"Little Ruthie, however, hides behind the sheerest of veils. When I hear the woman speak, I hear the child. When I hear her anger, her fear, and, most of all, her despair, I feel her baby tears. From my hospital bed, I could see the light of her innocent spirit. In the total darkness I felt the beat of her little heart. Sometimes I know things. From the first, I felt her soul. Knew her need. So when her mother and sister appeared at her bedside, I already had it all together. I would have turned Pam toward her anyway, but once I fully recognized who she was, there was no stopping me. I am here to help her learn the lesson of herself as Pam finds it necessary for her to know it.

"Please understand me, Arthur. Both Pam and Paloma assure me that you have no choice in this matter. They say you have already agreed to do as they will, but that you may need reminding. May I say prodding? Please be aware that these words are mine, but the substance behind them is theirs...."

"We can run...," pounces from the hidden speaker.

She actually grimaces. The gravel returns below the roll of her phrasing. "As I was saying before my digression, I'm an old Italian lady who does not appreciate most so-called popular music. Probably it's my parents' doing, but I far prefer opera. Italian, of course."

This trot is insufferable. Does any of this equine scat have any relevance to my present or future circumstances? She is correct. I cannot desert, cannot even harden into separation. I have enlisted in this crusade of theirs. If my Shanghaiing can possibly be misinterpreted as voluntary, that is. I have been most cleverly seduced. I am at sea without any hope of return except the cruel deck beneath me.

Captain Bruno continues. "There is a special message for you. From Paloma. I suppose she recognized my tendency to ramble, and so she has sent it thus. Mary Elizabeth fishes something from the smallish bag at her feet. It is a note. She offers it across the space between us. I reach out.

The moment the soft stationery slips into my grasp I am, as I should have expected, transported. Nowhere, no other when. Nonetheless, I am moved. The paper contains no words. Neither is it blank. At its center dwells a perfectly round red spot. It throbs with the beating of a present heart. I raise it to my lips. It is blood.

Paloma's.

DOCTOR MERRILL LEADS Ruth along a dark corridor. Her feet tick against each other as she walks, her neck twists, her eyes would be turned as far from each other as is possible without their disappearing into her skull.

Abscesses begin to appear upon her bare arms and legs. Others drain pestilence down her neck, over her bony bright shoulders and across her meager breasts. Were it not for Kenny's support, she would collapse into a stringless heap of empty clothing and disconnected sticks of fallen oak. She would cast herself into the fire, her nose grown longer than her legs.

Mary Elizabeth and Arthur sit in a well lit room with a panoramic western view of the valley. A rain streaked wall formed entirely of prismatic glass plays sunstreak tones of *musique concrete* with random bits of green, gray, and golden fibers, roiling blues and rainbow landscapes blending together as they clash upon the not so adamant surfaces of each other. The far sky is sunbrilliant while behind them thunder boils and gobs of lightningflash click and sizzle about the house. "This is so very real," Mary Elizabeth chants. "So very, very real. So, so, very real. So real." She might have continued into dusk's quiet incensed cloud had not the arrival of Merrill and Ruth interrupted.

Arthur holds Paloma's message tight against his cheek. Upon Ruthie's arrival, he allows it to move away. It leaves bloodstain.

Doctor Merrill allows his charge to disassemble onto the tile. Arthur approaches, something of the zombie in his eyes. His steps are firm and quick. His gestures subtle yet precise. He touches her forehead with the gift of Paloma's blood. Ruth emits a moan of volcanic proportions. One might imagine a dark cloud of ash and earthen gasses filling the room. The lights dim and fail. The far sky is no longer visible, and all the glorious actuality of the day hides itself behind the few props of this underfunded minimalist production we call reality.

Until Paloma slips through her own portal into this place of possible salvation.

The light grows more intense. The smell of rosewood overpowers the equally improbable sulfur and burnt iron of Ruthie's exhalation. Paloma takes Arthur's shoulders in her arm and leads him back to his chair. A quiet glow infuses the room. Its origin is Ruth.

Paloma and Arthur recognize the transformation. Ruth's features slip into disarray, her eyes sliding across her cheeks in black lines, her lips and tongue flaking into nothingness, her mouth and epiglottal leaf a dark gulf beneath which a living flame strives toward air and the freedom of its own consummation. Her form constricts, short and round. Violet ash swirls from her crown. She is becoming fire itself. She has become the trashcan.

Paloma, without so much as moving a labial muscle, without ever leaning in, whispers in Arthur's ear. "Remember?"

How could he not? Could he have been mistaken? He would have attested most confidently to the fire in Lenard's apartment being this beauty at his side. The divine Paloma. Most assuredly not the needy wastrel before him. It was not, but here in this room it is.

Again comes the musical voice of no vibrations, "It was me. It is me. Some time beyond this time you will comprehend the principle of non-locality. I am everywhere. There and here. Over, gone, and yet to be. I am granting Ruth that awareness now.

"By way of a small lesson in ancient history…. As Paul rode to Damascus I came to him, a being of light. The poor sap fainted dead away. Gave himself a concussion by falling off his ass and on to his head. Went blind just as the story goes. Jesus — another factor entirely — would have let him walk the roads blind and begging, but, for some reason, Big Daddy, intervened. Paul saw, came to prominence, and overthrew the true teachings of the one they call the Christ. Anyway, the point is that he never understood. Were I to reveal everything to you, neither would you. Ruth, however…. When the fire burns out and the black snakeskin of her present rags away, she will be a new woman. A new human being.

"Then she will die. Her revelation is personal and not to be shared with anyone, Arthur. Only you. I have a confession of sorts to make. Pam and I have both allowed you to believe that you are a mere bit player in this production, that the whole thing revolves around Mary Elizabeth and her Ruthie.

"Don't you believe it. You may have gathered, have you not, that I am not just a woman of fire, but that I am Fire. Well, Arthur, you, as you might have guessed, are my legitimate offspring. You are, as most in any of your groups would attest — even Lenard — all fucked up. They do not, can not, understand. The dark thing which sought to embrace you so long ago was evil. That force too knows your value. Love in the form of your mother rescued you, and it was I who lit the flame inside you to protect you, to purify you, to provide light in your night time, to engender rage within you, to open you to the consummate penetration of life."

Ruth burns. Makes not a sound.

Mary Elizabeth and Dr. Merrill neither move nor speak. Their respiration is undetectable. Their eyes register no awareness.

Ruth Burns. Arthur begins to understand.

Paloma smiles. Disappears.

288

SHE SHEDS AWAY to revelation of a woman of such beauty that the launch of a thousand ships would fail to do her proper homage. Or so she appears to Arthur. Faint within the volcanic dazzle of his mind's cavern, echoes of Paloma trip about, "She is yours, you're hers, she's you are her, are yours, are you.... Arthur would be sore afraid or more than a bit confused were not an overwhelming surge of raw desire engulfing him in the heat of a testosterone eruption of apocalyptic proportions. He stands. Erect. Ruth awaits. He strides toward her. They embrace.

Behind him he hears a stirring of garments, then pointed respirations, finally a polite, "Ahem," uttered conjointly by the two others in the room.

"Perhaps we might consider some options," Kenny suggests.

"Amen to that," murmurs Mary Elizabeth.

AND SO IT comes to pass that very evening. The two are afforded a suite at the Hilton Garden Inn to which they are chauffeured by Dr. Kenny and Mary Elizabeth in Merrill's low end CLA 250. Still a Benz however, and Ruth and Arthur snuggle most comfortably into the leather-upholstered rear. Physical intimacy grows on them block by block until the possibilities of their upcoming night together in a brand new room would have brought telltale roses to Mary's cheeks had she allowed her thoughts to stray into forbidden lands.

Instead, upon their arrival, she is first from the car, holding open the door and tilting her seat into a passable condition. "We're here!" she chirps. "Let's get you two crazy kids settled in. What do you say?"

Ruth and Arthur are mute, but they squeeze themselves past the seat and Mary out into the rain-fresh evening. Off across the river the sun casts its passing light from behind the hills. Overhead, a sliver of moon emerges from the gathering night. The four of them, not unlike a straggle of Canada Geese struck dumb by some fluke of impossible nature, manage their way to the desk.

The room has been booked. They have no luggage. The two keepers see the couple to the room, and, after a very few moments of trivial conversation, the exchange of phone numbers and e-mail addresses, after no talk at all of the future, Mary Elizabeth and Kenny return to the Mercedes and the familiar set of illusions they choose to call life.

HELLO, ISADORA. YES, it's Mary.

Yes. I assure you, Ruthie is safe.... And well.

No. I'm afraid I couldn't tell you that. You see, she's...how should I say it...? Met someone?

No I don't think you know him.

His name's Arthur. Very well spoken and highly intelligent.

I would guess they're in love.

No. don't worry. She'll stay on the right track. We'll see to that.

Yes. That does include Pam.

Now, Izzy, that's not worthy of you. Listen please. Ruthie will still be attending counseling with Paloma. Will go to meetings as well.

Of course. She needs Doctor Bhatti.

Yes, Isadora. We know she needs you too. Bank on it. You'll be seeing a much happier daughter in these next months. Let yourself experience all that entails, and I think you'll be most pleasantly surprised.

Yes, Isadora. I'll tell her.

We'll keep in touch.

HEY, LENARD. KENNY here. We've got it done. Arthur's outta your hair for good.

I know.

I'll tell him.

You'll see him around. Just don't feel any more responsibility. He's all taken care of.

OK, brother. See ya.

IN THE CRAPPY old house. Even the dank basement. Especially in the little car. It grew and grew. Hope, that is. Renewed belief in the possibility of goodness. Healing. Salvation.

IT IS NO deception. For just a blink she and I were one. I heard the Dove say she cared. She understood. She partook of my burning. How I burn!

I FELT IT in the basement. In the car. Now he looks at me with undisguised lust. It's all just another fucking rape. All night I would guess. Might as well get it on, all the sooner to get it over.

IF NOT FOR the two Bozos up front, I'd have taken her in the car. Her pheromones sang a song even that clot Merrill must have detected. I would wager there's a damp patch on the leather where she sat. I could feel it. Our surfaces slid all over themselves and each other. My tongue yearned for a taste of her aromatic vagina. My penis…? Well rock hard as ever even my ossificanic nature might imagine it, my generative member had regained thirty years of lost youth.

ARTHUR IS NO different. They're all the same. I see him stare. I could not mistake the nature of the pelvic thrusts against my knee. He's not that bad really. Simply average, that's all. Predictable. No doubt manageable. I know we're meant for each other. I suppose I won't find my situation far different from that of most brides. I've done it before. I'll put up with it again.

SHE DISAPPEARS INTO the bathroom. This affords me the opportunity to investigate the suite. Generic, I must say. Straw walls, peasant dresser, nightstand, desk and table. A huge TV, however. It must be seventy-two inches or even more. A generous closet, with a safe for the use of those who possess valuables. A small refrigerator, a bar — not for us Kenny admonished — a snack tray which he allowed would be covered. The carpet is softer than one used to such low-rent establishments might expect. I am certain that Pam, Paloma, and whoever in hell or heaven else is out there thought not a pico about the carpet. I would imagine a bed to have been the single indispensable element of their scenario. What a bed! It is huge with a multitude of cumulus pillows. I allow myself to fall back into its embrace. It is softer than Ruthie's meager breasts ever could be. It embraces me in four-hundred or better count linen beneath some sort of natural coverlet. I could explode.

THE INCIDENTALS OF womanhood, especially my own, have never ceased amazing me. We have already spoken at too great length of my invincible compulsion to submit, and here I am again. This business I am about is beyond incredible. I had hoped to be afforded a cure for my cancer. The fact that such will not be forthcoming has left me bereft, and should have given rise to at least a bit of the revolutionary nature present to some degree even in the worst of us. "*Je refuse!*" is not so difficult to say, translate or understand. But, Mr. Sartre be damned… I guess…. I am diligently cleaning myself for him. Regretting the wild and ratty growth of my pubes, scrubbing my armpits — thankfully hairless — and dabbing the curiously exotic perfume provided by the Hiltons with other amenities, including toothpaste and plastic sealed brush. Mouthwash as well. Oh, yes Mary, I am such a proper little bride. Or whore.

I HEAR THE shower. There will be time. Indeed, there will be time. I open an entire bag of miniature Reese Cups, uncap a bottle of S. Pellegrino, retrieve the remote from the stand, and begin to surf. The resolution is amazing. I allow myself to pause, move past, and then return to a rerun of *Lost*. Intriguing. Were one to understate the obvious, he might add "appropriate." Paloma would have me believe my fate involves some form of salvation, no doubt an alternative version, but salvation nonetheless. Damn it! I feel nothing like "saved" might suggest. Indubitably something awaits. Now "us" not simply me. Another appropriate term for "our" situation might be limbic. For here I am, she is, and we are arrived at the edge of something we neither perceive nor understand in either its concrete or abstract form. There exists, however, no possibility of turning away. We will cross over.

I never truly followed *Lost* and so I lose interest. Many complications. Few clues. No explanations. The shower scratches on. I could sleep.

THE TV PLAYS some jungle thing I don't recognize. My appointed companion lies asleep. For a time I am free. He has been eating chocolates.... With peanut butter. U fucking GG! And I'm not speaking of footwear. Chocolate is fine. In truth even at times angelic. Peanut butter is no better than baby poop. Thank god he sleeps. His breath must reek of the shit.

The goodie basket contains other treats of more appropriate consistency, color, and taste. I choose a dark chocolate/cherry granola bar and a can of diet Pepsi. Delicious. A commercial for Cialis defiles the screen. I wander about the menu for a time, eventually pausing at the Lifetime channel. A tale of confusion, abuse, true love, marital woe, salvation, and closure begins to unfurl. I neither recognize the title nor the actors. Nonetheless I know the story by heart. In Lifetime Land all truly is well that ends well, and all always does end well. Except, of course, for the brute responsible for the innocent-woman's brave and resolute victimization. May god forgive him for his sins against all womankind. May we all, women that is, give thanks for the salvation eternally present in the guise of the one good man god sometimes chooses to send....

Jesus H Christ! That had better not be my own story. I swear I'd rather die in a dumpster.

This thing beside me? Are we just some cheesy flic on some dreary eternal screen?

I'm telling you right this moment, I'm not playing that game. If anything I have observed is valid, he needs me more than I ever could him.

Hello, Lifetime, lull me into to something other than acceptance. Dull the sharp dissonance of my thoughts. I would drift into your melodramatic *Amales Potamos, Lethe*, should you prefer, and enter the dark land of my own dreams.

A DEAD QUIET engulfs the little room. Evening followed by midnight falls. Lifetime flickers away and is supplanted by multiple screens of clashing colors and frantic movement. Black walls echo colorless spiders of once was light. Two shadows, gray upon black, which might be women flutter together in a far corner. Their soft laughter neither mocks nor approves. Accepts. From each flows a trickle of inabsolute photons from individual shadow to individual matter curled atop the bed. Insubstantial Pamela to particulate Ruth. Probable Paloma to Arthur the observed. Man and woman do not stir.

The energy no longer light disappears into each, and for some time they remain dark within the darkness, but eventually trembles from each a glow quickly transmogrifying into radiance. The figures move not; each is locked into birth position. Nothing moves them. The photon flow from shadow to form eventually dims, ceases. The radiant figures soften into predawn insubstantiality. The shadows flit away.

THIS IS NOT real. It is no dream. I am imprisoned in the reality I have so often wholeheartedly halfheartedly wished to bring upon myself. *Fibrodysplasia Ossificans Progressiva.* Physically. Emotionally. Whenever has such condition as emotionality ever presented itself as an element of my most rational self? I am afire. Afraid. Trembling before an altar of my own sacrifice. Or beginning. It matters not a whit. I do not wish to be here. Then she arrives. Paloma, my dove. Paralyzed, I observe her as a divine blowball of feathers scattering shadows across my physicality and into the unmoving respirations of my life. She fills me with her seed. I am changed. I move again.

PAM ENTERS MY soul upon a tongue of flame. It does not burn. Will create no scars. She sears away my resistance and plants a seed of wonder. I feel joy. I am soon to be wracked with pain. Am soon to die. I rejoice. I await my crucifixion.

THE TWO AWAKEN to each other with the dawn. Arthur's eyes pool deep and warm. Ruth is ablaze, her eyes incandescent. Mute, Ruth, her towel fallen away, slips Arthur's pliant form from his clothing. Naked to the world as well as to each other, the two become a couple. Out on the Jersey Pike two women pass by a black man in a Mercedes. Pam flashes the thumbs-up. Paloma kicks her BMW past the pokey old man in his not so old guy's car.

ARTHUR, ARTHUR. ARTHUR!!!! I know it is you. I see your face, the silken threads of your morning hair tangled up in sunlight. I feel the soft satin of your fingertips glide upon the holy *antimins* of my newly woven skin. Your breath speaks of children as yet unborn. When you enter me I am sweet oil of juniper, liquid before you, and around you. All over you. Within you. I am the chrism of our sacrament of blessed union. We flow together. You and I are one and two, and all that is, ever was or ever will be. The mortal song of our consummation chants a soft Gregorian of hallowed exaltation.

I'VE NEVER BEEN anything like this. Never. I have always been, am, and shall ever be the Man of Fire. Until this morning. This, I must say it, blessed awakening into a state so far removed from *ossificans* that I might as well be water. Holy and pure, the ultimate liquid. My mind has sloshed down some heretofore unsuspected corporeal drain into my ill-equipped heart and eaten away its defenses. My manhood has ceased its accustomed crow and quietly seeks to offer gentle communication and comfort. The woman is open before me. I am upon and within her. I have been swallowed into immense natural gravity. I flow between her legs and into the place where death desecrates the temple of her life. For a time we jostle against each other. For this time the dark one slips away. She will not hurt me. I will bring her joy.

A SOFT ORGASM. This man is softer than the john of my fabled past. I have found a dream I must not let it get away.

I LOOK INTO her eyes and see her soul. I cannot ascertain whether or not I am actually looking upon her or if, perhaps, I see her from within herself. She could be me. Might always have been. And I her. Possibly a physicist would say our souls, spirits, consciousness —Who in hell cares? — are entangled. A mystic might spout an ancient word or two concerning *yin* and *yang*. Again, who the hell gives an Adam's fig? We are one and we are two. We are no longer separable. I love her as I would myself.

AGAIN THE COMPLIENT woman. You have succeeded Mary. I will do as Pam suggests. I cannot help myself. I am falling in love. Damn that freaky soft orgasm. I think I'm going to cry.

Smitty and Lyndi
1999

Smitty chose a most unbecoming pair of too large, too old gray sweats, another clean but hideous tangerine tee, topped off at the bottom by a functional but unattractive pair of rubber flip flops for her charge. Not even the fey Tricia could exude any serious appeal so accoutered. They could converse on their way along the Thruway. There need be no resurgence of libidinous imaginings. Smitty made herself safe. At least for a time.

Once past the toll booths and headed solidly south, Tricia unfastened her restraint, and appearing oblivious to the warning buzzer, tucked both legs beneath her, and turned those emerald eyes upon her new friend. "I've been thinking," she began, then paused as the annoying signal gibbered on.

"Shouldn't you buckle up?" Smitty suggested. That buzzer drives me insane, and anyway, it's for you own safety."

The little one was not without her ways. Deftly she slid the belts behind her, connecting them across the seat back. The annoyance came to an end.

Suspecting that any response to Tricia's earlier gambit might be the first step into a forbidden forest of some Freudian dimension, Smitty nonetheless felt compelled to ask, "Of what were you thinking, my dear?"

"Well," the tiny one drew out. "Well…. "Well, what the hell," at which point she drew herself up, sharpened her gaze, and, suppressing the lightest of laughs, plunged into the darkness. "You could be beautiful, you know. If you just tried even the littlest bit."

"Oh," Smitty blundered, "I've never paid much attention to my looks. I've always been a bit of a plain Jane. A very plain Jane." Then out of the blue, by way of both confirmation and explanation, she added. "You may not know it, but I was once a nun. I'm no longer so, but the old ways have stayed with me. I find them comfortable. Somehow pure."

Purity, she thought as the word tumbled from her. I have taken a lifelong vow of chastity. Purity, God, please, may I remain so both of thought and deed. Please, Jesus and Mary Ever Virgin….

"That's why!" the girl clamored, alive with the excitement of discovery. "I've been wondering why you're bein' so good to me. I even wondered if you were one of them…. Sorry…. You know what I mean, right? A lesbian? Or worse. Resucin' a girl in trouble so you could…. Sorry." Her eyelids squeezed upon themselves and, cheeks approaching the color of her hair, Tricia let one leg free and turned herself toward her window. "Sorry," she repeated to her reflection. Sometimes I got a really big mouth."

"No," Smitty countered. "Don't be. You have nothing to be sorry for. Why would you think you do?"

The girl's head drooped until it rested against the glass; her shoulders folded in upon themselves. "It's just.... Well, you hear all kinds a stuff. You're not some kind of monster or anything. Even drunk I could see that. At first I couldn't help bein' kind of afraid. I seen this movie once called *Eden* about a girl caught by some sex.... What do call 'em anyway? Anyhow, a bunch of really bad guys, and a woman too, kidnapping girls and turning 'em into who... prostitutes. My Fio says I'd be perfect meat for one of them. Anyway, it didn't take me any time to see you wasn't like that. The other thing though! You know? You just might a been. I'm sorry, but that's what I thought. Still sort of wondering about.... But you're a nun."

"Was," Smitty hastened to respond.

On down the Thruway they glided beneath deep blue July sky set to dancing by the sun. Shadows and reflections reeled about as they drove, rhythmic *Americana* to the *Abandono* pulsing from the speakers surrounding them. Words failed to move beyond lips. Individual hearts began to beat in unison. Various other basic elements of biology edged toward synchronization. The car thermometer registered 88 degrees and the radio played *Salsa*.

At least half an hour had passed this way when Tricia turned from her reflection, straightened her other leg and abruptly jammed the radio onto an incomprehensible mix of rhythm and bad poetry. "Tupac," she asserted. "Hope you don't mind," and without awaiting either affirmation or demurral, returned to her outside introspection. Except for Tupac and his brothers, silence once again reigned. The sun and shade, the blue and gold began dancing to a different tune, and Smitty was increasingly inclined to wonder if the adventure might best be scrubbed, when the *sylph* straightened around, smiled at her companion, and laughed soft and strong. "I guess I can be kind of a downer, can't I? Anyway, I'm feeling kinda queasy, and I need to pee. How 'bout we stop at the next stop? Ok?"

A hardy traveler with not a touch of senior incontinence, Smitty awaited her companion in the bustling anteroom, observing with lucid objectivity the common carnival of chattering voyagers. She knew them, knew them all, the chirping mommies with fledglings, the self-possessed and determinedly focused professionals of various natures, as well as the constant decomposing and recomposing clutter of those individuals around the edges of the common flow.

The too tired, nearly destitute, and the gravely wounded huddling in upon themselves, interweaving with the fat, the anorexic, the incapacitated both of body and soul. One of these in particular took her eye. Feigning sleep or at least a midday drowse, an angular youngish woman of indeterminate age leaned arrogantly against a green wall inscribed in bold letters MEN. Her shorts revealed legs tattooed from arch to hem; her sleeveless lemon top offered ink sleeves of complex design for all to see in passing. Her keen, bored face, green eyelids shut against all outside intrusion, the bold blue star on her forehead glared defiance to the world. Her neck was wound about by a serpent of malevolent jade, and FTW strode across her chin below her drawn, pale lips.

Whatever, Smitty wondered, could possess someone to so disfigure herself? All negativity aside, she was forced to admit, the girl was intriguing. One might find a world, a universe, of mystery locked up inside the tattooed one's so outlandishly shielded mind. Moving closer, Smitty detected the odor of marijuana. If only there were more time, no deadlines and inviolable commitments. Always the world moves on and all sorts of beings pass each other with no signs of recognition. Even in the daylight, and especially on the Governor Thomas E. Dewey Thruway.

What could be keeping Tricia, anyway?

No sooner thought than answered, the girl bounced up to Smitty's elbow as though from thin air. "Any chance of a diet Sprite?" she asked, gesturing to the machine to the tattooed woman's left.

"Of course," Smitty responded, relieved to be drawn from her own chaotic reverie. "Let's see what they have in the gift shop. I wouldn't mind a snack, and the junk in these machines is horrible." So it was that with very little further ado the traveling innocents rejoined their car, the car rejoined the highway, and Jesus in one of his greatest personae opened her vulture eyes upon the unmarked for anything but oblivion masses around her and smiled her secret smile.

"I COULD HAVE ended it there, Dad," the immortal Artoria rasps. "But you never…"

"Leave it, son," the Big Bear growls. "Fer My sake gwan off and do some kinda good. OK?"

NO MORE THAN a mile down the road Smitty is struck into volubility by an onrush of memory. Mary Margaret! Mary Margaret often traveled neither to New York, nor to Paramus for her quotidian shopping, but to the mall at

Woodbury. Not far from the Thruway exit and convenient to commuter rail. All this she explained to Tricia, expounding as well upon the fashion sense and extrinsic as well as intrinsic beauty of her non-sanguineous sibling. After a full five minutes of ecstatic testimony, she ended with, "We'll both buy new outfits. Maybe even have time for manicures or such. What do you say?"

Her companion's response was more muted than Smitty had expected, but the youngster at least smiled, sucked down the rest of her non-diet sprite, and gurgled a cheerful acquiescence of sorts. "Whatever. I never heard of any a these places."

As their time evolved, there was none suited for manicures. The shopper's moments in the boutiques, however, were most rewarding. Not until they were once again side by side in the automobile did the full effect of Tricia's transformation assert its dominion over Smitty's rational faculties. She had helped the girl choose the sundress, in fact had made the final decision between it and two others of similar cut and style, if not of color.

Sometimes Smitty found herself immersed in the minor details of an intricate tapestry to the point of either ignoring or completely missing the greater creation with which she had become involved. So did the dress hijack her more inclusive awareness. She fell in love. It was fashioned of the softest, most pure and organic cotton, of a light aqua so filled with sunlight that Smitty could never become aware of the dangerous shoals it might conceal beneath its dazzle. The contrast of Tricia's red hair set it off as would a brilliant Pacific sunset. Thin straps held a perfect — simultaneously demure and suggestive — bodice barely above the initial swell of the elf's immature breasts, and, best of all, when one looked closely, she would find hidden within the folds, just below the dazzling surface of the fabric, subtle yellow and blue flowers of such indeterminable genus as to stoke the imagination of even the coldest observer. Fashion can be art. This dress was a masterpiece.

Her mind drowning within its own imaginings, Smitty did her best to focus upon driving. They were bound for Harriman, overnight parking, and an adventure by rail into the wilds of North Jersey. The train would first deposit them in Hoboken, a mythical city of mystery and urban decay, home to rats and people she imagined might be indistinguishable one from the other. Mary Margaret who knew these things once remarked that, if it weren't for Newark and Jersey City, Hoboken would no doubt rank as the refuse heap of the east coast. Smitty had never been partial to these cities either, but, while suffering from no small degree of anxiety, she also became aware of a growing thrill of anticipation. *The drunkard's first drink*, she thought, *the Lotus Eater's feast*. The descent into sin and moral depravity of irredeemable nature requires an appropriate setting. Might not Hoboken New Jersey serve that function perfectly?

Of course her attention never ceased to wander to the little girl, her adorable knees doubled back and peeking from the hem of that amazing dress. Even while focused on traffic and road signs, Smitty's thoughts insisted upon straying to the forbidden place beneath the girl's clothing. Her new panties! Good lord, the most cheerful yellow, the skimpiest of substance, tight around her waist, soft and comforting upon her little place. Could anything be more beautiful? More terrible? Nearly as omnipotent?

Harriman. The station. Parking. Quietly and efficiently, Tricia slipped open her door and slid into the waiting world. Smitty took her time, collected their things, arranged her clothing, secured the doors. Quieted her mind.

The two began their trek across the blacktop to the depot.

No more than thirty seconds into the journey, the little one's fragile fingers found Smitty's lumpy palm. Tricia turned her green eyes up to her companion's. Smitty abandoned all hope. Conjoined, they entered the station. Plain, utilitarian in the non-Benthemic sense of the term, the Harriman station was essentially deserted. Their train arrived after a short wait, and despite a moment of confusion in the very seedy Hoboken Path, the daring duality soon found themselves escaped from one oppressive crowd of jostling bodies and thrust into another. Penn Station was impossible. Smitty could not for the life of her decipher the subway map, and so, always a decisive individual, she hustled her charge up into the human Maelstrom named Manhattan in hopes of hailing a cab.

Mary be praised, such occurred upon her first timid wave, and safely inside an herbal scented taxi, the two allowed their wonder to unfurl as they swerved, accelerated, bucked, and stopped up the avenue between unimaginably tall buildings which extended upward beyond the limits of their sheltered vision. "The Big Apple!" Smitty exclaimed.

"I never been here," Tricia whispered. "I never thought it could be like this." Then after a pause, "It's kinda scary. Isn't it?"

Smitty was more inclined toward "Exciting," and said so.

"I guess you're right," her companion agreed. "Just the same, I wouldn't wanna get lost out there. You're not thinkin' of goin' off anywhere without me are you? You know, when you meet these people or whatever?"

Touched deep past her heart, Smitty took the child's hand. "I won't leave you, Sweetie. Just stay close, and we'll both be safe."

The cab dropped them in front of the fabled Plaza half an hour before their scheduled meeting. "Let's just sit out here a while." Settling herself upon a sun bright concrete edge six tiers down from an elaborate fountain, Smitty trailed her fingers in the water and suggested. "We can go inside later. Don't you think it's nice? I just love the way the water springs up and then follows down through all these circles. I've always found it...I don't know.... Profound maybe? At least mysterious. I can't help but wonder about things when I'm here. You know. Greek. Or Roman. The woman is Pomona, you know, goddess of abundance, she was....perhaps I should say is...."

Grace

Oh! I have slipped the surly bonds of Earth…

TRICIA HAS DISAPPEARED from her side. The little adventurer, apparently carefree as a wayward breeze, is just vanishing behind the fountain as Smitty begins a frantic scan of the motile environment. Just a whisk of sun dress skips across the corner of her eye. And a tiny flicker of suede boot, grey as the concrete behind it. Smitty has promised. Hastening to catch up with her charge, rounding the corner just negotiated by Tricia, Smitty's hurried steps blunder her into the frozen form of her little one. Tricia has chanced upon one of the big city's more unpleasant realities. An old man, long white hair fringing a bald crown, stands beneath the abundant *derriere* of Pomona, refreshing her pool with   urine.

TOO WELL READ, Smitty was unable to banish a literary allusion from her response as the urinator turned their way, tracing patterns upon the walk. "Bottle green," blazed from overgrown eyes. His flow ceased, and a caressing began. His smile should have been toothless, but was not. His shaft grew huge in his hand. His smile offered paradise.

Smitty shrieked in horror as she grasped Tricia's shoulder in a vain attempt to turn her away from abomination.

The girl shrugged her off, squared around, and laughed. "What a fuckin' clown," she snickered, and turning to her protector suggested through little waves of humor, "Come on. Let's get outta here before we gotta see him squirt all over himself." Once they were back around the curve of things, she followed with a surprisingly adult exclamation, "Guys," she smirked. "They're all the same."

Away from the fruitful fountain and closer to Fifth Avenue, the two paused at curbside and prepared to share more traditional observations of the passing crowd. All around the waters swirled, the city spun about them, and the old man, unremarked, played upon his own satiric pipes. The day opened ripe for enjoyment, the mindless pleasures of a summer's day with a pleasant companion.

Of course….

From FAO Schwartz across the street issued a disturbance of pronounced although minor magnitude. Something akin to a seismic ripple waved through the crowd of tourists. Soon its cause became clear. A positively huge woman in motorcycle leather pushed past the outer edge of the human periphery of the toy mart. Close behind followed two riotous females, smaller of stature but not of effect, who joyously pursued their own disruptive course, randomly stumbling into unsuspecting individuals and waving hula hoops above their heads, not coincidentally, clipping the guarded edges of many a self-enfolded, self-defined innocent. As they progressed toward the street, their advance was arrested by a young woman of diminutive physicality and gigantic presence.

"Good Lord!" Smitty realized. "It's Amilee!"

In good time and heedless of downbound traffic, the triumvirate paraded across Fifth Avenue as would Psyche and her sisters while Amilee trailed behind.

"I know you from somewhere, don't I?" A young woman hollered across the streaming city noise, and when no response was forthcoming, called again as her feet stepped from the dark roadway onto the walk. "You are Agnes Smith, aren't you?"

The sometimes comfortable small world of Troy New York expanded into the immensity of the Colossal Malus, and Smitty knew that she very well knew the mysterious Pamela. "God help me," she came inside, "This is the Pam I'm supposed to meet? Another lesbian. I swear I must be cursed." *Or might that just be blessed?* God, can life not be intricate in its patterns and difficult in its calculus!

Once upon a time upon a time, Smitty, a former Sister of minor conservative views, happened upon a most holy woman, one Mary Elizabeth Foster, president and inspirational force of Women Of Mary (WOM), an outreach group focused upon the homeless, the hopeless, the blind and insane or however that line from somewhere outside Smitty's self went. Yes, the organization bore all the signs of the liberal wing of their most ancient church, but after only two chance meetings and one savory afternoon over hot tea and miraculous scones, Mary and Agnes recognized the sisterhood of magisterial purity within each other. In no order at all, Smitty became one with WOM, and her new friend and she walked secular paths of holiness together.

Pam had also been a member and friend of Mary Elizabeth. In her Smitty recognized something of herself. God help them all. It soon became too stressful watching and wanting, praying and sinning, hoping without hope.... Smitty eventually faded from the WOM sisterhood. Better the solitary life. A life of altruism. A life free from desire.

Nonetheless, her heart skipped a step or two as the ever egregious one bounded across the concrete distance between them, and threw her arms as far around the larger woman's person as was possible. "Smitty," she exhaled, cocking her head and shoulders back from Smitty's bosom. "Smitty! I had no idea "Smitty" could be you. Sister Agnes. That's how I remember you. From WOM wasn't it?" With that she halted. Reddened and relinquishing her embrace, stammered, "Well.... Maybe you don't remember?"

Not remember? Not remember? She could not not remember! Smitty had always found herself attracted to the word "nonplussed," and for a moment she found herself in a definite negative zone. Old longings and the wounds and betrayals of self had been tucked safely away, but what in the world was this one doing associated with Amilee? Whatever could have prompted her to request a meeting with someone she did not even realize she knew from older and more trying times? Smitty found herself unable to vocalize anything other than an exhalation such as she might have produced with a doctor's depressor prodding at her tongue. She too, however, manifested a revealing shade of crimson.

Amilee, as she would on more than one or six future occasions, breezed to the rescue. "I thought you two might know each other," she breathed into the paralysis of their discomfort. "In fact a little bird assured me that you did. So much the better, wouldn't you say? We're all friends. I assure you we share similar concerns and, that same bird tells me, destinies as well."

Then it was her turn to pause and perhaps turn a whiter shade of her own pink. Up to them lumbered Sis, trailed by the wilting figure of Lyndi, her hoop grown still. "Today, I speak for four of us, and for one who is not present," Amilee shot. "Now one of us may be principal in another tale." Just who might the little girl be?"

Returned to a semblance of awareness of the world beyond their knit up group, Smitty looked about her for the child she had enticed into this place, and found her engrossed in her own acquaintance with a troubling intrusion. The man from behind the statue had presented himself to the child in full masturbatory *delicto*. Tricia stood as if mesmerized, motionless except for the fingers of her left hand which slowly encouraged the hem of her dress to creep up her pale thigh.

"Hey, Asshole!" Pam called, and the Aqualung wackamoled beneath the surface of sensory awareness. "Hey, you! Little one," she called. Get over here before you find yourself more serious trouble."

Accompanied by a rueful smile, Tricia complied.

Across the avenue, the crowded square before the fabled shop of childish and childhood dreams throbbed with expectant life. The chatter of children abraded the sunlight into shrill streaks of lusterless photons and scattered shadows of impotent parental laughter about the fading July afternoon. A soft breeze feathered across Smitty's cheek, and her senses abandoned their temporary anchor. Jerry's voice, his haunting presence, the music from a long gone evening coaxed her from the shell of herself and set her adrift upon the wind of her own imagining.

I AM ALONE and insubstantial. I have nowhere to be and am nowhere now.

Of course she was wrong. Smitty drifted among the green leaves of 58th Street. She was able to see into the greater expanse of Central Park and beyond. All the way to Albany should she wish. Or Montreal should she choose. Instead she focused upon the husk of herself standing within the encircling group of women. Then upon Tricia. The girl had continued to raise her skirt to immodest heights. Pam had set her breasts free. The big and smaller two were engaged in pulsations of a most erotic nature while Amilee stood off to the side viewing the passing processional of partially clothed men and women, all intent upon one end only.

Old men pursued willing moorage with young women. Two stick figures, one most possibly deceased the other a dark personage from an alien sphere, had begun to do it in the road. Jerry and the boys scattered among the branches of Smitty's tree broke into a perfect rendition of *Friend of the Devil*.

Jerry caught her eye and directed her attention back to Tricia. The girl posed aglow in a halo of unrefracted sunlight. All red hair and pure dove skin she moved her fingers between her legs to the rhythm of the song and in concert with the manipulations of the man from behind the abundance. Smitty felt herself reaching her own rhythmic crescendo until all together the band, Tricia, and Smitty disassembled into incoherent pleasure while the old man, grown larger than the statue herself, splattered his anointing upon them.

Powerful enough to have reached into the topmost branches, his ejaculation smeared her cheek and forehead with....

"FUCKIN' JERKOFF," THE big woman hollered as she wiped away streaks of someone's Slurpee no doubt tossed from a passing car. Smitty too was covered in purple slush as was the big one's companion.

"What happened?" Smitty gasped, as yet unsure of the ground beneath her feet.

"Are you OK?" a fully clothed Tricia asked as she attempted to wipe away some of the stuff with her bare hand.

"Pli plink plit plas plon plurpose," the large woman's companion offered. "Plome plittle plid plom placross pla pleet pli'd plet."

Stranger and stranger. Smitty understood every word.

Plink, plink, platt pla plink plink, plut, plllop, an excremental storm of liquid droppings sketched a dotted line between the teacher and her charge. Smitty caught a fleeting glimpse of a flight of pale birds. Pigeons she would have guessed had not Tricia laughed out her own assessment. "Doves," she cried. "Where on earth'd they come from?"

"Squab's more like it," Sis muttered, wiping a stain from her bare forearm. "Goddamn rats with wings. I'd kill 'em all. Wouldn't eat one on a bet though."

""Try it, you might like it," Pam suggested. "Stephen loves that kinda shit."

Tight jawed, Smitty stepped across the dropping line and, hugging the airy form of Tricia to her own substantial hip and shoulder, turned to face the others. "It might be advisable to move inside," she suggested. "Things are getting a might uncomfortable out here right now, what with the birds…. Not to mention the heat."

The day had turned uncomfortably humid, and the temperature threatened a successful run at ninety plus. It need not be mentioned that the hotel would be air conditioned, bird free, and accommodating in numerous other ways. Wherever the disgusting old man had disappeared to, he most certainly would not be allowed to follow them inside the Plaza Hotel.

Should they have proceeded according to her suggestion, the sixth part of the sestet known as Agnes Smith might have been surprised to see the particular dirty old one she had come to loathe and fear disappearing behind the closing doors of an exclusive elevator reserved for the most private of the hotel's beyond upscale clientele. However, such enlightenment was not to be.

"I'm sorry, but I can't stay," Amilee announced. I have to be over in Brooklyn in half an hour, and as things stand, I'm never going to make it. My best hope, Agnes, is that all of us might ride together, and we can conduct our business on the train. "It's hot, I know, but we should be able to put our heads together and get necessary things done." Drilling her diamond keen eyes directly into Smitty's softer ones, she continued. "Brooklyn's coming back, you know. It's not so obvious now, but it's about to blossom, and I know a truly great diner, Bonnie's, where you can get an excellent early meal. Bobby Hunter eats there all the time."

"Fuckin' A NO!" Pam exploded. I've always wanted to meet him. Think he'll be there today?"

"It's not impossible," Amilee answered, but failed to mention that Hunter was meeting with Bobby Weir and her in Monte's, a great Italian place in Gowanus, and, even were he to stop by Bonnies for a late-night snack, the quintet, having become caught up in more essential matters, would have forgotten both about him and his favorite diner.

Past pretzel carts and cattwhining children, down sweaty steps they trekked to the Q which screeched them downtown, across nether Manhattan and off into the wilds of the as yet ungentrified City of Churches. From the first, while Sis, Lyndi, Tara and Pam shrilled subterranean introductions at each other and snuck glances at the unpleasantly diverse company about them, Amilee and Smitty huddled in a corner of the rollicking car and not without some difficulty groped about in the artificial illumination for a significant agreement.

Then from out the subway scuttle, they mounted the Manhattan Bridge, and Smitty spied the Crane's holy gull shedding white rings of sunlight as if they were blessings. Beneath the innocent bird, the Brooklyn Bridge. The teacher's mind slipped from its dark juncture with earth as her soul took flight. *To Brooklyn Bridge!* For the first time she understood. Beyond lay Liberty. Amilee, more than either Hunter or even Jerry himself, knew the way, the way for all of them. Home. Whatever that might be.

At the particular moment of awareness, Smitty would have felt a mortal shiver were it not so damn hot. As events unfolded, the train journeyed across the river glimmering with sunlight beneath a cloudless sky, and passed back into earth again. By the time they reached Amilee's stop her business with Smitty had concluded, and the company journeyed on with only vague inklings of where they actually should go or what they should do once they arrived. It was dinner time, and all were hungry, so Bonnie's Diner would have been a fine destination had anyone thought to ask Amilee how to get there. Sliding between two hostile Russian-speaking women and their assorted children, Pam addressed the map, "Let's see if I can help."

Of course it failed to list local attractions of any sort, but, engulfed by Sis's bulk, Lyndi's apologetic presence, and Tricia's wave of possibility, she began to trace the diagram of route and stations ahead of them. Upon their emergence into Prospect Park, a familiar old man relieving himself at the far corner of a platform attracted no one's but Tricia's notice. The ancient one would always be with her, his wrinkled penis, the taste of salt-hard urine two essential memories from her years-gone maiden voyage into womanhood.

As the others' attention focused upon such incidentals, Smitty found herself in company with significant matters of her own. Amilee's offer — or might it be more accurately termed imperative? — was highly intriguing, and, in light of her own apprehension of a reawakened manifest destiny beyond the simplicities of territory and politics, impossible to refuse. At the same time it all was more than a just a little unsettling.

SWEET LITTLE AIMILEE, in whose mouth sugar would never melt unless of course it carried within its secret self a healthy dose of lysergic, had begun in a brusque manner. "Forgive me," she interrupted as Smitty began an opening pleasantry. "I'm seriously pressed for time, and we need to get right in to this."

With those words the sweet one launched her attack, for "attack" was the only word Smitty would ever find an adequate descriptor. "You and your friend are pissing away your time with all the gypsy-van, traveling salvation show stuff. Thirty years after Woodstock you're still following an old path never intended as anything more than a preliminary to greatness. You help a few, maybe even save some. I'll admit that's no small thing. There will always be a Tara. Little girls and little boys will always die in strange and uncalled for circumstances. Most of them seek a shortcut to death way before any bad acid or overdone meth messes with their heads or their metabolisms to the point where it all shuts down. Or they just crawl in front of the next car. Anyway, and more to the point, even with Phish fans now or later-day Deadheads, most of them are just prospective yuppies looking for entertainment and some mild form of temporary rebellion."

Steel wheels on steel rails echoing in Manhattan's rockbound tunnels occluded the next few syllables, but Smitty never lost track of Amilee's accusations. To say she was nonplussed would be accurate but inadequate. To assert that she was hurt would identify another aspect of her reaction. "Resentment" might best describe her emotional response. Or "anger." This Queen of the Dead presumed too much. She was no Lazarus. Just a leftover groupie, a burnt out hippie. As Amilee's voice grew more shrill, Smitty gathered her dudgeon about her and prepared to put an end to the little freak's effrontery.

Just as that she might, Amilee's eyes snared hers, and Papa Bear's emissary spoke the magic words. "You still have the feather, don't you?"

Of course she did. A treasured memento. Home in a storage bag, airtight and secreted in the recesses of her sock drawer. She knew the feather was a message, that it was to be a guidepost of some sort, but it was not the kind of thing one could wear around her neck. Or weave into a bracelet. Anything else was just too risky. The bottom of her junk laden bag? A pocket? Hanging from her car's rearview mirror? Smitty had thought better of each of the choices. Her only option had been to preserve Jerry's gift and assume that whatever the foretold encounter with the mysterious Paloma might involve she would have ample warning of its imminence. There would be time, and opportunity to retrieve the feather. If that were even necessary.

Her anger and resentment fading, Smitty answered, "Of course I do, but it's at home."

To which Amilee announced, "Paloma's step sister is here today. Pam. You probably should have it with you the next time you meet. She hasn't said anything about it, but I think it is some kind of key or something

"Anyway, I have been commissioned to offer you my, I assure you, nearly unlimited access to certain venues and many as yet undiscovered or underappreciated artists. Hear this next clearly, without any interference from your thought processes. You passed a test that day in '95. The feather is Tara's symbol. It is Paloma's emblem as well. There are others you will meet along your way. Listen to me well.

"A new era in much more than music, a spiritual revival if you will, is upon us, and its associated social and psychological manifestations will alter, even negate many certitudes. As a whole it is a positive renewal of too often ignored human truths, but with it comes danger, for more than renewal it is a step forward into a new dispensation. Any such leap, think Jesus if you like, is inevitably accompanied by tragedy.

"My boys hoped to be in the vanguard. But the sixties fizzled, and the world settled back into the same old, same old....

A new nation seeks again to rise above the surface. Born of mud as was Woodstock, the new world order will blossom into the multifoliate lotus of human beauty and spiritual evolution.

"I would be certain you have never encountered the term "Dubstep...."

Smitty shook her head.

"Neither have you, I would bet, developed any knowledge of or appreciation for such genres as Electronic or House. But right now the muck is gravid, the flower forming. The scene needs you. Its people, performers and audience alike, need you. I hope you've at least heard of the 60's Hog Farm and Wavy Gravy."

Of course she had heard of them, although she knew little. Her expression remained blank. The train emerged into sunlight and mounted the Manhattan Bridge.

Amilee continued to the newborn consciousness beside her, "You're a teacher. A good one I've been led to understand. Now the time has come for you leave that behind.... At least most of it. Pam is here to explain it all. Just hold the thought, if you will, and let me get my piece of this done. I assure you,

Pam will make it clearer than I ever could. For now just let me state my own simple case.

"I'm quite a bit older than I look, you know. Pam tells me that's due to some cosmic connection or other, but I say it's simply because I take after my father's family, none of whom lived exceptionally long lives, but all of whom kept all their hair, never went gray, and maintained the skin qualities of people half their age. The last time I saw my father, he was forty-five or so and looked twenty-five. It's not just me saying that. Everybody did. Even my mother who hated him. I ask, would you believe I'm thirty-eight myself?"

No she did not. The girl could not be a week over twenty-five. If that.

Recognizing the denial in Smitty's face, Amilee simply flipped open her bag and, after some rummaging, withdrew her photo ID. It looked official enough, a California license, upon which Amilee's birthdate was registered as January eleventh 1961 which made her age to be thirty-eight.

Again sensing doubt, Amilee added, "No. It's not fake. Yes. It is real. I suppose there are ways you could check it if you were so inclined. On your own time, please. We have too much to do to continue this way. Sorry I brought it up. I just wanted you to know, I've been around and seen many things, have come to know much.

"I tell you, Agnes, even more than Hugh, you are fated to become a legend of your own sort. Your new mission, calling, I might even say vocation, will take you to places you cannot have imagined. You will save lives. You will save many souls as well. Or at least that last part is what Pam says.

"So allow me. There is a new dawn of concert experience. Now there are raves. Someday there will be giant festivals to rival Monterrey. Or Woodstock. The first of those are happening as we speak in Europe, and here in America. When I first met you and Mary, I had no inkling of your part in the grander scheme of which Jerry and the Dead, Kesey and Leary as well, were so obviously connected. I took Jerry's passing for it to come at all clear. Probably I should have guessed something when Papa gave you that feather.

"I guess it just wasn't the time. Anyway, I would have sworn that night in Albany that Mary Margaret was the Alpha while you were some Igorette or other. Was I ever wrong. You, my dear are a major player. No Pam, obviously, but pretty darned close. Mary has side issues and too many blind alleys to travel to be anything more than your, let me invent a name… River Girl, I think. She'll float along beside you and ease your passage, but, hear me well, that passage is for your steps alone."

The *überleher* could not refrain from lifting her eyebrows at the badly mixed metaphor.

Amilee shamed her automatic response into silence. "Yes, dear Agnes, little lambkin of God herself, you will someday walk upon the water. If you choose to, that is. Now listen carefully, but first, look at them over there. They're about to discover that this train takes them to Coney Island. They'll all want to go. You must accompany them. Not only that, but once there, you must listen to Pam and do as she suggests. Even if it seems strange. You need to know many things, and this day you are going to be taught two essentials. Originally they had only planned one, but you are nothing if not a woman of complications. At times, I think, even more than God himself feels comfortable dealing with.

"Anyway, I think you'll find Pam kind of a sister in such entanglement. You're going to understand a great deal more in just a few hours than you can even imagine now. Go with Pam. She will take you home.

"Now, the next stop is mine. Heed my words. Enjoy Coney Island. I'll see you again soon.

The Q jolted into the Atlantic Avenue stop, Amilee giggled farewell as though nothing more than a fanciful day of exploration and carnival thrills was afoot, and waved herself out the door. Confused and more than a bit dazed, Smitty joined the group, all of whom were already working themselves into a cotton candy sort of mood. Except for the big one. She held back, obviously resentful, shrugging off a tentative hand of Pam's and thudding onto a plastic bench with nearly enough force to crack it, and as Smitty settled herself beside the huge biker, she felt the other's halo of negativity. "Why?" she wondered, but had no time for speculation or even attempts at conversation. Pam slid in beside her, tugging the quiet one along.

"Agnes," she began. "I have someone you need to meet."

At this point the big girl grumbled, spat between her boots and twisted her frame away.

"Be cool, Sis," Pam warned. "There's no threat here. Chill. Will ya?"

Sis' answer was a muted "Yeah," and a resigned shrug of her shoulders. She did not look the others' way, however, nor did she speak again.

Pam seemed satisfied and moved into full hookup form. "Agnes," she began, "I think it's time you met someone more than just a little entwined with your life. You might even say instrumental." Turning to her companion she continued, "Lyndi, I think you know already. Agnes here's gonna be almost as important to you as Sis."

A stir of significant mass to Smitty's right captured their attention. Sis was on the move. Her fists battered into the plastic seat, a moan growled from her throat, and she quickly rose to her boot thick feet. Her lips parted, her teeth gleamed with saliva. There was no mistaking her intent. Smitty feared for her life.

Pam just laughed. "Watch it, Mama," she warned. "Why don't you just go on up with the kid and wait for us. She's cute enough to distract you for a while."

Fixing her friend with a stare sharp as a boner's knife, the big one turned toward Tara. As Sis lumbered away, Pam called after her. "Don't get too friendly. Or these two here just might twist their own panties into a knot tight as your own."

No reaction. Sis stood behind the little one, and the two of them remained a parochial distance apart as they stared at the route map.

Pam returned to business.

"Agnes Smith. Say 'hello' to Lyndi Stanley."

313

As formal as ever an *überleher* can be, Smitty nodded the silent one's way while mouthing below the railroad interference the words, "Pleased, I'm sure."

The other smiled beneath confused eyes and remained silent.

Assuming she had not been understood or perhaps even not been heard, Smitty tried again, this time loud enough to cause Sis and Tara to turn their heads her way. "Pleased to meet you," she hollered.

Again, no response other than zebra eyes darting Pam's way, then back to Smitty, and off to Pam again.

Upon the third rotation Pam laughed loudly enough to turn numerous heads her way and took Lyndi's hand in her own while addressing her eyes and words to Smitty. "Sorry, Agnes. I forgot. She's deaf.... Don't talk so hot neither," delivering the last with mock mockery as well as enough volume to attract attention from the other end of the car.

"Mind yourselves," she snarled, and, upon command, all attentions turned once again to the mindless rituals of passage. All that is except Sis'. The biker laughed even louder and offered two middle fingers before once again guiding Tara's attention along its predetermined route.

"Sorry," Pam whispered in Lyndi's ear. "This can only last for this day's time," at which moment the other's face grew wide and open with wonder, and Smitty understood. She once was deaf but now could hear.

"Oh! My God!" the woman exclaimed in the shrill voice of a teen age at a concert. Oh! My! God!" Then again. And again. And...."

"Enough," Pam cautioned. With good reason, for once again all eyes were directed their way as were all ears. The car echoed deep into the railing of their passing, and hooted above the high screech of metallic interaction. "Plo! Ply Plod!" the passengers heard. "Plo! Ply! Plod...."

Except Pam and Smitty that is. Each heard Lyndi in the standard English often so uncommon in a New York MTA conveyance.

Eventually the newly undeaf calmed into silence, and once again Pam began the introductions. "I would guess you have some inkling of what's going on here, at least for this minute, so I won't bother to elaborate. Just try again with your 'good to meetcha' or whatever you'd like."

More than a little bewildered, Smitty began again. "Agnes Smith," she stated, extending her hand half the way toward Lyndi. "I'm pleased to meet you."

In the clearest of syllables Lyndi responded. "Likewise," she said, a sense of wonder shining all around her margins. "You are able to understand me?"

Why shouldn't she be, Smitty wondered, but answered in the affirmative with the slightest hint of wonder in her inflection.

"Don't worry about the small shit," Pam intruded. "I've got things to tell you, after I'm leavin' you to your own devices." To Lyndi she added, "Try not to fuck it up, will you. Wrong things happen and it all falls apart. You two've got lots in common, but remember Sis. She's my friend. Only you know everything she is to you."

Then to Smitty, she directed, "You need Sis too. And Amilee, and Paloma who's a whole other thing. Alls I can say is be honest. Be natural. Be careful. If all else fails, please, be discreet."

With that, she directed herself back to Lyndi, "You too," she warned. "Both a you. Now listen up. We're almost there."

Having no idea where "there" was not even anymore where "here" might be, Smitty grew attentive. As did Lyndi.

Pam began. "The end of this line's Coney Island. We're, Sis, the girl, and me, gonna have a day of fun, junk food, and an extra or two that's sure to double the pleasure. Know what I mean? You two won't be with us though. You've got a whole other ride to take.

"So, to that end, allow me...," whereupon she extracted a wrinkled up sandwich bag from a side pocket and fished two capsules of something from it, at the same time calling across the space, "Hey, Sis," get me some water from your pack. These two' need a drink. Lots a drinks I'm thinkin'.'

"Git it yerself," the hulk shot back. "It's just the other side a the teacher."

The motorbike woman was mystery to Smitty. Not who she was so much as was her obvious intimate connection to Pam. How her former acquaintance could have degenerated, perhaps "fallen" might be a better word, into such company...? Her language was most troubling. If she remembered correctly, Pam had always favored the common side of everyday usage. It had become far worse. Surely she couldn't still be with....

"Get it for me, will ya Agnes?" Pam grumbled. "That one's crusin'. Know what I mean?"

Smitty wished she did not, but, Heaven help her, she feared she did. She was stuck. Committed. She had not promised Amilee in so many words, but knew her initial passivity had allowed the other to assume interest, and her silence as Amilee departed could no doubt be understood as tacit assent. The gull...the bridge, the "harp and altar," her own unstrung instrument of perception. She had no choice. So she passed the heavy bag over to Pam and resigned herself to seeing the whole thing through. The woman, Lyndi, was strange enough, but, all else considered, stood out as more normal than her company. What they might have in common that Pam found essential for them to discover might be as simple as gentility of manner and of expression. Possibly a sense of inarticulate wonder....

From such illusion springs the ambiguous reputation of hope. Neither sure and certain nor essentially false, Hope's only certainty is that it springs eternal while remaining as insubstantial as dry dunes in a desert wind, as tormenting as a jest falling from some mute gypsy's lips.

"IF YOU PLEASE, Ms. Stanley" Pam intoned, holding out one of the capsules which Lyndi ceremoniously slipped between slightly parted lips. This was followed by the offering of a plastic water bottle from which Lyndi took a delicate swallow. "If you please, Ms. Smith." Again the same procedure except Smitty's actions were neither ceremonious nor delicate.

"What the heck...." Abandoning all common sense while maintaining a tenuous grip on Hope, Smitty popped the pill down her throat and only took the water to please Pam who held it firm in her face until she drank.

"I got some drinks in the pack gonna help you later," Pam told them. "This shit might make you sweat a little. You know.... Keep hydrated with the things I'm givin' you. At least for a while don't eat anything. Just hang together and do whatever your joy suggests you do."

Joy? Smitty would have guessed a psychedelic of some sort. She would never forget The Dead and Jerry. And LSD. By all appearances, however, Pam was suggesting something else might be afoot. Just a minute too late, she thought to ask. "What have you given us, anyway? LSD?"

"Better'n that in oh so many ways," Pam laughed. "Just let yourselves go.

The train screamed against its rails as brakes held fast. People crammed the doors. "Next to last stop," Sis hollered across the noise. "Aquarium. Next stop Coney Island."

"Yeah," Tricia's mouth offered for no one to hear.

"Come on over," Pam called to the other two, "and wish these two adventurers Godspeed."

We have our own sacraments," she whispered across Lyndi to Smitty. "The little one old enough, you think?" and, before Agnes could respond, broke into a most disconcerting fit of laughter. "Guess you already thought she was, huh?" Her laughter drowned the beachgoing chatter of both steel on steel and breath upon cord. "Forgive me," she finally managed. I just can't help it. I find myself so freaking hilarious."

"Yeah," Sis muttered down into her rocking bosom. Don't we all."

Their train ground immobile, and sun and surf, cotton candy and enlightenment were waiting. Outside was sticky all over with the sugar of a summer's afternoon. Inside herself, Smitty felt the stirrings of an unbearable something a filmmaker of passing significance might have named "Being." Looking upon her assigned companion, she did not fail to note an expression suggesting a synchronous efflorescence.

"Think you can handle this?" Pam asked as she slid the bag across the platform to Smitty. "I'm sure glad I got Sissy here to tote such stuff for me. For sure you won't be travelin' far, but if we don't connect up, I'm guessin' you guys'll find your way back. Anyhow, don't lose your Metro Cards or your bags and it'll all take care of itself.

"Whatever... have a good time."

It didn't matter. Nothing mattered. Or so Smitty was beginning to realize. Stirrings of light beyond the probabilities of her accustomed range of sensory perception assumed particularity and her organs of reproduction gave birth to petals of moonlight. Her legs, her feet remained rooted while her higher self opened unto the universe. Or at least Coney Island. Beside her, Lyndi's eyes, open unbearably to the clamor of sun and sea around them, understood nothing beyond her own carnival mind. The two of them, radiant arm in improbable arm, all appurtenances unnecessary, ascended into the Cyclone.

Grace

"THAT THING WAS fuckin' scary," Tricia trilled as she, Pam and Sis returned themselves to softening asphalt from the world's preeminent wooden coaster. "I wanna go again."

12628

IN A BUBBLE of time all their own and coincidental with the cyclonic effusions of Tricia, Smitty and Lyndi discovered themselves high atop the not so infinite universe about them. The parachute jump loomed in the clouds of memory and unmet expectations which, mingled with pickled vomit, sour slurpees, and Nathan's Famous, hang winter as well as summer between the park and the sun. Closed and decaying, mocking a nation's Queens' pretentions, the paralyzed ride could not deny the two women. Unseen by the milling seekers of pleasure upon the beach, boardwalk, and blacktop, the ferrous giant collapsed an arm and effected the duet's ascension into the cosmos of Brooklyn. Side by side, eye to eye, heart and mind to heart and awakening mind, Smitty and Lyndi hung in harness. The world spun below them, the sea rolled slow as the rhythms of their perception. The sky, no longer blue, washed them in tidal breezes, and all that could be recognized as reality drained from their ecstatic eyes.

"I an fi," Lyndi hurled into the wind-torn-space between their intimately joined personas.

Smitty understood. "I know. I left my feather at home."

"ou tual avea eath," Lyndi responded, not a hint of envy to be ripped away from her words. "Mines olly n m ine...."

"Jerry Garcia gave it to me. It is very real. White and soft.... Beautiful in a sad sort of way."

Lyndi's voice cut through the wind, "I got mine from Paloma. Do you know her?"

"No. I don't. Amilee mentioned her and said she was important, but I'm afraid I've never had the pleasure."

Smitty lost any possible response in the uproarious air, neither did she feel any shift of weight upon their canvass perch. A raptor's shadow, however, blotted out the sun, and while those below continued to bask in Summer's beneficence, casting their own darkness into the swirl of light and shade patterned upon the pavement, boards and multitextured sand of the Brooklyn shore, Smitty and Lyndi knew only that which lay beyond their event's horizon.

From above and below, from within and around, the rasp of quill upon quill, talon upon innocent bone, and horn-rent flesh. Blood steaming into bitter August air.

"You two are too fuckin' much." Pam, of course.

"Look in her eyes, Agnes before the lightning strikes. Or the dove pecks you apart and then shits you out. Get it done."

"Coo, coo," mocked the not at all pacific avian as into Smitty's peripheral awareness a glimmer of unbound light prompted her obedience.

Ah those eyes! Those Mollywindow eyes. Lyndi's pupils had grown past dilated. No white, no brown, green or blue. Deep within the darkness of the room behind their own horizons blazed a song of Joy and triumph beyond the imaginings of master, poet or composer, creation beyond the formation of any sculptor even he capable of the most sublime David, even that most ginger painter of nights roiled with stars of madness and despair. As Smitty filtered her immaterial self through the nonexistent barrier between the two of them, she felt her own fire-song enkindle as awareness of superposition assumed pungency in the void of their interaction. In other words, Smitty's Mollified consciousness found itself totally in synch with that of Lyndi. No miracle at all. Simply a common effect of certain psychoactive drugs....

So, where in hell did the third party come from?

"Paloma," introduced the Mysterian to the most lucent dreamers of each other as well of themselves. "You will know me well," she pronounced. First you must comprehend each other and in so doing understand yourselves. Only then you will know me. For believe me or not, I am each of you and both of you together. And Pam...."

Laughter crazes from far off granite.

"Always the joker, aren't you. Your father knew what he was about when he gave you Stephen to carry. Now leave us alone, will you?"

A screech of cyclonic terror rattles off into nothing.

She knows how.... Forget her Loma. Yours is to take the higher road. Always until that never promised last syllable....

"Forgive me, please. Jesus wasn't the only one with a cross to bear, you know. Anyway, to everything... and everyone...there comes a season. Ladies, your time has come."

By her final word, Paloma's voice had returned from intemperance to serenity, and she whispered a soft short *ploo* as she allowed the Einsteinian potentiality of things impossibly aloft to assert its gravity upon the superpositioned accumulation of humanity hung from nothing upon nothing high above a most actual surface. Smitty and Lyndi plunged toward earth. Its deadly surface rushed to meet them as they fell to its deceptive solidity.

As all things need not end, and not every up must come down, neither was this Smitty and Lyndi's time for fatal conjunctions. They were, after all, seated upon the imaginary slingseat of a very real parachute drop. With a whomp, a belly flopping jump, and a subsequent NASA-like descent, the heart bitten women glided toward the safety of their own earth-crawling shadows. Dandelion fluff upon a gentle breeze they slipped through the streams of salted air toward a gentle reunion with the safety of their mortal selves. Until....

"Not so fast," cooed from everywhere. "Decide. The fall is fast and sometimes fatal. To join with your shadow is always the safest move.

"But! You were not chosen to play safe. In fact you were not *chosen* at all. The elect are special in their own way, but yours is a different state. Of your own merit you two are more than those. From the rich probability of everything human as humanity has existed since it has existed, evolution has taken its next step. It is not spiritual. Yet it is. It is not physical, but again....

"In you two, and to this point of time only in you two, has come about a creation of God but also of Man. Jesus... and, yes, Pam as well, are both human and divine, part God, part man and woman. The Father has made them all that they are. You two are not God made human by God's self or woman made divine by the divine. You are God raised unbidden from mankind by humanity itself...

"In a way that is.

"It is necessary that you understand something. The story of Lucifer, the angel of light, was never meant as a history, a metaphor or even an explanation of evil told to primitive people in terms they could understand. It was and is intended as a warning. Choice bears within its fundamental nature both triumph and tragedy. Lucifer is the embodiment of the best of all that is human: ambition, courage, independence. Lucifer whom we this day might best rechristen, Lucy, is not evil nor is she in Hell. As of the moment of your joining together, she has become two, and she must forge her own way, take her own path. She need not choose either the embrace of darkness or the bright hope of revolution. Nor that of Salvation. Her choices are not nearly so limited. Be aware that your forbearer brought humanity to humanity. Eve's choice was his triumph. As was it God's.

"With this in mind, tread cautiously yet boldly too. All choice is yours. Even the tragic. The time for your first newly conscious decision is upon you. Do we rise again? Or do we fall to earth and be not at all what we might be?"

Within their conjugated selves a babble of voices shouted questions across nonexistent distance to each other and to the raptor dove. The raptor had fallen silent.

"What do you...does she...can we....?"

322

The voices screamed themselves hoarse and faint. Darkness and light played among the dying echoes until from the emptiness arose awareness. Lyndi had never been meant to dwell in the comfortable world of Lyndi, wife of Edward Lapida-Vita, and Smitty had always been more than *überleher*. They just had not known it. A power arose from within them. Each and both. Paloma, the uncharacteristic dove, had awakened it. She was their mentor. Their friend. Perhaps even their spirit-guide. All the same, they were essentially on their own with the power to lift up or cast down, create or destroy. Within them dwelt the possibility, the certainty, of recreating themselves without need for biological intervention.

It became clear as well that the new experience of the rave, the transcendent togetherness of Kandy and Molly, while illusions, were also the world into which they had been guided. Old and comfortable ways had already been left behind.

Without effort, without Paloma's intervention, they rose again toward the top of the ride.

As they ascended, a darkness fell upon Agnes. An echo from somewhere. The babble of recent voices? Not at all. The newspapers, her car radio. Had she only indulged herself in a television set, she no doubt would have realized sooner.

"You're the one," she accused the other half of her duality. "You're the one who killed Tara!"

From the immensity of the consciousness of and about them spoke a familiar voice in unfamiliar tone and facility, "No one killed me. I lived and died as I was meant. I was a child of a different time and set of circumstances. Perhaps my primary purpose was to set each of you — most especially you, Lyndi — upon the road which has led you here. Again, especially you, Lyndi, without the trauma of our meeting, never would you have recognized your exceptionality. And, Agnes, had I followed your lead, become all that you hoped for me, I would have become an even more pathetic older version of the little one your heart has set itself upon these last few days. You would have sinned — in your own mind — would have found me increasingly unappealing and eventually sunk yourself into a mediocracy of aspiration and achievement such that your great sin would have been against your own true self."

"You can't be Tara," Smitty wailed, the wind of her rising whistling in her ears. You can't be saying this. You're too... too...."

"Stupid, perhaps? That's the Agnes Smith you would have become talking."

"No. I mean you're too.... Impossible. I mean.... You're... dead." As soon as the words cleared her immobile lips, the ride lurched to an entangled halt ten feet from its apex, and Smitty's objections fell away as might windblown ash from a spent torch. The girl's words were true. No doubt was possible. Her new awareness of all things assured her. How could she not have recognized Lyndi for who and what she was until this moment? How could she...?

"Tell her, Ms. Stanley," Tara laughed.

Smitty knew. By any other name a rose may still be a rose, but people are so much more complex. A Lapida-Vita whose maiden name was Stanley can become for most intents and purposes anonymous. Only the unlikely event of their shared consciousnesses had brought recognition.

"Curiouser and curiouser, ain't it?" chortled the dead girl. Now forget all that shit and get on with this. I got far better from the deal than you can imagine, and I'm gettin' ready to say farewell. Forever. I have just one last thing to say. I could never have become whatever it was you wanted from me, Ms. Smith.

"Lyndi, ask Paloma if you've forgotten our previous conversation. If nothing else, this Tricia needs some intervention. Remember?"

She was gone.

She needn't have been concerned, Smitty realized, as at the same time so did Lyndi. Pam was taking care of Tricia. She and Lyndi had a higher order of things to consider.

"It's a go," they heard as their selves slipped apart and opened into a world of future light.

ONCE AGAIN AT the top, they found themselves emitting autochthonic photons into a cold midnight neither could remember as resembling any July evening they had ever known. Below them amplified voices boomed, and the restless murmur of a crowd skittered about the dry air.

"It's New Years," Lyndi whispered through it all.

So it was Smitty Knew.

"A ball dropped, lights ran up and down and all above them in canopies of brilliance. The crowd roared. 2015 opened to those no longer confined to any time or place. Fireworks boomed and flared, lit the people, the land and sea in flashes of transient beauty. Lyndi gasped while Smitty held herself in close embrace.

"My parting gift. At least for now," Paloma cooed. Remember both of you that thou are light and unto light shall you someday return." Smitty hugged tighter. Lyndi laughed. She could hear it all and she could pronounce "fireworks" without any p's or l's. Her...their...new life had just begun.

They were back atop the rusting monolith of '99. Evening settled into shadow around them, but such incidentals were of no significance any more. Lyndi and Agnes were of greater moment than cycles of sun and earth. From each other's eyes they emerged. Into each other they gazed. Each knew. Each opened to the promise of the holy dove, the rapture of the innocent raptor who had ripped their reality from them so that they might see, that they might live.

That they might shine.

AS EVENING DESCENDED, and the tide deserted the beach, Pam, Sis, and Tricia spread two towels boosted from some cheesecloth rip-off shop upon the expanding beach. The air grew almost crisp, while the sounds of squeals and cross words, boxed music and distant metro noises faded. "I'm hungry," Tricia complained. "Ain't we gonna eat?"

"You already...," Pam began but was interrupted by Sis.

"Me too," she rumbled. "We ain't had no Nathan's yet. What good's a trip all the hell the way out here if we don't get a dog?"

There was no need for any one of the trio to conceal her secret smile as Pam suggested, "You two go ahead if you wanta. I'm good. I'll stay here with our stuff. Somebody's gotta."

"Want us to bring you anything?" Tricia called already walking away.

"I'm good," Pam answered watching the two of them walk toward light and satiation. They would not return, Pam understood, but such was as it should be. She could not have arranged it any better had she tried. Sometimes people do the necessary thing without prompting. Tonight would be such a time.

Only their incidentals had been left behind, and these Pam could easily accommodate. So it was that she wandered off into the urban margins of the Borough to the little park dedicated to the Spanish War Vets where she would sit upon a hard seat and play imaginary Chess with one of her imaginary selves. This night she was on a winning streak.

After several dogs, lemonade, and some talk of she and she, the biker nurse and her prospective mate settled themselves comfortably into the world of boardwalk-tourism and strolled about the island's wonders until their talk, their laughter, and their alternative circumstances resolved themselves into one inescapable awareness.

As such things often occur, the moment sprung from a most innocent even trite observation.

"You and Pam really are cool," Tricia enthused. I wish I could ride a motorcycle. And you're in a gang...."

"Club," Sis corrected, and all became as it should have always been.

Sis loved Lyndi. Whatever she did with the teacher, she could not forsake her. Not even for something as casual as this. Furthermore, the kid deserved better. Damn it all! She'd never wanted to be a fucking mother, but things were looking like that was meant to happen. She sure needed to get Pam for this. The little slut's time would come. "Come on, kid," she spoke into Tricia's ear as wrapping her strong arm around her charge's thin shoulders, she turned toward the west, the subway, and a colorful life only half as yet imagined.

Put out my hand, and touched the face of God.

A LIGHT SHONE within them out upon the midnight world, and, as unborn revelries and uncreated illuminations rejoiced about the fading park, Smitty and Lyndi sped in streaks of rainbow brilliance up, over, and out, the LED expression of the very Crown of Creation.

Upon their necessary darkling return to earth, ephemeral as the Leonid, their feathered tracings ground themselves into dew-drop turf. The unbearable 21 grams of their being, however, never having been lost also never returned itself and its light to shadow. As lover's voices expressed biological pleasure into the urban night, "Welcome back, sisters," greeted the *überfraus* with spasms of laughter. "Looks like the rook has exchanged places with the King. Just remember, you'll never be the Queen, and always will you need her protection."

Pam realized the new creations as they succumbed to necessary sleep, the morning's dew beginning to dampen the park around them, the ocean's call not for their ears.

Pam laughed and checkmated her King while laying waste her otherself's itinerant castle. "Goodnight, sweet princesses," she whispered. "I hope you never know all you might have to learn. In the end it all really does fall apart."

Grace

SETTING OUT UPON the Jersey Pike, a large black man in a Mercedes Benz found himself on the verge of becoming very well pleased.

MMM and Stephen
2003

The black velvet night is absolutely erotic. Mary Margaret rarely has felt so completely given over to her sexual nature as she does this sultry May evening. She has drunk too much, has sat with Stephen's friend Vinnie at a table in the overcrowded Daisy Baker's and flirted herself right into actually desiring him. Heretofore, she has pictured him with his lovely wife in compromising situations, but imagining herself with him is just as harmless, equally as much fun.

His last drink untouched, he weaves for home and spouse. Mary Margaret is once again on her own. That is not so bad. At least Stephen, this Thursday night, should be home with his wife as well, prepping or whatever it is he does for the next day's Bible class he and Vinnie spend so much energy upon. Thank God at least for this time he's out of the picture, and, if she has her way, soon for the rest of her life. He has become a trial, *a trial and a tribulation,* as her aunt Rita used to say, and she has already begun to show him the door. He wanted to be with her tonight, called her twice, once at the office, once on her cell. Adamantly, she denied him. Can't he take a hint?

Last Thursday he had spent the entire afternoon and evening indulging himself in his favorite perversion, bondage and punishment. Why she goes along with it, she really can't say, but some of it at least, she kind of likes. He has DVD's of various women in straited circumstances, and some of them, she feels forced to admit, are intriguing. She has read that sometimes being powerless aids women, especially those with a serious religious prohibition against sex in their backgrounds, in achieving the surrender necessary for optimal enjoyment of sexual congress and, perhaps, even accomplishing orgasm. For this reason she first allowed him to tie her, legs wide apart, and arms extended. That she has found interesting, not at all uncomfortable, but also, not liberating in the sense she had hoped. He, however, finds the entire experience compelling to a point, bordering upon obsession. Along the way he has added refinements of position and possibilities. As things now stand with them, for at least a month they have not engaged in intercourse without the aid of some sort of restraint.

Extremely boring.

Except the spanking. Why had she allowed him to begin that? Catholic guilt? The fetching lady on his favorite website? If she ever were to desire another woman, it would be her, Italian and Russian, as exotic and beautiful and strong as any woman could ever be. Her name (stage?), Victoria. Victoria allows herself to be bound, whipped and humiliated, experiencing pleasure and drawing strength from within so that she triumphs over the pain, the restraint, the men who abuse her. Maybe a woman's deepest power arises from such treatment? Who knows? In her own case, however, Stephen's fixation with such matters, especially the paddling, has engendered repulsion deepening into resentment. Her female nature aches for revenge of a most final sort.

The last time he took her, from behind as she lay frog-tied, her heels dug tight into her buttocks, her hands painfully clamped behind, her tender sex smarting from the snaps of the plastic ruler he had applied so diligently before harsh entry, she had actually contemplated shooting him, probably just in the arm or something, but really more deservedly, right where all he treasured would be destroyed.

She would never do this she knows. A woman can dream!

Along the half block to her car, not the least unsteady on three-inch heels, she feels the friction of her silk blouse, beautiful lavender in the sunlight, mysterious black in the darkness of ten P.M., upon her breasts, and almost hears the rough swish of her nylon-clad legs as they disturb the flow of her knee-length linen skirt. She'll get out of her pantyhose before driving home, and on the way, her windows down, air conditioner on, CD player singing her new favorite song, Van's *Wild Nights,* she will tug her skirt to the very tops of her thighs; perhaps she will remove not just hose but panties as well, and thrill to the night air, the music and intoxication as she sails free beneath the stars, bathed in the light of the moon.

Once in her car, off come her panties and hose, her sheer, little bra as well, and Mary drives home free as she has imagined, blessed as ever was a nymph on any moonlit night, as secure within the grasp of fate, the inescapable destiny of those chosen by God, as ever can a mortal be.

Along the back of her property lies the verge of the Rensselaer county forest, hacked to pieces now it is true, first by meadows and corn fields, later by tracts, developments running across the bowed and broken land. Now there is no forest, no primal darkness, nowhere for the Indian to hide, nowhere for the eagle to land, nowhere for the saint to fast. But memory provides the primeval with life even should it be long dead. So the shadows of the sparse trees, the hoots of the predatory night-birds, the rustle of passing deer may yet terrify, and Diana, Artemis, looks down, not with love, but with an expectant grin, upon the suburban clearing where her work will soon be done.

Amid the shadows lurks Stephen, a trifle stoned, a bit more drunk, roiling with anger born of jealousy. The bitch has been avoiding him? On more than one evening of this past month he has discovered her car outside some bar. How can he fail to imagine what infidelities she has been plotting within?

All of this fuels him as he clenches and unclenches his fists, as he paces in a small oval, never venturing into the weak lunar glow touching the tips of her lawn with delicate pearl drops, almost like the fragile lace of dew, but full of darkness and nearly divine mystery. He thinks of her and hardens. She will get hers. Good.

Somewhere, the cry of a loon is heard across the troubled landscape. Not at Pond Hill.

She draws softly into her oak deep drive and coasts to a halt. Her panties, hose and bra lie beside her, teasing the heavy leather of her briefcase with their ephemeral seduction. Unhurriedly, she gathers all together and cradles them in her arm; as she swings from her car onto the soft asphalt, her heels fumble just a moment for purchase before establishing their defiant victory over the vagaries of rough terrain, and the importunate demands of gravity which are destined ever to torment the stylishly dressed lady. Abruptly, as if answering the call the heels have ignored, her blouse swings open just a fraction wider, and one breast, the left, peeks its impertinent nipple into the very female night.

The shadow, the spurned lover, descends upon her. Stephen! His face, pale in the half-light, glimmers before her. "It's about time," he croaks, voice rough from weed, drink and desire. "Where the fuck have you been until ten thirty?"

Surprised, frightened, defensive, Mary stumbles, stifling a shriek as she does. Her things fly up into the air, her panties catching upon Stephen's left thumb as he reflexively reaches to steady her. She needs no catching. Weaponless, nearly naked, her breast now in full view, hidden no more, she takes a defensive stance and begins the simple and necessary process of removing her shoes. She is, however, stopped by her lover's growl, angry, it is true, but a familiar warning nonetheless.

"What the fuck!" he has exclaimed in that sexy, throaty way of his. "What the fuck is this?" He holds out to her the little satin string bikini once cuddled intimately beneath her elegant professional attire. "What about this?" he continues, lifting her bra with the toe of his Franciscan sandals. "Oh, God," he moans as he spots her hose all turned about as if removed in great haste. "Who?" he demands. "Who the fuck have you been fucking, you fucking whore? Who is it?"

Stepping forward, moon face breathing stale booze and weed upon her, he swings an open palm, but she is prepared and quick, parrying his strike with a forearm block, which will leave her bruised, but which causes the intrepid

Bruno to yelp. She has done the unthinkable, has not only defied him, not only disrespected him, but also has hurt him. His wrist really stings. Aches, for Christ's sake. *Fuckin' cunt!*

Halfheartedly, he slaps at her again, but she, more aggressor now than he, captures his wrist, senses a lack of will, and, carelessly drawing him toward her, deliberately allowing his limp, little hand to come into contact with her exposed breast, looks into the shadows of his eyes, notices a flicker there of something she does not comprehend, and asks the simple question, "What is it Stephen? What do you think I've done?"

Before he can answer, she knows. Now she is also without her shoes. He saw her remove them, she hopes, but what would any man think about the rest, her underwear in a bundle, obviously removed elsewhere, and her blouse loose enough to allow her breasts to show. Inwardly she chuckles, for had she not been thinking a little fling with Vinnie might be just the thing? Thankfully, both of them had thought better of it without even mentioning, without ever acknowledging its presence. Her state of *dishabille* has merely resulted from her desire to be cool, and, yes, to be erotic, but in a very chaste way.

Mary is not the type of woman to seek peace above all else, but this situation is ridiculous. She stands, unshod, unharnessed, and unclothed except for a scrap of silk, which hangs open now, allowing both breasts freedom to revel in the moonlight, and a little skirt, itself slit provocatively along its left flank. A woman in such a state, her panties twined about her lover's thumb, has no significant leverage. She is vulnerable. Needs to pacify. Lips tickling the lobe of his right ear, she whispers her desire for a cooling breeze in the humid night steaming in the high seventies, asks for his understanding. Suggests they go inside and share a drink as she further explains.

Laying her suggestive hand upon his arm, untwirling her panties and quickly slipping them on as her hand depends upon him for stability, a gesture she knows will win his heart or whatever it is that drives him, she urges her hip gently into his dark body, prodding him, suggesting their path toward the inside. She unlocks the door, his hands now upon her hips, his breath in her ear, unpleasantly warming the juncture of her neck and pale shoulder. They are inside. She switches the light, and brilliance blinds her as he rides her to the floor and quickly brushes aside her panties, inserting one, then two, three, and finally four fingers into her pouting vagina. She is on all fours. She moans. It hurts. In goes his thumb as well, and she is wailing now, begging him to stop. He does.

"Get up," he laughs. "You needed that."

Oh, no she didn't, but maybe it is enough, maybe this thing will end with their sleepily accepting each other's claims, his being her body, hers peace and early release from desire. To that end, she turns, kisses him, her tongue searching for the back of his throat. In response, he moans and once again, more gently this time inserts fingers into her. She twists, grinds her pelvis into him, accepts his invasion, and whispers. "That's so good! Take me, Stephen. I need you."

Is it possible for a girl to vomit emotionally without ever producing a physical symptom? She is disgusted with herself. He is hurting, abusing, raping her, and she gushes on about how she likes it. Maybe later, when he is within her she'll scream out, "More! More! Fuck me harder! Deeper...." Her hatred has turned upon herself, and in order to maintain even a last drop of self-esteem, she pulls free. "I think we need to talk," she announces.

Sucking his glistening fingers as if they were lollypops, Stephen grins, "I think we've been doing just fine. I hear what you're saying, and I like it."

"No, Stephen, I mean really talk," she whines, immediately angry at herself for being so typically femme, so predictably weak. Then, she is a psychologist of sorts, and is that not exactly what her kind does? She continues. "I think it ironic, don't you, that you're so quick to jump to conclusions about me, so prone to jealousy, when it's you who are conducting an affair, it's you who are unfaithful....?

"An affair?" He is momentarily puzzled, but then it dawns upon him, "Aha!" he exclaims, "An affair! With you." It slips over the horizon of his frown, turning gloom into sunlight, lighting up his adorable countenance, the most lovely of smiles. "I guess you're right," he gladly concedes, "but then, so are you. So are we both. You, however, are the one ignoring me. It's you who arrived home with her underwear in her hand. What am I supposed to think? How would you have me react?"

"Rationally," she jabs, and his smile disappears.

"So why did you avoid me? Why have you been avoiding me? Who is it, Mary? It has to be somebody."

Why she answers as she does, she will never fully understand, but she blurts out a name, the name of a near-innocent. She smacks him with the name of his best friend. "Vinnie," she shouts loudly enough to be heard by the neighbors were her house any less secluded. "Vinnie Romaine!"

Were this Pam, Stephen would strike first and deal with any fallout later, but Mary Margaret is of a different stripe. Rightly hesitant to act so, he stays his hand. His face livid and distorted by rage, arms twitching at his sides, fingers curling and uncurling against his thighs, he roars, "Vinnie?" "Vinnie? What the fucking hell were you thinking of? My best friend? Vinnie?" He is crushed, betrayed both by his woman and his best friend.

Mary Margaret has many tracks in her CD library exploring that particularly classic theme, and she cannot help but smile at Stephen's torrent of emotion, his confusion, his female ambivalence. Is he angry? Hurt? Sad? Devastated? Depressed? It is good to see him in such dire straits.

"He's better than you, too," she thrusts, "and quite a bit larger." He hits her then, a stinging blow across the face, and, instead of the reaction he would have expected had he been rational, she steps back, free from his grasp and taunts. "Is that the best you can do, big man?" She knows she's going to get it, but so what; the pain on his face, the helpless rage expressed by his distorted mouth, squinty eyes, and trembling fists pleases her. Excites her!

She expects that he will take her brutally, right there on the floor, attempt to demean her, to punish her by an animal's positioning and a few violent thrusts of that pathetic, narrow little thing he takes such pride in. She will take him, and, as he shudders into her, she will claw his little face into bloody stripes. Then she will banish him, send him into the outer darkness forever. Let him go back to his wife and his stupid, little job. She has better places to go and bigger challenges to meet. This will be his swan song, a much anticipated one at that. She is free.

He surprises her. "You want big?" he snarls. "You think you're missing something with me? Well let me know what you think of this" With that he pushes her to the counter top. Her knees bang into the hardware of the oak drawers; her head barely avoids clunking into the wall cabinets as he bends her over the workspace, not content with lifting her skirt, he hauls it, along with her panties, down about her ankles, popping its button and jamming the zipper in the process. "Step out of it," he commands.

Smiling inwardly, she complies, and then comes the unexpected. There is a stick of Land O'Lakes butter in a dish at her left elbow. This he grabs and unbelievably, disgustingly, rubs it between her buttocks which he is forcing apart with one hand. "Spread your legs," he commands. She complies. Tentatively. "Further." She is spread almost into a split and her weight is primarily borne by her elbows and forearms. He is doing something hideous to himself with the stick of butter; Mary is sure she knows what that is. "Here it comes," he sings, an anthem of triumphant revenge. "Don't think you haven't asked for it."

One finger first, its buttered length slipping easily up into her already spasming orifice. Then another. And another. He has inserted three fingers into her rectum, and is now grabbing her by the hair, pulling back her head until her neck cracks. He is attempting to peer into her eyes. To see the pain?

Eye contact, proving impossible, he releases her and withdraws his oleaginous digits. Another assault follows. Mary Margaret finds herself impaled by a penis, which in this particular receptacle feels not just big, but huge. She is choking back tears, just as he has always imagined she would, in pain and, yes, she hates to recognize it, fear. What is happening? What will the pig do next?

She is being slammed mercilessly into the counter and base cabinet, her face inadequately cushioned by her arms, themselves frictioning painfully across the hard granite. Her torment is not to end with his quickly ejaculating and withdrawing. No doubt triumphant, but, she hopes, more than a bit remorseful. Fearful.

Instead…. "Stick your fingers in your cunt," he barks. "Do it now."

Meekly, Mary slides one hand down and inserts the middle finger into her, *sick, sick* she thinks, vagina which is primed to take it. She hates the pig upon her; she might even hate herself a bit for responding automatically to the situation by providing natural lubrication should the cock sucker decide to befoul her further. Christ, she could get the world's worst case of *e-coli*!

"All of them! Even your thumb," he screams into her ear so loudly that it is actually painful. "We ain't even started yet, you fuckin' slut. The other hand too. I want both hands in there, you cunt suckin' whore."

He has lost it, she fears. He is ranting like a little boy now. A dangerous, a hurtful little boy. As she, almost timidly, rests her weight upon her ribs, partly upon her tender breasts, his assault intensifies. He has already forgotten his directive, simply assumes his edict will be heeded and mutely obeyed. Almost on its own, her hand goes not to her overfull sex; instead it finds the handle of the top drawer just beneath her arched form. It slips the thing open, slowly, unobtrusively, just far enough to slide itself inside, where it comes to rest upon her security. If he becomes, as she is certain he will, too excited by his rape, if he forgets her right hand, she will be safe. She will, indeed, have her revenge.

He lasts another minute or two, hours by her internal clock, abusing her tender flesh, tearing at her vulnerable tissues, producing swinish sucking sounds amidst the rising stench of feces and butter. He is finished.

She feels him release inside her. Readies her response.

With a pop he withdraws, and Mary Margaret whirls. His hand is already raised to her, his intention, she thinks, being to strike her on the back of her head, to drive her face cruelly into the hardrock counter. She is too quick. She delights to see the fear in his eyes as she faces him, will always remember his black eyes in the soft glow of recessed lighting as he registers the import of the pistol in her hand. The dawn of surprise, awakening of fear.

Mary Margaret squeezes the trigger, express-mailing a twenty-two caliber bullet right up Stephen's nose and out the back of his head. He jams backward onto the kitchen floor, a mind-blown jerk or two his abbreviated recessional as he and the One he has worshiped flit down an aisle of shadow.

If Jesus has a sense of humor, Stephen Bruno will become a eunuch in God's heavenly choir, but God is more merciful than vindictive, and, anyway, there is no heavenly choir, and so Stephen's fate, despite the circumstances of both his life and his death, is left to one who cannot help but love him. In fact, he ends up more than a little happy. For he has played his part well, as innocent as even the guilty may be.

For her part, Mary stands over his lifeless form splayed upon the tile floor, blood beginning to trickle from under his head and fill the grout lines chessboarding across the room. Her ears blare tinny notes into her brain; her nostrils and her throat sting from the smoke of firing; her rectum aches; intestines thunder with the promise of a violent storm. It is her bladder, its distress unnoticed until it bursts free, which disturbs the raucous silence. She hears rather than feels the stream of urine escaping her and at first is unaware of the origin of the sound. Could he be still alive? Making some desperate, inarticulate plea for help? She looks down and for a second fails to recognize the nature of the clear white fluid anointing him. She giggles finally in recognition yet fails to stem the stream. In fact, the need, the terrible, irresistible, aching compulsion to do as she will silences her consciousness, blinds her sense of decency, cripples her ability to see into the future. An animal, beyond or maybe before the tiger, the primitive ancestress of all she is, flexes her knees, assumes the universally appropriate attitude for defecation without benefit of commode and allows buttered thunder to erupt.

First comes a slight gush of bright pink, then a liquid stew of chopped and shredded excreta with corn bits, and finally, larger than ever was he, a pinecone size stool butts its way past the two totally relaxed sphincters and drops exactly where she would have directed it, should she actually have been aware of what she was doing. His rapist's mouth, the mouth which has bitten both Mary's and Pam's tender little clitorises, which has teased blood from their vulnerable nipples, which has bitten their ears, their butts, their necks and shoulders, hangs open, and into it slips at least halfway, almost as if it were a lover's brown phallus, the pungent cone of Mary's digestion, the quintessential shit of her absolute loathing.

BY THE TIME she has cleaned herself up and returned, clad in a very fetching little warm-up suit with PINK printed across her butt, the stench of her deed is everywhere. Sex smells. The discharge of a firearm smells. Death smells. Urine smells. Blood smells. So does shit. Her kitchen positively reeks, and Our Little Assassin knows not what to do. Call Uncle Mike, of course! But she absolutely does not want him to see this mess. She finds a rag with which to clean the blood and snaps surgical gloves upon her hands. She cannot do it; she cannot swab the blood from her tiles by hand, and so she secures a sponge mop and a pail. Christ, there is urine and shit all over everything. What to do about the turd in Steve's mouth? She will not touch it. Absolutely will not.

The question rearises. Who does she call? Who does she love and trust enough besides her uncle to deal with this? Who else is *capable* of dealing with it? If she can trust anyone it is Mike, her sweet, bi cousin, who will be neither appalled nor daunted by what she has done. She drops the mop, its handle coincidentally landing smack in a pool of mixed urine and stool which it splashes upon the dead man's cheek, hurries to her wall phone, taps in Mikey's number.

MIKEY IS HOME away from home when she calls and in an unusual position, hands and knees upon the large, soft ottoman which matches nothing else in his *pied a terre*, but which is absolutely essential for the various sexual adventures in which he and his menagerie of steady companions indulge themselves. Michael is in the process of having a sexual experience with, a very unique woman. They call her Nick. Some may address her as Nicky, "that's with a 'y.' No pussycrotch 'I' or fuckin' 'ie.'"

Nick's preferences are always respected. Her given name is Phyllis. She is the very large, muscular daughter of a large and muscular father. Her appropriately smaller mother is a plumber, her father a vagabond off in search of something this world is unable to supply. She has been nothing but gay–all her life. Butch to the core, Nicky has never so much as wondered what male/female sex might be like. She likes other girls; she likes them in all shapes, sizes and dispositions.

Like her father, Nicky has her free-bird ways. A biker without a club, a true nomad, she has roamed the continent from Mexico to the Yukon alone. She would have enjoyed the rough and tumble companionship of some of the outlaws she has ridden with, but, to them, she would always be an "old lady," a "gash" worthy of no respect and too ugly to fuck. Fucking men!

Not all men, she eventually discovers. Some *very macho* fags can be both understanding and pliable. Enter the quintessential example of that genre, *Mr. Macho Fag* himself, Mikey Ryan. He rides. Not often, but well. Afterwards in the quiet time of wine and smoke, he will allow himself to become the Scoot. This very evening, she towers behind him, a nine inch dildo strapped upon her burly form, the smell of anal musk and KY infusing her sinuses. As ungentle with his tender spots as ever has been any former lover, as only a man can be, she begins her play. He crouches, a humped-up kitten, offering himself for all he is worth, just knowing he can't take much more without coming....

Do bells always save us? His land-line rings. They ignore it, yet pause in the execution of their enterprise, and then his cousin's voice gasps into the dark chamber of love.

"Mikey, it's me. Please pick up"

He does, manhandled over to the phone, the extension of herself yet inside him, his entire pelvis screaming for relief. After but a few words, he pulls away, holds his fingers to his lips and motions the distressed Nicky back. A few more words and he is flaccid, all pleasure made impossible by the message she conveys.

They, he and his father, have been wondering how her insane affair, of which she thinks they know nothing, will end, and now he knows. To parody *Goodfellas* and he thinks *The Sopranos,* she has made her bones.

Mikey assures his *macho* lesbo lover that they will resume their intercourse upon another, non-too distant occasion, and, regretfully takes his leave, trusting the immensely honorable Nicky to respect his personal belongings, including the twelve odd thousand dollars she has to know nestles in his odds and ends drawer, and to lock up when she exits. Leaving her with a clean towel and washcloth, Michael speeds to the rescue of his distressed cousin, Our Own Sister Most Foully Stained.

His trust is not misplaced. Nick even tidies up and leaves an uncharacteristic little note for him on the kitchen table, a note with smiley face and all. They will be together again.

MIKEY ARRIVES BY moonlight, and the rosy fingered dawn is tracing the brail greetings of distant hilltops by the time he leaves. The oral traditions of many families are exaggerated and sanitized versions of the actualities which have spawned them, and this one will be no exception. Mary will ever be the heroine; her noble deed will be recounted throughout the generations; she will have valiantly defended her honor, and, with the aid of her heroic cousin, the childless patriarch of the next two generations, she will escape the slavering maw of the arch-fiend, Justice, who is a pretty lady, her breasts divine, but one wants not to find herself bent before her blind fury, neck bared to her keen sword. So thanks, in part, to the legendary Michael Ryan senior, and possibly even to the nurture of his wise father, Old Ned Of The Hill, the rapist's body will find its way to a Staten Island landfill, where, amid the most famous rubble of the twenty-first century, he will forever lie among those victims, animal, vegetable and mineral, of Allah's fury, buried beneath the forgetful skies of the brave new world known as America, having found a peace with those who died courageously, those who died pursuing their material ends, and those others, like himself, whose passing very few will mourn.

Mikey has feelings, deep and in some ways extravagant. His heart is torn by sad country songs, by little girls gazing adoringly at puppies or kittens on mall kiosk calendars, by *It's A Wonderful Life*, but most of these he has long ago learned to keep concealed deep within the wells from which they threaten to spring. He finds Willie Lowman tragic, and in the dark will someday sob silently as he drowns within the existential loneliness of the not-yet-released *Brokeback Mountain*, but he himself is always alone with emotions of that nature. Like all others of his kind, male and female, gay and straight, he allows only a violent anger and a just as violent sense of humor to define his emotional range. There are many flat and arid places within the man. He is not cold, just guarded, and, when the time demands it, exceedingly professional and supremely competent. Mary Margaret has always managed to reach a tiny ways into the dark cistern of his concealed self, and he enters her house visibly concerned and, possibly, a trifle fearful. Will he be able to undo the thing she has done? Will he be able to make it go away?

Doubt, however, is not his strong suit, and he enters grimly yet, at the same time, with an open and reassuring smile. She spies him, and the relief animating her face is touching. How he loves this girl! Then, hard upon her expression and his little surge of emotion comes the stench. *What the fuck has she done?*

She beckons to him, turns, and leads the way into the kitchen. Michael wishes he had brought a respirator. Mary seems oblivious to the odor. Then he sees it, the comically defiled corpse, and an old familiar feeling asserts itself, "You give new meaning to the phrase, Mary," he quips, "Eat shit and die!"

"Sorry, cousin. He died first," she responds.

Both, preferring to treat the incident and its attendant problems with humor, also understand that sober measures are required. Mikey, however, is unable to resist reaching for one last chuckle, "Holy shit," he exclaims in mock wonderment, "Holy fucking shit."

Mary laughs, although a bit perfunctorily, and the two of them turn to the task at hand, what to do with the earthly remains of one well known, and perhaps respected, college professor, whose demise is certain to raise a storm of unwanted inquiries. Mikey becomes all business; he has brought along a brand new, still in the wrapper, blue, plastic tarpaulin, which he retrieves from his Miata and spreads upon the floor, thereupon rolling the offending presence onto it, smushing the prodigious stool in the process, but that is of no matter. With Mary's help, he wraps the corpse completely within the womb of its cerements, and, again with his cousin's assistance, completely binds the entire thing together into one compact, little mummy-to-be, employing two full rolls of duct tape in the process. Then the two conspirators drag the package to the garage, depositing it convenient to one of the doors where it will be available for quick and efficient extraction.

Stephen temporarily, yet properly, disposed of, the clean-up of the kitchen becomes simple. Mops and pails, soap and water, sponges and elbow-grease soon render the space free of telltale stains. The two are exhausted by their efforts, yet deeply pleased and basking in the sense of closure a properly sanitized murder scene can provide. Of course, the work is not done. What are they to do with the neatly wrapped package in the garage? Bury it in the back yard? Toss it off a bridge? Mikey answers his cousin's wonderings with a simple, "My dad."

He has already alerted Michael Sr., and the father is awaiting his call. A truck stops by, a gray, nondescript van with no lettering or other distinguishing features, and stows Stephen in its box. Never again will Mary Margaret endure more than a fading memory of her one-time lover. Not even in dreams will his poisonous presence threaten the unfolding flower of her destiny. Stephen's journey to his final resting place on earth takes three more days.

He is forgotten.

Pam, Stephen, and Jesus
811

No more sleep wraps about her mind. Still, she must be dreaming. Perfectly comfortable with the existence of alternate everythings, especially after the turnpike, Pam tends to ascribe her growing number of paranormal experiences to the effects of high-quality drugs. Whether the sacramental initiate be waking or sleeping, currently using or temporarily straight, hallucinogens have lasting effects, especially on her. Those effects, she will eventually realize are colorless, antiseptic shadows, neither doors nor windows. Only hints. Reality — not just hers, but the REAL reality — is so much more than the most glorious of flower children ever imagined.

Curiouser and curiouser, she juggles beneath her surface, a syllable or two breaking water as might the tentative snout of a hungry Koi. *Cur, cur, cur...* is all she hears herself think, and whatever some doG might have to do with her bloody husband enters not upon her consideration.

"Got it backwards there," her asshole brother jokes.

Pam is not amused.

Mew the dead man mewls. *Mew, mew, mew....*

"The horndog sounds positively kittenish," our Lord and Savior remarks. I thought you chicks were the feline ones.

Pam is decidedly the underdog in this contest of overdone witticisms. Daddy's little lamb this mound of Venus morning is conjoined at the tail with himself. He's a firebird arisen into laughter.

"You make me wanna puke," she comments, reacting both to the nature of his apparitional self and to the reality of the stench he has brought into her room. "What's this shit with Stevie anyway? He ain't really here is he? And dead? I don't fucking think so. What's your game here? Just tryin' to annoy me"

"You know better," the hawk-faced savior clucks. "Our progenitor himself warned...."

"Cut the big words," Pam parries. "I'm not as dumb as I once was. Or as I might still seem to you. I know what "progenitor means. Anyway, I thought you still called him 'Papa.'"

"I have been known...."

"Stuff the cute replies, will ya? Just tell me is this other piece of shit here for real or not?"

"I assure you he's really...."

The putrescence once Stephen gives the lie to Jesus' assertion before the Savior is able to make it. Shambling forward until it halts not two feet from her bedside, the placental blob once her husband twists and stretches within itself much as might one fallen into an immense black hole —at least from an outside observers perspective. It escapes, no Hawking, no radiance. Suspiciously alive. Holographic at the very least. Before her, slumped into a classic stooped posture, shit smeared mustaache and all stands a Groucho Stephen. His brown fingers twirl a stool stogie between his dung lips. His spectacles sunsafe brown. Removing the stoolie from his mouth, the schmeared comedian remarks, "Man does not control his own fate. The women in his life do that for him."

Jesus caws a comment.

"You and that other slut," Groucho continues. I should have recognized my circumstances. I very well may have behaved in a more exemplary manner. I simply did not recognize the truth of human circumstances....

"Caw. Caw."

"Now I stand before you. My judge. My forlorn hope. May you have...."

"Caw, caw, caw...."

The murderous mockery of the ebony bird the enlightened one has become tosses Groucho back into his hole.

Twist and stretch.

Another emerges. This is a very chickenshit Foghorn, a truly white leghorn in the land of Black fathers, Jewish sons, and muddled sisters. Behind him lurks a grinning Dawg who occasionally laps at pools of bloody dribble and snorts up into its addicted sinuses the fresh droppings of the no longer peristaltic rooster.

Unfamiliar with this toonish presentation, Pam recoils from the overweening mess before her, its beak somehow as able to form English syllables as might any Cornishman. "I say. I say," he says. "This ain't no joke, son...."

Dawg's bloody canines reflect the darkness around them. He sneezes. A feather breaks free from the rooster's tail and wafts into a brief slip of carlight streaking through the window. Light as light it twirls and trails away into somewhere else. Pam becomes aware.

How do you know but ev'ry Bird that cuts the airy way, Is an immense World of Delight, clos'd by your senses five?

Damned Jesus. Her freaking brother. He sends her piece of shit husband smeared with the excrement of all his sins to her first as a comedian she never knew and would not have liked and then as a cartoon, again outside her reality or likely appreciation. He plays with images; he plays with words; he toys with her very sense of reality Then he lisps some words at her, words she recognizes from a book Stephen once forced her to read as she languished within the prison he had made of her room, a roach, a beautiful friend Jennifer, her companion, a galvanized pail her cloacal chamber. "Shit, piss, and corruption," the watchwords of her days and antarctic nights. "You will recognize the validity of your punishment" he had trumpeted while inserting the rough end of a plunger into her vagina. "You will someday appreciate the necessity of this," as he commenced to lash her back and buttocks, her tender breasts and thighs with the cruel nine-tailed cat he had procured from the depths of the worldwide web.

She had allowed it. She had allowed him to assault and rape Sally, her first and ill-fated true lover. Had held her power at bay as he did the things he had done. She easily could have stopped him. Killed him. Had not. Now. Now he totters before her, a pathetic rooster in need of salvation. A dog licking at his spurs. God cracking jokes like rotted eggs at his — and her — expense. "March your unwashed ass straight to hell," she should say. Instead....

"What exactly am I supposed to do," she whines at her brother. "Is this thing really my husband?

Jesus needs not answer. She recognizes affirmation. "Then, how'd this happen? Where'd all this shit come from?

If Pam is not special, she is nothing. She sees it all in a flash and understands. Mary fucking Margaret! She sees the woman's past with Stephen. Experiences the fatal moment and subsequent cleanup as part of the other's consciousness. Mary Margaret has done the deed the deadman's deeds have demanded. Pam's awareness moves past the everpresent into the fateful future. Mary Margaret will become her confidant, her marginal friend. Her mission's — whatever that is to be — protector. It's financial base. It's very human, infinitely resourceful manager. Can it be that such as she is capable of becoming the savior of the savior?

Jesus nods "yes."

Pam returns to the chickenplucked room into which a modestly presented Stephen, sans physicality of all possible manifestations, has been deposited. There is no more Jesus, Marx, dwag or cartoon chicken. Stephen stands before her. His eyes plead. His lips tremble.

"You preached penitence to me," Pam accuses. "I did betray you with Sally. With a whole bunch of others too. You could say I got what I deserved. At least, I felt that way myself sometimes. You..., you had to go too far, didn't you? With that one? You went easy. We both suffered. Anyway, I don't know about her. At least, can't speak for her. I do know about me. I condemn you!"

At that, Stephen sagged, a suspicious brown smear began its spread across his face, his lips puckered up beaklike, the darkness rolled into fragrant leafs.

"No!" Pam snarled. "I could condemn you to hell," but I'm not even sure what that is. I'm doing worse by you, although you might not see it that way immediately. I condemn you to the heaven of your own preaching. You always inveighed, *love what's happening to my vocabulary,* against mediocracy. Well, my once beloved husband, may you enter into a paradise of no more sorrow, no more hunger, despair, or loss. Also, be aware it is also the land of the unexceptional. All equal. All happy. All harmonious. A John Lennon land holding nothing to live or die for. A Mellencamp world of shady streets and little houses of blushing pink.

"Enjoy!"

Stephen winks away. Pamela returns to sleep. To dream incendiary dreams.

Rollin'

"Pli pleed pla plathroom. Plow!"

"Sorry...."

"Can, it Plindi. You don't talk like that anymore."

"Pli plan plear...."

"You can talk too."

"What's going on here? Where in all God's creation are we?"

Trucks grind, cars screech, bicycles wallow, motorcycles stutter, and the ragged subway drives the AM Beats.

"Plan...."

"You're fucking impossible.

"Here!"

Radiant in the cloudygloom park, a spirit takes her by the throat. Anime eyes stare lidless into her own shuttered ones. Lyndi understands.

"What has happened? We've slept on the ground...?"

"I can talk, and I can hear."

"Now let's get the hell outta here."

The radiance drifts unbound toward the street and climbs the elevated stairs. Lyndi and a disoriented Smitty waft none too far behind.

Plastic benches. Fastforward scenery beyond their shell. Dark. Artificial illumination. Rock and roll above the river. To dark again and then to station's light.

"Out we go. Grand Central."

Tide ebbs or else it flows. Drops rust above the beach. Smitty and Lyndi are transported from the place in which they remain.

"Wake the fuck up."

They do. Crowded. Loud. The island is nicer.

"No turning back."

THEY HAD BEEN up all night. Rides shut down. Concessions closed. The deceptive Atlantic rolls on. The sand dries. Stays warm. Stars swim in the sky and dance upon the calm sea. Souls connect and rock away margins. Sis and Tricia experience gestation. They becomes entangled. Are more than twins. Paloma, clad in the soft robes of predawning, breathes the love of God upon them. Their hair is teased. Their hearts grow calm. Their energy becomes eternal. They sleep aboard the Q as it shuttles them toward an uncertain future. Undetermined, yes, but the early Browning would see fit to write a line or two concerning deity, the world, and things going right.

Someday, possibly, Tricia might.

They reach the central station some time before Pam and her companions.

They doze in chairs staring at cooling coffee and untasted muffins.

The others find them there.

It has been arranged.

THE EVENING'S COMPLEXITIES resolve themselves quickly. Smitty gulps half of Lyndi's coffee. Pam offers Tricia a Zaro's muffin. The youngster breathes it in and aspires the crumbs before they can hit the table. A more traditional breakfast is in order. At least for the biker and the chick. Sis consumes two Belgian waffles with butter, maple syrup on one and vanilla ice cream, whipped cream, and strawberries, juicy red and of sharp-barbed taste on the other. Lyndi pulls apart a cream cheese slathered multigrain bagel; Smitty stirs about a paper cup of oatmeal, raisins and skim, while Pam tosses off three cans of San Pelligrino Blood Orange nectar. Only Tricia, miniscule as she may be, is able to approach Sis. She orders the same ice cream and strawberry concoction as her new friend, but chooses blueberries and whipped cream with chocolate swirls as her second. The two of them end with enormous chocolate milkshakes, again with whipped cream topping. As all knew it must, it comes to pass that Tricia fails. She is able to finish but half of her shake. Sis cannot resist. She scoops it away from the pufferbellied girl, swallowing the remains in one great gulp then snorting chocolate triumph through her nose.

The others desert the table posthaste. All, that is, except Tricia who gazes upon the magnificent woman she is coming to know with something akin to reverence. Lyndi turns away, a sigh of disgust pressing through her own nasal cavity.

They don't go far. Itineraries are already in place, but the company know none of the details. Well, one of them does. Sacagawea Bruno shepherds them to a deserted gate to an empty track, sits them on the floor before her, smiles her most engaging smile, and sets them straight upon their appointed journeys.

Of course Sis will be paired up with the little chippie in the childish sundress, her babydoll frame all bone and pale skin beneath it, her fake smile sitting there across the stuck-up table, whipped cream at the corner of her salmon lips. One night and away her newborn hopes for sanity have flown. Up under a flippant skirt....

"First off, Sis, if I'm not mistaken, Lyndi needs you to return her to captivity. Again, if I'm not, she's already past her deadline. Best beat your boots outta here. Amtrak's about to leave. I'll fill you in on whatever else we got goin' later."

Lyndi is saved. Sis takes her by the arm. Gently. Hip to hip, they sway away.

"Agnes, you have won the lottery. You, me and Tricia here'll head over to Penn Station. You can drive us on up the river. That is if that's OK?"

They find some Italian ice, and the three of them trek across the island to another subterranean pathway to the rest of the continent. Jersey Transit.

As much as ever could have Smitty or Tricia, Pam loves malling. A stop at Woodbury becomes essential, and Pam, at her essential best, finds a dress the equivalent of that worn by Tricia. Also translucent panties unable to offer more than token coverage. All the way up Dewey's highway her pheromones endanger their safety by slushing Smitty's concentration away from any reasonable attention to the details of driving.

Pam rides shotgun. Tricia curls asleep in the back, her pale half-moon visible only to Mrs. Bruno who sits, beltless at a most convenient angle. Smitty might drown.

"If you let your hair down and your skirt up a little, you might make it with Mangold, you know."

"Perhaps you aren't aware. She and I are former nuns."

"Exactly."

"Exactly? What exactly are you saying?"

The darkness between Bruno's legs threatens the daylight. "I'm saying that I know more than you can imagine. Well... maybe not. You must have some inkling of what I am. Anyway. I feel the tongue of your imagination. Here." She opens into spectacular view. "Back there at the conference. Oh, you two were so fucking chaste." Her legs clamp shut. "That doesn't have to be, you know."

"Never. We never. We will never."

"Too bad, cause after a more than minor interlude with my husband, Mary Margaret's gonna be your partner anyway. So.... Might as well enjoy yourselves the way women are meant to. Know what I mean?"

"Sex isn't everything, you know."

"Prim as shit, ain't ya? Well listen my girl" Those wonderful thighs loosen. "You and Lyndi are every bit as special as you discovered up on the drop. Sis and Mary not so much. They need you two. Lyndi and Sis might someday even get themselves married. Sis needs Lyndi to complete herself, and Lyndi can lean on Sis for a million necessary chores. Physical backup, know what I'm sayin'? Far as romance goes? Well that's sure physical, Makes it all better. Hot fudge and whipped cream, you know."

"Anyway, don't try and tell me you weren't gettin' physical with that one in back." Tricia stirs. Her breath stirs a wisp of hair. "Sure as hell, you were thinkin' illegal thoughts."

Smitty finds the highway suddenly engrossing.

"Come on admit it. If I didn't know better, I'd say you were afraid of Mary or something. You ain't are you? You think she's anointed or something? Holy?"

"I'll state the facts for ya. She's gonna meet and fuck my husband. He'll make her screech with pain and joy. Just like he does me. That much is for sure. There's more I gotta to tell ya. They'll break it off someway. She's for you not some man. Just like Lyndi and Sis, you and her are gonna be part of something me and somebody you know, Mary Elizabeth, are gonna light this old world on fire with. Don't know the details yet, but I do know. Lyndi and Sis. Mary and me. You and Mangold too. It's gonna be hard at times. Why make it worse? You ain't gotta do it without the pleasure. Come on, Aggie, join the fun. I tell ya, she'll be more than happy to oblige, and she'll make your life a whole lot better."

Smitty would often see more clearly than would Pam. Such was to be one of the many facets of her value to the revolution. This time, despite the god-child's certainty was one of those clearview moments. She and Mary Margaret would love each other more deeply as each year passed, but their kisses would be chaste and their love beyond the merely mortal.

"DON'T FORGET WHAT I said about Mary Margaret," Pam whispered back into the driver's window, as she and Tricia took their leave in the Amtrak lot where Pam had parked.

"Bye, Agnes," Tricia trilled over waggling fingers. "Thanks for everything."

A breeze toyed with the hem of the little one's skirt and Pam felt the same playful fingers trace wisps of longing about her own knees. For sure Smitty and this one would be wrong. Not necessarily for her. What could be the harm?

"Ever been to Lickety Split?" She oh so innocently asked. It's just up nine and twenty and better than you could ever imagine."

"Sounds kinda bogus to me," Tricia replied. "You got somethin' in mind I don't know about?"

Too wise. No fool, Pam knew the child was willing, but, god help her, she had something of Agnes Smith in her besides sexual leanings. She couldn't do it.

"No," she said. "It's a great ice cream place. Maybe even better than Snowman. I thought we could get cones…or anything you want, and decide just what we're gonna do about you. You know?"

"Sis says she'll take cara me, but she thinks I oughta go home and straighten shit out first. Said to ask you if I could drag your mind away from my boobs."

"Fuck her," Pam laughed. "Your boobs aren't your main attraction an' she knows it. Anyway, sometimes her head's a whole lot straighter than mine. Sounds like you got a plan. We can still do the Split though. Ever had a Root Beer Float?"

The Last Dance
2015

Last evening. Her final unaided stagger to the table. It sat a mere six feet from her bed, the full-bore hospital appurtenance Mother supplied. She leaned so mightily upon the IV pole, plastic ears flapping, tubes ripe for new entanglements, that Arthur was certain the entire apparatus and she would collapse to the floor. Instead, always the unpredictable one, Ruth not only gained her seat but settled upon it smoothly. The merest exhalation followed by a curt gasp might as easily have been a sigh of triumph as admission of exhaustion. She sipped the *chai* tea Arthur set before her, toyed with the soft boiled spinach with organic vinegar. The tiny cup of frozen vanilla yogurt liquefied unnoticed.

"Thank you, Artie," she smiled, her lips colorless, approaching dematerialization.

She could not stand. Bone and sinew pushed against gravity and threatened to rupture her parchment skin. A cough. The darkness around her eyes deepened. Color trembled upon her cheekbones. Yellow teeth and hollow breath begged release. Arthur felt her surrender.

He missed the pale trickle licked from the corner of her mouth, noticed not the watery streak across the root-evident teeth. Arthur did as he was meant to do. As he never chose to do. As he was blessed to be able. His love lifted her. His strength carried her eroding frame across the polished floor. His agility allowed him to shepherd the IV's before them. Softly he lay her down. Gently he tucked the fresh sheet around her. Sadly he turned to the hotel sized television, pointed the remote and brought to brilliant life the program she loved so much. "The Good Wife."

"Thank you," she whispered.

Before long she slept, dreaming, he knew, of Alicia. Such dreams had been denied him. Ruth was his one and only. He had been forbidden any others, including Paloma and Pam. God help him, he had tried. Without success. He and Ruthie had become celibate. Brother and sister, priest and nun…. He could, however, have her in his own imagining.

He could not!

Denial. Could your name be Love?

HER BED OVERFLOWS with blood. He strips her sheet away. A river of watery hemorrhage flows from between her legs, draining it must be direct from her heart. She hints at a cough. Speckles fly from her crimson mouth. Her nose sniffles something back. She is not expected to go like this. He is helpless. He will do as he has been instructed. Nothing. Not even 911.

Ruth's face spring to life. Her raptor eyes speak her hunger.

She spits her life into the air.

I KNOW WHAT I must do. I am free of the bitches' interference. My Ruthie lies before me. I loved her. I love her. I shall love....

First the preparation. I must unfetter her, remove the tubes, strip away the tangled rag she wore and wash her. I must kiss her once more. I shall heap her mattress and bedding in a corner.

I am prepared. With the assistance of her mother, Ruth and I found and leased a mini Cape situated on an undistinguished street in the hamlet of Berlin, New York. I never made the acquaintance of our neighbors, but my most casual and disinterested observations have assured me that the term "red neck" would in nowise offend them.

One lady one day appeared with a tinplate pie. Ruthie could perambulate then so she answered the door and asked the woman in. Dull-witted as the welcomedragon might have been, the cannulae, both nasal and intravenous so prominent upon her hostess worked their charm, Mrs. Welcome could not wait to get away. Ruthie was most amused. From that point on, our neighbors maintained their distance.

I most certainly have devolved. Such rumination does not speak well of me. I am unable to regret my time with Ruth, but, why did this blessing require that I wrap myself in this mediocracy of language and intellect? Somewhere I feel the words tumultuous in their confinement. They would be reborn. My mind? I know. I know. I know.... Unlike my true self, I understand. So godabandoned pedestrian.

I digress. I digress. Hello Eliot. No, I'll not wear my trousers, bottoms or too-wide waist rolled. I shall divest myself of trousers, of all earthly accoutrements entirely. I shall embark upon the final stanza of my life naked. Thus did I enter this world and bare as picked bones shall I leave it.

I prepare a place for my love. In the unfinished top space of the hovel I have stored a fresh mattress. I tug it down the crackling old stairs and lay it in the center of the room. I secure a fitted bottom upon which to lay the vacant edifice of my Ruth. Around her I place the comforter she loved so well.

From the backyard shed I transport the four five-gallon cans. We will not depart in darkness. We will take our leave bright shining. Ruth's face has softened. The dead usually appear so stark. She, however, may have moved a bit toward life upon the occasion of her death. I close her beginning to sparkle eyes, touch her reformed lips with my own. Stroke her cheek back to a semblance of color.

Grace

From a religious store in Latham I have purchased a chalice veil, a nacreous pall of the funereal sort embossed with a simple gold cross. This I most reverently place across her visage. I am free to proceed. Ruth knows. She accepts. She has done as she must. It falls to me to raise the curtain.

At the foot of the basement stairs sprawls the detritus of two years habitation. Plastic and Styrofoam carryout containers, wisps of supermarket bags. Miscellaneous newspapers, and paper bags. I douse them with gasoline. The rooms above are stocked with Isadora plush furniture and ostentatious draperies. Petrol sloshes everywhere. Saturated cushions obstruct both front and rear access points. A gallon and a half anoint my Ruthie. Her veil ripples above her approving smile. To the top floor I ascend. An old analog TV lurks before the double windows as does a cordless saw, one most appropriate for demolition Ace at the hardware assured me.

I cut away the centerpiece and hurl the television through the glass and skeletal framework. *Astronome Domine* begins to play from my anachronistic boomer. Below bakes a fresh-sealed asphalt drive. Clutters of wood, glass and gutted casing adorn its surface reflecting shards of sunlight. All is as it should be. I descend to the netherparts, snatching a butane BBQ igniter from the kitchen island. Innocent blue, it shouts incipient consummation at the heap below. A roar of rhapsodical appetite demands satiation. Leaving the door agape, I spread flame about the ground floor on my way to Ruth's bier. I shall not pray. I shall not cry. I shout into the fire I light about her, "We will not go gentle." May our rage burn away with fire green as grass the flesh holding us in chains. We sing. No longer are we imprisoned.

Cupric flames reach for me as I scamper up my penultimate stairway. The house begins to moan. Approaching the natal aperture, I catch sight of the first busy neighbors beginning to swarm about our pyre. I shout down. I care not if they hear. My penis is strong and straight. Fuckemall.

I have a pale blue mop pail into which I pour the remainder of my gasoline. I await countdown toward ignition.

My feet sense the heat beneath me. My ears hear the approach of sirens. I breathe smoke. Finally after an eternity of decision without indecision my time to fly arrives upon a tongue of organic flame.

I anoint my head with petrol. All systems are go. I step to the threshold of my nativity.

I detect a soft taste of my heel. Warm breath wreathes itself about my leg....

ARTHUR HAD IMAGINED himself soaring through the wooden gateway of his old life into the eternal sky of the new, afire, borne upon nonexistent breezes above the assembled multitude until, become little more than memory, he rained his phoenix ash upon them.

Instead, as he should have been aware, gravity asserted its dominance, and with a banshee howl he dropped to the ground a smoking, sputtering heap whereupon two brave citizens rolled him about until all the fire was gone. This was no simple task. He was after all drenched with 87 octane. Only in mythology, however, does fire last forever. He was eventually quenched.

Not extinguished. He lasted three and a half more days.

As for Ruth, Isadora and Felicia, after a most tasteful memorial service attended by Pam, Mary Elizabeth, Lenard, and others of lesser note not a few, laid her to rest in the family plot at Saint Mary's Cemetery, a perfectly appropriate and blessed resting place for a prodigal daughter come home at last.

Set the controls

I awaken in the dire, familiar place to which I have often traveled. Brightness abounds but dazzles not. No sun need shine its light. No shadows are cast. Flipfloppy condoms and sterile sharps fade from memory, misperceptions of my addictive consciousness. The imposition of that appurtenance, dedicated foe of genuine awareness has been removed. I have no need to see clearly or through any sort of glass darkly either. This is the land of Mister Ono's imagining. There is nothing to live for. I am not alive. Nothing to die for. I am no longer equipped to do so. What of all the people? Empty desert, Johnny O. This sand and duned horizon is one world. I am abandoned. I need not imagine. I feel memory fade. I am alone.

"Never alone," a rich contralto croons. "You'll never walk alone."

This is not Pam. Neither is it the other me. It comes from somewhere neither without nor not within me either. It is intimate and universal. I have heard this voice before. It belongs to Delphine Galou. I cast about for its origin, perhaps an angelic vision of the magical being who, my final visit to Lincoln Center, brushed aside my buzz and for an evening's brief interlude overpowered me with the ontological paradox of her music. It cannot be that she is here. She lives…. Is not her voice divine?

"I love her too, you know," Delphine's voice speaks of herself. "She knows no equal. In fact, in our more intimate moments Pam and I am inclined to refer to her as 'The Divine Miss D,' although Pam is more inclined toward Bette. She being so earthbound and all."

"Why am I able to hear you but not see you?" I demand of the deceptively mellifluous one. "You've already given yourself away, little dove. You might as well show yourself."

"No need," the abruptly reedy one responds. "You're in a place where within you and without you as well as above, below, and all around you are the same place and time. Were it necessary for you to visually perceive me such would be so…. Please excuse my attempting to sound like Arthur. Anyway, I have things to tell you before my *adieu*. Hear me in your own voice. I'm telling you nothing you do not already know. You simply don't remember."

Something begins to shimmer over the edge of things. I focus. The disturbance disappears. The Ruth within me speaks that which I know. I listen, compelled by some note of gravity in my dissertation.

"Atta girl," I encourage. "Never lose your love of self-expression. Now listen to yourself with the attention you deserve. Time does not exist in this land, and so, I employ the concept as metaphor. Whatever…. Within the next few moments Arthur is slated to join you. He has only inklings concerning the nature of this land and the special circumstances in which you two find yourselves. You will have need of instructing him concerning the nature of your mission. It is important that the two of you operate together. In life you were broken…incomplete. In this place you must become one while remaining two. If that sounds impossible… crazy… look back upon the lives you have led. Each of you has lived in a world of illusion, delusion is far the better term. All humanity wanders within veiled chambers, torn by intuitions and presumptions, blinded by logic and benighted by sight. You two were worse than most.

"To top it off, neither of you ever had a chance at anything resembling peace, understanding or salvation, not even the lobotomized Nirvana of Mr. Ono. By the way, Cobain is already here, as is and will in time be Courtney, along with all the Sids and Nancys of common as well as uncommon humanity. So many of you in so many pieces. So few of you fit to reassemble. Lobotomy Johnny sang of the world living as one. Such pretention! The world is the world, its people the incoherent particulate matter of probability. In this place some of those human bits can be drawn together into coherent unities. You and Arthur are such ones.

"Together you will come upon others like you, and eventually you will be drawn to an individual in need of no conjunction. Her name was Mary. Her presence speaks of reality beyond naming. Her band of preterite souls follow aimlessly as she searches emptiness for direction. You and Arthur, your own band of siblings as well, have been chosen to provide that for her. I have elected you. Do not fail.

"Mary Elisabeth hoped for your healing. Lenard strove to bring Arthur around to sanity. Pam, uxorious as any Macbeth, eventually would have wiped her hands clean of her failure had it not been for my intercession. The two of you have been in my sights for a long time. I saw something in your and his anger, rebellion and disdain for the normal. Sometimes Pam provides little more than an amusement. Her place is with the 'living.' Mine is with the eternal. Yours is to be no small part in the coming revolution. Remember Blake and you may find some hint of just what's afoot.

"Allow yourself and Arthur to meld once he is here. You will find he brings some of his own insight and most importantly he bring a necessary talent. Use yourselves wisely. Keep yourselves aware of your quest for Mary. Be prepared for more than you can at this moment understand.

"Say goodbye, Ruthie."

TIME FLOWS WITHOUT moving, without direction. The arrow is knocked, the target awaits. Ever released. Eternally pierced. I have always known this land, have forever stood alongside Ruth upon this verge. About to fly. Having flown. Eternal fire, I glow black as she explains that which we both have always known. I observe her stasis alongside my own. The sand does not whisper. Does not shift. Galou sings always at Lincoln Center. Studies at the *Sorbonne*. She is born whispering in Handel's ear. I know all that Ruthie knows. The obverse is so as well. We are the same coinage. Mortal and eternal, omniscient and invincibly ignorant.

We are each one and two. We lie at the quantum base of the new computing. Qbits we may be termed. We are all that is was or ever shall be....

"Shut it down," Lenard's harsh bark commands. "Save the profundity for different circumstances. Just take the girl's hand in your own and let it all flow. You'll be surprised."

"Fuck you," I mutter, but Ruthie is already reaching to me. I cannot refuse. Our fingers touch and intertwine. She moves nearer. I flare. She is not afraid. We move together. My flame coaxes her own to life. We meld impossibly above ourselves. Ourself. We are both and one.

Her voice is sweet as could any *chanteuse's* be. "Listen to yourself," she whispers. We must be off to where we have been."

Grace

WE ARE THE sun above this barren land. Together we step from the precipice and ascend.

MY BODY FALLS to the ground.
The bottoms of my feet burn. My flesh is ash.
Voices cloud about me.
One shines forth.

"WELL DONE, ARTHUR," she declares.

.

Ouroboros

As ever it must the world jolts from whimper to bang, and Time circumnavigates the universal curve poking the archer in the ass.

ABOUT THE AUTHOR

J.S. McInroy is wholly imaginary and every bit as real as you and me.

Visit J.S. @ The Wasteland – www.jsmcinroy.com.

If you enjoy the author's work, please consider sharing it with a friend or leaving a review at your favorite retailer.